The Thorn
by Doreen Zaiss

ISBN 978-0-9937911-8-5

encreLibre Publishing
Riondel, BC
Canada
encrelibre.com

The Thorn

SECTION ONE

The Thorn punctured the surface of the sea and rose through the fog that obscured the inky water. Impossibly pointed, the tip sliced through gravity, thrust upward to the clouds and then through them like the dorsal fin of some mighty sea beast made of metamorphic rock. Even in the dark, it stood as a reminder that life here wielded a keen edge.

Around the curve of the coastline stood a small red rorbu, one of many in the village that once housed fishermen who came from the south to work in the cod fishery. This one stood out because its shutters, pebbled pathway, and the thread of smoke hanging idly from the chimney all spoke of family. A raven flew over the house, then another, calling out to the first from deep in its throat. The sound of their wings was like sails flapping in a cross wind. Black birds announced the morning in a black sky.

Johanna stood over her first daughter's cot. "Rikka. Henrikka." She took the girl's hand and stroked it - a beautiful hand with smooth flesh. Her own hand was chapped, her knuckles swollen and painful, lined with cracks that opened and bled every time she touched something fine. They were the hands of an old woman. Thirty-three and old.

"Wake up. It's time to get the breakfast on." She knew her daughter was tired. She was young and needed the sleep, but Johanna would leave for work soon and all her children had to be up first. Johanna needed to know that all three were alive and well before she left. She lit the fire but there was no time for anything else. It would all be up to Rikka, taking care of the girls, the cooking and cleaning, the mending and minding, plus the heavy job of hauling and splitting firewood. But she had to go back to work after her time off with the baby.

Rikka rolled over and let her long legs dangle from the bed. Her eyes were closed. Her feet curled up to avoid the cold floor. She felt for the rug with her toes.

Hanna tucked the covers around little Agnes. The girl snorted in her sleep and mumbled a complaint about chickens pecking under her blanket. Their shared bed gave them warmth at night. Whenever Rikka turned in her sleep, Agnes turned with her. She was better than the heated stones Johanna sometimes placed near their feet. There was a line of sweat across the child's brow and her cheeks were a bit too pink. Oh no, Hanna thought, this again. Agnes seemed to swing like a pendulum between health and sickness. They had been told that she would never thrive the way other children did. There was too much congestion in her slight frame.

"How are you this morning, Mama?" Rikka asked.

"The same as ever. Is that fire hot enough for tea? Give it a poke."

With her back turned to Henrikka, Johanna pinned her long brown hair firmly in place. "I have to go now." There was such a tightness to those words that it was clear she was holding back tears, tears and rage. Johanna stepped out the door with her bundle and her dread.

No one should have to start their day like this, Johanna thought. As she slipped out the door, a twist of salty air stripped the shawl from her shoulders. The door slammed so hard that it rebounded and hit her in the back. She had a kilometer of this squall to fight her way through in the dark before reaching the Lorkman's farm. That wind was going to whip around doing all it could to trip her up. The cold had already worked its way through her dress and within minutes her boots were slurried with mud.

Her body flinched against October's worst. On a summer day, or even a cold-but-still day, she loved this walk, the sound of her own footsteps, the swoop of kittiwakes around the bay, the swirl of teal and turquoise waters, the pungent smell of dried cod in the air. But October changed all that, sucking her into its core. She tried not to trip on the path or be thrown sideways by angry cross winds. All that so she could spend her day working in someone else's house, making their lives comfortable, their larder full, their time their own. Her time, her children's time would have to wait, maybe forever. Their time belonged to others.

Head down, Hanna watched her feet and tried not to count her steps. A raven croaked. Was it complaining about the weather or threatening her? Maybe a warning? Another raucous caw. She looked up. The raven spun in the wind, feathers blown askew, maybe mimicking her clumsiness.

"Get on, devil. Stop taunting me."

The raven circled over her head, answered with a glottal cluck. An updraft lifted him straight overhead like a puppet on strings. He hovered, skreighed, and plummeted, wings pinned to his side.

"Scram, Munin! Or tell me something new." Her words splintered in the wind and the raven chuckled, chased those broken bits, and was gone.

There was only a dull hint of morning in the sky as Hanna approached the Lorkman's farm. She felt she had already done a full day's work just getting to the place. Her body ached with the tension of fighting the storm, and her hands were cramped with cold. She flexed her fingers inside her mitts and imagined Munin flexing his wings in the same way. Lucky creature. Where did creation go wrong to leave her grounded and trudging through mud? Gravity sucked at her boots. By the time she passed the gate to the farmhouse, the protective coating of seal blubber had been breached.

She entered the small mudroom that kept the kitchen free of manure, snow or mud, according to the season. Johanna wondered if she could sneak her boots into the kitchen and tuck them in between the wall and the tall column of tiled stove where they could dry out. She didn't relish the idea of pulling wet stockings and boots on at the end of her workday, though she also knew that bringing them to the inner sanctum of the kitchen was not allowed. But surely, she could dry her stockings there. She slipped the stockings over her hands and pulled them as high up her arms as they would stretch. Barefoot, she moved over to the stove and placed the palms of her hands on the tiles. The heat and moisture mingled to create a healing wrap. The steam smelled faintly of leather and seal fat. She inhaled deeply as her muscles loosened. If the owners slept in this morning, she could warm up a bit before the cycle of chores began.

Wednesday. Churning day. Stock-taking day. Milking day (always). Bread day. Mending day. Endless day. She pulled the damp but warm stockings onto her feet. They would have to do for the time being. She buttoned up her sweater as she entered the cold room off the kitchen, a good-sized pantry with baskets and crates of the summer harvest. Bins of potatoes, onions, winter squash and rutabagas, insulated with sawdust, lined the wall the cold room shared with the kitchen. Crates of stockfish, crocks of pickled herring, and canisters of various smoked fish and meats were stored on cooler walls. But the coldest part of the room was reserved for all that the cow provided: milk, precious cream, butter, rounds of cheese both soft and hard, mild, aged and herbed. The oaken churn had to be moved to the kitchen to warm it up. It was too cold in the room to do the churning. She could churn all day and never get the cream to come and the buttermilk to flow. She tipped the churn so it rested on an arc of its base and rolled it into the kitchen. A kettle of water had kept hot overnight in a cubby hole of the stove. She poured this into the churn. It should be ready after the milking.

Her boots were mired in mud and damp. As she stared at them, she heard them taunt, 'Don't sneer at us. We are the perfect boots for you, brown, sagging, listless. Pretty well done with life. We fit.'

No, not yet. Hanna kicked the boots aside and slid her feet into Dankert's boots. She refused to head out to the byre in her own. She wasn't that far gone. Three children to feed, her husband, drowned. She never thought she'd miss him so much. He had been old enough to be her father. But that was what she missed so much now, a steady man who would take care of her and the children. Fortunately, he had left her the house, small but sturdy. She still had that. But she no longer had comfort. Life had turned into a toboggan run through the dark, with no end and a sense of despair instead of exhilaration.

Hanna picked up the clean pails, filling one with warm soapy water, and walked out the door. Dankert's boots flopped around on her feet. The ridiculous size and orange leather reminded her of puffin feet. Feeling childish, but also feeling totally alone and unwatched, she tried out some puffin noises, the long moaning "aahs" from deep inside that sounded like laments even when the birds seemed perfectly content. Maybe they were just chronic complainers. Maybe she was too.

The light was dim in the byre. The sun's angle wouldn't light the area for an hour or so; bad planning on someone's part. Aiming the wide-open door towards the Thorn guaranteed that the sun would avoid it most of the day. She could just make out Bestemor nosing around in the empty hay trough. The old cow turned her head slowly and fixed Hanna with her doleful stare.

"Good morning, Bestemor. I'll make you a deal. I'll put some hay in box if you'll promise not to empty your bowels in the stall this morning."

The cow's head swung from side to side in agreement.

"Promise?" There was no response to that. Hanna kept up her part of the bargain, and the cow sauntered over to the milking stall where she tried to reach the hay without putting her head between the bars of the stanchion. "No you don't, Beste. I know your tricks. Come on now. Sure, we don't like our heads stuck between the braces, but we know it's the only way we get fed. Come on, old girl. Let's not make things harder for ourselves today."

Hanna pulled the milking stool in close to the cow, wrung the excess water from the washcloth, and gently bathed the cow's udder. This, Bestemor seemed to enjoy. A good omen. Next Hanna opened the small tin of lanolin which would protect both her skin and the cow's udder. Empty. Yesterday she had scraped out the last traces of lanolin and had told Fru Lorkman that she needed more. Without it, her hands suffered and, worse yet, the friction of the pull on the cow's teats angered Bestemor. The Lady of the House had insinuated that Hanna used far too much of the balm and wondered if she was in the habit of taking more than was needed for the cow. Wasn't that just the way with those who had more than their share? They feared losing even a dab. Maybe the old bag could spare a few grams of cod liver oil to rub into those teats. That would make the milk taste just fine!

Hanna held her hands out in front of her and stared at the damage. Bestemor arched her back and Hanna had to pull the pail away quickly before the cow could piss in it.

"All right, you old beauty, I'll get on with it, unless you had something more to say. No? Saving the shit for another day? Thank you for that." Hannah let fly one squirt of milk from each of the four teats just in case any bacteria had developed there that would contaminate the whole batch. The resident hedgehog peeked out from its nest behind the stanchions. Hanna aimed a few more squirts into the little bowl that she kept handy for the creature. She admired its prickled coat, a warning not to touch. Replacing the pail, Hanna took hold of two teats, squeezed the base of one to be sure the milk didn't retreat back into the udder, then let each finger in turn force the milk further down. The same on the other teat: squeeze the base, then one finger after another pulling down in rapid succession. She rested her head against the cow's flank. "Good girl. Let it go." This was the time in the day when she could relax into her task, the joint rhythms of her heartbeat, the cow's slow swaying and the milk filling the bucket. "That's a good girl. Just enjoy the release, Bestemor." Memories of her life with a man in it flashed through her mind. The rhythms. The melding of two into one. The tensions and the release.

The dwindling of the milk came sooner this time of year, before the next calf, before the new grass. Hanna probed the udder to be sure each quarter was empty before she patted the cow on the flank and moved the pail to safety. "Come Beste, time for your main course."

The sun, mostly subdued by clouds, managed to toss some spears of yellow light down on the farm, but the air was wet and chill. She set the pail down on a flat stone, hugged herself and noted the stiffness in her body. The milking stool had been too high. It was a bad pose to hold throughout the milking and she noticed the slight twist in her spine, forward and to the left. Inhaling deeply, she tried to straighten. Getting older.

Hanna eyed the flat stones surrounded by dung and water that led between the byre and the house and concentrated on placing each step exactly so she wouldn't get any mud on Dankert's boots. Just get through this mess without spilling milk and get warm. But as she picked her way across the distance, dizziness set in. She felt as if she were walking on the deck of their fishing boat as it left the bay with Anders at the helm, steering them towards the fishing grounds. She had never really gotten her sea legs after a lifetime on the coast and more sea passages than she cared to remember. It was always a contest with nausea and balance. Anders found it endearing, an excuse to take care of her. She hadn't told him that his hovering intensified the nausea. He would have taken it personally, and maybe he would have been right. But now, just now as the dizziness and bone chill were upon her, she could have used Anders's overbearing care. Anybody's in fact. Almost.

Four steps before the door, her foot slipped out from under her and Dankert's fine boot slid into the muck. She swayed, one foot on stone, the other in a whole ocean of water. The puddle seemed as bottomless as the sea. Her mind swirled in the maelstrom.

Would her leg pull her down into that other world where Anders floated through time? Hanna reached for solid ground on the next stepping stone, the hem of her dress soaking up the muddy water. She had to pull herself out of this mess.

The sun came out to show her reflection in the puddle. Her eyes were too big, bewildered and wild and her cheeks fell forward as if to slip right off her face. A madwoman. She could either laugh or cry at this horrid distortion. As quickly as it appeared, the image was erased by a dark mass sweeping back and forth, changing dimensions every second. A cloud of grackles, silent except for the murmur of their wings, flew free, headed for home. She couldn't let herself sink. She just couldn't.

After her mother left and they had all eaten, Rikka wrapped a long shawl around herself once and then wrapped it again, this time including Ragna. The baby gave Rikka a toothless grin knowing that they were to go outside. She loved the cold, always blinking and wrinkling her nose as the wind blew in her face. Ragna was oddly quiet for a baby usually so full of joy.

Rikka was still concerned about the trace of fever she felt on Ragna. Agnes should see a doctor again, she thought. She wondered what to tell her mother. She took Agnes by the hand.

As they walked, Ragna picked at the eight-pointed star woven into her shawl's fabric. The shawl was worn thin, a remnant of better times, but still lovely. Why did the Norwegian star have eight points instead of five or six like in other countries? Perhaps her people needed more light to find their way through the polar night.

As she did so often, she thought of her father, who, her mother said, had died at sea saving his mates. She said he used to play the fiddle, that he was a master of the instrument. He used to swing her mother around the floor and make her laugh. Rikka didn't remember him but she had the fiddle.

What she didn't know, and what her mother would never talk about, was what other man (or men?) had fathered Agnes and Ragna.

Their path ran in the opposite direction Johanna had taken to the farm. They passed the inlet where a few men were refitting and caulking the boats that would join the local fleet when the cod came in. Two men were replacing worn-out supports for their fish racks. In the rising sun, the new poles shone golden in contrast to the old grey ones. The drying poles wouldn't be laid across the supports until later. Agnes waved to the men who were too busy to notice. She called out "Hei" to them but her words were blown away behind her.

"They're mean," Agnes pouted.

"No dumpling, they just can't hear or see you because they aren't fairy people like you are. Just feel sorry for them," Rikka said.

Further along the shore they found a spot to sit on a flat slab of stone and eat an apple cut in thirds. The water here was a brilliant turquoise, the sand beneath it white. Agnes moved forward to put her hands in the water. "I want a dress this colour."

"That would be beautiful. It would match your eyes." Rikka was raked by regret for the little girl. Agnes reached for the sulphur yellow seaweed shifting sinuously just under the water's surface, then yanked back her hand as the tendrils seemed to grasp her fingers. The baby squirmed in its restraints.

She stared at the mountain, the Thorn, that towered over the whole village. A scar ran across it that looked like a smile. She wondered if it could be climbed. Had anyone ever done it?

Rikka looked up at the peak of the Thorn. Could she climb that high? She would need boots, maybe different clothes. *What if* coursed through her. What would people think or say?

Saturday and Wednesday mornings were designated butter days. Hanna had already skimmed the thickest cream off the top of the day's milk. She poured the richest cream from the last three days into the churn, added a bit of salt, and replaced the wooden lid, sliding the central hole down over the pole that extended from the wooden paddles, and began the churning.

Hanna slowly raised and turned the pole, slowly lowered and turned the pole, raised, lowered over and over. She used to hate this chore, standing in the alcove to the kitchen, the dull tedium, the pain in her feet and legs from standing still on hard tiles. All for the butter's sake. Without the right temperature, the cream might bind but the butter produced wouldn't store as well. She wished she had gloves; her hands suffered the most. But there was an element to this chore that she loved. The rhythm of each stroke, the slow thickening, the gradual change in the texture of the that rich cream from slack liquid to something with a resistance and response of its own. She would close her eyes and settle into the growing resistance. In this state, she felt the gradual pulling apart of elements, the thickening and breaking, the ultimate formation of pale ivory curds of butter.

At last, it had taken. Opening the churn, Hanna tipped it carefully to pour off most of the buttermilk into a waiting pail, affixed the lid and set the pail on the cold shelf where it would keep until needed for baking. Then she scooped out and strained the gobbets of butter into a cold bowl, covering them with icy water. She poured the water off and replaced it repeatedly with fresh water until it ran clear. She mouldeded and press the butter in her stiff hands until all the water oozed away. She checked the flat obsidian stone to be certain it was immaculate before placing the mound of butter on it. With two wooden paddles, Hanna slapped the sides and ends of the pat, turning it frequently until it was the perfect size to fit in the butter mold. With a spatula, she smoothed the surface and impressed it with the wooden stamp of a Pasque Flower. The job was finished. Now she could slip back into the kitchen to warm her aching hands on the tile stove.

Moving from the alcove to the kitchen was moving from one realm to its opposite, from shadow to light, from the settled smells of dried, smoked, stored food, to the rich and mellow aromas of simmering broth and wisps of birch smoke. The kitchen was the same muted yellow as the butter she churned. In both rooms, everything was in order, everything was clean and cared for. But only the kitchen offered comfort. Hanna gravitated to the kakelugn that stretched from floor to ceiling, its chimney passing through the upstairs bedroom on its way through the roof. She ran her chapped hands over the white tiles, many decorated with sprigs of purple heather. The glazer's hands had allowed minute variations in the design of the heather sprigs. She loved comparing them: this one had a few extra buds and that one leaned a bit more to the left, while on yet another the buds were a paler shade o purple. She knew them all and had chosen her favourites. Spreading her fingers wide, Hanna pressed her palms into the warmth of the tiles and stroked them back and forth until she could smell their earthy, faintly musky aroma, almost hear the bees buzzing around the tiny coronas. She spread her arms out and around the tiled body of the tall, tall stove and moved her own body in on the warmth: her cheek, her chest, her belly, all the way down, sinking into dreams of other days. There had been days of warm, tall grass gently bent by a susurrating breeze, releasing smells of summer. Warm days to lie down in the grass, to be loved. Stroked. Hannah exhaled the memory of pleasure.

In that moment of total emptiness, of her lost youth, her lost ability to feel pleasure, a claw closed on the back of her neck. Ice shot down her spine.

"No, don't. Please." Another hand, a practised hand, too

smooth, between her legs lifting her dress. "Please don't!"

"Quiet."

"Please," she whispered.

"Quiet!" hissed in her ear. His breath. Sour. Hot. His fingers penetrating. Johanna's body locked into rigidity. Shame and despair.

Then footsteps on the stairs. He withdrew his hands, first the one between her thighs, then the one crushing her neck.

"You owe me," he hissed in her ear. The master of the house, of the farm, of two fishing boats – the master of his son Dankert and the master of Johanna – withdrew to the kitchen table where he stood exuding calm authority as he wiped his fingers on a clean white linen. "Good morning, Fru Lorkman. I hope you slept well last night."

"Well enough, and you, Herr Lorkman?"

Johanna was having trouble moving. She felt trapped, unable to find a reason for standing face to face with the round column of the stove.

"And what is this one doing?"

"I have no idea, staring at those tiles like an idiot. But perhaps she could bring us coffee and sweet buns if she isn't too busy.

"Bring mine upstairs. I'm not quite ready to face the day," Fru Lorkman demanded.

Johanna summoned her voice. "Will you join your wife for breakfast upstairs, Herr Lorkman?"

"No."

Of course not, Johanna thought, certain that he wasn't finished with her.

"Be sure the coffee's not too hot, but don't let it go cold either," the old woman said.

"Yes, ma'am. Shall I put the butter on the side?"

"That is how we do things here, isn't it?" Her disdain evident in the raised eyebrow.

As she headed back up the stairs, Lorkman added, "I'll have mine hot and melting." One side of his mouth smiled.

Johanna turned aside to make the coffee. So much tension coursed through her neck and shoulders that she could barely move the kettle without spilling it. Her whole body wanted to run from the kitchen, away from the farm, back to her small home and her girls. No, further, she wanted to run out of her life. She could feel Lorkman's eyes on her. She knew that she was safe for the moment. Breakfast had to be prepared and brought upstairs or the wife would become suspicious. Johanna wished the Fru would be more vigilant, hover on the stairs and see what her husband was trying to do. But she suspected that the woman didn't really care. Her place in the house wasn't at risk. Johanna's was.

Moreover, if she actually did witness her husband's behavior, Johanna knew what the consequences would be. As terrible as the job was, as little as she received in turn for her work, Johanna knew that no one else would have her in their house. Her history, her secrets, and other peoples' accusations would close in on her. She had no family to support her and there would be no help from the church which had shunned her. She had to hold tight and hope that somehow, some way, some man who cared for her would find the strength to stand by her side.

Rikka had changed the soaking water for the salt cod twice and was trying to peel the potatoes with the dull paring knife. It gouged instead of peeled. She looked at the leather strop nailed to the wall. Her mother used it. There was a certain angle for the blade; she could imagine that the wrong angle could make matters worse. And just how much tension did someone use in holding the end of the strop? As she pressed hard on the first downward stroke, she managed only to nick her supporting hand. She watched a bead of blood form on her thumb. It built slowly until the mass of it broke form and spilled onto her skirt. Fascinated, Rikka watched for more. Another drop formed, grew, fell, and another. She opened her hand and closed it into a fist. If she stood here long enough would it just seep out of her, drop by drop until she stood in a pool of her own blood? But it didn't, the last drop sat on her finger. She watched the shiny skin develop. The squawk of a chicken followed by the thud of an axe blade on wood broke the spell. Her neighbour, Dagur, would have a feast tonight. In the meantime, she would just scrub the potatoes hard and leave the peels on, knowing there would be complaints.

Agnes came from the bedroom to shadow Rikka. She wished the little girl would go play somewhere instead of trying to help her. Agnes looked at the splotchy potatoes and said, "That isn't the way Mama does it." True enough, but Rikka didn't need to hear it from a four-year-old.

"Oh no, there's blood on the floor." Agnes was outraged. Rikka tried breathing deeply but instead of a flow of breath she was emitting tight little shards of breath, panicking. Was this what the rest of her life would be like? Would she run this house doing both the man's work and the woman's until her little sisters grew up? And then would she be doing the same in her own pathetic house with an army of small trolls and she their slave? Her breath sharpened still more. She felt suffocated.

Someone knocked at the door.

"Go away," she hissed, and the door opened. There was Dagur, a gutted and plucked chicken in hand. She placed it on the counter and in a moment her large old arms wrapped around Rikka. Even the stink of chicken on her sleeve was a relief.

"Sit down, Henrikka. Sit down." She lay her calloused hands on top of Rikka's head, bending her head towards her lap and breathed deeply in and out, in and out, until Rikka was able to follow the rhythm. She loosed the cord that held the girl's long pale braid together, and gently ran her fingers through the weave of hair, loosening, loosening. Finally, Rikka wept. How she loved this old woman. She was like a grandmother and also a bit of a sorceress.

"You have a heavy load now, darling. I know. I know. When the clouds grow heavy, they always piss on someone. Look at that. You have cut yourself. We'll clean that up, and I don't want you touching that chicken with that open wound on your hand. Where's the yarrow I gave your mother? Never mind. I'll find it. See? Here it is. I made this little bag for it. Now, remember what it looks like and where it is. You will need it for all the cuts and scrapes that children get ... and those that come with working in the yard and kitchen. It will suppress infection and start the healing. Now here's what we're going to do. You're going to put on your other skirt so I can get that bit of blood out of this one. Salt will draw it out. Then you're going to go out for a walk, a good long walk. You'll take your time and I'll use it to cook this chicken and take care of the little ones."

Rikka finally looked into the old woman's eyes which were almost lost in loose folds of speckled skin.

"Thank you," she whispered, unwilling to cry again, even in gratitude.

In the sleeping room was an old pair of pants, rough and

patched that she sometimes wore to keep out the cold. She took off her skirt, put them on and had to smile at the look of her legs in men's pants. Then she pulled her second skirt over the pants. Bulky, but comforting. And daring. A secret. Wrapping her shawl around herself, she gave Dagur another hug, a smile, and then she was out the door.

A fine cold sun illuminated the fjord and the mountains outlining it. Colours were sharp in the autumn light. Blues, golds, black. Wind blew, spiking a chill through Rikka. She took the same path that the four of them had followed so recently, but she travelled much further along it. The turn of the path was more protected in this direction. Sudden outcroppings of rock created little alcoves where green grass still hung on to the tail end of the season. The rock walls soaked up whatever sun was available and sent the heat back out to the soil. In one of these alcoves, she found crow berries growing close to the ground. It was a wonder that they could still grow in October, but there they were and she was glad to pick them, storing them in a twist of her shawl.

Rikka sat down on the slope of a black rock to enjoy the warmth and protection of the place. The wind-whipped surf sent up salt spray and the low sun illuminated the cascade as each wave crested and fell. If only she could live right here, right in this place, in this moment, forever.

She started to grow sleepy in this perfect spot, so Rikka decided to move further along, to a marshy spot protected from the winds where she had picked cloudberries in another season. She knew that the copper-coloured berries had been finished since early September and that they were far more fragile than the blueberries, but she just had to try. She wanted to take full advantage of this time to herself even though the self-indulgence was at the expense of others. Around another bend, the ever-present Thorn came into full view and glory with the golden sun blessing it. She thought of her idea. Climb the Thorn. As impossible as cloudberries in October. Or only as improbable as crowberries?

A flock of kittiwakes wheeled around in the spiral of an updraft. Their calls reminded Rikka of spoiled toddlers whining and complaining but the birds seemed to enjoy their ride. What could they possibly have to complain about? The ability to fly? The ability to be carried upwards with little effort on their part? The sun caught their white feathers so they glistened like day stars in the sky. Rikka couldn't imagine a luckier fate than to be born a bird. She lifted her body with no help from an updraft and moved on. She was taking too much advantage of Dagur's kindness, so Rikka decided to go only as far as the cloudberry marsh, not that she expected to find anything there, but because she had set it as a goal.

The marsh was as she had imagined. It marked the centre of another, larger alcove. She stepped from one small mound to another. On each were the remains of last season's cloudberries. The leaves had turned a deep burgundy and no trace of orange berries remained. Of course not. She couldn't believe that she failed to harvest any in August. The berries were a favourite when mixed with cream, their tartness contrasting with the silky sweetness. And in a good year, they could be sold to the farm families.

She focussed on where she stepped with each foot. A geometric form hid in the copse of birch on the edge of the marsh. She squinted to get a clearer picture of a tawny brown shape. Her mind turned the shape into what it really was: a lavvu. The tent was short and circular, and she knew that lavvu were the traditional homes of the nomadic Lapps.

But what was it doing here, so close to her village? She had been taught that the Lapps were thieves and drunkards, not to be trusted at all. She couldn't decide what to do. Were there Lapps in the woods or perhaps right behind her this very moment? She had seen the Lapps before when they came down from the tundra to trade reindeer meat and skins. The sight of them always excited her, but excitement had turned to fear. Which way to turn? She pivoted on the little mound, absent mindedly wrapped her shawl more tightly around her shoulders, and watched the collection of precious crowberries trickle out onto the mound. Well, Lapp or no Lapp, she wasn't going to let the berries just roll into the muck. One by one she picked them out from under tired mulder leaves and between sodden roots. She was just scooping the surrounding water for more wayward berries when she sensed someone behind her.

Rikka froze. She wanted to take back her foolish decision to retrieve the berries. She couldn't turn to face whoever it was. She just waited with her shawl still open. A hand reached around from behind her and gently let crowberries roll into the bowl of her shawl. That was all. A hand, an arm, a silence, a quick turn of her head, an eye, eyes, a turned back. A silent leaving.

Rikka rose, arranged her shawl more securely, and without looking back she stepped carefully, and with what she hoped was dignity, from the highpoint of one mound to the highpoint of the next. And then she ran, imagining it over and over again. The unbroken silence of his presence. She knew it was a man, his hand told her so. She knew she had just met a Lapp, and she felt that she would meet him again. A hand, his eyes. Blackbirds beat in her chest.

Dagur slapped the chicken carcass down on the counter and Agnes shrieked with delight. "Hold still or you'll topple. You sound like this old hen with her head cut off. Now I want you to go outside and find a piece of firewood about this long," Dagur said running her hand down Agnes's forearm.

"What for?" Agnes asked.

"To beat this old hen with. She's as tough as a loaf of bread lost behind your bed since spring."

Agnes shouted laughter and jumped down from her chair.

"Stupid old hen. I'm going to beat her and beat her until she's soft and squishy."

"You'll leave the beating to me or we'll end up with mashed chicken for dinner. I'll let you beat the potatoes though."

Agnes ran outside with more enthusiasm than Dagur had seen in her for months. It wasn't until she heard the coughing that she realized the little girl wore only her dress and vest to keep her warm. Dagur hurried to the door to call her back in, but Agnes swooshed past her with a perfect piece of wood to use as a mallet.

"Here!"

"Oh, fine work, Agnes." She hugged the child, mostly to give her a boost of warmth, and lifted her back onto the chair. She noted that Agnes's lips were no more blue than usual, a sad enough comment in itself.

"Please let me hit it once."

"All right. But try not to knock it all to pieces. She was a good old hen."

Agnes loved the chickens. Dagur often let her gather the eggs and throw kitchen waste into their yard. She even helped Dagur pull up certain wild plants to feed them. Her brow furrowed as she asked, "Is this the old hen, Sigga?"

Dagur saw her consternation and gentled her tone. "Ja, Agnes.

This was Sigga. I know she was one of your favourites, but she wasn't well. She had to drag one leg around behind her and she couldn't get enough to eat because the other hens were faster than her."

"But if she was hurt, someone should fix her. You fix people. Why didn't you fix her? You give me medicine. Don't you have chicken medicine?"

"Child, this old hen was soon to die. The best medicine I had for her was to help her die and leave her pain behind. That's what we do. We take care of our animals and then, when the time comes, we kill them as painlessly as we can."

"You chopped off Sigga's head!"

"Yes."

"No, that's wrong."

"Let me tell you how I did it."

"No, I don't want to hear that."

"I mean, how I took away her pain first."

Agnes looked doubtful but listened.

"I held old Sigga and stroked her. She liked that. If she weren't so sick she wouldn't have let me do it. Then I held her chest and her legs and I drew her beak through the soil, gently, slowly. She closed her eyes as I drew her that way several times. And then it was as if she were asleep. That's when I lay her down on the stump, stretched out her neck a ways and took her head off. She didn't even know."

"I would know."

Dagur decided that Agnes had heard enough about death and wanted to distract her. "Did you hear that?"

"What?"

"I think I heard Ragna making little noises. Maybe she's waking up. Why don't you go in and see if you can settle her down, maybe rub her back gently or kiss her on the nose."

Agnes looked suspiciously at the old woman. She stared at her crinkled face. Then she slid down from the chair and wandered off to the sleeping room. Dagur made quick work of the old hen, deciding not to pummel it at all but to dismember it and put it in the big pot to stew slowly. It wouldn't have done well in the oven anyway. Just too old, too tough, like someone else she knew.

Dagur pondered over what she could do to lighten Agnes's mood. Her spirits seemed erratic, just as her body fluctuated between weakness and vitality. Did the child fear death? Did it haunt her? Her sorrow over Sigga's death was to be expected at her age, but did she have premonitions of her own dark fate? Maybe a visit to Dagur's workshop would be helpful. It might help her to normalize death, even to see the beauty in it. A swishing sound accompanied by giggles caught Dagur's attention. Agnes had her arms wrapped around tiny Ragna's chest so that the baby's arms stood out to her side and her feet dragged the floor. Her eyes were wide and she chortled as Agnes manipulated her body.

"Look, Dagur. Ragna can walk." Dagur's hearty laughter encouraged the little girl to dance her puppet around the room. "See, she learned to walk in her dream. See?" All three of them laughed out loud, filling the room with a new mood.

"Agnes, you are a wonderful teacher. No one else could have taught Ragna to walk and dance at such an early age. Let's put our coats on and bundle up the little one. I want to show you something in my workshop." Agnes was delighted. She had never been allowed to enter the shed that looked like a fairy castle to her.

"I'll need to carry Ragna. We can't expect her to walk over the pebbles before she even has shoes." As if she understood the joke, Ragna shrieked with laughter. When they were all bundled up they made their way from Johanna's sparse and tidy rorbu over to the apparent chaos of Dagur's home. Pathways of seashells swirled into concentric circles bordered by flat black rocks and tiny gardens where herbs and medicinals grew in the light months. The workshop was a small stone structure which Dagur said a very good friend of hers built long ago.

"She must have been very, very short to get through that door," Agnes said.

"He was actually taller than most men," Dagur said. "But he wanted to be certain that anyone who was afraid to stoop could not enter."

"Who was he?"

"Never mind that. He has been gone for a long, long time. But he left me this workshop, and now it's time for us to go inside."

Agnes was shaking with anticipation. In her short life she had spun many tales about who lived inside this miniature palace, about the wonders that must be inside, and why she wasn't allowed to enter. Dagur led the girls inside and left them by the open door.

"Wait here a moment while I make some light." Agnes stood in the tiny doorway with Ragna still dangling like a puppet. Soft swishing sounds came from Dagur as she moved through the darkness. Then the thin sound of metal scraping. Dagur was making fire with a tinder box. A spark of light followed by more scraping and more sparks managed to light up bits of the room a flash at a time. Dagur blew on the tinder and then lit a twist of paper, then a candle and another candle. She put glass chimneys over each candle so the light danced around the little room. Agnes's eyes followed the dance. The flickering of the candlelight on the uneven surface of the stone walls made the stones appear to float lazily in water.

"Look Ragna. It's moving. The rocks are swimming! It's like we're under water." Ragna answered with a shriek of delight and swayed back and forth between her sister's legs.

Agnes moved to the centre of the room where the table holding all the candles was laid out with tiny skeletons. She touched one of them with just one careful fingertip, then ran her finger down the length of its spine. "It used to be a bird?"

"Yes. How could you tell?"

"I see its beak. I see two tiny feet with long fingernails. And this must be the inside of a wing and only some tiny, tiny bones are there."

"What you see is a skeleton. That's what most animals leave behind when their flesh has fallen away or been eaten. You've seen fish bones many times.

"Yes, I know. We eat fish for dinner really often. Mother usually cuts the fish down the centre and pulls out its skeleton. They are different. I don't think about them. They are just dinner and sometimes I get tired of fish."

"Can you guess what kind of bird this skeleton came from?"

Agnes moved in more closely and touched each part of the skeleton. "Its head is quite round. It seems nice. I think it's a dove, but it seems too small. Maybe it's a baby ... or maybe it's so small because it lost its feathers and its skin."

Agnes was gaining momentum as she began to visualize the living bird. "The doves sometimes sit on our windowsill. When it's cold they puff up their feathers and get bigger. Maybe they can get smaller too." She turned to Dagur with a light in her eyes and the smile of discovery on her lips. "Is it? Is it a dove?"

"Yes Agnes. You are right." Dagur didn't want to praise her too enthusiastically. She liked the little girl's power of reasoning and didn't want it to bloat into arrogance. It might be that she was exceptionally bright; then again, it more likely was just that fay quality which small children sometimes possess and then lose, just as the full moon wanes. Dagur took special care of her little aviary of dead birds. There were kestrels and kittiwakes, ravens and doves, waxwings and godwits, and in its own special nook in the rock wall, a puffin too large to perch between the other skeletons. These were her private treasures, and she was pleased to see the care and love that Agnes showed. She had laid the smaller birds in a circle with their heads pointing out as if each were to fly off in its own direction.

"Where are they flying to?" Dagur asked.

"That one will fly over the water and sit on a rock. This tiny one will fly in circles and then sit on your windowsill. These two aren't strong enough to fly anywhere, and this one will fly around the whole world."

"I guess they're just like people then, Agnes, each one going its own way and some not going at all."

"What about me?"

"Are you asking where you'll go in your life?

"Yes."

"Only you can answer that. And time will tell you."

"I think I might die."

"Why do you say that?"

"I'm always sick. My sisters aren't sick. I am. I think I might die."

Dagur couldn't think what to say that would be both true and kind. More than anything, she wanted to be kind to the child. No, more than anything she wanted to help her thrive. And so she was silent.

"Dagur, what do you think my life will be?"

"I think it will be whatever you make it."

"How do I make my life?" The child looked at Dagur with hope in her eyes.

Dagur drew in her breath. She must answer the child from the perspective of someone who truly believed that she would survive her childhood.

"You are good at looking at things and understanding them. Like these little skeletons. You can see what their lives were like. Try looking into the sea, too. There's so much life under the water. Look at what they are made of and what they do to survive. Just watch and listen and then ask your questions. I think you will have much to teach others." Dagur didn't know where this was coming from. Was she just fantasizing a rich and healthy life for Agnes, or was she seeing a glimmer of the child's possibilities?

"Can we go to the shore now? I want to watch."

"It will be dark soon, but perhaps we could go down to my tide pool. The tide is out now but the little pool should hold plenty for you to see. And it will be safe there."

"What can we do with Ragna?"

"I'll hold her. She is only barely awake as it is, and my body will keep her warm and safe. See? Her eyelids are fluttering."

Agnes laughed. "They look like moth wings."

Dagur looked back at the circle of bird skeletons Agnes had made. Almost a perfect circle with the birds evenly spaced; but one bird's head reached out of the circumference.

"That's my favourite," Agnes said stroking it's bald head. "I think I know where it will go."

Dagur blew out the candles, took a circular disc of clear glass down from a high shelf and tucked it into her apron. The three headed out of the little hut, shutting the door behind them. Dagur's tidepool was at the end of a small inlet that reached into her property, just a short way below her gardens. The pool was made private by the surrounding rocks. Dagur had heard the rumour that she bathed in the pool. Whether they thought it was true or just someone's idea of a great joke, she could imagine them visualizing the old, wrinkled hag floating in her private basin under the aurora borealis. The mere thought of it could inspire hilarity among a tavern full of sailors. And it probably had. Dagur sat cross-legged at the pool's edge with the sleeping Ragna cradled in her lap. Agnes knelt at the water's edge. She leaned forward and held her gaze steady on the water which was rippled by the tendrils of wind that worked their way between boulders.

"I can't see down," said the disappointed child.

"Ah, you just need a little help," said Dagur as she pulled the glass disc out of her large apron pocket. She blew on it and then polished the surface with the hem of Agnes's dress.

"What's that?" asked Agnes.

"It's a looking glass," Dagur told her in a tone that signified she was surprised the child didn't know. Then she bent forward with the disc, much the same size as a big Easter pancake, and said, "Pretend the sand here is the surface of the water."

"Okay."

"Now hold the edges of the pancake, just with the palms of your hands. Don't touch the surface but press your palms firmly on the edge of the pancake. Now lower it down to the surface of the sand and hold it steady." The child giggled but did as she was told. "Now what do you see?"

"Sand... through a window."

"Right. You're doing well. Now are you ready for it to get a little more difficult?"

"Yes."

"You will do just as you already did, but this time you will lower it onto the surface of the water in the tide pool. Are you ready to try that?"

Agnes couldn't have been more ready. "Like this?"

"Almost, Agnes, but see how the water is sloshing over the edges of the pancake? We don't want a wet pancake. See if you can hold it just a bit higher so the water doesn't flow over it but touches it nonetheless."

Agnes's tongue was set firmly between her teeth and the concentration on her little face was intense. A few times she tried, still not understanding why, and a few times the water covered her pancake. Then she set it down on the sand, shook out her arms and said. "I will keep trying." Dagur laughed.

When it seemed as if they'd soon run out of light, Agnes gasped. "Look! I can see into the water. I can see what's at the bottom of the pool. This is not a pancake, it's a magical looking glass."

"Congratulations. What do you see?"

"Something. What is it?" Agnes had to lift the glass off the water and use her skirt to wipe off the top, and then she set it perfectly on the surface again. "There's a round white stone down there, and there's a jelly fish resting on it. I couldn't see well at first, but it's a clear jellyfish, almost as clear as my pancake. I can even see some tiny little bits of red… like threads in it… Is that its blood?"

"No, jellyfish don't have blood."

"It has to have blood, doesn't it?"

"Most animals do," Dagur confirmed.

Agnes looked deep into Dagur's eyes and then shrugged, setting this information aside. Then she had to wipe off the disc again and place it back on the surface.

"But something funny … let me look a little more. There's a black circle right at the center of the jellyfish." Agnes gasped. "It looks like an eye."

Dagur was becoming suspicious. Had the child's imagination gone wild? "Hold steady, Agnes. Think about what you're seeing."

"It's not a jellyfish, it's a huge eyeball." She gasped again. "No, the jelly fish just lifted of the white stone. It's floating away. I can't follow it."

"Don't even try. We don't want you falling in the water. Now what about that black circle. Have you figured that out yet?

"I'll look again. Steady, steady, little hands," she prayed. "Oh, that's funny. It's just a pebble, a black pebble resting on a white stone … and then a jellyfish … or a giant eyeball." Agnes and Dagur laughed together.

"Well, that's enough of looking for one day, little one. What have you seen today?"

"I've seen things that I never saw before, and they turned into other things, and then turned back into themselves."

"You've seen more than most people see in a whole lifetime. Just keep looking."

Rikka sat on the front step, reluctant to go in even though she knew Dagur needed to get home. She studied the Thorn, its impossibly sharp peak, how ominous it looked this evening. And there was that scar, or smile, as some people liked to call it. Illuminated by a dying sun, the lighter rock of the gash grinned dull orange. The house was silent. Ragna must be asleep and Agnes just curled up by the fire. Rikka gathered an armload of stove wood, wishing they had coal stored up for the worst of the winter. Her mother often brought home bits of coal from the farm. She foraged the waste pieces, never enough to make a real difference. Some years Lorkman brought a load on a cart pulled by his horse. But the amount varied from ample to stingy, and one year he didn't bring any at all. Rikka wondered what this depended on. He made no explanations, just called out for all hands to shovel the coal while Johanna served him dark bread with precious butter and a glass of aquavit, a rare treat for anyone else in the house.

Rikka's thoughts shifted to the specter she encountered in the marsh. He didn't seem real. Her memory moved to the one part of him that she had focused on: his hands, tawny skin, long fingers, palm gently cupping the berries and then slowly opening to slide them one by one into her shawl. In her mind she watched those berries slide, over and over, always more slowly. Who was attached to that hand and arm? A flash of something else about him was interrupted when Dagur broke into her fantasies by opening the door.

"I'm sorry, Dagur, I took too long."

"Never mind. I'll come again. It does me good to hold a baby."

"It does me good to walk. Tusen takk, Dagur," answered Rikka.

When Hanna came home, the house was warm and smelled of chicken stewing. The whole day changed. Her daughter had managed to keep the house in order, and where did she ever get a chicken? They sat at the table, just four of them, Agnes busily chewing every bit of chicken off a bone. Her face gleamed with chicken fat. The baby ate bits of bread soaked in milk. Until recently, Ragna was breast fed and Hanna could take her to work, but Fru Lorkman had recently announced that it was time for the child to be weaned and left at home. This would free up Johanna's time to get more work done. Johanna could not argue with the decision. She would have to limit nursing her baby to first thing in the morning and the time just before she put her to bed at night... and only eight months old. Now the baby sat in her highchair and stared big eyed at her mother of whom she saw far too little. She banged her hands on the tray.

"Where did you get that highchair? It seems like it's been here forever," asked Rikka.

"It's beautiful, don't you think?" replied Hanna. She stroked the satin smooth surface of the wood. "It really is a piece of art."

"But how did you come by it?" Rikka could tell her mother was evading her question. "You know, it looks like Onkle Dankert's work. That detail on the back of the seat, the flying dove, it's just like the one on the alms table that he made for the church. I never thought about that."

"You're right, Rikka, your uncle did make the chair."

"So why are you so secretive about it? Are you reluctant to give him credit?"

"Maybe. He does annoy me sometimes, you know."

"And how is he, my uncle? I've been wondering about that. He isn't your brother. Was he your husband's brother? What's the connection?"

"Oh, stop it, Rikka. He's an uncle in name only. Not related."

"Did he make it for you?"

"I suppose so. I don't really remember."

"How could you not remember a gift like that? And speaking of relations..." Rikka knew she was exasperating her mother, but she also knew she was weakening her and that she might squeeze some information out of her. "I think we should put together a family tree. I would love to see that, and the little girls will appreciate it someday, too. We could even embroider it and put it on the wall."

Hanna's head slumped. She was exhausted, as much by her daughter as by work. She started tapping her fork on the table, a slow rhythm growing in intensity.

"Yes," she hissed, "you could do it in hardanger, counting threads and embroidering satin stitch around the edges of the little squares. White thread on white cloth; you'll have a good time with that. Oh, and then you could take those tiny, tiny scissors and cut the fabric away from inside the frames. You could create miniature windows for your ancestors to stick their heads out of. Yes, this would be our family tree, all lopsided and ready to fall over sidewise. Oh, my bleeding eyes!"

Rikka stared at her mother, but Agnes, totally delighted by the silly story began to giggle, and they all laughed.

"I'll wash the dishes," said Hanna. "I'm sorry."

Rikka cleared the dishes and then sat down on the daybed. "Mama, I'll sleep on this bed. From now on, I'm the night watchman."

Rikka controlled her impatience for two days before calling on Dagur to help her out again while Hanna was at work and Rikka was home with the little girls. She stepped lightly as she made her way through Dagur's garden, careful not to crush any hidden treasures. She knew the soil itself was the old woman's greatest pride, even more than what grew out of it. She gathered seaweed, food waste, scat, fish scales, and shells to grind up.

"Gotta make it yourself. There are more stones than shit on this island, and that's saying a lot," she claimed.

And still, even in October, a few wild onions and medicinal herbs bravely held their place. Dagur made a nice little living for herself working up remedies for everything from aching bones to insomnia. In a community with no doctor, her skills were invaluable, even to those who claimed she had a touch of the witch about her.

The inside of Dagur's little rorbu looked more like a factory than a home. Bundles of herbs hung drying from the ceiling. A pot of something vaguely sweet and yet astringent let off steam that seemed to work against the drying process, but clearly, she knew what she was doing. She never took her boots off, which was just as well since she refused to put a wooden floor over the pounded earth, claiming it kept her in contact with the subterranean forces, whatever those were. A fisherman's jacket that wouldn't button up over her belly and old gloves that left her fingertips free completed the look.

"I was just headed out to see what treasures I might find along the shoreline. Do you want to come with me?

"I was actually going to ask you if you could watch the little ones for me, but put it out of your mind."

"Oh, I can watch them alright. Ragna can sit in the cart and Agnes can run alongside." That proposition sounded less than safe: an old woman pushing a one-wheeled cart filled to the gunnels with a baby while a four-year-old ran alongside.

"I can see that you have doubts, but I've handled wild chickens and tame otters in my life. I guess I can handle these two. We'll be just like a little family, and I'll be the great uncle."

Despite her doubts, Rikka fell for temptation. She was anxious to revisit the cloudberry mounds, just for a quick look and for curiosity's sake. "Alright, then, I promise I won't be long."

"I want to go with you, Rikka," Agnes chimed in.

"Not this time, Agnes, I'm going to move really fast."

"I can run faster than you," the little girl argued. Her hands were clenched, her feet ready to fly, and tears welled in her eyes.

"Alright then." Rikka was disappointed but couldn't come up with a good enough excuse for either Agnes or Dagur. "But you must mind me. You'll need to help with gathering driftwood and putting it in little piles. Later we'll pick it up in Dagur's cart.

"She's not Dagur," Agnes said. "She's Great Uncle."

There was little new driftwood along the shore but enough to make Agnes think she was doing a real job. Rikka wondered if she would ever get as far as the marsh at this rate, and if she did, what about Agnes? Was she exposing the child to danger? Well, she probably wouldn't get that far moving at this four-year-old pace.

Just ahead were the Sentinels, a group of tall, jagged rocks standing in a ring like members of a coven, angular, sharp, dark. But within their circle, driftwood often lay at the feet of those guards. They stood within the tide line, half the day catching flotsam and half the day tossing it back to sea.

"Look, Agnes. The tide is out, and I'll wager the Sentinels have trapped some firewood for us." The little girl ran down squealing with delight.

At the slit of an entrance framed by two hovering pillars, Agnes stopped. She looked around inside the circle, looked up at the guards, and simply froze in place.

"It's alright to go in. They'll protect you."

"But there's lots and lots of driftwood in here."

"Good then. Let's pull out the smaller pieces. Don't try to lug that great monster. He needs to go back to sea."

"Yech, I don't want any sea monsters. Here, is this little enough?" she asked holding up a piece the size of a clothes peg. Then she laughed, but the laughter brought on a spurt of coughing, reminding Rikka that she should get the girl back into the warm rorbu.

Rikka could hardly believe her good fortune. So much firewood, and so much in lengths that she could handle if she borrowed Dagur's cart. Many would have to be cut to fit the stove, of course, but perhaps she could borrow Dagur's saw. As she pulled more and more pieces further up the shore, she noticed that the tide had turned and she picked up her pace. She wondered to herself if the wood would still be there if she piled it all up and came back with a cart.

She thought of sending Agnes for the cart, but the child couldn't possibly manage it on a path, much less on the bumpy shore. Ridiculous thought. Maybe if she ran all the way back, got the cart and rushed back with it, Agnes could wait at the top of the beach for her. She'd get her to straighten out the pieces of driftwood just to keep her busy and safe.

Rikka watched Agnes working intently, light brown curls stuck to her cheeks and forehead, nose running, but nothing unusual there.

"Agnes, I have an important job for you, but maybe you're too little to do it." The response was as expected, outrage at such an idea.

"This is wonderful wood we've gathered. It'll keep us warm for at least a week. We've done a great job gathering it. Now, do you think that you could lay these sticks out straight, side by side and then on top of each other? It's a big job and maybe too much for you."

"I can do it," Agnes replied. "I can keep us warm for a year!"

"Alright then, I'm going to get the cart and I'll be back really soon. Then we can lay your tidy pile of wood in the cart and head back home. Will that work?"

"I can do it."

"Just don't go in the Sentinels again, Aggie. The tide is starting to come in. Stay way up on the shore, right here." Agnes nodded and got to work.

Rikka felt tugged in two directions as she ran down the shoreline. Get the cart. Mind Agnes. Get the cart as fast as you can. Stay with Agnes. It became a silent chant so convincing in two directions at once that she felt as if she were tripping over her own two feet. It wasn't so very far to the cart, though. There, she could see it up ahead.

The seagulls had suddenly grown raucous, circling over the Sentinels, uttering shrieks of warning, of concern, or of victory. Rikka heard the tumult, spotted the circle of birds, dropped the cart on the path and ran, calling out Agnes's name. No answer. The birds showed Rikka where to go by their circling over the Sentinels. Her little sister lay face down, her faded blue dress floating in shallow water. Her head rested on a piece of drift wood with an odd animal-like face at one end. An otter? Rikka turned Agnes over. She seemed to be alive. But blue. She picked the child up, heavy with sodden clothes, and ran back towards home. She would get her to Dagur. Save my sister, please.

Dagur was running from the opposite direction holding little Ragna close to her chest. Her run was staggered and slow, but she put all her will into it. The birds had told her to run.

When they reached one another, a panting Dagur commanded, "Take off your dress, "and she set the baby down and took off her own. "Take off her wet dress and wrap her in both of these. We have to get her warm."

She turned Agnes over on the path and pounded on her back

repeatedly to expel any water from her lungs. There wasn't any. She looked at the bump on her head and announced it was essential to get her home right then. Dagur carried the baby, and Rikka pushed the cart with Agnes in it.

Although Dagur lagged behind, she was quick to get together the herbs she wanted and take over to Hanna's house. "Build the fire up. I want it hot in here. Get a small pot of water boiling. Don't you have any muslin? Never mind, I can do without. Bring me that sieve."

Rikka ran from one task to another. She could hear Agnes's breathing now, raspy and thick. She needed more to do, right now. She pulled a stool close to the stove and draped blankets over it to warm. She brought Dagur a large old sweater to pull on over her undershirts. Standing back Rikka almost laughed when she saw the old woman, muffled in baggy layers on top with her bulbous legs and saggy elephant skin hanging below. Rikka shook herself. Where was the urge to laugh coming from? She had almost lost her little sister, the frail one, the one who needed even more protection than baby Ragna. Yet still this urge was boiling inside her, pushing up from her gut to her throat. And then an ugly laugh burst from her mouth… like vomit, like the Devil spewing out from her guts.

Dagur froze, but only for a moment before her attention returned to what she was grinding with a pestle. She did not even look up. She didn't see Rikka slump down onto the edge of Agnes's bed. The smell of garlic filled the room. Rikka waited for the silence to break.

 "This is for killing the foul things in her. Here, mix some of this honey into it. We'll make her a tea of that. In the meantime, I want you to make a tent over her bed. We'll steam her with fenugreek. That will open her lungs and let the snot out. The turpentine will have to wait. Go sit by her. Watch her carefully. Do not let your attention stray."

Rikka sat on the edge of the trundle bed, stroking Agnes's

hands, kissing the delicate curve of her ear. Time passed and more time passed, marked by the uneven breath of the little girl. Eventually Rikka heard Dagur her call from the other room.

"What is she doing?"

"Sleeping, I think, and her skin is not so blue now. Will she be alright?"

"Her system is weak, but you already knew that," Dagur responded from the doorway. "And, in fact, you knew it when you left her on the beach. Maybe this could have happened anyway. Who knows? For now, I will watch her closely and wait." Dagur closed her eyes, as if waiting for something from Rikka. Nothing came.

"So now," she continued, "I want you to go outside, take one of your walks if that's what you're inclined to do. Think about it all and leave me here to deal with the little ones."

Rikka wanted to protest, to help, but Dagur's tone told her that she was no help at all. She was being shunned by the one person who always supported her. But now all Rikka could do was obey, and so she went outside. The October sun was sinking into the sea leaving behind a drapery of gloom. She sat down on the splitting stump. Realizing self pity was just an indulgence, Rikka gave her head a shake, shook out her hands, her feet, stood up and shook out her whole body until it stung with looseness. It was time to have a talk with herself. She had only wanted to get firewood but trying to do it with a four-year-old was not a good idea. Trying to be efficient was a good idea, but her way of accomplishing efficiency had almost brought disaster. She should have found others to take care of the children. Rikka turned around seeking out an answer from the sea but it had little to tell her, its constant only waves hit the shore in ever darkening succession. Never a mistake, just wave upon wave perhaps until the end of time. Always the same shore, always the same waves, growing less distinct in the gloaming.

She turned again, this time facing the back wall of the rorbu. What was left of the wood was stacked under the eaves on the leeward side of the house, out of the fiercest of the elements. It was loosely piled and insufficient. Then she noticed that at the far end of the pile, a pillar of wood. Each length was identical, and the column was built by overlapping the ends at ninety-degree angles so that air passed between and around each piece. She walked over to the strange column. Who had done this? It was a lot of work and very precise. She ran her hand down the column, feeling the stability of the structure. It made sense. She noticed that one of the pieces at the bottom, larger around than the ones from Agnes's pile, had that same knot that looked like an otter's face.

Dagur came out of the rorbu, wrapped her shawl around her shoulders and headed home without another word.

In the house, Rikka noticed that Agnes's breathing was still rough and that she was sleeping once again. Should she wake her up? After she fed Ragna and herself, she found the baby a warm rug to loll on. Then she picked up the bag of mending and set to work. She committed to working on the task as long as candlelight allowed. Then when Hanna came home and noticed a finished job, it might go a ways as an apology.

The baby was all smiles and chortles. Rikka couldn't resist picking up the Hardanger fiddle to amuse her. She attempted to tune it with no idea how close she had come to getting it right. Then she tried a simple melody. Ragna slapped the floor, but Agnes called out from her sleep, "Rikka stop! Stop the seagulls. My ears hurt."

Rikka took a clean cloth soaked in warm water and washed Agnes's face and hands. The little girl hugged her in her spindly arms, asked for something to drink, and fell back asleep.

Rikka set to work on the mending. She had learned her skills from her mother. She thought often if they had one of those new sewing machines, they could start a business together. She knew they could. She had seen treadle machines that joined the fabric pieces with stitches as even as her mother's or her own but much, much faster. She liked the sound of the treadle, the quiet rhythm of it, as if it would carry her thoughts away.

It was quiet outside. The wind had died down, had blown the clouds clear so the low autumn sun skimmed the horizon. This day, it lifted from the sea for seven hours. The next week it would be six, then five, then four. Maybe things would fall into a place of acceptance when the sun gave up altogether in December. It was the fear of the falling into winter that was difficult.

A knock at the door, crisp and assured, not a common thing. Rikka and Agnes both stared at the door, until finally Rikka dropped her mending and opened it. Three women stood there: Fru Lorkman, Fru Bergsen, the priest's wife and Fru Haugmen, the shipping agent's wife. Their posture was uniformly straight and their clothing immaculate and appropriately dull.

Rikka greeted them and invited them in although they had already entered. The three wandered around the room scrutinizing everything, one with her eyes, one with her fingertips and one apparently with her nose. Rikka regretted the acrid smell of the coltsfoot and hyssop that Dagur had left steaming on the stove. Fru Lorkman threw open the drape that hid the sleeping room. She didn't enter. Fortunately, everything was clean and tidy.

Rikka kept her head down and her thoughts to herself. Fru Lorkman picked up a piece of mending that Rikka had finished. She asked one of the others, "Do you think a child should be doing this job? I thought Johanna did it herself." The others tut-tutted. The Fru examined it closely, impressed but not saying as much, then looked at Rikka. "You did this work?"

"Yes, ma'am."

"Hmm. Not bad. You may continue to do so."

The priest's wife approached the daybed where Agnes lay quietly but with that telltale rasping breath.

"How is the child?" she asked Rikka.

"Not well at the moment but improving daily. She sometimes comes down with this condition," Rikka said, sensing that she should say as little as possible.

With a sweet and understanding smile, the woman asked, "And does she usually come down with this condition when she has fallen into the winter water? Does it sometimes happen when she has been left alone on the beach?"

Rikka closed her eyes. She couldn't answer. The question was meant to shame her. Long ago, her mother had once screamed about her children being taken away. Still smiling, the priest's wife turned away from Rikka and stroked Agnes's forehead. "Poor little thing. She deserves better medical care. And proper love."

The women poked around and asked questions about firewood, food stores, about where they all slept and when Rikka would go into service.

"Service?" whispered Rikka.

They even asked about the children's father, "or fathers," with a knowing look at each other. They knew plenty already, more than Rikka knew, and they made that evident with sly smirks and nods. Rikka fought the impulse to spit at them, or worse yet, to beg them for what they knew.

The priest's wife suggested that they all sit down, as if there were that many chairs in such a home, and pray together for wisdom and the child's recovery.

Rikka bowed her head but the words travelling through her mind were anything but holy. "God bless Agnes and God bless that icy puddle at the foot of the stairs. May they not notice it in time. Amen."

On their way out the door one woman handed Rikka an old dress and told her to see what she could make herself out of it. "Fix it up. Alter it to fit yourself. I don't want it anymore." And they were gone.

49

Rikka examined the fabric closely. It was a fine wool, warm but not itchy. The colour bothered her. Brown. She could not make a brown dress; it would be far too sad. Maybe Dagur could help her dye it. She knew that the old woman kept a store of dried flowers, bark and berries that she used as dyes. But what colour can you dye over brown? Darker brown. Maybe black, but she knew that was hard to achieve and she wasn't ready to announce her mourning to the community. But maybe she was thinking all wrong. Why would she make a dress when what she really needed was warm clothing for the winter, for the jobs she needed to do outside? This fabric could surely make a good pair of warm pants. She could even use them for climbing the Thorn, if she ever did. And she could modify the bodice to make a jacket to go over her vest. Yes. That was what she'd do. Let people criticize. Just let them.

The next day, Rikka was out at the woodpile when she heard the scraping of boots at the door and rushed to see who it was. Dankert had already entered the house and was holding Agnes in one arm, Ragna in the other. He smiled at her and she pulled a chair over for him.

"Thank you for coming, Onkle. I've been hoping to talk to you. I think I have a bit of coffee left. Sit down. Please." Then imagining what he might be thinking she added, "I was only outside for a moment. I need to work on the woodpile any time I can find."

Dankert kissed Rikka on the cheek and tried to slough off his jacket. Agnes didn't want to leave his arms, but the baby was glad to get free. She was just on the verge of crawling and liked to practise whenever she could.

"Yes, I heard you have a tendency to slip away. No, don't look at me like that. I know too much responsibility has landed on your shoulders. But remember, your mother's burden is even greater."

"I know. And it's breaking her."

"You have to let me know what you need. I'll always try to get it for you. I see you need more firewood."

"Yes, Onkle, thank you so much for what you already brought."

"What? I didn't."

"That doesn't make any sense. Where did it come from then?"

"Was it cut and stacked?"

"Beautifully, yes. You should see it."

"Well, you must have another benefactor. Still, I'm sure you'll need more."

"What I really need is coal. Lorkman hasn't brought any."

"That's the game my father plays, a sick game. I'll try to get you some when the supply boats come in. And I'll teach you how to cut the wood to length without amputating your hand. You look sad. What is it besides too much work, not enough coal, too little time to yourself?"

"Mother."

"Tell me," he said shifting in his chair.

"Something is happening at work that makes her crazy. I know, I know, I make her crazy when I fail her. But I mean really crazy... mad. She left today in complete disarray and was outside trying to strike the wind with her fists. She doesn't even look at or touch Agnes. Lately she doesn't seem to see anything except what's going on inside her. She's been betrayed so many time, by men, by death, by I don't know what. How could she ever have expected life to be like this?" Rikka knew she was touching on forbidden territory here, the unspoken land of adult loss, but she deserved to be acknowledged as an adult if she were to carry the weight of one. In the silence that followed, she traced spirals in the oatmeal dust on the table.

Dankert seemed frozen. He cleared his throat, but no words came out, so Rikka took another step. "Onkle, tell me who my father is. Tell me or I'll grow into womanhood without knowing what to be or who I am. Maybe I will repeat my mother's mistakes. Tell me."

But for the moment, Dankert was saved by a distressed child. Agnes was restless in her bed. Rikka attended to her, tried to get her to sip some of the rose tea. She massaged her feet, kneading faster and harder in her frustration. The child coughed and coughed again, a fit coming on, so Rikka took boiling water from the stove spilling some of it on her hand. She shook her hand and added thyme and pepper to the water, then placed a light cloth over Agnes's head to create a steam tent. Agnes pulled it off screaming and choking. The baby woke up crying. Every cell and nerve in Rikka wanted to run away.

Dankert put his arm around her shoulders and whispered in her ear. "Calm now, Henrikka, calm. I'll handle Agnes." He took her from Rikka's clutches and walked around the house rhythmically pounding Agnes's back. "You take the baby outside and get some air. Good for both of you."

As Rikka wrapped a shawl around herself and the baby and opened the door, she heard Agnes vomit a glob of mucous, probably down Dankert's back. Better Agnes should spew on him than I do, she thought.

Beneath a fuzzy blanket of cloud, the sun roamed westward, sliding along between the sheet and the shore, looking for a place to set. Its pale light threw dim shadows on the land wherever it met a rise. The Sentinels, far down the shoreline, cast the eeriest of shadows, taller than their stony heights, jagged and attenuated. The sun's rays reminded her of a starfish, it too travelling west.

"Thank you, Onkle," Rikka said when the chill forced her back inside.

He had settled Agnes who sat up in the bed pretending to read an upside-down hymnal. Putting on his coat, Dankert said, "I want you to know, Rikka, that not all men are bad, not even all the men in your mother's life. Men die at sea, men run because of fear, men are not always masters of their fate. For now, you'll have to settle for an onkle who cares for you."

"I'm happy and grateful to have you for an onkle, but I wonder what kind of onkle you really are?"

"Look around you. Look at everyone on this island, and the next and the next, all the way through Lofoten. We are all somehow related if you look back far enough."

"Yes, I see that. But that's not the real answer. Someday soon you will tell me all that you know. Sometimes I feel that I am the only person who doesn't know, and yet it is my life that is affected. I'm the one who needs to know, yet I'm totally ignorant. You may as well set me on an ice floe and wish me good luck in my life. And I don't believe in that luck. I believe only that I will fail."

"You're being dramatic, Rikka, but if there is something you need to know in order to face the world, then I will tell you when I can. For now, you'll have to settle for something material, something you can hold in your capable hands."

Should she continue to plead or should she take up this offer, asking for something that would help in her present circumstances? She looked him in the eyes and said, "Boots."

"Boots? What kind of boots?"

"Men's boots. For working. For my life as it is now. I don't care if they're old or new. I just want them to fit, fend off the rain and snow, and they should have sheepskin linings. That will give me some help and some safety."

On Sunday morning, Rikka watched Hanna awake in the morning to something soft against her cheek and to the sound of suppressed coughing close to her ear. Agnes was standing by her bed, her little hand on Hanna's cheek. She shifted to make room for the child. It was Sunday and she could stay home.

"Good morning," Rikka called from the other room. "Why don't you lie and rest for a while? Everything is in order."

"Wonderful, will you bring me Ragna, please?"

Rikka nestled Ragna in close to Hanna and on the opposite

side from Agnes who smiled at her mother and baby sister. Hanna had pulled her bodice aside and Ragna grabbed eagerly for her breast as if she had been starved. In a way she had.

"Rikka, why don't you go out for a walk after breakfast? Give yourself some time alone." Since Rikka had already eaten she thanked her mother and walked out the door feeling better than she had in a long time.

She picked her way along the beach, skirting larger rocks and looking for places that wouldn't trip her up. She wanted to watch the shifting layers of early light. Layers of pale pink woven through dark strands of cloud. Not yet the sun, but a premonition of its rising. The Thorn loomed, a black mass on a still-night sky. There were so many sounds, the surf, the breeze past her ears, the far-off hammering of an early builder, animals waking in their byres, the flapping of wings. But the Thorn was silent. It needed no sound to announce its position in the universe. Rikka still wanted to climb it. Each time she looked at it, whether it dominated the daylight scene or dissolved black on black in the darkest nights, only visible as the negative triangular shape that blocked out the stars, she wanted to climb it.

A story ran through her mind, a myth she learned in school. The sea god, Aeger, had a palace under the sea. She could imagine the palace as a web of subterranean caverns in the submerged base of the Thorn. Water flowed freely through the halls and rooms of the palace, illuminated by phosphorescence caught up in lanterns made of opalescent seashells. Aeger and his wife hosted opulent and raucous parties in their palace, and Aeger being a powerful god, held sway, often good willed, over the gods he invited. However, Ran, his wife, was cruel and vindictive and both gods and sailors feared her wrath. Rikka couldn't remember the rest, something about nine daughters scudding through those caverns. Imagine being one of them, she thought, with all that wealth floating in all that salty water, and nowhere to spend it. Rikka decided that she would rather climb a peak than dive in the depths.

In the distance the sound of hammering, chopping, the dragging of something heavy across the shore came from the furthest end of the inlet where the fishermen kept their boats. It was almost completely enclosed, a safe port in a storm. Fishermen were refurbishing, tightening up, sealing with fresh coats of tar. They were preparing for the arrival of the cod.

As she picked her way through the feeble light, she knew that she was once again headed for the cloudberry marsh. A chill ran between her shoulders and up her neck as she imagined meeting up with the stranger. And yet she walked on, away from the shore and into the great shadow of the Thorn. The darkness was receding, giving way to a pale violet morning light. Patches of frost caught the light and invited her onward, like stepping stones into a different world.

At the edge of the marsh, Rikka sat down on a boulder, and wondered at the force that drew her here. She inhaled deeply, trying to calm her heart, and watched the sun emerge from the sea. Its light caught on the crests of waves while the quiet valleys beneath were indigo, nearly black. She shook her head; so much of the time she saw her island as a place she needed to escape. And then this beauty.

She had learned that there was a boundary around the beauty and that on the outside of the circle there were places in the world that had no beauty or had only that which was contaminated by evil. These places were not rich in sea life, lichen and grasses. They were places where people breathed sand and dust and insects unknown to Lofoten. Her island filled her with love, and yet, it was a love she wanted to rip herself away from. Imagine if what she was looking at this morning, the sun rising over cold blue water, was a sea of hot sand, of scorching foul air, of skeletons stripped bare of life. An opposite world. In school, she had seen pictures and read about foreign lands. In her nightmares, they triggered anxieties; in her dreams they enticed her. Awake, she faced her own world; anything outside its boundaries was illusion.

Rikka turned to the marsh. Frost-coated pools of slushy water lighted her way. She watched her step closely, through the area where cloudberries would again grow in the summer. A small alder shrub caught her skirt and as she turned to free it, she noticed something small and white hanging from a branch. It was no longer than her little finger, and it had a slight curve to it. A needle. And it was threaded. She ran the thread between her fingers and felt the life in it. What was it made of? Not wool or cotton or silk. A bit thicker, soft. She gave it a tug and then another: strong. Could it come from an animal? She had only used threads derived from plants. Maybe a fisherman lost it. Not likely. She scanned the marsh. Opposite her, sitting on a boulder was the Lapp. Biting her lip and pushing down a small fear, she smiled at him and held up the needle, reached out her arm in a gesture of offering it back.

He shook his head, pointed at the needle, then at her, and left. She stood still, running the thread through her fingers, testing the sharpness of the needle. It was hers. He had given it to her. She had seen his face, kind, young, different from all the faces around her. She had a secret now, this knowledge was hers alone.

Hanna was still in bed with Agnes, and the baby was crawling on the floor, a look of studied intensity on her face. She rocked back and forth several times and then slid her hand forward a few inches. She then rocked herself again and brought one and then the other leg forward. "She doesn't know if she is a horse or a plough," Rikka said. There was laughter in the house.

"You must've had a good long walk, Rikka. Now isn't it time to get cleaned up? You can't be late for church service." Rikka's heart dropped. Of all days, this was the one when church would be more stifling than any other. She felt she had already been to church, and it was there in the marsh under the power and shadow of the Thorn.

"Mama, please, not today... not without you."

"Yes, today, for our standing in the community, if not for God."

"What about your standing in the community, Mama? Shouldn't you be there? Maybe Dagur could watch the little girls."

Hanna raised one ironic eyebrow in response. "I have no standing in the community. I hardly exist except as a handmaid to the holy Lorkmans. You, on the other hand, are still an innocent."

Rikka realized that Hanna had not been told about the cause of Agnes's severe turn of health. She hadn't heard about Rikka's almost fatal lapse of care for her little sister. Maybe that proved Hanna's contention that she was nothing to the community, to the church, to anyone.

On her way, Rikka reflected on her mother's attitude towards the church. She never said anything outright, but it was clear that she despised it. A necessary evil, at best. The little church stood on a rise, perhaps to make it look larger than it was. Or maybe to bring it closer to God if one were to be more generous in their thinking.

It was square and sparse except for its steeple which was disproportionately tall and aspiring. The rest of the building resembled a hen's roosting box. The colour was odd. The community had raised funds to paint it the ubiquitous red of the rorbuer and most of the other homes and buildings in the area. But the wealthy farmers and ship owners hadn't been satisfied. Their church should reflect their wealth. So, they dug deep into their pockets to buy the much more expensive white paint that they used on their own homes. The result was an oddly mottled shade of pale rose. They weren't rich enough that they were willing to dig deeper for another coat. Pockets only ran so deep. Instead, they saved face by christening it The Rose Church. Thus inspired, they carried the theme inside. The wealthiest of the lot, an owner of four fishing boats and the store that provisioned all the other ships, commissioned a stained-glass window depicting Christ with tears running down his cheeks, a crown of thorns, and clenching a pink rose. Aside from that dubious detail, the church was all warm wood and hominess. Both Dankert and his father had been instrumental in building pews with rounded tops and end arms. The result was simple, comfortable and perfectly waxed.

No one smiled or even nodded at Rikka, but some looked around her as if to point out that she was alone. They would have liked to see Hanna there, too, if only to snub her.

Rikka found a seat by herself in the back, not far from the door. She thought she might enjoy the service a bit more if only the singing were better. With the exception of a few croakers whose voices sat in the rafters demanding attention like crows, there was a general reluctance to let one's voice ring out in the hymns. Why so rigid? she wondered.

Just before the service started, she noticed Fru Lorkman turn around slowly in her front row pew. She was looking for someone. Rikka was surprised that it appeared that the woman's attention was on her. Fru Lorkman smiled at her and gave a little nod. That, apparently, was the signal for the other women seated around her to do the same. Pernille, Dankert's sour-faced wife, nodded ever so slightly. Rikka had no idea what it all meant, but she was unnerved by it and glad to be close to the door.

The service did not run its usual course because there was a new mother ready to be reintroduced to the congregation, and the priest realized a new mother could stay for only a short time before the baby made new demands upon her.

Bjørd's infant was forty-two days old, just two days over the minimum for an infant to be introduced to the congregation, and for a woman to be reintroduced. Her husband sat by smiling as Bjørd was accepted back, deemed to once more be clean.

Rikka wondered about her mother. Had she ever been reintroduced? She knew that she didn't bring Ragna to church for this ceremony, and she was pretty sure that Agnes wasn't brought either. What about herself? And if not, why not. Was this why her mother stayed away? Rikka would have to ask Dankert. No, she would ask her mother, give her the chance to explain.

It was announced that there would be cake and coffee after the service in celebration of Bjørd, her husband and the infant. Now Rikka was glad that Hanna forced her to come to the service. She wanted to learn more about the idea of being reintroduced. Why would a woman who had gone to this one church all her life need such an introduction? At any rate, Rikka did love cake. Maybe it would be rich in butter and even spiced with cardamom which she couldn't resist. That would make sitting through the sermon worthwhile. But she suddenly felt dull pain deep in her abdomen, maybe even a little lower than that.

The priest offered his blessing and stepped forward to the pulpit. He was a small man with a wiry frame hidden under his cassock. He didn't look strong enough to lift his Bible, much less move a congregation. But he stood in the spot that was his alone, looked at his congregation, tried to make eye contact with every one. At one person he paused and nodded, to another he gave a look of questioning, and so on around the room until even the most edgy and twitchy of his flock sat still and focused all their thoughts and expectations on this little man. And then he opened his mouth and out rolled a voice of such resonance and depth that if he had asked the Norwegian Sea to part its waters, it surely must have done so. And so, the sermon began:

"My brothers and sisters in the Lord. We have at our gates a new threat and an old one. The old one I will speak of in time. The new one must and will be dealt with now."

Rikka's discomfort had turned painful.

"I fear there are those in our presence who have allowed to cross their doorstep a new breed of devil, and he is a devil in the disguise of a saint. In fact, he calls himself a Latter Day Saint. Do not be fooled for this is the devil with all his hot breath and sweet speaking who wishes to lead you down the pathway to Hell itself. These Mormons are an insidious breed who pride themselves in taking many brides on whom they beget as many children as their seed will allow.

'It is not enough for them to have spread their evil over the great plains of America. No, now they must cross the seas to gather about them still more brides for their lecherous men. Ah, and they especially covet young brides of fair skin and wheaten hair. That is why they have come to Norway, even to our far reaches: to steal away our healthy, strong and beautiful women and make them slaves to their satanic ways."

Rikka didn't think she could sit there any longer.

"Therefore I ask you, Who here has seen them in our fields? Who here has crossed them on our paths? And who here ... and this is hard for me to believe ... has opened their doors to them? Stand up if you dare and repent in front of this congregation of good men and women."

Rikka felt something wet between her thighs. Sticky.

No one stood but some squirmed in their seats.

"This is just one of the sick and evil practises of the Mormons. If we want to protect our families and our island, we will rid ourselves of this plague in whatever manner we can devise, and the good Lord will sanction. Let not the Infidel pass through your door!" he shouted, and the silent congregation let his words echo from wall to wall.

"As is written in the good book Leviticus18: For whoever does any of these abominations, those persons who do so shall be cut off from among their people. Thus you are to keep My charge, that you do not practice any of the abominable customs which have been practiced before you, so as not to defile yourselves with them; I am the LORD your God.' "

With that the priest lowered his head and led his congregation in prayer.

Head down, and her shawl hanging lower than usual, Rikka fled the church. She didn't know what to make of this pain or of whatever was leaking from her body. What she did know was that those low flat clouds of the morning had turned into much heavier clouds with shredded undersides, and they were blasting their way onto shore. Snow was coming, and it wouldn't come gently. This was a big storm. November was known for these monsters. It was time to take shelter, but Rikka wanted to be in the storm. She knew something was changing inside her. This leaking she felt, was it her old self being cast out? She wanted to see what it looked like, this sloughing, this cramping. She squatted down, back to the wind and crossed her arms over her gut. She was being ripped to shreds by whatever was within her. Without straightening up, she turned to face the sea, already black in the middle of the day. The clouds had menacing edges. What was she doing there?

The next blast bought sleet which stung her face and penetrated her shawl. She had to get home. The sudden blasts would propel her in one direction and then break off. A trickster wind. She lost her balance and fell, knocking her mouth against a rock.

This was all a mistake. She didn't have the strength or courage to change her life. What had she been thinking? Befriend the young Lapp? Climb the Thorn? She cried from frustration more than from pain. Then she could see her home. She saw her mother standing in the light of the doorway, shouting to her. Her words were blown back into the cabin.

A little closer still; her mother raced out to meet Rikka, her head bent into the wind and driving forward like a bull. When they could talk, arms around one another, Hanna shouted at her,

"When a storm comes, you have to get away from the sea. Never challenge the sea. Don't let it beckon you."

Hanna pulled Rikka into the rorbu.

"What were you trying to do? You are a foolish girl. Stupid."

Frowning, Hanna examined Rikka's cuts and scratches. She was soaking wet and far too cold for Hanna's liking. She stripped Rikka's sodden clothes off in a fit of panic. Rikka tried to stand, which was a mistake. Hanna saw the blood between Rika's legs.

What had happened? Had her daughter had been raped? Rikka shook so hard she couldn't speak.

Hanna shrieked. "Get Dagur. Call her. She'll have medicine. Get her. Get the filthy herbs." It seemed way out of proportion to Rikka. She wished her mother would stop yelling and just let her curl up in bed.

Mokci sat cross-legged in the lavvu and scanned his surroundings. Everything in its place. The burning birch sent sweet smoke straight up and through the cross poles into the sky. The stars faded and brightened due to the smoke. He imagined his grandfather sitting next to him, patiently waiting for his decision. Would Mokci return to Sapmi and his place as a noadi for his people, or would he travel further and further south searching? Mokci could smell the scent of his grandfather, moss and wisdom. He inhaled the scent and held it deep in his lungs. His grandfather rocked back and forth and then sat straight, his thoughts etched into the hieroglyph of his brow.

"Where are you going?" the old man asked. "What are you looking for?"

Mokci shook his head. He didn't know.

"Something has pulled you away. You have to know what it is or you will wander in circles. Your life will seem long, but it will go nowhere even as your body moves around and around."

A long silence. Mokci wanted to explain, but explain what? How he needed to know more, needed to know if he could carry the inherited burden of a noadi. His grandfather breathed the wisdom that allowed him to lead the siidu. He could read the signs of the weather, the night sky, the reindeer in their corral. For years Mokci had watched his grandfather and memorized each posture, gesture, phrase and chant, but he couldn't understand how that deep wisdom could be passed on to him. The people respected and believed his grandfather and at the same time they accepted the Laestadian priest whose message was to follow a new path laid out by the church through the teachings of Christ. Most of his family and neighbours could nod assent to the priest and still follow the old ways. Mokci couldn't. But he had not yet figured out what he could do.

"Will you sit here until you can answer your own questions? Will you travel with the reindeer or with the sleeping spirits? You have the power to heal, to lead, but that power lives in Sapmi. Not here. Come home when you're ready, but understand that you are ready and come soon. I will not be around for long."

Mokci inhaled sharply. This is what he had feared. His grandfather's time was near. The old man touched Mokci's face and rose with the smoke into the night. Mokci withdrew into his loneliness. He could not expect to leave his calling without leaving behind the love of his siida.

He shifted his focus to that other form of love, that of a woman. The girls in his siida were shy of him, aware of the lineage that set him apart spiritually from all others. Yet there was one girl who never flinched. She was different from the others, unafraid to tease him. She was the only person in his group who would jump out of the boat and swim with the reindeer as they crossed an icy river. He could hear her laughter as she threw herself onto the back of a thrashing buck. Why wouldn't she appear now and burst this throbbing loneliness?

"You must call to me," she said. "I have called to you, but you are afraid."

He murmured, "Siri, are you there? Siri?"

She leaned into his lavvu, just her shadowed face at first, then a sinuous glide into his contemplative retreat. Her feet were bare, and he held his focus on them, unable to look in her eyes.

"What do you yearn for? Me. Reach out. That's all. I don't care whether you are a noadi or just a man. Be something! Touch me. When I touch you, you will not forget. We will run with the reindeer and, like them, we will couple on the side of the mountain, on the ice bridges that may at any time crumble and send us to death in the wild caverns below. Touch me. Everywhere. The sky is falling into our arms and nothing matters. Just us, the two of us. Why not!"

He knew why. She was a distraction and one he yearned to embrace, if only he were not who he was. He withdrew his hand from that pole that rose between his thighs. Spilt seed. It would never reach Boahjenasti, the North Star. It was just the feeble ejaculation of a weak man. And who was he? A wanderer? A seeker? A holy man? A fool? He would love to live unbridled, run with that wild woman across the mountains and rivers of the Sapmi.

Life in his homeland was hard, but the community of his people was something he didn't know if he could live without. He didn't know if his search would help his people or just abandon them. In fact, he didn't know what he was searching for. Mokci poked at the fire. With a sigh, the wild woman rose in a pillar of sparks and disappeared in the night sky. Mokci let out a cry to call her back, but she was gone.

He could just as well be poking at the fire in a larger lavvu somewhere around Jukkasjarvi. There the birch trees would already glisten with icicles this time of year and the whole family and neighbours as well would share the stew pot. The dogs would lie around, just inside the perimeter of the lavvu, their noses aimed at the pot, ready to pounce on any dropped shred of reindeer meat.

And then the singing would begin. Mokci rocked back and forth inhaling the images of home. When his body found a rhythm that it loved, he began to chant, not in words but in sounds that expressed his love for his sidda, for the immense dome of night sky shot through with stars revolving around Boahjenasti. He sang with love and sorrow for the loss of his uncle, buried in a snow drift with just his ski set upright so others would find him. He sang of the power of the wild woman, of the seed he would plant in her. He sang of something far off and unknown. Mokci's joik, his song of sounds, reached out as far as he could call for someone to touch him.

He closed his eyes, listened to the silence, and reached into the bag that always hung just below his hip. His fingers touched the small smooth stones that lay at the bottom of the bag. They reminded him of the autumn blueberries he had poured into the Norwegian girl's hand. She had been afraid to look at him. But they were only berries he offered. These small spheres now in his hand were solid, they had no juice in them, and instead of deep blue, they were blood red. Thunderstones.

Hanna

The soft snowfall had ended. The storm side of every home and shack had been coated white. Along with the snow came silence, but a silence full of secrets whispered just below the threshold of hearing. The snow muffled and hid sins within its cold indifference. Even the sea had little to say. It lay still in the harbour and merely whispered to the shore.

Johanna tied on her cap and drew it tight over her ears. The house was asleep, but she had to go to the farm. Bestemor would not be sleeping. She would be waiting for hay and Johanna would have to go through the motions of milking her even though only the slightest trickle of milk was likely to ting in the empty pail. She tucked her leggings carefully into her long stockings, the black ones Rikka had made for her. Her dress would still drag through the snow,

She stepped outside and still the world lay silent. That didn't make any sense. The sea always spoke and so did the wind. Maybe her ears were deaf to the sounds of the island. Maybe it was all that screaming last night. About what? Who had been screaming? She must tell them it was not allowed. One cannot scream like a naked Lapp if one wished to go to heaven. Heaven, where had that gone? Wasn't it supposed to be here on Earth? Isn't that what they all said about this island? Heaven on Earth?

She walked on, pushing the snow ahead and to the side of her. It was like walking through clouds but colder. She knew it was snow, but couldn't it be clouds, too? She tiptoed, hoping not to break through and fall to earth. Then the clouds became snow again and she knew herself to be back on the path but still took care not to step too heavily and break through this crust that divided earth from hell. The fallen snow gave the only light. None came from the skies. She wondered about that. Where did the snow get its light?

"From hell!" Hanna laughed out loud. How could the truth have been there all this time, yet she didn't see it until now? She shouted out, "The light of hell. The light of hell be with us all." She hadn't known this truth before, but her mind was open to the wondrous and miraculous today. Did others know the truth? Did the good priest know about the light? She certainly hadn't known it until this very moment, but it was perfectly clear. White hot light seeped up from Hell and lit her pathway to the farm. Of course. Something happened last night. What was it? She would remember soon, but whatever it was that was hiding from her memory, it was the cause of hell's light reaching her feet. She would find out and she would denounce it. No force could stop her.

What was this, a barn? What if it caught fire from hell's light; what would happen to the animals inside? Johanna entered. It looked familiar though she couldn't quite place it. But there was Bestemor, her old friend, swinging her head from side to side. Johanna frowned and listened. The cow was sensible and wanted out of the barn before it burned down. Of course. Save the cow. Johanna opened the gate to her stall and gave Bestemor a quick slap on the rear. The old cow sauntered out, turned her head at the door as if asking permission. "Go on now. Before it's too late. Save yourself."

The farmhouse loomed heavy in the dark. There was no light inside except a candle in a sconce burning in the kitchen window. Johanna walked in and went directly to the stove without taking off her boots. She fed the fire and put water on to boil, decided that she would have a cup of coffee and some cake now that she had taken care of the cow. She got a jug of cream from the cold room. She would put plenty of cream in her coffee. She would put cream on the cake, and she would take the rest of the cream home with her for the party that night. She frowned trying to remember what the party was for and who would be coming. She would take the cake home and the pretty knife with the carved handle, too. She ran her hand over the raised motif in the handle. Heilag konag Olaf was at the bow of his ship leading his men to battle against the Danes. Someone was screaming again. Couldn't they just stop that screaming? Who was it? The shrieking kettle laughed at her. She poured it slowly onto the floor, then made beautiful patterns in it with the cream. A swirling sea of white.

But Herr Lorkman had heard noise coming from downstairs where Johanna, wild eyed and dishevelled, had strewn the morning cake, cream and a pitcher across the floor.

Johanna held a knife in her hand. When she saw the fear in his eyes, she lifted the knife so that the sharp edge of the blade touched her face from forehead to lips, as if to slice her face in half. Slowly, slowly, she ran the blade up and down, teasing her flesh. Lorkman positioned himself so the table lay between them.

"Dankert," he called out to his son. Thank God he had spent the night at his parents' house due to the storm. "Dankert. Come at once."

Johanna could see the devil's fangs, orange like flames. She stepped closer to him, but not too close. He could probably leap over the table and drag her down. Her body tensed and then tensed some more.

"Johanna," said a soft calm voice. She had heard that voice before. Did it belong to the devil or to that other man, the younger one? Now she was confused.

"Johanna, I'm here to help you." It was a voice she wanted to hear, a voice she loved. She carefully lowered herself to the floor, set the knife down in front of her and then leaning forward, she pushed it away.

"Dankert?" she asked her voice filled with hope. "Is it you?"

"Yes, Johanna. Here, let me help you up. You've had a very difficult night and morning, too. You need to rest now. I'm going to take you into a bedroom where you can lie down under a warm duvet and sleep. You will be safe. You just need to sleep."

She followed him, still confused but calmer now. He took her shawl, unbuttoned her dress and hung it over the chair by the fire. He laid her down and pulled the covers up over her, stroked her wet hair back off her face. Kissed her forehead. She was almost asleep already but she could still hear the voices.

Lorkman yelled. "She held a knife up to me. She's a madwoman. I won't have it."

"Leave her alone, Father. I'll get Henrikka and the two of us will deal with it."

"You know the conditions...."

"Yes, I guess that under the circumstances I have to agree with them."

"Don't let the girl sway you. You are weak around her."

"I am her ... she is my responsibility. I will take care of her in whatever way I can."

"Did you lock the door?"

"What door?"

"The one to your room. The one she's sleeping in."

"You can do that, Father."

"Be sure that I will!" He turned his back on Dankert and left the room.

The snow fell heavily on Dankert's head as he bent his way toward the little rorbu. What could he tell Rikka? Had her mother gone mad? Completely, even violently mad? But wasn't that just what Rikka had told him? He had thought she just meant difficult or odd or strange, but this was so much more. That knife, the broken china on the floor, Hanna's face twisted into an unrecognizable form. She was so beautiful, had always been beautiful. Where had it gone? He knew. He knew where the guilt lay. And now there was guilt upon guilt.

He would have to lie to Rikka. This wasn't just protecting her from the truth as he had always pretended. This was cruel deception and cowardice. His cruelty, his cowardice. The snowstorm shoved him. It slowed his progress down the path, wanting to push him inland. He would gladly let it push him away from his goal, but on an island, one can only be pushed so far before meeting land's end on the other side. There was nowhere to hide.

Dankert stopped, looked into the face of the storm coming off the Norwegian Sea, turned his back on it and faced the land that eventually ran into Vestfjorden. No escape, just more water. He stared into what he could not see but could not deny the existence of. He was trapped. A figure moving in the dark drew his attention. It wasn't human … too long, rather than tall. It swayed slowly carrying its blanket of snow. He watched its slow progress in a line parallel to his own, but where no path lay. He watched how it just kept plodding along. A cow moving through the rocky terrain where no shelter existed.

"No," shouted Henrikka. "You can't mean it!"

"Rikka, your mother is terribly sick. I can't even tell you what I saw. She is not in control of herself. She's a danger to your sisters.

She is completely incapable of taking care of them."

"Who says so? Who has the right to tear our family apart?"

"They are good people, Rikka."

"You mean they are people with power and money. Let me guess, the priest, the storekeeper, Dankert, not your father! He hasn't made this decision, has he?"

"No, I don't think so. He might have expressed his opinion...."

"Of course he expressed his opinion. He always does and he usually gets exactly what he wants. It's just a bunch of men who know nothing of the heart."

"Not just men, Rikka."

She stared at him until the answer settled on her, then she nodded, looking him deep in the eyes. "The three women who came sniffing around here, touching things, touching the little girls, looking down their noses at all that is ours. At us. Your mother, Dankert. She was one of them."

"I know how much this hurts, Rikka. It hurts me too. But something has to change. And they take their decisions seriously. They want the best for all of you." He fidgeted, looking down, away from her.

"Isn't that just so very good of them!" Dankert could see some of her mother's intensity in Rikka but, of course, the situation was dire. She looked down. "Tell me. Who are we being given away to."

"Not given. Agnes will be with my parents."

"No. They are so rigid. They treat my mother like a worthless slave. I don't care if they are your parents. They are horrid. They'll just work that four-year-old body to death."

"You're wrong, Rikka. They will treat her like a granddaughter. They will keep her warm and well fed. They'll get her proper medical attention, not just steam filled with bitter herbs. Mother will teach her to read and bake. She will love her. She has always wanted to be a grandmother."

"Then why doesn't she take Ragna, too. Oh dear God. What is

happening, Dankert? How can I accept all this? It's my fault, all the stress I put on our mother. That's what's broken her. Last night I got caught in the storm. She was shouting into the wind trying to call me home. When I finally managed it she was so distraught that she was screaming out nonsense. I don't know. It made no sense, but I do know it was my fault. And now we are all torn apart, tossed into the maelstrom."

"Rikka, it is not your fault. She's sick. You've had too great a burden."

"And how will you lighten that, Onkle? Put me into service?"

"No, Rikka, we need you to take care of your mother. Her care will be your only concern. And no one else can do it."

"Oh my God. All the joy gone out of this house. No little girls. No father, just the mad woman and her daughter in training to grow mad. Thank you so much. And what of Ragna, who will be snapping her up?"

"That hasn't been decided. I will make it my personal mission to be sure she is loved. It should be someone who has suffered loss and will cherish Ragna."

What else could Dankert say? He knew better than anyone that the decision had been made, but he couldn't tell her just yet. Let Rikka deal with one loss at a time. There was nothing to make it better. Someday the girl would find out -- perhaps he would tell her — just how bad things were.

"I will bring Hanna home as soon as I can."

But his father was a step ahead of him. When he went to check on Johanna after dinner, Lorkman had filled a sack with food to send home with her. He had opened the casement windows and tossed the down duvet that he had stripped from Hanna's sleeping form onto the floor.

Johanna had initially curled herself in a ball against the cold, like a kitten, a dirty kitten, a stray. Lorkman had locked the bedroom door, assuming that Johanna would escape out the window.

But when she left by the window, Hanna went all the way to the inlet where the fishermen worked by firelight on their boats. The fires were spaced one after another along the shore, each situated near a different boat. There was a second layer of firelight cast by lanterns on tall poles, as high as a man's reach and then some. The smoke smelled of fish oil. Their flickering light cast dancing figures on the snow. The men's faces reflected the light and absorbed the shadows as Hanna walked by them. Some stopped work to watch her while others laughed at her strange gait and appearance. All the sawing, the caulking, the hammering and chiseling stopped as she passed. She was bad luck. No women ever came aboard, and for the most part, women didn't come near the boats except to bring food.

"I wonder what she has in her gunny sack," one said.

"Get her outa here," called another more superstitious than the first.

"Go home, go home," one said, as if to a troublesome cur. Men picked up the rhythmic chant. Hanna stood, mouth slack, turning in spirals of confusion. One young man, over in a dark corner stirring up a pot of tar, saw her fear and confusion. She was lost.

He cleaned off his brush and walked quietly over to her. "Let me help you," he said. "Come on, this way. I'll lead you home." He took her arm and put it through his.

As he led her back up the path they were followed by catcalls. "Got yourself a woman there, have you, Lapp Boy?"

"Better do it quick before your tar brush droops." Laughter.

"How's that for a sight? A crazy bitch and a Lapp walking like lovers."

The whole community would know by morning that she was stark mad and incapable of keeping her family together. And a strange man who said his name was Mokci went with her to the door of their home. Hanna tried to tug him inside, but he refused.

Rikka came into the kitchen.

"Who were you talking to, Mama?"

"Mokci."

"We don't know any Mokci, Mama. No one on the island is named Mokci."

But Hanna went on talking about this kind young man who had helped her home. He had saved her from a bunch of evil men and helped her find the right path. These were probably the sanest words she had spoken in days.

"Let me help you with those wet clothes, Mama."

Hanna put her hands high over her head like a small child ready to receive help from an adult.

Rikka smiled at her. "Thank you, Mama, very helpful." Would she be talking to her own mother like this for the rest of her life? She would miss the talks they had always had in the past, free flowing discussions sparked by something that Rikka had learned at school like the way the moon pulls the tides and pushes them back, or a poem that Hanna had read that perfectly described the aurora borealis in Lofoten. She remembered a line from it even now: "Like the iridescent wing of a dragonfly caught in the sun's rays, the night sky cast filaments violet and green through the Milky Way."

Would they now be talking only of washing her face and cleaning her teeth? Would Hanna become more confused and infantile, or would she wake up one blessed morning free of this ailment in her head and heart?

"Let's get you to bed, Mama." She was glad Agnes was already asleep. Just how confusing would this strange order of things be for them? Then she remembered that Agnes wouldn't be with them after tomorrow. She took the warmest blanket and put it over Hanna, who seemed to drift immediately into sleep. There lay the woman who had sustained all of them these past years, now sucking her fingers in her sleep.

Rikka picked up the sack of food Hana had brought back with her. Had the Lorkmans tried to assuage their guilt by sending home delicacies on this last night of Johanna's employment? But the sack was filled with dried cod heads, the only food of which Rikka had a surplus. Cod heads were fine for soup when one was cold and hungry enough, but if one wanted to fill a sack as cheaply as possible, it would have to be with dried cod heads. No cream or butter or cake or even cabbage. Just cod heads. Of course, she didn't expect cod tongues, that great delicacy the young boys extracted from the new cod once the season had started. But one might expect something more as a thank you for years of service at such low pay. Rikka sat down by the stove, opened the lid and, one by one, threw the cod heads on the fire. What a fine crackling sound they made. Like tiny bones snapping.

Rikka washed Agnes's little nightdresses and stockings in their largest cauldron and stirred it with the wooden dowel. She pictured etchings of witches stirring a similar pot. They were in a book of Shakespeare's plays. She knew he was an old-fashioned English writer whose plays were very difficult to read even though they had been translated into Norwegian. But she had memorized their chant, both in English and Norwegian:

> *Double, double toil and trouble;*
> *Fire burn and cauldron bubble.*
> *Dobbel dobbel slit og trøbble*
> *Brann brenne og gryten boble*

She always recited it either to amuse Agnes and Hanna or to go into that imaginary world all by herself, inside her head, where witches could not only see the future, they could change the future. Maybe even the past. Right now the witches' lot seemed like a perfect one. They had control. They were usually old and ugly, much like Dagur, she thought. They were hated and feared, and maybe that was the way to walk through this world. Instead of trying constantly to do the right thing, they revelled in chaos and perhaps that was the natural state of the world.

Rikka took her time stirring the cauldron. There were no eyes of newt or toes of frog in it to distract her imagination. What she could see instead was Agnes growing up in a wealthy home, and she could only hope that she would grow up happy and healthy.

Rikka was, in fact, a bit jealous of her little sister's fate. But Rikka wasn't going to cry in the cauldron. She didn't want to break her vision with tears.

Finally, Rikka packed a small bag for Agnes. She was so full of rage that her hands wouldn't fold the clothing, just mangle it. She looked at the pieces, smelled them, stroked the embroidery that she and Hanna had spent so much time on. She especially loved the little black vest with its red, blue and yellow flowers all worked together through a wandering trail of green vines and leaves. Would the vest just be thrown out? She could just hear Fru Lorkman saying, "Toss it all out, all of it. We'll start afresh."

She packed Agnes's little doll. She had no idea who gave Agnes the doll, but Agnes had loved it since she was born. It seemed to just appear one day in her crib, or that's what Rikka remembered. The doll was crocheted in bright pink wool with black braids, and despite its strange looks, Agnes loved it. By the time she was one year old, Agnes had chewed one hole after another into her favourite toy. It was an ongoing joke in the house that it was once again time to mend Poona, as Agnes had named her. Since they had no matching wool, they got in the habit of mending the doll with every bright colour they could find. Poona looked like something halfway between a clown and an unlucky warrior. Rikka decided to let Agnes carry Poona to the farm so that no one would dare to wrest her from the four-year-old's hands. Agnes sat on her bed wheezing, unaware of how her life was about to change.

By the time there was a knock at the door, Rikka had pushed her emotions down so deep that she was able to ask Fru Lorkman to enter, if not graciously, A man stood outside who Hanna knew acted as bailiff in cases where there might be trouble.

Also outside, sitting on a stump in the dark, was her mother. She had gotten out of bed and slipped outside while Rikka was washing and packing.

Just as well she isn't inside right now, Rikka thought. Fru

Lorkman stood by the door, afraid of a scene and wanting to make a quick exit. She had her no-nonsense face on. Agnes stood by, doll in hand, looking back and forth between her sister and the tall woman with the tight lips.

"Come with me, Agnes," the woman said. "I'll take you to a doctor who will make you well. And then we'll go to my house for cake with apples and almonds and currants inside. Won't that be good? Then I'll show you your new room. Wouldn't you like to leave this old doll here? There's a brand new one with yellow hair at my house."

Agnes squeezed Poona. It was clear that she wouldn't be letting go, but she did take the woman's hand and followed her out the door.

Once she knew Agnes would be out of sight down the path, Rikka went outside. Hanna sat rocking on the stump. She didn't seem to have noticed Agnes leaving, but who could be sure? Maybe she had given up on everything she had thought belonged to her. Maybe nothing mattered in the world she inhabited now, not even her babies. Rikka sat down next to her, rocking her mother in her arms. Back and forth, back and forth, following her mother's rhythm. It offered Rikka a pathway for her own rage.

The sky swayed with them, the northern lights flowing like green sand down to the sea and then shooting back up again. As she watched, the whole sky began to dance with colour, mostly emerald green, but then the purple shot through, working with the green cascades to eradicate the depths of night. Then came golden shards and the pink of rosa rugosa, all the colours of Agnes's vest enlivening the black canvas. Rikka ran into the house and brought out the hardanger fiddle. The instrument shrieked under her bow. Under her chin it screamed to the night. Shrill cacophony directed the colours to sing her rage.

Out of the dark corners of the night, a man moved across the snow and sat down next to Hanna. He took her hand, rigid as a claw, and began stroking it, smoothing it. Hanna looked at him and smiled a weak smile. She leaned over and picked up a length of driftwood, then handed it to Mokci. He examined the stick as if to read from it what Hanna's intent was. He picked up another piece from the ground, this one flat, and tapped it with the stick. The energy in his hands built on the rhythm he found in the stick, built and built, until it matched the manic energy of Rikka's fiddle. The sky danced with hectic electricity. The sound was terrible, it was beautiful. Rikka could not sustain it much longer. Mokci took control of the pace, moment by moment slowing it down, letting it breathe, and the fiddle followed.

Rikka looked through the dark at the drummer who had brought her dreadful music to a resting place. He stood still, nodding at her, then dissolved into the night.

The next day, Rikka was glad to see Dankert. Perhaps he would visit with Hanna for awhile so she could go for a walk, get out of the house for a change.

"Actually, Rikka," he said. "I was hoping to convince you to come to my parents' home to help with all their work."

She looked at him with one eyebrow raised. "Surely you don't expect that. Who was it who told me just weeks ago that all I had to do was take care of my mother and baby sister? As if that were no small thing."

"I know, Rikka. I did say that."

"You mean, you promised that."

"Did I? But you see, it's a lot of work for my mother — she isn't so young anymore, you see. She said I must find help for her. She can't deal with a child and milk the cow twice a day and churn the butter."

"So, she isn't so sure about how much she wanted to be a grandmother. I guess she isn't used to getting tired. Or maybe she expected to go lounge on her down mattress every time my little sister required attention. I thought she didn't want me anywhere around. She said that it would make the transition more difficult. Look how things change. And no!"

"All right, Rikka, you've made your point. I'll find someone else to help in the house. But could you manage to come for the morning and evening milking? It's just old Bestemor, and she isn't exactly flooding the buckets with milk these days. Could you do that, please. I'll be sure that you get paid in milk and cheese."

"And meat! Every day."

"All right. And meat."

And so Rikka walked to the farm every morning and every evening to milk the sweet old cow. Each morning she came home with milk or cheese and a cut of meat, which improved the quality of their meals.

The job had other advantages. She was not allowed to visit with her little sister, but she and Agnes managed to catch glimpses of one another through the upstairs window. Clearly Agnes knew what time in the morning and in the evening her big sister would come out of the barn. Agnes, transformed by one or another frilly frock, would wave to her using the hands of both Poona and the brand-new Blondie doll.

On her way home that evening, Rikka noticed a dark form settled on the rock seawall that jutted out from the entrance to the inlet. She stood, watching for any movement. The form was totally still. It was unusual for someone to be just sitting and staring out to sea at a time when all the fishermen and boat builders headed straight home to the warmth of family and hearth, to a hot dinner and perhaps a cup of ale.

Rikka froze, just as she might to watch the dark shape of a minke whale hovering just below the surface of the water. What was this curiosity towards a stranger, a man? She moved towards him as quietly as she could, not wanting to be noticed in case it was someone to be avoided. So many people were to be avoided. But this one sat with a posture that seemed foreign, relaxed yet aware, peaceful. After a deep breath, she braved a tentative "Hei."

He turned his head, and she recognized the Lapp. "Your name is Mokci, isn't it?" He nodded. "I think you know my mother. She speaks of you. You've been kind to her."

He smiled but said nothing.

"Do you speak Norsk?"

He nodded.

"You came around to take care of her at just the right time. Thank you."

"You are welcome."

She stood silently. Rikka looked down at her old boots and wriggling her toes to fend off the cold.

"May I sit with you for a moment?"

"Yes." He shifted sideways to make room for her on the flat slab of granite. It was warmer than the neighboring slabs. She glanced at his profile, the straight nose and prominent cheekbones, then turned back quickly, afraid of being rude.

"How do you know my mother?"

"I have met her sometimes. In the wind. She is like my mother's sister who is also very sad. And lonely. I feel at home with her."

"Is your mother's sister sick, I mean, sick like my mother?"

"She has … I do not know your word … but her spirit is dark. I do not know if it is the same with your mother. Maybe. Maybe you know."

"My mother has been hurt too much," Rikka said. "That's all I know. I think she has broken under the weight of her sadness."

Mokci now turned to look at her, unsure of how much he should tell her.

"Sometimes when my mother's sister sits before the fire, she

just stares, stares and rocks. I place my hands on her shoulders."
He held out his gloved hands as if to comfort the icy air. "That
seems to help. Or I put my hands on the sides of her head and I
sing to her." He shifted his hands upright so Rikka could almost
feel the warmth of his hands on her own head, hear his song. "If I
could do that all day long, she would be well."

"But I can't do that all day long," Rikka whispered, exhausted
by the mere thought of it.

"No, you cannot." Mokci looked at Rikka, just long enough
that she had to shift in her seat. Sensing that, he turned back to the
sea. "Who made this wall?"

"What wall?" Rikka was thrown by the change in the
conversation.

Mokci stretched out his arms sideways, smiling. "This wall."

"Oh, I thought you meant … never mind. The men, I guess, I
don't know really."

"How did they move these huge stones?"

Rikka thought about that. She had never considered how the
breakwater was built. It had just always been there. "Maybe they
used a stoneboat. You know? Like a flat sleigh with runners? That's
probably it. Maybe a horse, no two horses, pulled it."

"A stone boat," he laughed. "A stone boat pulled by horses.
Those men wanted to hold back the sea," Mokci said, shaking his
head.

Rikka laughed, "It looks like they did just that."

"Does it work always?"

"No, I've seen the sea breach the wall, and when it does, it
claws at the shore with vengeance."

"Good," Mokci whispered, "no man should stop the sea."

"But they will try."

"I wouldn't."

"Not even if the sea might wash away your home?"

Mokci laughed. "We pick up our homes every time the reindeer are on the move. They are like your sea. They move in great waves like your sea."

Rikka could visualize a whole rolling sea of reindeer, hear their legs thrashing through the breakers.

"Look how the moon has moved as we talk," Mokci said. "Now it is time you go home. Take care of your mother and baby."

Rikka was shocked when she realized what he thought. "She isn't my baby, she's my sister."

"That is good," he said smiling.

Rikka could feel the smile on her face the rest of the way home. I have a friend, she thought. A friend. I never had a real one before.

The next day she decided it was time to make some pants. She looked closely at the old ones someone had left behind. The way the legs went straight up into the crotch and the waist. That would have to change. She drew out a pattern modifying the shape to fit her own body. She used a string to take measurements. The pants could button on the left side where her right hand could easily do them up, instead of front and centre like men's pants. The legs could be a bit shorter, the waist definitely smaller. Finally, she felt ready to cut into the fabric. Kneeling on the floor in front of the daybed she reached under and ran her hands over the wooden box, over the intricate carving of whales swimming nose to tail, nose to tail, nose to tail all the way down its length. With a gentle tug, it glided out from beneath the bed as if skimming over clear ice. The box was as long and deep as the bed itself, and it held the treasures of her family: her mother's wedding dress, and four intricately embroidered babies' frocks with white French knots on soft white linen.

The dull brown dress that Fru Lorkman had condescended to give her lay behind those treasures. It felt good in her hands. The wool was soft and warm, a fine gift from the sheep that studded the mountainsides during mild weather. The colour was deadly, but she decided to view it as the warm and fertile soil at the foot of a rocky bluff.

Deeply into her project, she didn't notice Dankert's arrival.

"What's this you're doing, Rikka?"

"I'm making pants."

"Good, did one of the fishermen give you a commission?"

"No. I'm just doing it so that I know how, in case."

"In case of what?"

"In case I feel like keeping my legs and rear end warm in the winter."

"They're for you?"

"Yes."

"Next thing you'll tell me is you're planning to wear them to church."

"Only when it's really cold outside."

"I sincerely hope you're joking. You'd start another scandal."

"That seems like an easy thing to do, don't you think? But don't worry, I'll wear them under my dress just to please you."

"Well, never mind then. And I promised to try to find some boots for you."

"Oh, thank you, Onkle. They'll make such a difference walking to and from the farm."

"I haven't found any yet that would suit you, so I brought you this instead." He pulled out a satin vest, lilac in colour, with tiny pearl-like buttons. "I thought it would be beautiful with your eyes."

"Keep it."

"What? I know you wanted the boots, but this is just for now."

"Keep it. Why can't you understand. I am not that pretty girl you want me to be."

"Yes, you are, you're beautiful."

"Keep it. Beautiful is easy. It's just chance. My life is hard. I need warm pants. I need coal."

"Oh, the coal. I forgot to bring it. I'll need to get a wagon together for that. Maybe early next week."

Hanna had been listening to this conversation from the next room. She cackled aloud. Dankert went behind the curtain to her, alarmed by the harsh noises coming from her throat. Alarmed even more by her appearance, he patted her on the arm. In return, she swung at him, hitting him hard in the stomach. He called to Rikka to come and help him.

She ignored the request, calling, "Leave us alone. You have nothing to offer. Go to your wife. Take care of her. We have no use for you."

She stood up to look after her mother. Hanna's eyes squinted at Dankert, mere slits exuding malice. Hissing like a snake, she retreated under her covers. Rikka was taken aback. She had never seen this outright hatred towards Dankert. She attributed her mother's mood to the craziness that had a hold on Hanna. She tried not to wonder about the venom in their relationship, the strike, and the recoil.

Rikka accompanied Dankert out the door. He looked stunned.

"Is she like this all the time?"

"No, I think that was especially for you, Onkle." She noticed that he was wearing a new jacket with seal skin around the collar. She had only her shawl. She pushed the imbalance to the back of her mind and asked, "How is Pernille doing?" Even though she didn't really care. He explained that she was relatively healthy. Rikka wondered why that was all he had to say about his wife. He spoke instead about the new house they were building and that he would like a child to keep his wife contented. "She is well enough now, especially since we hired a neighbour woman to help her."

Rikka wondered how a woman in a new house with modern plumbing, a flush toilet, hot water in the kitchen even when the stove wasn't burning, could possibly need two women to help her run it. Dankert explained that Pernille simply wasn't cut out to do much in the way of housekeeping and she suffered from headaches when stressed. It sounded to Rikka as if he was apologizing for his wife when he added, "The modern way is to build larger houses, but they also mean more work. I want everything I build or buy to make her life easier." Rikka could not even respond but said goodbye in as gentle a way as she could muster.

Rikka knew that her onkle was respected in the community. He was the very finest woodworker in all the islands around. He had finesse with the wood, a sense of what it wanted to become and what was fitting for it to become. He also counselled the leaders of the community in the best way to go about their building plans. They listened to him. So why, why, did he bumble like a fool around Rikka and her mother?

That night Rikka confided in Mokci about her confusion surrounding Dankert. Mokci said that Dankert was one of the very few men who spoke to him at all, and that he took an interest in the way Mokci approached his work. He told her how they had been working side by side on a warped stave that looked as if it might not hold up in a storm. Mokci suggested that these beautiful fishing boats with their upturned bows might weather storms better if they were a little looser in construction. Dankert had replied that it sounded as if Mokci was suggesting sloppy craftsmanship, and the younger man told him that the boats the Sea Saami built were designed to give and flex in a storm rather than to rigidly confront the waves.

"Warrior waves will always win," said Mokci. "So, do not fight them. Bend. Let them have their way and they will let you have yours."

Dankert had laughed, not the laughter of derision but of discovery. Mokci said that Dankert had told him. "I've never seen a Lapp boat up close. Will you draw me a picture of it with lots of detail? Can you do that?"

And Mokci had drawn the boat with ink on paper.

Rikka was curious about Mokci's sea knowledge. "I thought you followed the reindeer back and forth across the tundra."

"I always did, as a baby on my mother's back or on my own feet as a child. One year my grandfather, the noadi, decided that I should learn the ways of the sea people, so he left me with distant relatives on the coast. I did not return to the highlands at all that year or the next. Instead, I learned the ways of the fishermen. Their boats were very different from yours."

"Are they smaller?" Rikka asked.

"Yes, and faster. Much faster. And lighter," Mokci said with pride. "We sew together with reindeer sinews and overlapping seams. That is why they can shift and give in the water."

"Don't they bog down with water?"

"No, the water flows in, so the water flows out too."

"But do they break up easily when you get caught in ice?"

"No, they shift with the ice," Mokci said smiling. "We fish all summer, not like you, waiting for the cod in winter. That is when we hunt walrus and seals."

"With guns?"

"No, with bows and arrows, from our boats." Mokci stood up and mimicked aiming, drawing and letting fly an arrow. He made a sound of a walrus dying.

"Sometimes breaking ice can be dangerous, but the skins of these animals make strong cables for our boats."

"Do you eat those beasts?"

"Sure. Why not? Nothing better than hot blubber on a cold night."

Rikka still dreamed of, wanted to try to climb the Thorn. Despite all the chaos around her, or because of it, her idea was becoming an obsession. She could see the problems. She could imagine the hazards. She admitted to herself the implausibility of her desire. Instead, she focused on each step that she had to take in approaching the climb.

She made her pants, reinforced the knees with an extra layer of sheepskin. She adjusted and readjusted the fit as she realized how flexible the legs had to be and how nothing could be allowed to bind. On the other hand, if they were baggy, they might get caught on snags. She redid the pockets when she realized she had made them too big. The idea was to be able to carry food, a knife, an extra hat in them; and then she realized that those pockets were as big as saddlebags on a workhorse and filling them would weigh her down and throw her off balance. But now she had a pair of pants that would work for her. She also made a warm vest from the bodice of the ugly dress. This she allowed herself to decorate with some embroidery, not too much, no flowers, just feather stitching, like bird tracks in the sand, so they wouldn't look girlish. She still had no boots. Dankert had a hundred excuses, but she suspected he just wanted to slow her down.

One evening, sitting with Mokci on the sea wall, she said she had something she wanted to show him. In a gesture that was both sudden and impulsive, she pulled up the hem of her skirt, all the way up. Shocked, he could hear her laughter muffled behind the fabric. Instead of legs, he saw an odd pair of long brown pants.

"Rika, you have turned into the tree with two trunks. Did the stallu cast a spell on you?" Rikka hid her face in her skirt, unable to let it fall because then he would see her face. But now he was looking at her legs instead. All the closeness that had built up between them, the trust and friendship, suddenly felt endangered.

She lowered her skirt and lifted her chin. He wasn't laughing at her anymore, in fact, his face just showed a sincere interest in the ugly pants.

"You made these, Rikka?" He reached out and pinched a bit of the fabric, rubbing it between his fingers. Then he brought his face close and sniffed it. Rikka almost jumped away but caught her reaction and pushed it down into a safe place.

"Yes, I must admit I did," she laughed with relief and maybe a bit of pride. She did a little double-trunked tree dance for him, swaying in an Arctic flow of wind.

"This wool is very fine. Does it come from this island?"

"Oh, here or Paris, France or maybe Persia," she laughed. "Off a rich woman's back."

Then she grew serious. She told him of her need to climb the Thorn. How she was planning, sewing, imagining. How she felt this urge in her body to tackle the face of the mountain.

"But I don't have boots, and I don't know how to get any. They have to be good boots, too. Flexible, sturdy, warm, and they can't slip on smooth or wet rock."

"All right," he said. "We will make them."

"Can we? How? What'll we make them of?"

"Reindeer hide. You will see. You have to come to my lavvu and I will show you. Bring the needle I gave you. If we both work on them you will have a pair of boots soon. Good Saami boots like the ones we wear crossing the mountains in the winter."

Rikka reached for his hand, and growing soft and serious, she thanked him. "You are my best and only friend. So now you need to be honest with me."

"I am always honest with you, Rikka."

"Then, do you think I'm foolish to want to do this thing?"

"I think you are brave. And I think you need a quest to prove to yourself that you can do a crazy thing."

"I just wonder, though, do I know how to do it? It's not like climbing an apple tree. Are there things I need to know? How strong do I have to be? Things like that."

"I can teach you what you need to know. We will practise together if you like. I will not offer to go with you on your quest. It needs to be yours."

"Yes. You're right." For the first time, Rikka was terrified. Mokci was making it real and possible for her, but he wouldn't pull her up the mountain; he would stand below and watch her climb or watch her fall. Now she had to do it, and dread oozed its way up from her belly to her throat. She felt as if she had swallowed a raven's nest. It stuck in her throat and threatened to choke her, either choke her or spur her on.

SECTION TWO

Sunday was a frigid morning. The fire had gone out, and deep into winter was no time to let it die at night. Rikka lit the candle in her little window and watched it soften a small circle of frost on the glass. She pulled the bed covers tighter around her, reluctant to get up and relight the fire. It looked as if it would be one of hard cold winters in the islands. Usually, the temperature didn't drop far below freezing. The Gulf Stream chased away much of what might be expected of winter cold. But that was most years.

There had been signs that this winter would be different. The fish lay deeper under the water; the cormorants left earlier; there had been frost in the beards of the fishermen out working on their boats in November.

The circle of cleared glass grew to the size of a Sunday pancake. Rikka knew she had to get up. She wrapped her blanket around her shoulders and let it drag along the floor as she did her morning chores. Rikka decided to go to church without even being coerced. If she got the house warm enough, Hanna and baby Ragna might sleep longer. The church would be warm because the keeper would have gone early to start a good fire. The church always had sufficient firewood and coal for its two large stoves. Maybe there she would find some comfort and even a bit of clarity. Maybe there would be coffee afterwards. Maybe the priest would have something comforting to say, something about loving each other, helping those in need. A blessing would be welcome.

New snow lay deep on the path and the world looked cleansed. As she walked through the church doors, she thought that maybe one day the women would welcome her. Why shouldn't they? Jesus would. Wouldn't he?

She looked around the congregation. The front rows were filled and she could recognize people only by the backs of their best Sunday clothing. They sat so straight, heads faced forward towards the pulpit. Others, latecomers, brushed past her. Some would whisper "Excuse me" as they edged around her. None looked her in the eyes or asked her to join them. Gradually, the pews were all claimed.

Rikka reverted to her usual spot near the back of the congregation, far away from the warmth of the furnace but also from the chill of the congregation. She paid scant attention to the service. It seemed to vacillate between old prayers and incantations vying with new pronouncements on the priest's part. Rikka repeated the prayers and bowed her head when appropriate.

As she investigated the lap of her green dress, she imagined a field where Mokci and his family and friends lived in Finnmark. His life seemed so gentle and natural. His people wouldn't sit in these rows of rigid pews, looking straight forward and singing off-key. They would be sitting in a circle in a lavvu with a fire burning in the centre. There would be food and drink to share. They would welcome anyone who came by for warmth and kinship. She was thinking about the tales of his life in the high north. She loved his stories about the mountains and the animals, especially the reindeer. His stories were rich in details with the way they would hunt wild reindeer during the winter. A hunter might lay his bow between the antlers of a tame reindeer. Then hunkering down close alongside the animal he could move right up to a herd of wild ones and easily make a clean kill. He even told her about how they would castrate the herd's young male reindeer. Mokci had looked at her with a twinkle in his eyes as he said, "You wrestle the young buck to the ground, roll it onto its back, spread its legs apart and then sink your teeth into its testicles."

Rikka, having scant knowledge of testicles but getting the gist of his story, looked at him in horror.

"Don't worry, Mokci said, "we do not bite them off, just crunch them enough that they will never develop. Very tame reindeer."

Rika found herself biting her lip to keep from laughing aloud as she sat in her pew. She still didn't know if Mokci was teasing, but she did know that he said he'd never lie to her.

"Black magic and the spawn of Hell knock at our doors, wanting in," the priest said leaning over the pulpit, knuckles white where they grasped the edge. Rikka wondered how he could speak with so much force that his words grated and bounced off the back of the nave.

"A Mormon man: what does he look like? In the daytime he might be mistaken for one of you good men sitting in the congregation today. He might look like a hard-working farmer or fisherman. But what about at night? My good women, I don't wish to frighten you, but it is my duty to educate you regarding the dangers these men bring. At night, in the dark, where your bedroom becomes a torture chamber..."

Rikka felt her attention being drawn away from Mokci and into a nightmare.

"...claws and talons and body parts grossly..."

His words were pulling her down into something like the most gruesome and terrifying of old myths. She decided she would not slide down there with him. She tried to block the words and return to that lavvu in her imagination. Bending forward, she returned to the green field of her lap. Breathing deeply, she fought down the priest's voice, quieter, quieter. Had she stopped him? Rikka was startled by the silence, then startled again when it was shattered.

"Today's collection will go to education of the Lapps. Missionary efforts in Lappland to teach them our mother tongue have been more and more successful. The importance of this mission is obvious. Through our language, our common language, we can bring the Lapps out of their darkness, away from drunkenness and debauchery, away from their thieving habits, and towards the light of God. We must live with them more closely as they come south and we Norwegians settle northwards, but we can only live with them when they have seen the light. For your own safety, for love of Norway, give what you can. Then give again. In the name of the Father, the Son and the Holy Ghost, Amen."

Rikka raised her head, perplexed by the priest's words. She knew nothing of the Mormons. They weren't her concern. And she didn't need to listen to gossip about what they did in the darkness of their own homes. There was no room in her mind for such gossip. Life was hard enough. But the priest's sermon had been virulently against the Mormon missionaries. He said they had no right to impose their religion on Christians. They should return to America and leave his people alone.

Yet his request for offerings was based on the virtues of his own mission to change the lives of a race of people who he would draw down into his own darkness. She would not be part of it. One of the church men stood at the end of her aisle holding out the basket filled with the congregation's offerings, waiting for her donation. She had nothing to offer. Rikka stood up quietly, no blood this time, no shame, just leaving.

Rikka walked home alone, the rest of the congregation still behind, maybe drinking coffee in the meeting room. Maybe still praying to ward off the invading forces. The day was clear now, the sun igniting sparks of light in the snow. A narrow strip of ice delineated the water's edge like a window into the blue. Would the low sun melt that ice or would the dropping temperatures reinforce it? She had heard of winters when the bay was blocked by ice, but that was before she was born. How would that affect the cod fishery? Would the boats get locked in before the cod arrived? The men must have plans for keeping their boats free, but she couldn't really imagine how. If they anchored them further out, they would be vulnerable to storms, and how would they get out to their boats anyway? Would the ice be so thick that they could safely walk over it? These matters, which she had never considered before, now seemed more vital to her than any of the fears emanating from the church. Everything, everybody on the island was dependant on the cod, not just for their own food supplies but also for trade. Cod meant money, meant survival. Even the farms were dependant on the cod fishery. No one could buy beef, lamb, butter, and milk from them if there was no money to change hands.

Rikka entered the path to her house. Smoke came from the chimney. That was a relief, a sign that Hanna had been up and thinking about what was needed. Even more promising than the sworls of chimney smoke were the sweet faint notes of a lullaby wrapping around Rikka. Hanna was singing to her baby:

> *Now roof and rafters blend with the starry vault on high,*
> *Now flies little Ragna on dreamwings through the sky.*
>
> *There mounts a mighty stairway from earth to God's own land*
> *Where Ragna with the angels goes climbing hand in hand.*
>
> *God's angel-babes watch your cot, the still night through.*
> *God bless thee, little Ragna, your mother watches too.*

Rikka found herself singing along with the lullaby. She remembered Hanna singing it to Agnes and she remembered it with her own name inserted. She used to think Hanna made it up but she learned much later in school that Edvard Grieg had written the lullaby, and her mother had replaced Grieg's names with her own babies' names.

Rikka came in the door and ran to her mother who cradled Ragna in her arms. They smiled at each other. Hanna had made attempts to tame her hair. Her face was washed and she wore a clean dress. Except for the dark deep circles under her eyes, she looked like the girls' mother once again.

"Mama, would you like me to braid your hair?"

"Is it such a mess?"

"Of course not, it's just that it looks so beautiful in a braided crown. And you deserve a crown."

Hanna smiled. "Would you wash it first? That's what I'd really like."

"Of course. Let me see if the water is warm enough." Rikka felt a rush of excitement. Could she dare hope that a real change had come about? Hanna nursed Ragna while Rikka made the preparations. Hanna's milk flow had ebbed when she wasn't able to be with her baby for most of the day, but by the look on little Ragna's face and her legs kicking in the air as she grabbed Hanna's breast with both hands, it seemed that the milk was again flowing.

Rikka mixed some cold water in with the hot, trying to find the perfect temperature. She laid a towel next to the stove so she would be able to wrap Hanna's head after she washed it. She had never done this before; Hanna had always been so self-sufficient, but Rikka tried to remember the steps that Hanna had followed in washing her daughters' hair. It was such a treat to lean her head over the sink and have her mother's agile fingers massage her scalp.

Once she was sure there was enough warm water, she called to Hanna who laid Ragna on a blanket on the floor and came over to the sink smiling. Silently she bent her head and covered her eyes with her fingers. Rikka slowly poured the water through all that thick light brown hair, running her fingers through the length of it, loosening the tangles. She used the camomile shampoo that Dagur always made for them. Hanna sighed, and the muscles in her shoulders visibly relaxed. Rikka took a moment to massage Hannah's neck. Then she rinsed her hair again and again until the water ran clear of soap and of bits of weeds and splinters of wood. Then the warm towel, wrapped and wrapped again.

"There, Mama, sit here by the fire, and when your hair dries a bit I'll comb and braid it for you. Ragna had crawled across the floor, until she reached up and tugged at Hanna's skirt. Hanna laughed and lifted the baby onto her lap again.

"I'll make the meal," Rikka offered.

"Thank you, Rikka. And ask Dagur to join us. She's been kind."

"Yes, she has." Her mother was noticing the good things people did. She couldn't do that when she was lost in her world of grief. Maybe things would be all right after all.

Rikka thought about the midday meal. She wanted to make something special to celebrate the new turn in Hanna's condition. She had fresh makarel that Dankert had dropped off instead of coal. She would pan fry them and warm up a sauce spiced with cranberries. If she added a bit of sugar to those, the sauce would thicken and create the balance of flavours that she knew Hanna would enjoy. That and mashed potatoes with butter from the farm and a bit of Dagur's horseradish would make a festive Sunday meal. As she boiled the potatoes, she imagined Mokci sitting around the table with them. She realized that she would have time after the meal to go to Mokci's lavvu and work with him on the boots. She slipped the reindeer antler needle in her pocket, and smiled at the way a bad day had turned so good.

The meal was a success. It felt like a party with Hanna laughing at Ragna's attempt to stand holding onto one set of chair legs after another. The baby begged food from those sitting in the chairs, and Dagur was delighted with the invitation and her good friend's happiness. Dagur made things easy for Rikka by suggesting that she go for a good long walk while she and Hanna cleaned up. Rikka was out of the house as soon as she could pull her pants on under her skirt.

The sun lay low in the sky, ready to drop into the sea. Stars were barely visible between breaks in the clouds, but as Rikka walked towards the cloudberry swamp, the clouds drifted further and further apart revealing a thousand more stars, brighter by the minute. No moon, but enough light from the stars to help her along a familiar path. She was confident that she would find Mokci at his camp; the boat works were quiet on Sunday, and he never seemed to have anywhere to go. She wondered how much trouble it would cause if she invited him to their midday meal next Sunday. It would probably cause another scandal, but only if it were noticed. She knew that Dagur and Hanna would both enjoy his company.

And there he was, no more than a dark shadow in the darkness of the evening. He was standing on the edge of the birch forest, back facing her and arms raised to something hanging on a line there. Warmth suffused Rikka as she watched his arms moving back and forth, arranging whatever it was in front of him. He looked as if he was conducting a chorus of birch trees, their slender trunks pale and still. She picked her way through the marsh which was frozen over now with just the tips of the cloudberry mounds peeking out above the ice. In one step her foot cracked the ice sending a warning to Mokci who turned slowly and silently to face a possible threat.

"Rikka, you have come. I hoped you would. Careful, there are more weak spots in the ice as you come closer." He moved towards her, holding out his hand.

"I have good news," Rikka said.

"Yes, your smile tells me so."

"My mother's better. She's happy today. I washed her hair and she's nursing Ragna again." Rikka was so happy to tell someone this, especially someone who cared for her mother.

"This is very good news. Did something happen to make her glad?"

"I don't know. I haven't had time to even think about that. It's just as if a warm wind came through and blew away the sickness." She stared into the darkness and then a glow from the lavvu pulled her attention in that direction. "I think she saw a light. I don't know."

"Come this way, Rikka. Let's go in where it is warm." He took her hand again and led her to the lavvu. He reached up to the line and took down one of the objects he had been arranging when she arrived. They were round coils, almost like small Christmas wreaths.

"What are those?"

"Soon you will see."

"Are they made of straw?"

"Where is your patience?"

"I left it at home, under the door mat."

"I will make you coffee," Mokci said as he opened the flap to his home.

Rikka looked around the tent. The rock slabs under her feet ran in a straight line to the fire at the centre of the lavvu. The fire gave off a flickering light that cast golden streaks on the hides that kept the inside in and the outside out. Mokci's shadow danced on the hides as he bent to make coffee and lay out cups. There was no furniture except a wooden slab, curved up at one end with a deer skin over it for his bed. She sat down on the springy layer of birch saplings and dried moss carpeting the floor. One pot and a bowl hung from pegs on the centre pole, and a smaller pot was suspended over the fire. Most of Mokci's possessions were organized in tidy piles off to one side. He poured a bit of cold water on the coffee to make the grounds settle, then poured the coffee into the cups. He set them on a flat board just back from the fire.

"Are the cups made of wood?"

"No, walrus tusk. Feel the cup. You can tell it is not wood but animal. And you can smell the difference, too. But right now, it smells like coffee. Try some." Rikka sipped; it tasted rich and mellow even without cream and sugar.

"I brought my needle."

"Good. We will start the shoes tonight. I have already cut the skins and softened them."

"How do you do that?"

"I paddle them until the stiffness leaves them. Feel the difference," he said handing her two lengths, one pliable, the other rigid. "I think I have cut them to a size that will fit you. Give me your leg."

No one had ever asked her to give them her leg before. Laughing, she pulled up her skirt to reveal her pants leg.

"Do I have to take my pants off?" she asked, then felt her face heat up with embarrassment.

"No. This is fine. There has to be room for the sedge anyway."

"Sedge?"

"Here. These coils that I brought in. They are sedge that I cut before winter came. They will make the boots warm."

"Won't they be itchy?"

"No, sedge is soft. We always use it in our boots. And when we travel, we bring coils like this with us for when the old grass is no good."

Rikka stretched out her legs and Mokci rested her feet in his lap. Her mind was spinning in one direction and then in the other. She could not imagine that this closeness could be acceptable, that any of the island boys would ever touch her legs like this. And if they did, she would beat them off. But this was Mokci. It was so natural, wasn't it? She couldn't always read him and yet he was … what? He was Mokci. A brother, a friend, what else? Rikka told herself to breathe as Mokci spread the skins over her feet and calves.

"What part of the reindeer do these pieces come from?"

"Their legs of course. Their legs are now your legs, strong, fast, able to run and climb and swim across fast flowing rivers." Rikka laughed at the idea, but she loved it.

"Yours boots do not have the turned-up toes like mine. They would not work for you when you are climbing."

"Why do yours have them?"

"They are good in the snow, good when I am skiing, too." He set two skins aside and trimmed both of them. "Your legs are very thin. I cut these too big. But now we can place them together. I will show you the stitch and we can both start joining the pieces. Here is the bundle of thread, as you call it. It is made from reindeer sinew."

"What is sinew? I've always heard the word but don't know where sinew is in the body."

"It lies between muscles and bone, between bones and other bones. Without sinew the reindeer and us, too, would just be skin sacks filled with a pile of bone and meat."

"All right, sinew is just fine with me. I never aspired to being a sack of slop,"

Rikka laughed. "How do you turn sinew into thread?"

"Mostly the women do it. They beat it with the back of an axe if the axe is not busy cutting down trees somewhere. If it is, they have to settle for a stone. Then they start ripping the long strands into thinner ones. And then they have to spin it."

"How?"

"So many questions."

"How?"

"With their teeth. Ripping them thinner and thinner. Then they roll and twist it on their leg and it gets longer and finer. If they keep going, they can make it very, very fine, or they can stop sooner and it is like this thicker thread for your boots."

"That's amazing. When I'm sewing, the thread comes off a wooden spool. I never thought about where it comes from or how it's made. I had silk thread once and didn't even think about it coming from worms and how people managed to turn it into the beautiful thread on my spool. Do you think some woman in China had to chew worms to make the thread?"

They both laughed, but neither of them knew how it was done in China.

As they sewed, the two talked more about their lives. As Rikka reached the end of her first long line of stitching, she realized that too much time had passed. Her mother would be worried. Maybe frantic. Hanna could so easily slip back into her terrible state.

"Mokci, I need to go. I wasn't thinking. I have to get home right away."

"I will walk with you. It is a dark night and I want you to be safe." They both bundled up and headed outside to find a night sky that had turned to emerald green. The waves of colour would light their way. The sky was dancing and Rikka wavered between dread and delight.

"There is something I want to give you," Mokci said as they walked along the shore.

"What would that be?'

"I want to surprise you with this gift. You must find a time when we can be together for more hours."

"Why?"

"You will see. You will like it."

"It's hard to get away."

"Have trust in me. I will leave you now before we are seen together. Good night, Rikka."

"Good night. I'll see what I can do."

Just one candle stood in the window absorbing the waves of green light from the sky. The house was silent. Rikka went to the bedroom and found Hanna smiling in her sleep with Ragna in the circle of her arms. The baby's head rested on Hanna's chest. She took the blanket warming near the stove, ready for her own bed, and put it over Ragna. She picked up her baby sister and, bundling her in the warm blanket, moved her to the cradle. There had been nothing to worry about. No reason to rush back from the lavvu and from Mokci, but Rikka was glad that she had. She lay in the daybed watching the dance of the aurora as the tendrils of light draped her house in dreams.

When she woke in the dark of early morning, Rikka saw her mother standing by the stove watching her. "God morgen, Mama."

"God morgen, Rikka. You were out late last night, weren't you?"

"Yes, there was a lovely green sky, just green but beautiful. I was entranced."

"Were you with anyone, a boy?"

"I was learning how to make shoes, Mama."

"Who was teaching you?"

"Mokci."

"Aw, Mokci, I like Mokci. He wouldn't do anything bad with you, would he?"

"No, Mama. We worked at sewing reindeer pelts together to make boots. We sewed them with sinews. It was really interesting. I want to do more of that."

A mix of feelings on her mother's face; she had to convince her mother that her relationship with Mokci was safe.

"Did you know that they use the forehead skin of the reindeer to make the soles of their boots? And we will use two pieces for the soles with the hairs on one side running against the hairs on the other. That's to make them less slippery."

Hanna still looked doubtful, so Rikka continued. "Just think, Mama, we could learn to make these boots ourselves and sell them. We can decorate them with ribbons just as the Lapps do."

"No, Rikka. We will not take advantage of the Lapps that way. And I want you to be sure that one certain Lapp is not taking advantage of you."

"How can you say that? He's my friend. And he's your friend, too."

"That's different. You know that's different. I have to worry about you. When you came home covered in blood, I thought some man had attacked you. It can happen that easily, that quickly, and then your life is hell. Just hell."

Rather than argue, Rikka went over to her mother and put her arms around her. "I know, Mama. I know I have to be careful. But I don't have to be careful with Mokci. He is careful with me. He also has a lot at risk. And now I'd like to eat some of that rice porridge you've made so I can go to the farm with something in my stomach."

The skies were clear and dark, hard as obsidian, as Rikka headed towards the farm. Wisps of snow skittered across the ice in the bay stopped only by the jagged rocks guarding the shore. There the snow continued to pile up until a cross current would once again lift it and shift it down onto another drift. A sharp-edged sickle of moon threatened the Thorn, and Rikka looked forward to leaning her forehead into the warm flank of old Bestemor. This cold snap bore into her bones.

It's not supposed to be this cold, Rikka thought and then laughed at herself. Supposed to? Was nature supposed to follow her rules? From down the shoreline path, she saw a dark-on-dark form moving towards her, growing larger as it approached. A horse pulling a wagon. Could it be Dankert? Had this unusually cold night reminded him to bring that coal he promised?

Rikka stepped aside as the horse and buggy approached. Her path was his road and there wasn't room for both of them. It wasn't Dankert, she saw, but Herr Lorkman in a hurry. She nodded to acknowledge him. No response, he passed her as if she were nothing more than a pile of dung in his path. Hardly even that. Well, no hurt feelings there. She had no wish to get closer to the man. His rushing buggy whipped the early morning cold and dropped it a few degrees. His face worried her. Grim determination. Snow dust swirled behind him, obscuring the phantom buggy.

When Rikka got to the farmhouse, she collected warm water in a bowl and retrieved the milking bucket from the pantry. Even the pantry felt warm after the icy outdoors. She had no desire to linger inside but said a silent I love you to her little sister, no doubt asleep upstairs. She realized that she had not given much thought this last week to Agnes and her absence in their home. Was it that easy to let go of someone you loved? She made a promise to herself to find a way to spend time with Agnes. Was she happy here? Was it enough to have rich cakes and a different dress for each day of the week, or was the child's heart yearning for her real family? Rikka considered sneaking up the stairs to the room she figured Agnes slept in, the one where Agnes stood at the window to wave at Rikka. She knew Lorkman was not around, but where was the mistress? Still asleep? Probably. But what if she were caught? Of course she didn't want to get caught and perhaps sent home without her usual parcel of food and probably without a job anymore.

Rikka moved through the kitchen, admiring the warm round tower of the kakelugn with its heather sprigs in bloom even in the depths of winter. At the bottom of the stairs, she stopped and listened. Silence. She took one step up and stopped again, alert. Still nothing.

Step by careful step she made it halfway up the stairs before her weight on the next step made it creak. She froze, then heard a rustling of sheets. She knew she had to retreat, but as she stepped down backwards, the same stair creaked again as her weight left it. Again she froze and heard nothing, continuing backwards, one by one, keeping her eyes on the landing above.

What was this thing in her that made her take chances lately? Sneaking around in someone else's house, spending an evening alone with a Lapp in his tent. Looking for trouble, her mother would say. Or was trouble just looking for her? Was trouble all too easy to come by? Back in the kitchen she walked over to the kakelugn and ran her hands over the warm tiles. Imagine having a stove that stayed warm all night, that needed to be fed only once a day. The heather, along with all that warmth, made her hungry for summer: flowers, hot sun, light. But for now, winter edged in and froze the fantasy. Time to milk a cow.

Bestemor was lying down on a bed of straw in her stall. Usually she was standing, ready for breakfast when Rikka arrived.

"Poor old thing. Are your bones aching today? Calf kicking you in the ribs? Come on girl, time to face the day. Come on now." Bestemor shifted her weight and slowly managed to stand. Rikka laughed to see that a hedgehog, seeking warmth, had been curled up next to the cow. "Is that a dirty look you're giving me, Pin Cushion? Stay around and I'll see if there's a drop of milk for you."

Milking was a short job. Very little milk collected in the cow's udder. There was so little, in fact, that Rikka decided she might as well leave a bit of it for the little creature. No cheese or butter would come from today's milking. She didn't want the cow to dry up. That would mean an end to the little contact she had with Agnes. Then what? Could she make herself indispensable in some other way? Rikka ran her hands over Bestemor's belly. She could feel the small bundle of calf inside the old girl. She draped herself over the cow's round side, resting her head on her back, sharing warmth with her. "Will this be your last calf? Have you had just about enough of life?" Bestemor swung her head back and forth, an answer that Rikka could not read.

As she closed the barn door behind her, Rikka looked up to Agnes's window. No little girl there. But she caught motion in the next window. Fru Lorkman stood waving her arms to catch Rikka's attention. Her eyes were spectrally large in her face and her mouth was open, lips trembling. She gestured for Rikka to come in. From the kitchen Rikka heard Fru Lorkman's shaky voice calling her to come upstairs. Was something wrong with Agnes? She bounded upstairs, past Agnes's room and into the next. The mistress stood in her dressing gown, ashen and shaking.

"What's the matter, Fru Lorkman?'

"Someone is in the house!"

"Who?"

"How should I know? I heard them. Herr Lorkman went out early, but someone else was in here. I heard them on the stairs."

Rikka wanted to laugh. Had the mistress been standing there shaking like that ever since Rikka stepped on that creaking stair? She couldn't disillusion the woman, so she'd have to play along.

"When did you hear that?"

"What a silly question. I've been in such a state of terror. Here I am all alone with not so much as a useless husband to protect me."

Protect you? Rikka thought. What about Agnes? If the mistress was in danger, did she give no thought to the child, only herself? Rikka breathed deeply, trying to still her feelings of contempt so they wouldn't show on her face.

"It's an old house, Fru Lorkman. Perhaps the stairs are just complaining about the cold."

"No, I know the difference between the house's sounds and the sounds of an interloper. It could be one of those Mormons. It could even be more than one. They may still be in here. I want you to go look."

Ah yes, I could risk my life for you, but you couldn't even look in on Agnes, could you? Rikka could not argue with the fool. Instead she told her to sit down, keep perfectly quiet and let her check the house out.

"Don't forget to check the larder and the pantry. They could be hiding anywhere. And the coal bin."

I'll check the teapot too, if you like. Oh, how Rikka wanted to speak her thoughts aloud. "Lock this door once I'm out of here."

"There is no lock. I asked for a lock, but no one ever listens."

"Then tip this chair so the back is under the handle."

"That won't work."

"Yes. It will. Just do it, please." Rikka left the room and made noise going down the stairs. She was utterly silent coming back up and entering Agnes's room. The little girl was sitting up in bed, rubbing the sleep from her eyes. Rikka put a silencing finger to her lips and whispered in her ear, "Don't let the mice know that I'm here." She gave the giggling child a hug and promised to be back in a few minutes. "Just curl up here with your doll and rest until I can come back. It's our secret."

She saw the pink doll with blond ringlets at the foot of the bed and tried to hand it to Agnes, but Agnes reached under her pillow and pulled out Poona who she kissed and held next to her cheek. Rikka kissed her and left silently. Downstairs she made a point of taking her time and making noise in each room she entered. It was a good chance to take inventory of all that the Lorkmans had accumulated over the years, and she comforted herself that it hadn't made them the least bit happy.

Back upstairs Rikka convinced Fru Lorkman that no one was there, but the woman cried about how she was alone and unprotected. "I want you to come and work here. There's so much that needs to be taken care of. I can't do it all myself."

Rikka had no intention of being their full-time slave, and she told the mistress that it was impossible. She was far too busy at home. Fru Lorkman countered that Rikka soon would not be nearly so involved at home. A wave of dread flowed through Rikka, but she didn't ask any questions. Instead, she tried to appease the woman because an idea came to her.

"I'll come every morning to take care of the milking. Then I'll get your breakfast and bring it up to you. Agnes will come downstairs with me for breakfast, washing up and getting dressed. That will have to be enough for now. And you won't have to worry about intruders if Herr Lorkman has to go out early. But you'll have to pay me."

"I'm sure that can be arranged."

"I will want money as well as the food I already get." The

arrangement was made, much to Rikka's advantage. Maybe someday soon she'd be able to buy a treadle machine and start her dressmaking business. Then she would never again have to work for others. Maybe she'd even make pants for women. Rikka could finally enjoy the coming Yule season.

Hanna stood in the doorway, watching, as Herr Lorkman pulled his horse and buggy up to the little house. He looked around for somewhere to hitch the horse but could find nothing in the dark. Instead of getting down, he shouted out to Johanna from his seat on the buggy.

Hanna's clean brown hair fell to her shoulders and she wore a clean dress. She would not invite him in, not in a thousand years, but she also would not slam the door in his face although she had to anchor her hands to her hips to keep from doing just that. The desire for revenge pulsed through her body, but no, she would act with dignity, and she would not let him see her fear.

"I have come to tell you what the council has decided," Lorkman pronounced in his magisterial voice. "Your infant, Ragna, will be taken to live with my son Dankert and his wife, Pernille. They will adopt this infant who you are not capable of caring for. The decision has been reached and the bailiff will arrive after the evening meal to take her. You needn't pack anything. This is the decision of the council."

Hanna looked straight in his eyes. She held her face and body steady, a picture of serenity. He would not have the pleasure of witnessing her fury or her tears. Hanna turned and silently closed the door behind her. Shut him out. Shut the evil out.

Ragna was sitting in her highchair, making pictures on the tray by running her fingers through a mess of porridge. She laughed at the sticky stuff between her fingers and waved her hands in the air. So precious, Hanna thought. How utterly precious, as Ragna ran her gooey fingers through her angel fluff hair. Hanna would have to be especially cautious now, take care in hiding her sweet baby. She licked the palms of the baby's hands and sucked the porridge off her fingers, much to Ragna's delight. Hanna would miss the closeness.

She looked at her shawl hanging by the door. Time to go. Hanna lifted Ragna out of her highchair and wrapped her in the red wool blanket she had knitted during her last pregnancy. Ragna curled into her mother, full of breakfast and growing sleepy. By the time they were outside in the dark morning, the baby was sound asleep.

Hanna headed down to the shore and picked her way carefully over and around black rocks bedecked in slimy seaweed. She knew her destination, the Sentinels, and all the protection they offered. She reached out her free hand and stroked the pillared rock that marked the entrance to the refuge. The tide was out and the Sentinel's floor was a small carpet of charcoal slate and white sand, damp but not sodden. Hanna chose a smooth rectangle of slate to sit on. She sat crossed legged and lay Ragna in the cradle formed by her legs.

"No, my child, you will not go to Dankert's home. That dry stick Pernille will never be your mother. Only I, and then not I, and then not you."

And so she sang one more time to her daughter:

> *Now roof and rafters blend with the starry vault on high,*
> *Now flies little Ragna on dreamwings through the sky.*

Hanna tossed blessings towards the baby floating far above the rooves and rafters of farmhouses and rorbuer. Far above the Rose Church and the sheep in their pens. Her baby rose above the cod swarming the seas of the Barents Straight heading down towards Lofoten in masses. And still higher in the sky there appeared a spiral made of steps to take her further up.

> *There mounts a mighty stairway from earth to God's own land*
> *Where Ragna with the angels goes climbing hand in hand.*

Who were all those winged creatures around her? Little white souls holding her hands? Look at how they danced and led her to her bed, watching her the still night through.

God bless thee, little Ragna, your mother watches too.

Hanna lifted Ragna from her cradling lap and lay her gently in the sand. As Hanna rose and stepped out of the Sentinels, Ragna slept undisturbed. Hanna moved to the water's edge and watched it inch forward with each breath the sea exhaled. She thought she might sit there for awhile as the Sentinels kept guard. She too could guard.

Something white and silver caught her eye under the shelf of ice that gripped the shore. It was round, bobbing in the back-eddy. She leaned forward squinting to make out what it was, but the sky was dark, the water was darker and the ice distorted her view. One wavelet, a little bolder than the others, slid under the ice and brought the orb closer to the surface. Just for a flash of a moment, the orb rolled and she saw that its other side showed a disc of blue. An eye. Just an eye all by itself, not attached to a face, but surely a human eye.

And then she thought … Anders. It had to be his. That blue, the deep intensity of it. She used to tease him about his eyes having been painted by a bluebird's feather. Had Anders, the man who used to protect her, been rolling through the sea all these years? Had the cod sucked his eye out of the socket? Had he been enticed by the nøkken to leap over the side of his ship and then been pulled under and further under? Was he sucked into the maelstrom and spun centrifugally till his limbs were ripped from his torso? She needed to get at the eye, to hold it. She lifted a stone and dropped it on the ice. When it didn't break, she picked up larger rocks and threw them with force until the ice shattered. Dipping her hands into the chill water, she scooped around trying to find him. Where was he? She hurried to her feet and started running up and down the shore looking for him, calling his name. Anders. Anders. But no, it was only his eye watching her. That was all that was left, watching what she was doing. But she no longer knew what she was doing. She reached in the water trying to scoop out the eye, but it rolled away, time after time, it simply rolled back into deeper water. Squatting at the water's edge, Hanna watched the eye and began to doubt. It couldn't be Anders; it had been too long. The eye kept sliding back just out of her grasp. Just as Anders would do if he could. Her skirt was wicking up the frigid water. When she tried to stand up the weight of it held her there, tugging at her to reconsider.

And then she realized, that's what unlucky fishermen did ... died at sea. The eye drifted under the sheet of ice. Looking up at her the blue iris was milky, warped. Was everything to be taken away? Every source of love and comfort? Was she so vile that she didn't deserve love? Hanna scooped up double handfuls of salty water and poured them over her head, again and again, until she was cleansed. Walk alone. From now on, she would walk alone.

The boots were almost finished. Mokci beat the bundle of dried sedge grass with a birch stick, softening it. The sweet aroma of summer wafted through the lavvu.

"Did you bring some ribbons?" he asked.

"Yes, which colour should I use? I guess mostly red with touches of yellow, blue and green would be traditional, right?"

"They would, but I like that purple. You do not have to follow the tradition. Let us see how that would look." He unrolled the small ball of purple ribbon, ran it through his fingers, then hung it around Rikka's neck. "Now I have lassoed you, my very own reindeer."

Rikka's laugh caught in her throat. Something had shifted. Mokci held both ends of the ribbon around her neck. He pulled one end and then the other. The satin rubbed lightly against the back of her neck and sent a charge down her spine.

"Some night soon I have a surprise for you," he said, "when the moon is full and the snow just deep enough."

"Deep enough for what?

"For the surprise."

He picked up the finished boots. "Let me help you." He had packed the soles with sedge grass and as he pulled the boots over her feet and up her legs he worked in more sedge to keep her warm. His hand ran up and down her calf, smoothing the sedge in place. She shivered, not accustomed to being touched so casually, so lovingly. Mokci took the purple ribbon and wrapped each boot securely. Rikka looked down at her feet and laughed. The boots felt wonderful, conforming to her feet perfectly. The grass, warmed by the fire and his touch, was soft.

"Thank you Mokci. I love them."

"Yes. Hurry home now and do what you must do. I will see you when the light passes tomorrow."

"If I can...."

But Rikka was not at all sure she could. Her mother's words came back to her, and although she had pushed back against her mother's fears, they had become her own. Maybe a little time alone, a little time away from him. She almost whimpered at the thought.

But maybe she was headed right down the path her mother warned about. Her mother, that vibrant woman, so sad, so deserted by the men in her life. Rikka knew that she had to acknowledge how they were the same, how vulnerable they both were. In the mornings she was full of optimism, of the new ways the world could unfold for her, and then she looked at her mother, that beautiful woman who had been full of hope and love. She knew her life would be better than those around her.

And then things fell apart.

There came that terrible day when Lorkman announced that he would take Ragna, that terrible afternoon when her mother, distraught, abandoned her baby on the shore, confirming the righteousness of Lorkman's decision, that terrible evening when Dagur, sensing disaster, followed Johanna and scooped up the baby just before the tide took her. She rushed to her house with Ragna and rubbed her whole body ruthlessly until the skin turned from blue to purple to rose. And then she trundled all the way up island to Dankert and Pernille's house to deliver Ragna to her new parents. All of this misery coloured Rikka's perceptions. She felt that her own blood had been frozen

Rikka's feet were warm within the beautiful new boots. Her heart brimmed with new love while her shoulders caved under her fear of the future. She would go to church again tomorrow. She didn't have to listen to the priest. She would listen to her heart and hope it would straighten out her mind. The night had grown colder and colder since she had set out for the lavvu. A new level of deep cold had gripped the island. Rikka wrapped her arms around her breasts and shoulders and ran the rest of the way home, noticing that her new boots gripped the icy patches along the way.

Rikka jolted awake. What was it? Not a gunshot, but it sounded like one. She tugged the blanket tight around her body and, in stockinged feet, tiptoed across the frozen floor to the window. Ice patterns swirled like the skirts of flamenco dancers on the glass, backlit by a crystalline moon. The rorbu skreaked and shuddered. The cold which had gripped the night would not loosen its hold this dark morning. She shuffled over to the kitchen stove, hoping for a bed of coals, but had to settle for some shadowed hints of orange.

She found the small hatchet hidden safely beneath the firewood, out of the sight of children's eyes, a pointless precaution now with no child in the house. She shaved slivers of pine wood to urge the cinders to life. The rorbu cracked again like a rifle shot, and she heard Dagur's old rooster curse at the challenge. Rikka split more fine kindling from the pine, glad to have its sappy bark. And, feeling small gratitude, she gave silent thanks to her onkle for the modest store of coal he had brought in a flour bag and the promise, no matter how shaky, of more to come. It was that coal, placed sparingly in the centre of the wood fire that had kept a spark or two alive through the night.

This morning was so cold, she could remember nothing like it before, and she realized that if she were to keep her mother as healthy as possible, she would have to gather the fortitude to challenge Herr Lorkman. He would have to deliver a generous load of coal if he wanted his cow tended and the kakelovn stoked. She knew well that her escalating list of duties in the house and barn made her indispensable.

She had made it clear that more time with Agnes was an absolute condition of her own continued presence on the farm.

Agnes' presence made the work go quickly even though when Agnes insisted on mopping the floor it only meant that little pools of soapy water had to be attended to when the eager child had turned her back. Rikka worried whether she was teaching Agnes practical skills or just how to be someone's house slave. She was certain, though, that she had to protect the bond between herself and her little sister. It could be that for want of contact, Agnes might eventually forget her mother. Considering Johanna's fragility, her fits of outright madness, it might be best for little Agnes to be away for a time.

The old woman wasn't so bad, just useless, pampered, frustrated. But Herr Lorkman ... there was something gone rotten in him. Rikka avoided him, would slip around corners when she smelled his presence. Even thinking of the man evoked nausea, as if his whole being exuded something of the underworld, something from the depths below the depths of the sea. It seemed a blessing that he kept a careful distance from Agnes, sending her upstairs to his wife's territory whenever their paths crossed.

He kept a much closer eye on Rikka. That had taught her to be ever-aware of his whereabouts. She could slide behind the milking stand before he appeared in the doorway of the barn. In the pantry's weak light and shadowed recesses, Rikka could dissolve into invisibility. Or if Agnes was with her, she could simply tickle the little girl so her tinkling laughter would send him off in a different direction. The sickening aspect of these careful evasions was the burgeoning awareness that her mother hadn't always been able to hide. And then what? For the first time, Rikka could imagine the hell of her mother's time at the Lorkman estate.

Rikka blew on the coals, blew harder and blew again until the flames took hold of the sapling pine. Now she could see to her mother. See to her, but could she ever fix her? Rikka pulled back the curtain that divided the bedroom from the rest of the rorbu.

How barren it was. The top bunk of the trundle bed lay empty, perfectly made up, as if waiting for a guest sleeper. Johanna had pushed the lower bed back under the top one. She had tucked a discarded sheet, a tablecloth and an old nightgown into the bottom boards of the top bunk so that the pieces hung down like a ragged curtain. Hanna lay within that cave, curled up as tight as a seasnail. Her long hair spread out around her like pale seaweed. Rikka bent over and stroked her mother's spine. How thin she was. The vertebrae sharp and prominent, formed an archipelago down her curved back.

Silently, Rikka cried. She needed to talk to someone who could understand without judging. Mokci wouldn't do for this; it needed to be a girl or a woman. But aside from old Dagur whose rough compassion she didn't want right now, Rikka had no friends, just an all-consuming family that had dissolved in the last few months, leaving too much space and too little company in her tiny home. Where the laughter had been, now there was only the groaning and cracking of frigid walls. She needed to break out.

She pulled on her pants, with two long skirts over them, then the new boots. They made her smile. It was a morning for emptying the clothes cupboard and putting on every available layer she could find. She stoked the fire one more time, damped it down, and left the house before her conscience could trip her up. The moon had hidden behind the Thorn but left a trail of light on the black water. Rikka felt her way along the path, resisting the turn towards Mokci's lavvu. Instead, she headed past the boatyard where a few fires still burned near the larger fishing boats. As she neared the church, she could see the rosy glow that emanated from the stained glass window. Sunday again. A sleepy morning service. It would be warm and light in there. Rikka knew that if she tried to join in, she would inevitably feel displaced. Nonetheless, she followed the adjoining pathway up the slope to the church's front door. She stood there breathing deeply, trying to imagine help for her inside. She opened the door just a crack and had to smile at the croaking of an old hymn.

> *When the waters part, cast your net, cast your net*
> *when the waters part, praise the Lord*
> *Join me in this boat, said the Lord, said the Lord,*
> *I'll swiftly cast my net, Simon cried.*
> *When death comes to me, by my side you will be.*
> *When the waters close, I'll drag my net.*

The usual sopranos were letting their tremolos soar while the rest of the congregation tried to sing as quietly as possible and without moving their lips. Right at the peak of "I Will Cast My Net," a tremendous tolling of the church's bell obliterated even the strongest vibrato. There was a great hustling for coats and many of the men wore huge smiles of relief and anticipation as they ran out the door. The women also hustled about gathering this and that and bowing quickly, sometimes apologetically, to the priest.

"I thought they'd never come."

"Sven, don't forget the parcel with your extra gloves. Were you thinking the one pair would last you?"

"Finally, finally, some peace at home."

"Fine for you to say, you have those strong boys to help you out. And I have no one to warm my bed on the coldest night of the year."

"Friedrich, did you and Oli finish the mend on that sail last night?"

"What a time to start. It couldn't be colder."

"We'll wait and see about that now, won't we!"

"Come on, let's get going. It's all ready."

"Take it easy, you know that they'll leave us lined up for another hour or so."

"Ja, but we don't want to be at the back of the pack when the flag goes up."

"Come home and get a cup of hot coffee first."

"O, hot coffee, when will I see another cup of that?"

"I love you Brit. You are my own true wife."

"Good thing to hear as you sail away. You take care now, you old bugger. I don't want to hear that you've been tossed over to feed the Minkies."

"Good luck, may the cod leap into the boat for you."

"Take care, you bag of bones."

"Hei, hei, hei all of you. Bring back a whole sea of wealth. Make us rich, or don't come back at all."

Some of the women ran down to the shore with their men. Others rushed back home hoping to find one more useful item, one more memory to send off with the men who they wouldn't be seeing until the cod ran out. Some cried, some looked out to the sea's horizon, some looked down at their feet. And in time, they all moved home to stoke their fires, to worry or pray or give flight to their nervous laughter. But they all held their children close, stroking them or shaking them with a passion brought on by icy trepidation. They may or may not have heard the call of God in the morning service, but they all heard the call of Cod.

Rikka stood still as a stone as the congregation divided into two streams, those who would stay and those who would sail away. Even then she could not fit into a flow, but only watch and marvel at the commitment to one direction or the other. The sea blew angry gusts at the shore, but next to her Rikka heard the counterpoint of a slow, deep exhalation.

Pernille turned her head and looked into Rikka's eyes. Rikka stared back at the woman who had become surrogate mother to Rikka's baby sister. She was tall and bony, with hair pulled back so tight that her eyes slanted upwards from the bridge of her nose.

Rikka barely knew Pernille. She was older than Rikka, but not nearly as old as Rikka had thought her to be. Her skin was smooth and flawless, her hands showing no signs of wear. Pernille was married to Dankert but had always seemed far too upright to compliment his playfulness. What sort of a mother could she be to Ragna?

Pernille broke the silence. "Looks as if the whole island has scattered far and wide. And here we stand, two women who have no one to send off."

Rikka wanted to protest. Pernille had her husband, her parents, and she had Ragna who should be home curled into her mother's chest. The unfairness left Rikka stunned.

Pernille saw the storm in Rikka's eyes and in the sudden stiffness of the girl's body. "I'm sorry, Henrikka. I was thinking only of myself. How stupid. Please forgive me. My mind doesn't work at all when I get one of these headaches. You must think I'm completely callous and cold."

Rikka wasn't ready to forgive the woman anything. Why should she give her the comfort, just because she had a headache?

"Really," Pernille continued, "I am just stupid sometimes. I guess I spend too much time thinking of my own problems. Could we walk a ways together? It's too cold to stand still any longer. Please. Forgive me and give me a chance to get to know you. We're practically related, yet I hardly even recognized you. You've grown so much, not the shy girl I remember. Really, almost a woman." She finally stopped talking and just looked at Rikka with interest and something like longing.

Rikka softened a bit. At least if she walked with this woman, she could get an idea of how Ragna was faring. If there was just a hint of impatience or ignorance on this woman's part regarding Ragna, then she would see just what lengths Rikka would go to save her tiny sister. "All right. I don't mind walking on some more. I need the air, however cold."

"Well then, perhaps you'll walk in the direction of my home.

The path will be plenty cold any way we go. Do you need anything at the commissary?"

"No, we rarely buy anything there."

"Well, where do you buy your food? Do you have some secret source that no one else knows about?"

Rikka held her jaw firm and her pride in hand as she said, "The Lorkmans always paid my mother in food. Now they pay me the same way."

Pernille frowned. "How did they know what your mother wanted?"

"They didn't."

An uneasy silence accompanied their steps.

Eventually Pernille said, "That's wrong. That's just humiliating."

"Yes, if you let it be. But one gets tired of feeling humiliated. It's easier to pretend that we got just what we wanted. And it's better now that I am helping them out. My mother was too frightened to make a request, much less a demand."

"And you?"

"I demand."

"Good for you. What gives you the courage?"

"Guilt, their guilt. And my outrage."

"Tell me more. I don't know the story behind you and your mother and the Lorkmans, but I do know they can be difficult. All except Dankert, of course."

"Of course," Rikka responded with some ambivalence.

As they continued along the coastline path, their conversation slowly became more comfortable. Pernille admitted to being overwhelmed by the huge house that Dankert was building for her; Rikka laughed at the odd idea of a house being too large for comfort.

Rounding a curve in the path, Rikka called out, "Pernille, look at that."

Pernille gasped, "What, they weren't there when I came to church this morning."

"My God they're beautiful."

"It's the light. It was so dark when I came, and now there's that little bit of rosy light. They almost look … spectral."

The little inlet was filled with frost flowers, white, delicate, spindly and leaning, reaching to the east in the wind. They floated on top of the water like a fleet, as if they were there to accompany the fishermen.

"They look like ferns, delicate white ferns, uprooted and searching for home," Pernille whispered.

"They look like long skeletal hands. Just look at those bony fingers reaching out for help, as if their bodies were sunk below that icy water," Rikka whispered.

Pernille looked at her.

"I've never before seen a whole flotilla of them," Pernille said. "I so want to scoop one up and take it home."

"Sure death," Rikka said bluntly.

"I know. I know. I still want to do it even though I know they'd melt in my hands."

Then Rikka knew. This was a woman who recognized that life was disappointing. It didn't matter that she had a good husband, a big new house, and a baby that really belonged to Rikka's own mother. She had a sour look on her face, her eyes were impossibly pale, barely blue at all, her skin whiter than seemed right, as if there was no blood behind it.

"The frost flowers are beautiful, but we won't be if we stand here staring at them much longer. You look frozen."

"Of course, the whole world looks frozen. It is frozen. Let's move on."

The subtle midday light washed the island, like the beauty of dawn and dusk wrapped all in one. Not the cheery pastel of spring, the vibrancy of summer, nor the gold saturated tones of autumn, but a time unto itself, a time of violet and orange brevity.

Rikka and Pernille looped their arms together as they walked: an unexpected sense of friendship bound them. They were nothing alike. Rikka was brave, resilient and pragmatic. Pernille was fragile and discontent, but with a bitter sense of humour that could make Rikka laugh. And now, without notice, they were friends. They walked along in silence, infected by the beauty of the day and by the exodus of half the island. Looking ahead, they saw three figures coming towards them on the path, three men dressed in dark overcoats and hats, and walking with a confident sense of direction. Pernille and Rikka pulled closer together and conversed in whispers.

Pernille's lips froze in a tight line. "Dear Jesus! Who are these lumbering souls trampling our path?"

"Really, who are they?" Rikka asked.

"What are they? Pernille giggled.

"I don't know, but they appear to be well fed."

"Shhh."

"Maybe they've come to cast spells on us?"

"You and me?"

"Everyone. The whole island will follow them into the ocean but they'll soar away, the wind filling their huge coats."

"Shh. Shh. Really. They'll hear us."

The three men approached with big smiles across their faces. "Good day, Sisters."

Pernille and Rikka looked in one another's eyes. Sisters? They had to stop because the men blocked their path, apparently unaware of their impropriety.

"How are you good ladies on this good day?" The roundest one tripped over the Norwegian words that were brutalized by his teeth and tongue. So, they definitely were foreigners.

"Bra, takk."

The second man looked horrified at this response.

The leader gave his companion an elbow and tried again to speak in the language of the natives.

"The good Lord has blessed us all. Now, can you answer a question for us?"

"Kansje," Pernille responded. Both Pernille and Rikka had studied English in school for years; however, speaking it was another matter.

"We heard a loud clamoring of the church bell awhile ago. What was the meaning of it?"

"The cod are in. All the fishermen have left the island to fill their boats with fish," Rikka answered.

"Please repeat that more slowly. I have only studied Norwegian for a short time."

Pernille repeated Rikka's response, enunciating her words.

"Really, they all leave at once, together?"

"Yes sir, and now my friend and I must ask you kindly to step aside so that we may proceed on our path." He stared at her blankly while his mind tried to catch up with her meaning.

"Oh, yes, of course," the largest one said. "Forgive us for making you stand still in this cold wind. God bless you both. Good day."

Rikka was glad to be able to make out a few of his words and gladder still to be free of the men. Their presence was overwhelming, especially the leader's. And they stood too close to her and smelled odd, milky and sweet.

After putting some space between themselves and the men, Pernille and Rikka glanced back to take one more look at the odd ones. Their heavy coats billowed out around them.

"What do you think? Are they really that large? And their accents... well, I don't know where they're from." Rikka asked.

"I think I know," Pernille whispered. "They have to be the dreaded scourge that the priest warns us against."

"Mormons? Should we run?" Rikka laughed. "They seemed

vicious, don't you think?"

Pernille couldn't quite laugh at the joke. "Maybe they are. I've heard horrible things about them."

"In church, I suspect," said Rikka. "Maybe the rumours are true. But maybe they're just one more group with their own beliefs and rules. I'll bet that's what all religions have in common, rules. Rules to say who can join in and who must be shunned. Rules about who must bow down and who must be bowed to. But don't they all say they have the only true God?"

"You're not much of a believer, are you, Rikka?"

"No. Maybe because I'm always on the wrong end of those rules."

"Well, then, let's talk about something more enlightening, like what we'll have to eat when we get to my ridiculously large house. Maybe we should change it into a church that follows your rules," Pernille laughed.

In a more serious tone Rikka asked, "May I see my baby sister?"

"You may hold her as long as you like. I'll bet she'll laugh for you."

And there it stood, Dankert's house. She shouldn't have been surprised. Pernille told her it was huge. A downstairs and an upstairs. One big cube sitting atop another. The windows were strung tautly across both levels, square, all the same size, five across the top floor and four across the main floor, the door claiming the spot where the middle window would have gone. The whole thing was a flat white wall, reflecting nothing of nature, in conflict with its surroundings. She closed her eyes and turned her back on it. Rikka knew she was holding her breath, or her breath was holding her. Dankert's house, Dankert and Pernille's house, could swallow six of her mother's rorbu where most of her life she could not turn from the stove to the table, from the bed to the stove without bumping into a child playing on the floor. But now her little red home was hollow. Those who belonged there had been swallowed by big white houses with too many rooms and not enough love.

When she opened her eyes, she was facing the sea, down the island past her home. There was the Thorn anchored in the Norwegian Sea and thrusting towards the North Star. The Thorn was charcoal grey, almost black in this low light, and surrounded by an amethyst glow emanating from its surface. Its impossibly sharp peak drew her eyes upwards.

Pernille's voice broke the silence. "Would you like to come in? Please?"

Rikka turned back to Pernille and back to the wall that defied nature in contrast to the Thorn that was shaped by it. In front of her, the wall. Behind her, the Thorn.

"Yes, excuse me Pernille. I was lost in my thoughts." She would rather turn around and run home or, better yet, to Mokci's lavvu.

Pernille knocked on the door to her own house. With a cringe in her smile she said, "It's locked. I just want Ragna to always be safe."

"From the Mormons?" Rikka laughed.

"Well, you never know. I hear they do come calling on people." Pernille laughed at her own nervousness. "What would poor Urd do if she had to open the door to that lot?"

Just then Urd's face appeared in the door's tiny window. She didn't look to Rikka as if she'd fall into a fit of terror at the sight of those wholesome faces. She looked more like a square muzzled guard dog ready to pounce. Not one but two separate latches clicked and the door opened. Urd curtsied and stepped aside.

"I have a visitor, Urd. Find something suitable to go with coffee." Pernille's tone held traces of her mother-in-law's chilly manner.

"The cardamom cake? I made it this morning," said Urd.

"That will be fine," Pernille said, her tone softening as if she had heard the hardness herself.

Rikka looked around the entry: more white walls, honeycomb

candles ensconced on the bare walls. She saw Urd lighting candles in the next room and on a table that drew Rikka into that space. The table dominated the room. It was a massive honey coloured oval. On both of the two long sides of the oval were matching benches with backrests and soft curves all in that beautiful wood. She recognized the beguiling curves that let a hard surface seem soft.

"This is Dankert's work?"

"Yes. It's his greatest pleasure these days, chipping and sanding and endlessly polishing. Can you smell the beeswax? I hope it doesn't turn you away from the cake."

"No. Definitely not. It's lovely, and nothing can turn me away from cardamom cake. But what kind of wood is that? It must not come from the islands."

"He's says it's oak, imported from England. It arrived as huge lengths of tree trunk which he had to have milled. That's about all I can tell you about it. That and the fact that it kept him out of the house for months as he worked on it. Thank heavens he didn't do that work in here. Men make such messes, intolerable noise, too." She noticed Rikka's expression. "I know. I sound like an ingrate. It's as lovely as any work of art I've ever seen. I'm grateful to have it … him."

Rikka wondered if they actually sat across from each other at this amazing table. No wonder Dankert forgot to bring coal to Johanna. No wonder he brought ridiculous gifts like that silky lilac vest instead of the man boots that Rikka had begged for. His brain was not in his head but in his hands, and it was brilliant.

"May we take our coffee and cake here?" Rikka asked.

"Well, it's that or sit on the floor," Pernille answered. Rikka liked Pernille's acid humour. "And I should add that there are no carpets yet, so you may want to settle for the benches. Don't you think," she whispered, "it all looks a bit churchy, as if the priest would hold council here? Especially with all these candles?"

"Dankert's work in the church is the only thing that feels welcoming there. If it weren't for those rounded pews, nothing could drag me into the place ... well, except cardamom cake.... which, in fact, I never stay long enough to enjoy."

"You really hate the place."

"I do."

"Maybe someday you'll tell me why."

"And maybe someday you'll tell me your secrets."

"I want to believe that we'll be that sort of friends. I think we both need a friend."

"Yes. I do have one friend, but he can't answer the questions I have about my family."

"I don't think I can help you too much, but maybe we can piece something together between us. Finally, the cake arrives. Did you remember to warm the cream for the coffee, Urd?"

"Yes, Fru, I did." Her look clearly said, 'Do you think me an idiot?'

When Urd was not quite out of hearing Pernille added, "She's good enough in the kitchen, a bit of a drudge when it comes to cleaning, but what can you expect?"

"What about Ragna? Is she good with Ragna?"

Pernille heard the anxiety in Rikka's voice. "Forgive me Rikka. How could I forget! Urd, Urd, come back in here. Is Ragna sleeping? Where is she?"

"Yes Fru, she's napping. She was awake most of the time you were away and then she had some milk, warm milk of course, and she fell asleep not long before you came home. She is content."

Rikka felt uneasy about Ragna. Clearly, she was taken care of. But was she loved? Rikka wanted to run through the house until she found her baby sister, wrap her up in a blanket and run back home with her. But she inhaled deeply and, instead, she praised the coffee and, of course, the cake, which was delicious. Something in that exotic flavour with its hints of sweet herbs and smoke never failed to take her away from herself and into the heart of a mysterious place that she didn't yet know.

"I do hope to see her before I leave."

"And you will. I promise. It will be good for both of you. But since she's sleeping.... more coffee? Urd, more coffee here! Hmm, she must be upstairs. Shall we venture into the kitchen? I call it Urd's domain."

"Sure, but do you think we can manage a small pot of coffee on our own?" Rikka asked Pernille slid the door open and Rikka noticed that it glided into the wall and disappeared. Again, Dankert's work. Rikka stood in the spot that the door so recently occupied. She stared at this new room. Would it be like this each time she entered a different space in the house, in this great breathless expanse of space?

Rikka imagined it filled with horses, just milling around, munching on long strands of copper coloured hay. You could fit four, maybe six stalls in this room and still have room to store all their gear, all their hay, why, maybe even oats. Imagine bins of toasty smelling oats, imported from the south just for these horses' breakfast. Rikka shook her head. What was she thinking? It was a kitchen, not a stable, and where had this image of horses tossing their manes in that superior manner of theirs come from? This house was the source of her wild imaginings.

Its dimensions and marvels were so alien to Rikka that she felt her footing in the world was slipping, as if she were sliding down a slope into another world filled with wonders yet apparently quite normal in the eyes of its residents. This was a small island unknown to most of the world, yet it could hold this mansion of excess just up the path from her rorbu which held so little, and further down the path one could fold back the hide door to Mokci's lavvu. Three totally separate worlds in such a small space. So why not horses in the kitchen?

Rikka opened her eyes to what really was just another white

room, this one with a whole wall for hanging utensils: copper pots reflecting the candle light, black iron kettles, ladles, whisks, long handled forks, all suspended from iron bars that traversed the far wall in the shape of inverted chevrons, all in very deliberate order and all looking as if they had never been sullied by soot or grease.

"Do you like it?" Pernille asked.

Rikka nodded.

"I worked on the layout for days and days, and poor Urd has let me know that there is no logic to it. 'No cook in her right mind would put a heavy kettle high up and a whisk next to a colander.' Pernille mocked Urd's gravelly voice and rough demeanor. Rikka knew that Urd made a valid point. She also knew that Pernille's design was more beautiful than Urd's complaint.

A massive black range balanced on silver lions' paws dominated the right hand wall, and an icebox large enough to hold a lamb carcass stood next to the door to the outside, the coolest spot in the kitchen. A long work table, the surface built of thick planks that had been buffed and sealed with beeswax, dominated the centre of the room. Unlike the beautiful oval table, this one was all about functionality. At one end a mountain of yeast dough was set to rise on an inlaid marble slab dusted with flour as white as fine beach sand. A matching marble rolling pin lay at ready to shape the dough. At the opposite end, a set of knives ranging from paring to butcher knife were aligned in slots worked into the table's end. Several cooks could perform completely different tasks on this table with ample elbow room and no contamination of their ingredients.

On the left hand wall were two doors. Rikka wondered where they led. Between the two doors was a work in progress that demanded her attention: a tall and stately kakelovn. Its surface was greyish-white and rough. Rikka remembered the soft pattern of heather on the Lorkman's kakelovn and wondered at the raw state of this one. Then she noticed the faint lines of an imminent design sketched through parts of the tall column. She turned to Pernille for an explanation. Pernille was looking down at her feet as if they held the answer.

"You have a plan, don't you Pernille?"

"Yes," she whispered, "a landscape."

"What do you mean?"

"A rendering of our landscape."

"Of the island?"

"Of the most important parts of the island."

"What will it include?"

"The sea, the sea wall, and the Thorn."

Rikka stared at Pernille in surprise. "The Thorn? Why?"

"Because it's the most important element, along with the sea. It's what makes us who we are."

"What do you mean?"

"It's the greatest challenge in our lives. We think the cod are the greatest, whether we have a good year of fishing or total disaster. But the Thorn is what we should aspire to, what we either ignore or respect. We can drown at its feet, or we can face its peak."

"Yes. Yes, that's what I think too. That's the challenge, the ultimate challenge."

"Yes."

"But what does that mean to you, Pernille?"

"That I hadn't found my challenge. Until now."

"So you have decided to have someone depict the Thorn, the challenge, on your kakelovn?"

"Me."

"What, how?"

"The only way I can. I will draw it — I can draw really well — and I will create the tiles."

"Really? How will you do that?"

"I've studied it. I've ordered the minerals I need for painting the tiles. I'll have to travel with them to Trondheim to be baked. It will take a lot of test runs, but I will not stop until I've found the right combinations."

"You're determined! Oh, wonderful! Show me."

Pernille walked over to the kakelovn and running her hands over the surface, starting down at sea level and standing on a stool when she needed to reach the heights, she told the story of the island, of the land and the sea and the struggles, the defeats and the possibilities. Rikka could see it all as if she had imagined it herself. She turned to Pernille, this woman who she had thought was hard, bitter and aloof, and she hugged her.

"Yes, you will do it. And I'll do it, too," Rikka promised.

Although Pernille didn't understand Rikka's half of the promise, she held her tight, knowing that a bond had been forged between them.

"Shall we have that coffee now," Rikka asked?

"Yes. No. I don't know where anything is. I've never made the coffee and I don't want to call Urd down here."

"That's fine, Pernille. I don't care."

"But I know what we should have." Pernille opened a high cupboard and drawing the stool over to it, she reached far back and brought out a bottle. "Have you ever had aquavit?"

"Just a sip once. It's not something that fills our shelves at home."

"Well, let's fill our brains and warm our stomachs. It's a fine bottle and has crossed the equator twice. It's only for special occasions, but this certainly counts as one."

"I've heard of that, how once a barrel has traveled to the southern hemisphere and back it's the finest drink in the world. Is that true?"

"Yes, you can bet the Lorkman fortune on the truth of that."

"Well, I won't be so rude as to refuse a sip. Not that I have much to compare it to," Rikka laughed. Pernille hoisted herself up onto the long table, poured two tiny glasses of aquavit, patted a space next to her for Rikka to claim, and handed her new friend a shot of the alcohol. They looked into one another's eyes, nodded gently and then said,

"Skøl."

"Skøl."

They tossed their heads back and the aquavit followed, as well as some coughing on Rikka's part and laughter on Pernille's.

"Can you believe that came from a sack of potatoes?"

"Best potato I ever tasted," Rikka said.

"Want another one?"

"Ja, just a sip. I like the hidden flavours, like a meadow in July."

"Like a meadow in July with the wild dill and fennel blooming," added Pernille.

"Like a meadow in July with no chores to do."

"Like a meadow in July with a sailor boy."

They began singing drinking songs that belonged to drunken fishermen. Their favorite was the one about running off with the neighbour's drunken wife and to hell with anyone sober enough to object! And then they were dancing around the table, Pernille pretending to be the drunken sailor and Rikka the neighbor's wife.

"My turn now," slurred Pernille. "My turn to be the runaway wife."

"My drunken sailor can hardly keep up. He's never going to catch you."

"Stupid sailor, I was afraid of that. Hey, you, get off the floor," demanded Rikka with a sharp kick in the sailor's ribs. A third, and then a fourth tiny glass went down as they lay side by side on the floor. Rikka still had enough wit to recognize that her head was leaning against a bucket that smelled foul. "God, what is that? Yuck, it's horrid. Take it away."

Pernille was laughing uncontrollably. "It's lovely, what do you mean? It's Urd's bucket."

"Did she shit in it?" asked Rikka.

Pernille reached across Rikka and removed the lid. "Take a look."

"Rikka pulled herself into a sitting position and stared at the contents with her hand over her nose and mouth. "What is it?"

"Whale blubber. Don't you just love whale blubber especially when it's floating in sour whey?" Pernille's eyes sparked with sarcasm.

"What? Why? Why would anyone have a bucket of that?"

"She's a Finn."

"Oh...." Rikka thought she should understand, but didn't. Maybe just too drunk. "Anything left in that bottle?"

"A little. Let's lie down."

"We are lying down."

"Decent farm wives don't lie on kitchen floor."

"But drunken sailors do," Rikka countered.

"Come on up here. The table's big enough for both of us," said Pernille as she patted the table. Pernille lay spread eagled with a crown of knives at her head.

Rikka hoisted herself up with some difficulty. Her legs had grown heavy, unwieldy in fact. She meticulously fit the soles of her feet against those of Pernille and then fell backwards onto the surface of the table, her head rolling languidly in the cushiony, fragrant pillow at the opposite end. And then, as the world spun around her head, Rikka fell asleep, the last sound she heard being the deep throated snoring of her new friend .

"Get off that table," a furious voice shouted. "Get off. This is my room. You've ruined half a day's work for me. Get out of here!" Rikka woke with no memory of where she was. A sweet yeasty smell surrounded her head. Her head, oh her aching head. She tried to lift it, but it seemed to be glued to this sticky pillow it was lying on. Then another shout, another command, another shriek of anger. Urd had found her bucket of precious whale blubber knocked over on the floor. The white gelatinous masses squirmed and jostled with indignation.

Urd was screaming. Obscenities hit the white walls and echoed back around the room. Rikka's head rang with pain. All the noise, all the screeching. She tried again to lift her head. What a weight! And spinning! Her head was sucked into the maelstrom but her body wouldn't follow. And that smell, worse than the sour whale blubber, that sweet yeasty smell. She put her hands on the side of her head to stop the pain, stop the nausea. What? Her hands stuck in her hair. Gud i Himellen! What sort of punishment was this?

"I'll never drink again. Never. The priest was right. The Devil's work. Never," and she vomited all that was evil in her stomach.

"Get out of here right now," Urd screeched. "Into the bathing room, and don't expect me to clean up in there, too. You are dirty .... dirty..." Urd struggled to find a word offensive enough to be scathing but not so strong as to lower her to their level of depravity. Or to get her fired.

"Likainen huoria!"

She dragged Rikka off the table, taking care to twist her wrist until the girl cried out. Dragging her across the floor, she opened the door to the right of the kakelovn and pushed her in.

"Stay there," Urd growled and slammed the door.

Rikka complied. She lay curled like an infant sea horse on the floor, trying to breathe anything except the smell of yeast. The smell of wax filtered through. Rikka kept her eyes closed, tried to limit the intrusion on her senses. Never again. Never again. She was not at all sure that she would even survive and have to live up to her vows. Well, that was one way to escape bad decisions. Rikka's fingers reached for her hair and touched goo. She lay there trying to make sense of it, but her thoughts were gummy. Sniffing her fingers brought only confusion so she touched the mess with her tongue. It was like home, like sweet bread rising. Her mind began to rise out of the depths of drunkenness. No wonder Urd was irate. Anyone would be, even a drunken sailor.

"Urd," she called, "Forgive me. I'm so sorry, please forgive me. I'll help you make a new batch. Just as soon as I ...."

The next thing she knew, Pernille was sitting slumped next to her on the floor. The room was filled with fog. Or was that her head? Pernille gave her a shake. "Wake up. Come on, girl, you need a bath."

"Bath?"

"Yes, a bath, in the bathtub."

"Bathtub?" That concept helped Rikka open her heavy eyes, and she looked around the room which was, in fact, filled with fog. No, steam. Why? Rikka squinted and held her hand like a visor over her eyes, scanning the room as a mariner might scan the sea's horizon. "Where are we? I feel seasick."

"Come on, you aren't even in your ship yet. Let me help you." Pernille seemed none the worse for drinking the exact same poison Rikka had. She did look a little blurry, but that might be the fog. Pernille tugged at Rikka. "You'll have to stand up. I'll help you, but I won't carry you. Your ship awaits."

"Where is it?"

"Right over here."

"Too far. Can't stand."

"Then crawl, you lazy fool."

Rikka crawled through the fog and over to her ship. It was small. It was made of tin. The fog was rising out of it. Oh. All right. It was maybe a bathtub. She had never seen one before. A bathtub was way bigger than a basin. All right. She would get in.

"Wait," Pernille said. "First your clothes. I'll help you."

Pernille took Rikka's clothes off, piece by smelly piece. Rikka could not have undone a single button herself with her fumbly hands.

"Why do I have to take my clothes off?"

"Because they stink. Because you are getting in the bathtub. Because no one wears clothes in a bathtub."

"Oh." Holding onto the gunnels of her ship, and under the orders of the captain, Rikka lifted one naked leg over the edge.

"Oh, hot."

"Too hot?"

"No, just hot." Rikka slid her foot back and forth and sideways in that water. She couldn't believe how so much hot water could be collected in one place.

"Are you going to stand there all day with just one leg in?"

"Maybe."

"Rikka, lean on me and put one hand on the rim …

"The gunnel?"

"Sure, the gunnel. Now you can lift the other leg in. That's right. And now you can sit down. Down girl. Sit."

"Aaaah. This is the best boat on the whole Norwegian Sea."

"Well, at least it's the only one of its kind. Now scoot down and let your whole body go under. No, you'll have to bend your knees. You are a slow minded anemone, aren't you!"

Rikka bent her knees and slid as much of her body as possible under the warm, warm water. Pernille laughed. Rikka's boney knees rose out of the water like two sharp peaks, almost like two Thorns. And her head, oh her head. Her face had turned red and her hair was like that of a sticky nøkken. Her sighs could turn the tides.

"Slide down further and tilt your head back so I can wash the bread dough out of your hair."

Rikka complied, sighing again with each further centimeter. As Pernille's fingers worked on the mess of Rikka's hair, little islands of bread dough were set floating around Rikka. "Does this water come from a hotspring?" she asked.

Pernille laughed. "We have no hotsprings on this island that I know of."

"Oh, I thought maybe there were hotsprings only the rich knew about."

"We've been accused of many acts of selfishness, but not of that." Pernille laughed

"Where then?" Rikka persisted.

"From the kakelovn."

"There's hot water in it?"

"In a way. I watched when they built it. Long coils, long long ones wrapped tightly around the firebox. The kakelovn fire never dies so there is always hot water."

"How does it get into this tub?"

"More copper tubes. We can have a bath every day if we want. Of course, once a week is sufficient."

"I would live in this little tin boat. Never get out. Do you want to get in too? I could curl my knees up?"

"Nei, takk. I would come out dirtier than I went in. Little clumps of bread dough all over me."

They laughed together, both feeling far better, the fog lifting. And then a cry broke the spell. Rikka cringed. Her little sister, her whole reason for coming into this house. Not to drink, not to get sick and rude. Not even to soak in this tub. She was here for Ragna, and now Ragna was outside this room crying. She called out the baby's name just as the bathroom door swung open. There was Urd filling the doorway and holding Ragna out in front of her as if she had become drunk like her mother. "You take her. She's yours, isn't she?"

Rikka nodded and held out her arms to take the baby. "Please, bring her to me."

"Naked. That's how you end up with one of these...." Urd said through clenched teeth. Rikka, happy to take little Ragna in her arms, paid no attention to what Urd implied nor to the fact that Ragna was diapered and dressed in a lacy white nightgown.

"What's this," asked Pernille, "are you going to baptize her?" Give her to me for a moment. I'll get those things off her."

A reluctant Rikka stopped kissing Ragna's face and let Pernille prepare her for the bath. "She's never been in the tub before. We always bathe her in a basin. Here you go."

She handed Ragna back to her sister. When Ragna heard the

laughter and felt the water on her naked little body, she joined in kicking the water and sending a fine spray and then a whole tide over the sides. She kicked her feet, slapped the surface of the water with open palms, and blew bubbles in the water. And when that water got in her eyes she just blinked and blinked and laughed some more.

Pernille helped make a happy mess with no thought of consequences. Ragna patted Rikka's face with wide open hands and screamed with delight at Rikka's make-believe horror. But they could hear Urd slamming pans and mops around in the kitchen.

"I think it's time to get out of your boat," Pernille said. "The water is cooling. that's no good for Ragna."

Rikka felt that she took half of the bath water out with her and slopped it onto the floor. She turned Ragna over to Pernille who looked around for a safe place to put this wet puppy. Ragna sucked her thumb. Pernille bit her lip.

"Where's a mop?" Rikka whispered.

"I don't know."

"We need one, and a bucket. Or no. I guess I can squeeze it out in the tub." She looked behind herself at her boat, empty now except with long drools of dough stuck to the bottom and sides. Sea slugs.

Pernille opened the doors on a tall cupboard and stared at the contents as if she had never ventured there before. Her shoulders pulled in towards her neck. Then she reached for one bundle of cloth after another, settling on a thick quilt. She looked around the floor, gave the fabric a shake, and let it fall. She placed Ragna on her little island and then pulled out other bundles of cloth, throwing some to Rikka and spreading others herself.

Rikka was puzzled. Why not a mop? Maybe Pernille was avoiding running into Urd in the kitchen and really didn't know anything about where another mop might be stored. Pernille kept her eyes focused downward. They were each standing on a piece of fabric and scooting it around the room to absorb the spill. Neither spoke. Not a sound except the swish, swish.

Leaving was hard: pulling clothes on over her damp body, dealing with the swimming sensation in her head, all the time looking down on a perfectly contented Ragna sucking her thumb.

Rikka wanted to scoop her up and run. She stood weaving, aware of weaving, over her little sister. Ragna would stay in the white house. There was no one she could count on in the rorbu, just a demented mother and a drunken sister. Rikka tried to pull her wet hair out from where it was caught in her vest. If there were scissors handy, even a dull knife, she'd cut it all off and never be bothered with the weight of it again. Just one more burden shed.

Is that how she'd grow to feel about Ragna if she were to take her home? She'd be tied to the care of her mother and her baby sister. She could imagine where that path would take her. Never have time to herself, never sit on a moonlit rock with Mokci, and never climb the Thorn.

She was visited by a vision that could have risen out of an old myth: Rikka ascending the Thorn with Ragna in one arm and dragging her mother behind her over sharp rocks and across crevasses. No, she was no Valkyrie. She wasn't even brave. As she knelt on the floor to kiss Ragna good-bye, her sodden hair fell forward curtaining the baby's head. Their two faces, one with eyes closed, the other with eyes wide open, were cloistered in an underwater cave festooned with long tangles of dripping lichen hair.

Outside, full darkness had fallen and no moonlight lit the path. Rikka's progress was awkward; her head thumped in time with her feet. She kept losing her footing yet and something in her stomach wanted to come up. When she gave into the vile taste, it came from deep in her gut. Alcohol was not for her. She could do without the fun of laughing hysterically if it meant feeling this sick and full of misery. She wiped her mouth with the back of her hand and then wiped her hand in the snow. She scooped up a handful of virgin snow and stared at it; how perfect it was. She lifted a bit of it on the tip of her tongue and then some more until she took the rest in her mouth, moved it around with her tongue, spit it out and felt finally somewhat cleansed. It was time to get home and take care of her mother. Maybe she could ease her mother's heart by telling her that Ragna was well and content and safe in Dankert and Pernille's house. Or maybe that would only intensify her sorrow. Was there anything on this island that could make Hanna happy or, at least, less miserable?

The cold threw knives at her. Rikka had to get moving, walk fast, create her own warmth. Her legs were shaky and her lips frozen. The wind picked up and blew the shawl off her head. When she recognized the curve in the shoreline where the frost flowers had delighted her and Pernille, had drawn the two of them closer together, she left the path and moved down to the water's edge. The delicate flowers should be visible even in the late afternoon darkness. They were not. Then she scanned the water up and down the shore and spotted the flotilla further out. It had been shattered by the wind and broken into smaller bouquets. Maybe, she thought, they were following the fishing boats and would protect and bless all those men on board. Or maybe they were just shattered.

Rikka shook her head and regained the trail homeward. She grew colder as the minutes passed. She knew she needed to rush, but her legs didn't comply. Her eyes were running and the tears freezing on her face. This was wrong. Now was the time to push herself, but her legs refused, and she stood in the wind wondering why, why?

"Girl. Miss? Ung dame? Are you all right?"

"Clearly she is not!"

"Look at her. She's frozen. She can't even move." The three men looked at one another in confusion.

"What can we do? Quick, take your scarf off," said one. "I'll take off my coat. Dear me, my fingers won't even undo the buttons. Can you do it? Thank you, Brother Cecil."

"Here now, sister. We are going to put this coat on you. Don't worry. We shan't hurt you."

"No, certainly not. We're here to save you," the third reassured her.

"Just look at yourself. You're frozen stiff."

"I've never seen anything like it."

"Just let me move your arm so I can get the coat on you," said one.

"Forget about that. Just button it up with her arms inside. Hurry."

"Get the scarf on her head. Look at her hair. It's frozen solid."

"She's a statue."

"Yes, like a statue of ..... of a Norwegian goddess."

"That's bl...bl...blasphemy!" one stammered through chattering teeth.

"Sorry. You're right."

"Of c...course I am!"

"It's the cold."

"Of course, I'm sorry Brother Otten. You have no coat now."

"It does make it difficult to think. What should we do?"

"Take my coat, we'll trade off."

"W...won't fit."

"We could make a tight circle around her and give her our warmth."

"You think so?"

"That could be an invitation to trouble!"

"Doesn't matter. J...just get her warm." Otten was adamant. He would appreciate any warmth himself. He let the other two strategize as he maneuvered himself as close to the centre of the circle as he could.

"Couldn't we get her to walk?" asked Cecil.

"Obviously not. She doesn't bend."

"Could we carry her?"

"Now that would look even worse than encircling her. Besides, there's no one here to take it amiss."

"All right then. Let's see if we can thaw her out."

Rikka heard everything they said, but little made sense and none of it mattered. The three men encircled her. One rubbed her arms through the fabric of the heavy coat. She could hear their teeth chattering. and then she could hear them pray through the chattering. She would have laughed if she weren't frozen. She knew it wasn't just the cold that paralyzed her. It was the thought of going on, just going on and on and not getting anywhere. The frost flowers knew how to float, how to be moved by the tides and the wind. She didn't have their wisdom. So she'd just stand here with the three Mormon missionaries giving her warmth.

"My goodness, this is a strange turn of events," one said.

"I'm still not comfortable with it," the other added, shaking his head.

"Maybe it's the sinner in you that's troubled."

"Maybe."

"I know the sinner in me is struggling."

"Listen to you two, get a hold of yourselves," said the third.

"I'm trying. I'm praying. Just let me pray."

"Call on the Angel Moroni."

"What? We can't do that?"

"Whyever not?"

"Why, he's Joseph Smith's angel."

"And?"

"And, wouldn't that be blasphemy?"

The three men looked back and forth at one another trying to find an answer.

"Go ahead, but I'm going to sing," the first one insisted. "That might keep me warm. I love to sing when temptation hovers near. You can call on Moroni, but I'm going to sing. That's safe, isn't it? And comforting. and warming. Come on now. Don't just stand with your mouth open. Join me."

I need thee every hour
Stay thou nearby
Temptations lose their power
When thou art nigh.

I need thee every hour
In joy or pain
Come quickly and abide
Our life is vain.

I need thee, O, I need thee
Every hour I need thee!
O bless me now my Saviour;
I come to thee."

A nervous silence followed.

"That was all wrong,"

"I know, I know. I just left out some lines. My mind kept skipping to the most important arts."

"My important parts say it's time for us to do something else, and quickly."

"Let's see if her arms move. There, that's an improvement. Miss? Miss, can you talk to us? Tell us where you live? We'll get you home if your legs can carry you."

Maybe it was the home that brought Rikka back to her senses. She nodded. They cheered and gave her a three brother hug.

"Praise the Lord, Miss. I am Brother Otten. This small fellow who sang that unfortunate song is Brother Rose and the one with the admirable streak of freckles across his brow is Brother Cecil."

"And your name, Miss? asked Brother Cecil.

"I'm Henrikka ... and I'm very ... very cold and I want ... to get home."

""We'll be glad to accompany you there."

"See you safely to your family."

"Thank you ... but no. I'll be fine once ... I get moving."

"We won't be comfortable until we know you are safely home. You've had some sort of a spell and this weather has done you no good," Brother Otten said and the other two nodded.

Brother Rose reached out to touch her frozen hair. "Excuse me. I shouldn't touch, but your poor hair looks as if it could snap off. Does that often happen in this climate?"

"Why yes," Rikka responded. "Each year we ... shed our hair just as .... the reindeer ... shed their antlers."

Brother Otten slapped his well-padded knees and said, "Very well then, Henrikka, if you don't trust our company, we will hold back a ways. But don't despise us for keeping an eye on you. It can't be safe in this weather and in your condition."

Rose turned a shade of pink befitting his name.

Cecil tried to ameliorate: "We promise to stay twenty paces behind; no more, no less, until you reach your home. We want to protect you from the wayward habits of strange men."

Rikka said "You will find few enough of them on the island since the ringing of the cod bell. Mostly just the priest, his sexton, a few too rich to have ... to fish .... and yourselves. Good afternoon, and watch your step along your way." Rikka hoped to insult them just enough to rid herself of their company. These Mormons seemed an earnest lot but no company that she cared to encourage.

There would be whisperings on the island. Surely someone had stood ten steps back from the path and witnessed this strange interlude. It could be a horrified housewife or the all-too-nosey sexton. A child, perhaps, coming home from his auntie's house. The story would be kneaded like Julekaka, sweet and bubbling with dried berries and nuts, tastier each time it was told and another tantalizing bit had been added. All those lonely, frustrated women left behind to deal with absolutely everything from diapers to teenagers who could not be bothered to get up in the morning and light a fire. Already they would have a juicy bit of rumour to savour, stretch and pass on for further embellishments. And it would all be for the betterment of the community, this drive to prove the evil intentions of the Mormons.

The missionaries seemed oblivious to the dangers of the situation. Rikka thanked them for their help and moved on down the path, never looking back.

Mokci stood at the southernmost point of land, looking across the strait to the Thorn. He had spent the day close to home waiting for Rikka's visit. She had not come. He thought back to her last words of the night before. "If I can." Possibilities ran through his head: problems had arisen involving her mother; she had been pulled to the Lorkman farm to work on a rare day off; the ringing of the bell announcing the start of the cod run had somehow complicated her day. And then he thought what he didn't want to think: she didn't want to come. Mokci sat down on a boulder the leeward side of which had been pummeled by wind, wave and weather for millennia. Now it wore a coat of ice that flickered in the starlight. It could be liquid, its surface flowing and changing as if time and erosion were speeding up. The stone grew molten then froze and crackled like ice snapping. When he thought about how his life had changed, he only knew that it would continue to do so. And how was he to live within this change? Did he have any control over the shape of his life, or was he just meant to fall into place in the preordained order of things? Whether or not he actually had the power to control anything at all, he knew he must take the steps.

He had told Rikka that he would teach her to climb. Now he stared at the Thorn, its pointed peak a solid black form on the dark pallet of the polar night. Black on black, but the black of the sky was peppered with starlight, whereas the black of the Thorn was uncompromising. What was he thinking when he told her he could teach her to climb? Certainly, climbing was as inherent to his life in Sapmi as it was to the reindeer but climbing the Thorn would be quite a different challenge.

He stared at the silhouette. No wonder it was called the Thorn. Just like the one on a wild rose, it had a solid base though this base was rooted deep below the sea, and the whole upward thrust of the mountain was aimed toward a point that only a high flying sea bird could alight upon. Not a tree or even a shrub on the face of the mountain, nothing larger than the sporadic veins of lichen. Where the Thorn rose above the water line, there was no beach, no apparent foothold, no invitation to climb.

It would be easy to think of the Thorn as a two-dimensional thing, flat as a whetstone. Perhaps the view from a different angle would reveal a point of entry. He could get a rowboat to familiarize himself with the possibilities. Maybe from Dankert.

Mokci tried to calculate how long it would take to row around the mountain. It would have to be during low tide and it would have be in the small window of semi light. A full moon would be helpful but that was sixteen days away and he wanted to explore right now. But why wait for light? His eyes were keen. He knew that if he sat totally still and controlled his breath, he could see in the dark, even the small details, even where a beetle ratcheted its crooked legs across a lichen path.

"Find shelter," Mokci whispered to the insect. "This is not your time to be out."

A sense of urgency drove him to find Dankert. As he picked his way through the slick rubble of rocks and boulders it occurred to him that he didn't even know if Dankert was still on the island. Most of the men must have left in the fleet of boats seeking out the cod. Or if he was on the island, where? That great white house of his was well up island and if anyone else answered the door, they would almost certainly shun him. Dankert could be visiting at Johanna and Rikka's house, but he, Mokci didn't want to give away his intentions there. Dankert could be anywhere or nowhere.

He walked along the water's edge, trying to conjure a solution. When he neared the inlet which had recently been filled with sailors and their boats, he saw emptiness, almost complete emptiness. But he noticed an exception: a rowboat lay inverted across two logs.

Mokci examined it. The old boat had been patched with tar to the extent that its red paint was mottled by black, but he decided that the patches were probably adequate. But were there oars? He lifted the bow and found the oars lay waiting. Mokci hunkered down behind the boat and scanned the shoreline. No one. He thought about the consequences of what he was about to do. The fishermen were gone. Darkness was his ally. Who else would be looking for a rowboat in the dark?

He flipped the boat over, and tossed the oars inside, pushed it into the water and levered himself in with one boot dragging in the water. The water would never breach the walrus fat. The inlet had iced over, a rare condition on the island. His navigation had been eased by the exodus of the cod boats which left a network of channels through the ice. At times, Mokci had to kneel on the cross plank of the boat in order to break up jammed ice with one of the oars.

Midway through the inlet, the wind off the Norwegian Sea picked up so that the ice shifted and clashed with force. Mokci had a hard time keeping the boat balanced as a sheet of ice slid under the boat, tipping it sideways. He shifted his weight and used his oar to ply the ice and regain balance. Time spent hunting walrus with his cousins on Tromsø was paying off. He needed to navigate the inlet and gain open water before the little boat gave in to the force of ice. He knew he could do it, but did he know if he could do it if he had Rikka on board?

But he gained his way into clear water, though the force of the wind needed to be constantly evaluated and adjusted for. Mokci tapered the angle of his oars and stayed focused on the shoreline as his guide in the dark. At times he could see nothing more than ocean spray but even that told him something of his direction. This was not the sort of weather he would challenge when Rikka was with him. That thought echoed through his mind … when Rikka was with him. And then the shoreline disappeared altogether. He was beyond the southern tip of the island and surrounded by nothing more than sea.

There was the rorbu. Rikka felt as if she had walked all night dragging her sour body along with her. And now, there was home and her mother standing just outside the door, her hand over her brow as if she were shielding her eyes from the ceaseless light of June. She was scanning, looking out to sea and looking down the path along the coastline. Surely she could see nothing in the darkness, but she kept looking. " Rikka, Rikka," she called, and Rikka called back. "Yes, Mama, I'm here. I'm coming."

"Oh, I thought you were.... I thought you were.... there you are. It's been such a long time. Come home. Please."

"I'm coming, Mama. Just a minute and I'll be there. Go inside where it's warm."

But it wasn't warm inside. The fire had gone out and the door was open. Rikka brushed past Johanna and ran to the little girls' room. She gasped when she saw that both of their beds were empty. Then she remembered; they didn't live here anymore. How could she forget? Was she mad? Mad like her mother? She had been with Ragna just a few hours ago at Pernille's.

She turned away from the empty room, walked over to the wood stove and looked around for kindling to start a fire. Then she paused, slowed her breathing. No, she was not mad, just drunk and sick and paying for her crimes, like the crime of abandoning her mother, of enjoying the company of a friend, of bathing in Pernille's boat with her little sister on her lap. No, she wasn't mad, just selfish.

She felt her mother's hands in her hair. "This is not beautiful hair," Johanna said.

Rikka laughed, remembering how the missionaries seemed distraught by the way her hair stood out around her head. She took hold of a skein of her icy hair and bent it sending tinkling shards of ice falling to the floor. She went to the tin mirror hanging on the wall, and laughed at what she saw. Johanna laughed as well. She grabbed more of Rikka's hair and twisted it, freeing more ice slivers, then blew and blew the cold off her hands and off Rikka's also. The two of them held hands and danced in a circle.

Johanna sang songs that seemed to rise from her imagination. Her voice was like a flock of songbirds tittering, more manic than sensible.

"Sing me a song, Rikka," she begged.

And Rikka sang the lullaby that Johanna had sung to her a thousand times.

> *Sulla meg litt, du mamma mi*
> *Skal du få snor på skjorta di*
> *Vil du ha gule, vil du ha blå*
> *Vil du ha blanke, skal du det få*
> *På skjorta di*
> *Du mamma mi*

> *Cradle Me a Little*
> *Cradle me a little, you my mama.*
> *And you shall get a cord on your shirt,*

> *Do you want yellow, do you want blue,*
> *Do you want a shiny one, I'll give it to you,*
> *On your shirt,*
> *For you, my mama.*

Johanna encircled Rikka in her arms. "Thank you, Mama," she said. Rikka accepted her thanks. She could no longer be surprised by her mother's confusion.

"Do you know what your father always said about you?" asked Hanna.

Rikka held her breath. Was she about to hear who her father was?

"He said that you were the person he had always waited for."

Rikka gasped. What did that mean? "Waited? He waited for me, Mama? Then why did he leave me? Why did he leave you?"

Johanna sat down on the daybed. She picked at the woolen pills on the blanket and hummed "Sulla Mi" again. Rikka held her breath. She would wait. She would hold this moment for as long as it stretched.

"Because men can."

The water here was calmer than in the inlet. Not only had the wind subsided, but Mokci thought that some vortex, triggered by the wind and tide had worked to pull him in directions that he hadn't anticipated. This little boat was far too broad for its length, making it especially unwieldy. Now, in the open sea that lay between the island and the solitary mountain, the going was slow but predictable. He would have preferred a sleeker boat, one that flexed with the wind and tide, one that didn't balk at the waves hitting broadside but canted with flexibility. He would prefer a boat he could sit forward in, watching where he was going rather than where he had been. The Thorn was further away than it appeared from the shore and his arms, stressed by the work in the inlet, ached. He decided the Norsemen must pride themselves in designing boats to challenge their strength rather than to ease their travel.

As he drew near the base of the Thorn, Mokci dragged an oar and focused on the line where water met rock. He let the waves butt him into the side of the mountain, none too gently, but allowing him to run his hand over the surface. The mountain was dark, massive, foreboding. He pulled off his gloves, the better to acquaint himself with the rock. Ancient beyond all time. This rock had been many other rocks before they fused into one. Each line, each subtle change in colour and texture spoke of violent upheaval. What was dark grey or even black from a distance, now closeup, was a melding of eons. Tiny specks of silver and even (could it be red?) lay beneath his fingertips. Mokci's life felt so little and inconsequential that he felt shame for his small miseries. He leaned his palms and his forehead against the immensity of time and space and had to laugh at the trivialities of his life. Whatever he did, whoever he loved, was of no consequence. Mokci walked his hands along the rock and with the help of the current, he worked his way around an arc of the perimeter. How different this would all look in the light of a spring day or even in a bit of moonlight.

At times, the rowboat would smash against the Thorn and he would worry about damaging this boat he had stolen … borrowed?

Mokci continued to explore the base of the Thorn for a path or an outcropping to help a climber launch his climb. His hand slid around and inward. He reached further into the darkness, pulled himself and the rowboat in this new direction. Further into absolute darkness. And he said what everyone says when they find themselves in a dark place they don't understand, "Hello…?" And the answer came: 'Hello? Hellooo?'

Mokci realized that he had entered a fissure in the mountain; he reached out his other arm in the opposite direction and found that his hand reached another wall. He used both hands then to propel the boat further along the crevasse until his arms could stretch no further. What had been a channel leading into the guts of the mountain became a vaulted pool in which the tide created a gentle whirl, circling and circling in the cold and echoing darkness. He sat while the boat made its rounds in the dark. He thought of his grandfather waiting in Sapmi for him to return. Return, or just turn.

A flash, a mere glimmer entered the space, accompanied by a swoosh of movement in the water. A swirl and a reversal of the swirl. A dance. Some presence in the spinning water and a light that flashed and swirled tinting the darkness an emerald shade of green. He looked back towards the entrance and realised that the northern lights were dancing a bright and hectic dance and they had danced right into the cave.

And he heard a voice, perhaps his own, for who else could it be calling "Rikka ka ka, Rikka ka ka ka ka." And near the surface of the water, tiny silver-green forms, thousands of them spiralled in the green light. The herring, shoaling and hiding in the cavern from their predators: the cod, the Minke whales. They flashed silver then green, then swirled deeper. And Mokci's boat circled just like the herring hiding from all that threatened them. "Rikka," he called one more time. It was wrong that she wasn't here with him, here where they could hide in the cavern's swirling light.

RIKKA

Rikka sat in the green light pouring from the sky. She had chosen the east side of the rorbu and leaned back against the woodpile. Light was streaming from some distant portal above Vestfjorden, a swooping bridge from the heavens down and across the fjord to the mainland of Norway. The air was filled with soft whistling sounds, not exactly like wind, more like restlessness. Her lap filled with a pool of swirling green light. Rikka decided to sit silently in this place until the dance ended, no matter how cold, no matter how much she wanted to visit the lavvu. She imagined Mokci lying back by the fire and watching this heavenly flow of light through the smoke hole between the birch saplings. How different his perspective must be with just that small porthole framing the magic of the lights.

Her head rested on the top row of the woodpile. It was not enough, this pile of wood. Within a week she would be using the carefully built structure that Mokci had created. It was more air than wood. It would be drier and burn faster and hotter than her messy pile, but it would not last long. And would Dankert ever remember to get more coal to them? Would Lorkman deign to leave off a load? Rikka shook her head. This was no time for worries, not when the green light flowed over her, over her island and her whole world. She would just sit here and bathe in the light, banish her worries. A ribbon of intensely violet light poured like a river down through the emerald green skies.

"Rikka," she heard. "Rikka, where are you?" The voice intertwingled with the whistling of the skies. "Rikka ka ka ka ka." She jolted up straight in her seat, listening, wondering. She didn't know that voice, and yet she did. Calling her. But who? Where?

"Rikka, I need you. Come inside. Where are you? Rikka, help me." The faraway timbre of the voice homed in on her, coming closer with each repetition.

And then it was a shriek. "Rikka, help me!" Rikka ran around the corner of the house. Her mother stood on the stoop, her head twisting back and forth, searching the sky. Johanna's eyes passed over Rikka, unseeing.

"I'm here, Mama. Don't worry. I'm just getting wood for the fire."

"Where? Where are you? I can't see you in all this … colour. Why is there so much colour? Who is doing this to me?"

"No one, Mama. It's just the aurora. You know them. You've seen them a thousand times. These are especially beautiful."

"I want the sky to be blue and filled with sweet birds."

"It will be, Mama, just not yet. Like you've always told me, the sun cannot rise until night has had its reign. There is no light without darkness and no darkness without light."

"I said that?"

"Many times."

"That was wise, many times wise."

"Yes Mama. It is wise. And it's our way of life. Just imagine, all those people who live on Earth's belt halfway between the north pole and the south pole, they don't have our long, long night nor our long, long day."

"I didn't know that. What do they have?"

Rikka smiled. Of course, her mother knew that. She had the same education that Rikka had. One-time Rikka had picked up a text book on the classroom shelf and found her mother's perfect signature inside. She had been proud to put her signature right below her mother's before taking the book to her seat. But now Hanna's mind was that of a child, and Rikka must be the adult.

"Come inside right now, Rikka. You will turn green and purple if you stay out here any longer."

Rikka laughed and put her arm around Hanna's waist as she entered the rorbu with her. The fire was low, the air chill. Rikka stared at the green and violet sky through the single window in the kitchen. Ice crusted the glass on the inside and formed swirls of its own adding depth and opacity to the counter swirls in the sky.

"Cover that glass!" Johanna demanded.

Although mesmerized by the strange beauty, Rikka took off her shawl and draped it over the window. Even so, the light played through layers of ice and shawl.

Rikka turned to the door. "I forgot the firewood. I'll be right back."

"Don't go."

"Only for a moment, Mama. I want to make the room warm."

"You won't come back. I know."

"Yes. Sit down and count to ten. I'll be back when you get to nine." Rikka was fully aware this was a child's game she played with her mother. But a child she was, at least for now. Aa she arranged a load of firewood in her arms, Rikka again noticed a whispering coming from the lights. Through the soft whistling she heard the ka-ka-ka sound she had heard earlier. Almost the call of a raven but softer. Could it be Odin's raven, Huginn?

The myths spoke of how important Odin's ravens, Huginn and Muninn were to him. Apparently, he sent them out every day to see what was going on in the world, who were his enemies and who his friends. She had learned a lot about mythology in school because it was said that understanding their myths led to a deeper understanding of who they were as Norwegians:

"Our myths reflect our national soul," her teacher had said. When word got back to the priest, such talk was never more repeated, at least not within his hearing.

Rikka raked the dwindling coals and carefully laid the fire. Johanna's lips were blue, and she sat on the edge of the daybed with her whole body shaking.

"I can't think. I can't find my way," she cried. Her eyes were rimmed in red. Rikka thought it was better when her mother simply didn't recognize her own state, but this was awful, this profound anguish, and it was contagious.

"Mother, let me hold your hands," Rikka whispered.

Johanna looked at her hands as if she didn't recognize them, and then slid them under her thighs. Rikka held her mother's wrists and slowly freed her hands. They were deeply chapped. Traces of blood spoke of the way Johanna would scratch and pick at her hands as if trying to rid herself of them. These were the hands that could stitch the most delicate detail on a vest: seven stiches per centimeter. They were the hands that could lift the pain from a sick child's tummy just by passing her palm over the pain. Now, these were the hands of a crone, brittle as dry twigs in August.

Her first real talk with Mokci as they sat on the boulder overlooking the breakwater came back to Rikka. He had spoken of his tormented aunt and how the sickness in her mind might be the same as what Johanna was experiencing. What had he said? His hands. Yes, he put his hands on the sides of her head and rocked her gently, slowly. And it helped. Could Rikka ease her mother's distress in the same way?

No, she should wait until Mokci could come to their home. He was the one who might help her. Let him rock the sickness out of her. But when would that be? She needed his help right now. She could run to the lavvu and find him, bring him back here. But that would take time. Did she have the time? Would he be willing to help? What if he were seen entering their home? What if someone - Dear God in Heaven, no! - even Lorkman, were to arrive at the door? Mokci would pay heavily, probably be driven from the island, or worse. Rikka felt her own agitation building. Were the seeds of her mother's madness germinating in her own mind? From mother to daughter? From something creative to something gone rotten? She needed to find a remedy for both of them.

Rikka knelt on the daybed behind her mother. She put her hands on Johanna's shoulders, surprised by the frailty, like bird bones. When had this happened, this dissolving of flesh, this meagreness? These shoulders had carried such a load for so long, had carried children, had carried worries, even abuse.

Rikka knew so little of what had gone on in her mother's life. It occurred to her that had her life been a happy one, Rikka would have heard happy stories. She would have heard her mother's singing. She would have seen her mother chatting about everyday things with a friend. But Johanna had no friends, except perhaps Dagur who was a blessing but not a confidante. Her mother was always too busy with work and the responsibilities of raising her children. But Rikka had not seen her as a woman living in a void. There had always been so much noise in the house, with Agnes's coughing while she danced around; with Ragna's cries for milk or a dry diaper. Oh, and of course, Rikka's own self-absorbed chatter.

Rikka ran her fingertips down the sides of Johanna's neck and along her shoulders. She felt her mother shiver.

"Are you cold, Mama?" She nodded. Rikka pulled a lap cover out from behind her and put it over her mother's lap. "Is that better?" No response. Rikka rubbed her hands together to build warmth before continuing to stroke her mother. She ran her hands down her mother's arms and then, reaching further around her, Rikka gently massaged both of her hands.

Johanna pulled her hands away. "Ugly!" she said.

"No, Mama," Rikka countered, "you are beautiful. Everything about you is beautiful."

Tears ran down Johanna's cheeks. Little damp spots appeared on the lap cover. Johanna pulled her hand away and wiped at the tear spots. "I made this. I put on every kind of fish I could think of. And a whale. Now I've spoiled it with my stupid tears."

"You have spoiled nothing, Mama. We will always love this blanket, and we will always love you. The tears will dry and disappear."

"I saw an eye in the water."

"No!"

"Yes, I did! I thought it was that man I was married to!"

"Oh Mama. It was something else, something that terrified you, but it wasn't your husband."

Rikka didn't know where all this fantasy was coming from. But she knew that it came to help turn her mother's mind. An eye in the water; this picture needed to be washed away along with this madness.

"Mama, why don't you lie down and let me rub your back." Many times, Johanna had done this for her. Rikka missed those backrubs, the tender friction of her mother's work-hardened hands on Rikka's skin. She didn't know if her mother felt it inappropriate now that Rikka was grown, or was she just too tired to care? Rikka had other comforts now, her mother had none. Johanna unwound the tight knot of her body onto the daybed, sighed and lay straight as a plank. Rikka sat on the edge of the bed. Rikka loosened her mother's twisted knot of hair. She tried to run her fingers through the pale brown strands, with hidden streaks of silver, but it was all tangled with knots. She must not have brushed it since Rikka washed it weeks before. The hair was an odd mix of brittle and oily. Her scalp was patchy with dead skin and bits and pieces of what looked like seaweed tangle. Would scissors be the answer? Just cut it all off and start again?

Rikka smiled, recognizing the threat that she had heard her mother utter when a very young Rikka had played too boyishly on a summer day. She remembered that she had urged Johanna on.

"Yes, please Mama. Cut it all off. Make me like a boy." Johanna had danced around with the scissors, pretending to be a wicked witch. The scarier her act, the happier Rikka's screams. "Make me a boy! Make me a little boy." It was a favourite family story which pleased all of them.

Her fingertips stroked Johanna's neck, over and over slowly. When she continued the stroking around to the front of her neck, Johanna shook her head.

"No!"

"All right, Mama. Are you sore there?"

"Just … no!"

"I understand."

"No, you don't."

"I mean I understand that you don't want me to touch your throat."

Johanna relaxed a bit. Rikka ran her fingertips down the back of her neck and along her shoulders. Johanna sighed deeply, expelling tension through her breath.

"That's better," Rikka said. "Just let me know any time I'm doing it wrong. All right?"

Johanna hummed her acceptance and Rikka proceeded cautiously. There was an odour in the room. Had she failed in cleaning the place? She had always been reluctant to do any more housework than she had to, and Johanna had always been ready with the broom, a dust cloth or old cocoa tin filled with seashell grit. She never seemed to mind scouring up even the stickiest messes others made. At least not in her own house.

Rikka resented picking up every bit that the Lorkmans idly dropped or spilled. She had complained that they both seemed to do it intentionally, always looking back over their shoulders to be certain Johanna was quick to take care of their mess. Did they think she was a dog, trailing after their every step in hopes of snuffling up a tasty piece of dinner?

"What do you think we pay you for, sitting around and hiding in the pantry, taking a break to gossip with old Bestemor? We know how you shirk your duties. You'd better watch out or we'll find someone reliable, someone clean." Rikka had been horrified to hear of the humiliation they subjected her mother to.

Johanna shifted her position so that Rikka could better reach her arms. But there was that smell again and now it was obvious: it was Johanna's body that smelled, the odour of indifference, of neglect.

A bath was greatly overdue, in fact. Rikka's hands rested on her mother's back as she tried to figure out how to make it happen. The bathtub, as they called it, was just an oversized metal basin that sat at the far end of the trundle bed in the other room. It stayed there collecting the dirty clothes and linens until washing day or bathing day. She would have to empty it and drag it into the kitchen.

Then she had to heat up enough water on the woodstove. There was always water heating this time of year, but she should start the large kettle going too. Hot water into the tub, then enough cold water to make it comfortable. She didn't want to leave her mother, but the pump was over at Dagur's and was troublesome during hard cold spells. She thought of the long icicles dangling from the roof. Problem solved.

But the bigger problem was how to get Johanna to stand steadily in the tub while Rikka sluiced her with warm water. A child could sit in the tub, but grown people had to stand. She looked at the chair; no, its legs were spread too far to fit. Johanna could kneel with her knees and thighs supported by the sides of the tub. Then she need only lean forward a bit and hold onto the edges so Rikka could soap her and rinse her. Rikka shook her head remembering Pernille's bathtub. How ridiculous. Unfair. Life was unfair.

Johanna had fallen asleep. Her shoulders were loose. Rikka had managed that, at least.

Perhaps it was best to let her lie. Maybe she could wash her mother as she lay there. If the water was warm enough, if there were still clean rags in the basket to dry her with, if there was a comforter large enough to cover Johanna and small enough that she could hang it by the stove to warm. She would need two: one to cover her while the other warmed up. Rikka pulled out the chest from under the daybed. She carefully lifted precious baby clothes, embroidered table linens and other treasures until she found a small rose-coloured blanket woven with a pattern of green vines twisting across the warp. Out of the vine grew a few yellow flowers, but far more thorns than blossoms. Nonetheless, it was soft, perfect for her purposes. Rikka set to work gathering clean rags that used to be clothing: a shirt minus the buttons, and a vest that belonged to her and then to Agnes. Sad remnants of their mother's skills, now relegated to drying off dishes or bodies after washing.

Rikka lifted the hot water pot and poured it into the basin, then ran out onto the stoop and broke off an icicle that reached from the eaves to below the window frame. Its top was the diameter of an otter's head and the tip as sharp as a darning needle. It would make a fine walking stick for one of the nøkken trying to lure them underwater. She carried it across the floor and set the tip into the basin. The icicle crackled in response to the hot water. She stirred the hot with the cold, imagining herself as a ragged witch reaching into the cauldron to check the temperature of her brew. When the water was still hot but not scalding, she dragged the icicle outside and laid it down in the snow.

She started with the shirt, tearing the weakened fabric along the seam lines until she had enough handy sized pieces to dip in the water and wring out. She had to reach under Johanna's blouse to wash her back, but her sighs told Rikka that it was fine to go ahead. She dipped the fabric in the water again, then she repeated the careful process. Her mother's spine was prominent, and the ribs stood out like rocky ridges. So thin. It seemed that all the vulnerable parts of her were right on the surface, indefensible.

Rikka felt around for the softest piece of fabric and used it to dry her mother's back so she wouldn't get a chill. She took the rose and vine blanket down from the line above the stove and buried her own face in it. Relishing the warmth and softness, she draped it over Johanna's back. Then she moved on to her legs, bypassing her haunches for the time being. Her legs were long, thin and white. Had she ever seen her mother's legs before?

She washed them with care and even ran her warm cloth down the front sides of them, her hand between the leg and the bed. No response except a slight deepening of breath. But Rikka knew she had to go back to her mother's haunches. So much of the rank smell came from there. Never before had she smelled anything bad on or around her mother. But this was wretched.

Rikka took care. She slowly went over Johanna's hips, noticing that her hands gripped with a new tension. Gently, slowly, Rikka hoped her stroking would be reassuring. She dipped the cloth in the warm water again and wrung it out, then repeated the motion. The tension eased a bit, but a certain wariness remained. Rikka decided to repeat and repeat this stroking until she could feel her mother's complete release. If she were to get this done, she knew that each step had to be slowed down. Rikka was aware that she was trespassing. With utmost care she dipped the rag again and dared to move her hands just over the rise from Johanna's hips. She rested there, listening for a change in breathing. Maybe this was okay. She moved her hands like a whisper, up and down from waistline to legline. And then a handsbreadth towards the center, up and down. Johanna's breathing deepened, evidence of a calm acceptance. Rikka warmed the cloth again. She stared at the base of Johanna's spine, the tailbone with a smear of brown and crusty flecks surrounding it. Her mother? This was not like cleaning a baby's bum. That was bad enough. Time to grow up, Rikka, she lectured herself. Just clean up the mess.

But from deep inside Johanna, a rasp, a roar, filling the room with her anger. "No! Never again! I'll kill tear your eyes out!" Johanna rolled over tossing the rose coverlet aside and stood up with fire in her ice blue eyes.

"Mama. Mama. What did I do? I'm sorry Mama. Don't hate me."

But Johanna didn't see Rikka. Her focus was somewhere far off, not confined to the rorbu's walls. She strode over to the door and beat on it. Rikka ran over to her and put her arms around her waist.

But Johanna had pulled herself into something large and monstrous and with a shout she pushed Rikka to the floor, opened the door and stalked outside. Rikka was in tears. Terrified. What had she done? Her mother stood naked, her skin stained green by the night. Rikka called her, ran after her and stopped short as her mother picked up the splitting axe and hefted it in two hands screaming at the skies.

"Dagur!" Rikka called. "Dagur, help."

She saw a dark form rushing towards the house. "Dagur? Help. Watch out. She has an axe. Careful! Dagur?" But it wasn't Dagur.

"Johanna," he said quietly. "Hush, hhshh, it's all right now. Let me walk with you. Here, this is my hand. You can take my hand."

"But she has the axe," Rikka warned.

"It's all right. She is bringing it to me." His voice was so soft that it melted the sharp edges from the night. "You have the axe because you needed it. Now you don't need it anymore, Johanna. Now you are with those who love you."

Johanna stood still, looking up at the sky. Her arm reached up as if to take something. She bent her knees, using the axe like a crutch, and lowered herself into the snow. In her other hand she scooped up a palmful and watched the lights play on it. Just kneeling there, naked in the snow.

This is my mother now, Rikka thought. She looked at Mokci, who was completely calm. Rikka tried to match her breathing to his, slowing it, trying to let it fill her with no catches along the way, just smooth inhalation, smooth exhalation. It took several cycles to tame her breath and then she noticed that she was breathing with him, that Johanna was breathing with them both.

Mokci stepped closer to Johanna and reached out both hands. Her hands in his, and slowly he helped her to stand. And there they stood smiling at each other, Mokci in his reindeer hides and Johanna in absolutely nothing.

"Well now, there's a sight to stir up the locals. And is this what you were shouting to me to join in on?" It was Dagur. "And are we all to take off our clothes and scandalize the whole island?" She laughed. "Wouldn't that be a sight!"

Mokci smiled and Rikka broke into shaky relieved laughter.

Johanna smiled. She turned, still holding Mokci by the hand, kicked the snow from her bare feet, entered the rorbu and closed the door.

"Well, if that isn't a scandal waiting to spread far and wide, then I've never seen one." Dagur said, still smiling. Rikka bit her lip and joined in, though not as wholeheartedly.

"Dagur, it's been ... it's been black chaos all night. Let's go inside."

Dagur put her hand on Rikka's shoulder. "Do I dare?"

"Don't you dare laugh."

"Don't you dare snivel, and let's not go inside just yet. Let's sit here on these elegant stumps and you can catch me up on all that's going on."

Eventually when they entered, they saw Johanna sitting in a chair with the rose blanket around her shoulders and another blanket over her legs. She was sipping a cup of something hot. Rikka couldn't remember anything steaming on the stove. It smelled of cinnamon and coffee. There hadn't been coffee in the house for at least a month. Mokci leaned against the tabletop, his legs stretched out in front of him as if he lived there.

"Are you alright now, Rikka? Your mother was worried about you."

"Fine." She could say no more. She felt like she was still wading through a nightmare. Dagur watched from across the room. Rikka knew she could see the swamp and would like to help her through it but didn't know how. Quietly, the old woman left the rorbu and returned home.

Mokci gently urged Johanna into the bedroom and closed the door behimd him.

Rikka didn't know where to go or where to stay. She looked around her. Her mother snored softly in the sleeping room. Or was that Mokci? Her mother never snored.

And what was Rikka to do, sleep on the daybed, guard the door? She had heard the whispers that chased her through childhood. Her mother was a whore, unworthy to enter the congregation or any decent home. And the Lapps, it was said, were godless, drunken people, who stunk like their herds of reindeer.

Rikka inhaled deeply taking in the familiar smells of spruce and smoke and fish guts, and behind them the eternal smell of salt spray. These were the odors of every day of her life. Right now, they nauseated her. Every part of her body ached. The alcohol was still doing its damage. Her breath smelt foul and the aftertaste of vomit lingered. Sleep. That was what she craved right now, the sweet oblivion, though she imagined it would run to nightmares.

But where to lie down? Not here. Pernille's! Pernille was her friend now. Her friend or her aunt? She hadn't thought about that. If Dankert were her onkle, but then, he really wasn't, was he? But they would welcome her, and maybe she could sleep with Ragna in her arms. To hold someone she loved, that would be a good thing.

Rikka pulled on her boots and the ragged sweater, plus her shawl. This might be the coldest night of the year. The rorbu's painful creaks and grunts said so. It was a long walk in such weather. Maybe she should go to Dagur's workshop. No, that would be colder than the old woman's rorbu though without the questions Dagur would ask.

Then she noticed the great woolen coat the missionary had wrapped around her. It had saved her once, and it could save her again. He had been a generous man. She only hoped he had a spare coat for himself or at least a warm place to sleep. She picked the coat up from the chair next to the woodstove. It was as warm as it was heavy, as heavy as it was long. As she slid her arms into the massive sleeves, she could hardly believe that she had carried the weight of this beast all the way home. But it was so warm, like wrapping a sleeping bear around her body. And it weighed as much. She sank her hands into the great pockets. Candies, in little paper twists. She smelled a handful of them. Peppermints. She felt a pang of guilt because she knew she'd eat them all along the way. "Thank you, Brother Otten."

She opened the door to a blast of ice shards. The wind had swept away the green lights like dust under a carpet of snow. Rikka stepped back, reconsidering. The wind was armed with needles. She put her full weight against the door to shut it. Now what? She wrapped her head with the shawl, covering her mouth and nose in layers of lamb's wool and tucking the ends deep into her new coat. As she set off, the coat dragged an ever-increasing load of snow along with it. When it became too heavy, she stopped, lifted the hem and gave it a shake. It was heavier than the thick, room-sized carpet in the Lorkman's house. The path behind her looked like it had been cleared by a narrow plough. She reached into the pocked for a peppermint.

This long long night, this long long path: Rikka dragged herself and her load of snow as if through a dream that would not give way to sweet sleep. She passed the church, a flat form inscribed on the landscape, dark on dark. Another heavy step. Past that place where the frost flowers had bloomed, joined one on one on a thousand others, and moved on to … where? Somewhere... Was it before or after the church or the forest flowers, that she had first met the missionaries? They had been incongruous forms, not natural in their surrounding. She had laughed about them, failed to see anything of danger in them. They were pictures in a child's book of elves and trolls rollicking together in black coats and foolish hats. Now she had passed that spot and somewhere, ahead, was Pernille's big white house where the smell of beeswax and sweet yeasty buns... soft wax, dripping butter ... awaited. And the big kakelovn whose base she could curve her body around ... warm, sleeping, god natt little Rikka, god natt.

And there it stood, the great white house, white even in this dark, dark night. A path ran straight to the front door, its way lighted by ice candles, each formed in a lard bucket with a hollow core in which a golden candle glowed. Welcoming her, asking her to please enter. Twenty-four candles, twelve on each side of the path. What could they signify other than "Welcome Rikka. Welcome home."

She stood there at the base of the path, her huge black coat with its burden of new-fallen snow, holding her to the spot. Then, step by step. she moved up the path. Music, the sound of hardanger fiddle and flute came out to meet her. The faint sound of laughter followed the notes. She walked slowly up the path, the music growing as the weight of her coat diminished, leaving its burden behind step by step.

There was the door. There was the window that Urd had looked out. Rikka had forgotten about Urd, the guardian who had banned her from the premises, and rightly so.

And then she could see the housekeeper's doughy face in the window like a gruesome decoration meant to fend off all evil. She stepped back off the path and into the dark hole of night. Things were coming clear. Inside that white house, people were celebrating the return of the light. They were singing, dancing, toasting the waning of the polar night. Tomorrow there would be a brief visit from the sun. Tonight, there was good cheer among those who could afford it, and Rikka could not. She had been wrong to think she would spend the night with little Ragna huddled close against her.

Rikka backed further into the darkness off the path. She had missed the chance to make a pitiful spectacle of herself. One step inside that door would have brought all the merrymaking to a halt.

There she would have stood, dripping mounds of melting snow off that ridiculous coat; head and face wrapped in a scarf like a bandit. So pathetic that even Urd would have felt remorseful as she pushed her back out the door. And what now? She hadn't the strength to return home.

Rikka looked around full circle: nothing but fenced fields and an outbuilding. She lifted the hem of the coat and, giving it a shake, walked around the corner of the house. Yes, there was a building back there. Not the barn, although she would have been glad for the presence of a barn with a bed of hay and a Norwegian Red cow to lie down next to. A bit of warmth. She slid through the shadow of the big house until she could get to this other building. It had a fine, heavy door with carvings on it, Dankert's work. The door slid open with little effort and Rikka stepped in. Her eyes were already adjusted to the dark. There were shelves, tidy piles of milled wood, as many tools hanging from the walls as there had been culinary tools in Pernille's kitchen. And there was even a kakeloven, giving off a slow and tender heat.

She went over to the towering stove, let the burden of Otten's coat slide to the floor with a slow sough, and put her arms around the column of warmth. Her forehead, her breasts, her belly and her legs, all embraced the heat. She tossed off the long scarf and let her hair flow. Nothing more mattered.

When Dankert found her in the late morning, he thought his eyes deceived him. She was a lump covered in the canvas tarp that should be covering the oak planks. She lay on a monster of a wool coat that came from lord-knows-where, and all of this laid out around the kakelovn which he had just come to stoke. What was she doing there? When did she arrive? Why?

As far as he knew, she had never seen his house, a thought that brought him shame. She must have come in the night, come when the house was full of music and laughter and people of a different class. She had come to visit, and he had not been at the door to welcome her. Dankert went around the kakelovn to where a pot of water steamed in readiness. He had tea, he had coffee, he even had cocoa if that's what she wanted. He opted for the cocoa, mixing it with some sugar and whipping it into the boiling water. The steam did its job, snaking its way over to where Rikka lay entombed in wool and tarpaulin. Dankert put his hand on her shoulder. She blinked. He put his arms around her, lifted her into a sitting position. "Rikka, it's me, Dankert. Are you all right?"

She nodded and yawned. "Is that cocoa? For me? "

"Well yes, for both of us. It looks as if you need a little something."

"Looks as if you don't, Onkle, but you can have some of it if you like." He handed her the large mug. She fumbled around in the pocket of the coat, pulled out two twists of brown paper, unwrapped them and placed one in her mug and one in his. He sipped at the cocoa.

"Peppermint? Where did you get those? I haven't had peppermints in years?"

"Uhm, the Mormons gave them to me. Sort of."

"The Mormons," he laughed "Where did you run into them? Why?"

"Maybe I'll tell you later."

"Maybe? Don't you think you ought to tell me now? Right now?"

"Not really. Right now, I want to drink my peppermint cocoa," she said.

"All right then, why are you sleeping out here?"

"You never invited me in."

"I would if I knew you wanted in but I thought you and Pernille felt cold towards each other. It was awkward."

"Pernille and I are friends."

"Really? When did that happen?"

"When we took a bath and drank aquavit together?"

"You're joking!"

She looked at him with one eyebrow raised. "Is there more of that cocoa?"

"Maybe you don't deserve it. You've been keeping secrets from me."

"Secrets? Secrets, Onkle? Between the two of us, who is the one with big, big secrets. Mine are no larger than I am. Yours are ten times your size."

"I suppose they are, but who would want to hear my secrets?"

Rikka looked him straight in his blue, blue eyes, held his nervous gaze and didn't let go. "My mother says you are too old to be so dishonest with your love."

Silence.

Rikka looked at Dankert.

Dankert looked into the steam rising from his mug. "She's right. Your mother is always right, even when she is not right in her mind. She told me that I should either help you grow up, help you find out how to live in this world of ours or I should step away. She's right. I've not done any of those things."

"And why should you? Is that an onkle's duty?"

"Maybe it is ... when no father steps forward."

"Oh yes, fathers. That great secret you, my mother, the church, the whole island for all I know... you all hold that secret from me. Do you know what it's like to live in this community when every man I come across who's old enough, I wonder, is it you? Did you impregnate my mother and then skip out? Or was it one of those corpses that wash in every now and then. Is my father fish food? Is it the priest? The shop keeper? The miserable drunk lying by the roadside? Did she want him or did he rape her? Was she in love? Yes, I have a few questions about my father. The one thing I can't quite believe is that he might be a good man. A good man wouldn't do that to a good woman and wouldn't do it to me, his daughter."

Rikka dissolved in exhaustion. There, she had said it all and now she wanted to go back to sleep, hide in Otten's great coat and cry until she withered. Rikka dragged the coat around her. She would make herself invisible, cover her head, her eyes, her ears even.

Dankert was fixated on his mug. Somewhere down there, under a skin of cream gone cold, lay the promises he had made. No matter how he tried to puzzle things out, he could find no exit from the web of lies. He could not own those lies. They were not his, and yet, here he sat, wearing them, always wearing them for the sake of others, and always understanding they did no one any good. Almost no one.

"Onkle?....Onkle!"

"Yes, my darling girl."

"You aren't paying attention."

"What ... what did I miss? I'm sorry ... I just got lost there."

"Lost intentionally?"

"All right. Do I get another chance?"

"Just one, and you'd better not waste it. Where should I start?"

"The last thing you said before...."

"....before you floated away, I was trying to attach an anchor to you. I want to hold you in one place," said Rikka.

"What place?"

"The place where you've hidden the truth."

"And what good do you think the truth would do you?"

"The issue isn't whether it would be good or bad."

"Then what?"

"Real. It would be real. That's all I want."

"That's what you think, but it may not be what you need. You know, Rikka, sometimes the truth is just ugly. It doesn't get pretty."

Rikka stood up, pulling the coat behind her.

"What do you think I am, a princess? Oh, never mind. I'm going inside to talk to Pernille. She'll understand why I need to know."

"Pernille doesn't know anything."

"Pernille knows far more than you give her credit for. You don't think much of your wife, do you!"

"Of course I do. I take care of her, try to give her everything she wants."

"Onkle, you aren't very bright."

"And you are far too bright for your own good. Come on, let's go inside together and have leftovers from the party. There's so much food we don't know what to do with it all."

"Poor you."

"Please, Rikka, just accept what I can offer. Please let it be for a few minutes."

"Yes, a few minutes. Only a few minutes, Onkle, and then of course you'll inform me of my birthright? Thank you for letting me sleep here. It's good to know there's a warm place for me when things are impossible at home."

He stared at her standing there in that ridiculous coat that she wore like a king's robe. "What do you mean by things being impossible at home? Is your mother going through a bad spell? Why didn't you tell me?"

"Oh no, I'm sure she's having a wonderful time" With that, Rikka headed out the carved doors dragging her train behind her.

"What? Rikka, stop. Wait for me! Please." Rikka did stop. She didn't know where to go. It was still dark, moonless and hopeless. She could see a dull light coming from the kitchen of their house, and then a door opening to let out more light, and then Urd blocking the light from the doorway. Urd with a bucket of slops that she swung outward with amazing force. Rikka flinched. She'd find a drooling attack dog more welcoming. Now she would have to trudge through the deeper snow to get around the house and onto the main path. But there was Dankert, barking at her heels. He picked up the train of Otten's coat and began shaking the snow off it. "Wait, Rikka, why are you going that way. I insist that you come into the house."

"Well then, call off your dog!" she said through her tears.

"What dog?"

"The one called Urd."

"Urd is fine, harmless."

"Oh no, she isn't. She despises me. And I deserve it."

"I don't know what you're talking about, Rikka. Urd never hurt anyone."

But Rikka knew better. "Well, you never vomited on her bread table. You never tipped over her bucket of fermented whale fat. You never…"

"What are you talking about, Rikka? You sound as mad as your…."

"…mother? My mother? Yes, maybe I am, or maybe the whole island is just drunk out of its wits. Crazy from the darkness. Starving for some light. I hate this, this moving through darkness. Through lies. I want to talk to Pernille. I want to apologize to Urd for not respecting her. I want to slap your face. I want to kill Mokci… I want…. God, I just want!"

Dankert caught Rikka in his arms, held her tight. He rocked

her back and forth. He lifted her along with the burden of her coat and its trail of snow and carried her to the house.

Urd just watched the coat slough off its burden of snow onto the kitchen floor. She glanced at the poor colour of the girl's face, scooted rolling pins and wooden spoons out of the way and patted the long table.

"Here. Lay her down here. Get blankets, a pillow, put the kettle on. Hurry, sir. She needs attention."

Urd took Rikka's hands and rubbed them vigorously between her own.

"She's blue. Where did you find her? Quick, there's a small bottle of Rhodiola tincture in a tin on that top shelf. Get it. Here, give it to me," she demanded.

She rubbed the phial between her hands spinning it with warmth. "For heaven's sake. What has happened here? More blankets. Heat up that one. Wrap it around the kakelovn."

Urd tipped Rikka's head back and pulled on her jaw to open her mouth. With one finger she lifted the girl's tongue, and with the other hand she squeezed six drops of the tincture under her tongue.

"There. Yes, that's good. Now get your wife. The girl will want her by her side when she wakes up. Tell her to bring the babe."

Urd continued to rub Rikka's hands, her arms, her neck. She never asked what she should do; she knew. She had seen this before, seen it in lambs, in children, in everything that got caught in the cold or trapped in their own misery.

"Should we move her somewhere more comfortable?" Dankert asked.

"No, she's fine here. Now go on, do as I said," Urd commanded.

"Stupid man," she mumbled to herself. 'Somewhere more comfortable!'"

She shook her head and gave him a shove to break his paralysis.

Dankert felt that he was spinning uselessly trying to follow Urd's commands. He wasn't accustomed to receiving orders from the likes of Urd, but he would do anything and everything she demanded. At least she knew enough that she could give orders.

Pernille rushed into the kitchen having heard the commotion. She gasped when she saw Rikka lying on the table. She held back a burst of nervous laughter as she realized that this was not a flashback to their drunken folly but a serious situation. Urd ordered her to get the warming bricks they kept by the kakelovn in the wintertime.

"Pernille, bring me that roll of butcher paper; no, just tear off a length of it and roll it into a tube, about as big around as a kroner. Make it a little shorter, about an arm's length. That's right. Now I have someone who can follow directions at least."

Urd opened the great coat that still entombed Rikka. She hushed everyone in the room as she stroked Rikka's chest. Her hand found the spot she was after and she placed the end of the tube just above the girl's breast. Urd's tilted head lay lightly on the other end of the tube and with another 'shush' and one hand raised to ward off any interference, she seemed to listen to some message coming through the tube. Whatever she could hear was the only sound in the room other than the soft murmur of the kettle. Time held.

Dankert tapped the table lightly as he shifted position and Urd's head jerked, the expression on her face threatening death. Dankert was caught in an eddy of confusion. What was this madwoman doing and why was he standing here allowing it? They needed a doctor. Rikka might be dying, and here was Urd leaning over her with nothing better than a roll of butcher paper between her ear and Rikka's heart.

No sooner had he thought it than it made sense to him. She was listening. What did she hear, the rush of blood pumping through Rikka's heart? The wind of breath moving through her lungs like a low tide? It made some sort of sense to him. She could hear what was going on inside Rikka's chest, and the frown on the woman's face told him that she didn't like what she heard. Right then Dankert would do anything that Urd asked of him. He would hand his trust over to her with every blessing he could conjure up.

"I need chaga," Urd said aloud. "I didn't gather any before the freeze came. No chaga!"

Pernille and Dankert looked at one another. Chaga? What was chaga?

First the paper tube, now the chaga. "Dagur. Dagur has it. She showed me a whole bucket full. Go get it. I need it now!"

"But…. what, Urd? What am I to get?"

"Chaga. From Dagur. Right now. Hurry."

"The horse and cart are at my parents' home."

"Then run. You can run, can't you?"

Pernille lifted the blanket off Rikka's legs. Rikka was wearing those new Sami boots that she and Mokci had made. She unlaced them and pulled them off Rikka's feet, kicked off her own useless slippers, and pulled on the boots. A bit short. She took them off and removed some of the sedge lining before putting them back on. They were warm and comfortable, flexible, perfect. She stamped her feet on the floor to get the feel of the boots, how they might do in the snow. Satisfied, she took Dankert's coat from the wall peg, wrapped a shawl around her head and shoulders and ran out the door.

"What? Where's she going?" Dankert asked Urd.

"After the chaga. She'll get it done. Now you need to focus on helping me here. Can you follow some simple orders? Good. Feed the fire. Get that down comforter off your bed and bring it here. The baby's crying. See to her."

"Yes, Urd. I will see to that."

"Well, finally, you're sounding sensible!" Urd returned her attention to the girl. She had not liked the sound of her heart. The rhythm had a broken quality, a tripping or stumbling. She had heard that same stuttering in her old dog's heart during the last year of his life, and she didn't want to hear it here. For now, Urd sat by Rikka, stroked her, sang old Finnish healing songs to her, waited for Dagur to arrive.

DAGUR

The old woman, who had been an old woman since Pernille was a small girl running past her witch's cove, was sitting on a stump in her yard, watching the first light. She whistled to Pernille. "There now, I see you've found your legs again, tall Pernille. Come join me if you need a rest."

"I've come for the chaga, Dagur. Urd sent me. Rikka is very sick and needs your help as well as Urd's."

"I'll get my gear. You go into the workshop and get the chaga."

Dagur disappeared into her rorbu.

Dagur was too busy making lists in her mind to hear Pernille's question. "Why are you following me. It's in the workshop. Hurry.."

"But I don't know…"

Dagur slammed her door.

"What are you doing, girl? Can't you read? Don't you know what a mushroom looks like?"

"A mushroom? What good is a mushroom to Rikka?"

Dagur brushed past Pernille, picked up a cloth bag secured with a drawstring, which she loosened and held under the young woman's nose. "There, that is chaga. They didn't teach you much, did they! Come on now. We need to hurry. See if you can beat me back to the house."

Pernille tied the sack of chaga inside her shawl, waved goodbye and ran.

The kitchen was so warm when Pernille entered, she thought she might melt on the spot. Dankert stood at the foot of the slab holding Ragna against his chest and patting her back. Ragna whimpered and tried to twist around to lunge for her sleeping sister. "Kaka, Kaka," she cried.

"Well, get her some cake if she wants it," Dagur urged Dankert.

"No, she doesn't want cake, that's her name for Rikka."

Pernille's head snapped to the end of the slab where Urd and Dagur stood together whispering to one another. Pernille was incredulous. "How did you beat me here?"

"I told you I would."

"But how? You didn't pass me."

"You have the chaga. Bring it here," Urd commanded.

Pernille reached inside her shawl where the mushrooms were tied in place. She freed the sack and handed it to Dagur without ever taking her eyes off her. In turn, Dagur smiled sweetly.

"I keep my promises. And you did too. You brought the chaga safely. Now, perhaps you could make some coffee for everyone and find something to distract Ragna. By the by, Dankert. I think I found your father's old cow, Bestemor. She made a new pathway across the fields. It's very handy, quite the shortcut from my house to yours."

Even Dankert had to laugh, albeit quietly, and then everyone's attention returned to Rikka.

"You'd better be careful, Dagur. My wife is no gossip but between the mushrooms and your ability to fly over her head unnoticed, she just might need to pass a story along. The priest would love to hear that one. You might become the latest sensation of his lurid sermons."

They didn't laugh aloud this time.

"Let's focus on how we can help this girl," Urd snapped. "Is the chaga sound? How do you want to deal with the chaga, Dagur? Is it pulverized?

"Not yet. I beat it down to the size of pebbles. Used the back of my axe. But now is the hard part. It needs to be like coffee grounds, and that takes forever."

The two women had forgotten about Dankert standing quietly behind them and learning more than they meant for him to know. He was upset to hear about Rikka and Pernille's indiscretion, but he pushed that aside. "I can do it. I have a grinder out in the workshop, I can adjust it to any size you want," he said.

"Good then," said Dagur. "Grind us about half a teacup full to start. Then run it back in here and we will steep it. Then you can go back out and grind the rest of it for later. That's a good man."

"What about Ragna?'

"I'll take care of her," Dagur said. "This will give Urd and me a chance to start the healing."

Dankert gave over the baby to Dagur. She stroked the child's flossy head and when Ragna stuck her fingers in her old friend's mouth she giggled as Dagur sucked and nibbled them. Then Ragna turned her head and touched Rikka's hair in the same way Dagur had touched hers.

"Kaka, Kaka, Kaka," Ragna said. Dagur laid the little one down next to her sister. The two lay side by side, one falling asleep and the other too deeply in sleep.

Dankert cleaned the grinder meticulously, taking apart and removing the locking ring and pulling out the grinding plate. The cross knife should shine, and he saw to it that it did. He usually left his tools as clean as the night sky, but the plate had a crust of ... what, he couldn't remember what he had last used it for. He twisted a soft bit of muslin and ran it through and around each part, reassembled it all and making sure the eye screws were tight. Perhaps he should oil it, but that might contaminate the chaga. He anchored the grinder to his workbench and poured in a handful of chaga chunks. He left the tension loose assuming that he would need to run the desiccated chaga through several times, tightening the tension each time, to get the results the women would expect. He enjoyed the sound of the grinding, the way it changed each time he repeated the process with an increasing tension. First pebbles, then gravel to grit, then powder. He wanted to go ahead and process the whole black and orange chunk but stopped himself. Take in the sample; see if it pleased the healers.

He heard the creaking of icy snow outside and the door opened. Pernille entered, a rare sight in this retreat of his. Dankert nodded to her and gestured for her to enter. "Did it work?" she asked.

"I think so. Come and feel it. Do you think it's the right consistency?"

"I don't know anything about it, but it seems very fine. I like the melding of the colours. It was such a homely chunk, like a tumour. This should dissolve in boiling water, don't you think?"

"Yes, I do. Let's take it in, Pernille." Dankert brushed the powder into a twist of clean paper and looked at his wife appraisingly. "I didn't know you could run."

"Well, I can."

"I don't think I could."

"I don't know why I ever stopped. I've never been as happy as when I ran."

"What do you mean?"

"It's something I did as a child that made me feel alive. I felt that I was being myself when I ran. No one approved, certainly not my parents, but then they rarely knew that I ran."

"Where did you run? When?'

"Mostly at night when I was supposed to be in bed."

"When did you stop?"

There was a long pause while Pernille decided whether or not to tell Dankert. Finally, looking him straight in the eyes, she said, "When I married you."

"Why?"

"It is not a thing a married woman does." She looked down at the floor, at her feet, those long lost friends.

Dankert was stymied. She was right. It wasn't a thing a married woman did. Why? Because it was not a thing a married woman did. He had to admit to himself that he would not have approved had he known. Why? Because it was not…. Why not? It was unseemly.

Why? Because married women didn't. They might hurt themselves. They might look dishevelled, red in the face and panting. They might be ignoring their children or even their husbands, their duties.

They looked at each other. He hadn't chosen her, and she hadn't chosen him. Their parents had made the decision, and it was a profitable one, increasing both of their holdings. Pernille knew that Dankert had submitted; she had not, but no one had listened to her.

"You should run again."

"I intend to."

"I never saw you looking as beautiful as when you came in the kitchen door."

"Red face, frozen tears? Panting? You like that, then?"

They both laughed. They didn't just share tight smiles; they laughed out loud. Together.

He handed the twist of chaga to his wife. "Here, you'll get there before me." He smiled at the image of himself tagging along behind her, always the second to arrive even in his own home. It was the two of them living together in their own way, a way that seemed to be opening up and making room for each to grow, much more satisfying than the portrait of the stiff couple taken after the wedding. The two of them were trapped in an oval frame on the dark wall at the end of the hallway. Neither of them ever looked at that portrait.

Hanna heard the Mormon brothers come in and she slipped out of the room, across the floor, right between two of the large men, without so much as a nod or a word.

"I'll start a fire. It's colder than ... than... never mind. It's cold." One of them headed outside to the woodpile. He came back inside with an armload of wood. Another was peeling withered potatoes that appeared to bend under his knife. He had stacked a small pile of dried cod's heads next to an onion.

Hanna sat down across from the third, who introduced himself as Brother Otten. Hanna's worried hands twisted and contorted on the table's surface and then flew loose in the air. Her shoulders were raised high and curved in towards her ears. She couldn't settle her body. Her eyes scanned the room, never lighting on a single object.

Brother Otten nodded to her. "Now, my good woman, I want you to be easy. We are here to help you. Put your fear aside. We will simply keep you company and make you some wholesome food. We will warm this place up, and look, Brother Cecil here is building you a fire. Soon the room will be cheery. And now he will find something warm to put around your shoulders. Brother Cecil? Do find her something, won't you?"

Hanna nodded and pointed to a wooden box under the daybed by the door. "Is there something warm in there?" Otten asked.

She nodded. "The rose blanket," she said in a voice as thin and fragile as a spider's web. "Maybe my baby is there, too."

"Your baby?"

"I don't know where she is. Maybe down by the Sentinels. Maybe in that box. No, Lorkman took her."

"How old is your baby?"

"Old enough to take five steps. Then she falls. How old would that be, do you think?"

"Maybe one year?" Otten ventured. "What's her name?"

"Henrikka, darling Henrikka."

Otten looked down at his large hands, cracked from the cold but capable of helping. Tears rushed to his eyes. The woman noticed them and reached across the table to brush them away. She licked her salty hand and smiled at him.

Otten said. "Cecil, Rose, please be seated at this table."

"Could it wait a bit? My fire hasn't taken hold," Cecil said making a last stab at the kindling.

"And I just want to get these cod heads cleaned so I can get the soup brewing," Rose said.

"There are greater matters at hand," said Otten nodding towards Johanna.

Brother Rose threw the musty looking fish heads into the water and found the only other chair, a stool really, while Cecil had to settle for a skimpy stump of firewood that he rolled over to the table and balanced on end. They looked at Brother Otten, wondering what important matter eclipsed their preparation of food and fire.

"Let us pray," said Otten. The other two and bowed their heads. "Heavenly Father, we are blessed by your presence in this humble home and by the mission you have given us in this beautiful land. I pray that you hear the words of a simple man, a humble missionary, and endow these rough working hands of mine with the power to bring succor and relief to this frail woman who needs whatever help we can lend her. I am your child. I am unworthy. But, I pray you give me power this one time to release the chains of misery that bind her. This we pray in Jesus' name, Amen."

Brother Otten said, "When I look at this poor woman, lost in misery, alone and unsupported by family and community, I feel compelled to help her if I possibly can. Do you think the Lord might loan some power to these hands? Just once?"

"But...."

"Just once for her sake?"

"But what are we to do?

"By supporting you, we too take on this presumption."

"And maybe the Lord is watching and knows there is no one in this land, no one ordained, no one else to help," Otten countered.

They all looked at each other, unable to say yes, unable to say no.

"Then you will be by my side?"

"I will always do so, Brother." Rose nodded, however hesitantly.

"And maybe we will be forgiven for helping this woman, if help we can."

Otten stood behind Johanna. Hanna could feel his hands hover over her head, not quite touching her tangled hair. She could feel a surge of energy that swirled in that small space between her head and his hands.

Johanna shivered. She looked around her at these three men who looked so comfortable in her little house. Who were they? Why had they come? Should she fear them? They looked as if they had known her, or she had known them, forever. They poked around the kitchen and the stove as if it were their own. The one called Rose dabbed at the bits of potato peel left on the counter and Cecil opened the door to the stove just a crack so that the air could encourage the flames. Were they cousins? Uncles? Vagrant fishermen? She didn't really care. They felt familiar, even with their terrible Norwegian and odd way of dressing -- and she felt safe with them. Later they could explain what they were doing in her kitchen. For now she felt surrounded by warmth.

"Are you feeling better? Look at you, you have colour in your face," said the big man. "What can I get for you?"

"I want to eat, sit by the fire. I want to sleep and then find my daughters."

"You sound much better. Your voice is stronger. Do you feel well?"

"No, I will never feel well, that I know, but I feel better."

"That's something," Rose declared.

"Yes, praise the Lord." Cecil said.

"No, I will praise the Lord when he returns my girls to me, when he sends them home safe and whole. Until then I will praise no one, nothing, except that wretched soup you have bubbling on the stove, and the fire burning bright, and your friendship, all of you. Thank you. Who are you?"

Brother Otten looked at his hands, held them out in front of Hanna and turned them one way and another. Then he left, walked outside. Hanna could see through the open door as he stared at the sky and at the sea which once again had melded together in darkness. Then he knelt in the snow, clasped his hands in front of his heart and raised his eyes to the heavens.

Dankert looked at Rikka and Ragna. Their bodies melded together. He listened to the two old women talk about their mushroom magic.

"Here. You should have seen it, Urd, a whole colony of them nestled together on the bark. Big chunks of black and rust. The tree looked like it was dying, rot coming from the core. Some say the chaga kills the birch. I don't think so. I think it settles on the dying tree and makes use of it."

"Hmm, maybe the tree and the mushroom help each other out. Maybe the mushroom finds a tender, softer part of the birch to attach to, and maybe the birch takes sustenance from the chaga in its struggle to survive longer, to drop more seed on the ground for future birches to flourish in. What I do know is that it cures anxiety, and this girl has more than her share of that," said Urd.

Pernille wrapped a scarf three times around Dankert's neck and tucked the ends into his jacket. "Hurry now," she whispered. "We don't know anything but will hope for love's help."

Dankert kissed her on the cheek. "I'll be fast ... almost as fast as you."

He was not much of a runner, but he could make good time on skis. A pair of pine telemark skis from his days in the Norwegian Army still hung in a cross on the outside of the door to the workshop. He hadn't worn them in several years, but he looked forward to having a reason to do so now.

He brushed off the skis, stroked on some wax as quickly and carelessly as time demanded. He laid them side by side, slipped his feet into the bindings and tightened them. He freed the old birch poles from their hook by the door and pushed off, at first awkward but soon with a sense of grace. Dankert imagined himself to be like Pernille, to float over the ice and skim the snow; to inhale through his nose in long controlled pulls and exhale through pursed lips. He smiled at the thought of them moving side-by-side, Pernille with her long-legged stride and he with the smooth stroke he had developed in training.

How little it had taken for his perception of his wife to slide from necessary convenience to friend, maybe someday something closer. She had changed in one day by simply letting him see who she really was. He had looked, looked right into her eyes. By God, they were green. He would have guessed gray if asked. No, she probably hadn't changed a bit. He had. He was learning to see this other woman, not as the duty that had been foisted upon him but as another human who had been pushed into a marriage that had no meaning for her.

His breath fought against the demands he was forcing on it. It became ragged and shrill. There was so much within him that he wanted to change: the sense of duty that was really a sense of fear; the lies he agreed to in order to keep the peace, a peace that was really just a tattered truce. He stopped and his vision of Pernille stopped with him. He toppled backwards, freed his feet from the bindings and sat on his skis.

She smiled and rested on the white white snow that gleamed in the moonlight. They were silent, this man and his wife-vision, and they both lingered looking at all the space around them. To the left was the house that Dankert built for them. To the right was the house that his father had built for his wife and his child. They were almost identical.

All around him was but white space, space that his family owned. But why did they need that space? What did they do with it? They just owned it. No one loved it. Yet look at the beauty of it. Empty beauty. I don't need this, he thought. My parents need it to feel safe, surrounded by what they own. An insulated emptiness. He would have nothing more to do with it now. He wanted to encircle his home, his share of all this space, and draw it tight. Like his parents, he too was afraid, though not of strangers or thieves, but of his parents. Unbidden images passed before his eyes: his mother shrieking at Johanna, calling her a lazy slut; his father lurking in the background, amused.

And there it was, the Lorkman estate. The house, a large white box with a door in the centre and square windows perfectly spaced and symmetrical, so much like the house he had built because that's what houses were supposed to look like, at least the houses of the upper class. Why hadn't he noticed? Why hadn't he realised that he was copying a mold that didn't even please him, didn't reflect his own sense of beauty or function? It stood there like a set of beliefs that he didn't subscribe to. Nor did he subscribe to marriages arranged for financial benefit. But he had built the expected house and he had married the woman who would increase the Lorkman status. And then, the worst of it was that he had treated her with utter indifference, paying no attention to what would please her. He had ignored both of their needs, his and hers. He was his father. The shame of realizing this to be true was coupled with the shame for how he had failed the others he loved.

He would like to sit here on his skis in this billow of snow and think about what he wanted and what he wanted to change. He looked out the corner of his eyes to watch this illusion of a woman who he had never bothered to look at before without resentment. She smiled at him. When he turned towards her, a cloud covered the moon, the white snow dimmed and so did she.

Dankert pulled himself up, sorted his bindings, beat the snow off his legs with the poles.

"I will make things right," he said out loud, "at least for Pernille and for Rikka if I can." And then the image of Johanna, so sick, so torn, perhaps beyond all help... she above all others, he had failed. Dankert pushed the poles into the snow to give himself a strong start. He was looking for a new rhythm, a strong and determined one. A sense of urgency pushed him towards his father's house. He would face his parents, insist on taking Agnes to his house. He would not tell them why. He would simply do it.

And now the skis propelled him as if with a zest of their own. He moved straight towards his target, the Lorkman estate. With each thrust of the poles and swish of the skis, Dankert watched that oppressive white block inflate, breath by breath. A fingerling of smoke scratched its way from the chimney. There would be no warm welcoming. Shutters covered any light that might have invited a guest. Were they all asleep inside?

Dankert really had no idea what time of day or night it was. There had been that moon, or was it just part of his imaginings like the chimera that had come to sit beside him as his wife, both disappearing behind the same cloud? Small Agnes could be asleep in her room drooling on the doll with the silly name, what was it? Poona? Yes. Or she could be up making the morning breakfast cakes with her grandmother. Either way, Dankert wished he could avoid this meeting. There was sure to be fury when he insisted on taking Agnes, and he planned to do so without any long explanations. He would just say he was taking her to his house to visit with her sister. He didn't need to specify which sister or how many. Pernille would feed her there, let her play for awhile, and then he would return her clean and smiling. They would have to admit that he had the right as her onkle to take care of her for a half-day.

Dankert looked around. He was more drawn to the barn than to the house. He would just check in there to see if Bestemor ever made it back. He worried that the old cow might have collapsed in the snow and given up on her life of servitude. She had certainly done her duty to the family. He remembered her as a calf when he was a boy. She had been bright red with a white mask for a face. She must be at least sixteen by now and her coat had dimmed as had her eyes.

It was darker in the barn than outside. A pail lay on its side in

Bestemor's milking stand. She was not curled up in the straw where she often lay; just a tiny pin cushion of a hedgehog emerged from there and scurried across the floor to hide from him. And there was something else in there. He took off his skis and leaned them against the wall. There was a stirring, something alive and larger than a hedgehog. Keeping one ski pole in his hand for safety, Dankert poked at the floor, trying to avoid a fall in the dark.

He searched for a lantern and found it where it had been kept forever, but it was clearly out of coal oil so the tin of tinder meant to light it was of no use. I'll just close my eyes and face the darkest corner for a minute, he thought, and then the dark will seem lighter. Because he had no idea what he would be facing in the recesses of the barn, he started to sing a gentle tune, very softly at first:

> *Bæ bæ lille lam*
> *Har du noe ull?*

He could hear rustling off to his left, so he repeated the question, and heard a soft reply:

> *Ja ja kjære barn,*
> *jeg har kroppen full.*

"Agnes?"
"Onkle?"
"Ja, ja ja!"
"Here I am. See me?"
"Yes, I can almost see you, like a shadow in the dark."
"I can't see shadows in the dark, Onkle. That doesn't make sense."
Dankert used her voice to lead him towards her. "Yes, you can. I'll bet that right now you can see a tall dark shape coming over to you. It's a little darker than the things that stand still, right? It's a

friendly onkle shadow."

"Good morning, Onkle."

"Is it morning?"

"I don't know, but I think so. You wouldn't be in a barn in the night, would you?"

"Yes, I would, because I came looking for you. Why are you sleeping out here, Agnes?"

"She told me to."

"Your grandmother?"

"Yes. She was mad at me and said I didn't deserve to sleep in a fine house so I could sleep in the barn."

"Were you naughty?"

"No."

"Was she naughty?"

"Yes, horrible naughty. She threw Poona outside and said Poona was dirty and ugly and I am dirty and ugly too and I had to wash my hair and sleep with the Blondie doll instead of dirty Poona, and I said no, no, no, no. And I said, 'I hate you.' And I do and I want to go live with my Mama and Rikka like I used to, or with you or with Dagur. I'll even live with Pernille if I have to but it isn't as much fun with her, but yes, I'll live with Pernille."

Dankert leaned down and scooped the crying child up into his arms. "Yes, Agnes. I am taking you to see Rikka. Dagur is there too. And Pernille will love to have you in our home. It is your home too."

The child stopped crying and hugged her onkle. "Can I stand on your skis?"

This hadn't occurred to Dankert. "That won't work, but I can piggyback you home. It might take awhile, but we'll stop and rest."

"I won't need to rest," Agnes laughed.

"No, but I will. Now have you found Poona?"

"Yes, she was sleeping with Pinsy."

"Umm, Pinsy the hedgehog?"

"Yes, how did you know his name? Can he come, too? He doesn't like Grandmother or Grandfather either."

"No, but he knows how to get away from them and this is his home. He might miss Bestemor."

"Grandfather says Bestemor is dead and he doesn't care. She's useless, he says, so let her die in the snow. I hate him too."

"Come on darling. I'll get the skis on and then you can climb up on my back. I'll be Bestemor and you can ride me home."

"Will there be breakfast there?"

"Breakfast or supper or whatever we have at this strange hour, yes."

"Good then. You'd better give me a whip so I can strike you when you slow down."

"What about Poona?"

"She must be at Pinsy's house. They're getting married."

"Do we leave Poona behind then?"

"Just for this week. They're having their honeymoon."

It was the blue hour. It announced both the beginning and the ending of the sun's appearance along the horizon, an appearance that splashed tropical colours – violet, orange, crimson – onto the canvas of the sky. The blue hour lingered so that a sleeper awakening in it might wonder if the bright colours had yet to appear or had slid off the canvas while he slept. The blue hour coloured everything so the world was composed of blue snow, indigo water, blue and violet houses and the blue faces of citizens either going to their day's work or heading home for a hot meal.

MOKCI

Mokci sat on the boulder where he first met Rikka, through the blue hour that followed the sun's display. He cared no more for it than for any flamboyant display of aurora borealis. He only wished to see Rikka. Where was she? He had been by her rorbu night after night, listening at the door for her voice, watching the pathways for her footprints. He had seen Johanna through the window, but he was warded off by his own shame. He had not been able to help Johanna when she needed support and kindness. Who else was there to help her, to hold her hand when the world tipped and tried to toss her off into the sea? She was like a fisherman trying to balance herself on the deck of her boat while the gunnels sprang off and the prow crumbled.

And today he had looked in that window again and saw three men in the room with Johanna. They looked foreign in clothes made from somewhere far away. At first dismayed by these strangers, Mokci kept watch, and he saw the men doing the chores, cooking, tending the fire, sweeping the floor. Who were they? No one Mokci had ever seen, but they sang in an unknown language as they worked. After watching them for longer than he could justify in his own conscience, he focused instead on Johanna who sat doing needlework and chatting with them. Whoever they were, they had brought peace and laughter into the house.

But where was Rikka? He had left messages for her, bits of brightly coloured ribbon tied to the fragile stalks of crowberry shrubs leading towards his lavvu. These were the same coloured ribbons that adorned the boots they had made together: the favourite Saami colours of red, blue, green, yellow, but also the purple that was her preference. He hoped she would come across the ribbons and know that he awaited her in his lavvu. She must be all right. If she weren't, surely Johanna wouldn't be laughing and singing with the three odd men. But where was Rikka?

Mokci sat rocking back and forth on the boulder that he should be sharing with her. The rocking found a rhythm, one meant to soothe and to clarify his thoughts. But his thoughts, running in concentric circles, could only repeat the question "Where is she? Where is she?" Over and over. His head lolled back and he watched the layers of blue grow darker and darker and become black as his focus reached Boahjenasti, the point of origin of all life. He thought of the pole that reached from that northernmost star down to Earth and how all life revolved around it. All the generations of his people, the reindeer, every plant, rock and animal in his world swung around that pole, and so did he, and so did Rikka, so where was she tonight?

A dark jealousy crept in. He had been pushing it away for days. Was she with someone else? Had she tired of him? Maybe she was afraid of her own feelings or of his. Maybe those feelings were too strong for her.

But Mokci could only know his own feelings and as he sat on that blue-black boulder, his feelings wrestled to be set free, to be heard by the sea, the sky, and anyone who might hear.

Finally he sat straight and still, relaxed his body and let the air expand the depths of his lungs. The first sounds left his body and moved through the darkening air, the sounds that expressed his yearning; the tones that reached out for expression. Each inhalation brought the sting of salt into his throat and lungs. Each exhalation tempered a new sound seeking the wellspring of love. Whoever might have been walking the path behind him, whoever might be opening her door to hear where this strange music was coming from, whoever might try to translate the syllables of his heart's language, he could only hope that Rikka was among them.

He asked the rocks, both the enormous boulders and the minute particles of sand. He asked the sea that pushed the shore relentlessly and without fatigue. He asked Boahjenasti who oversaw everything that happened on the land and in the sky. And he thanked them all for hearing him. And then his joik ebbed and found its ending, and the night was still. Mokci stood atop the boulder because he could sit and wait no longer. The sea could send in one wave after another, always coming to the same shore and always pulling back from it, but he had to move.

He knew what he would do now. A new way had come to his mind, sent to him by his grandfather, or maybe by the tall standing rocks down by the water's edge. They had responded to his song, his joik, sending him new knowledge and a more patient way of being. He would stop looking for Rikka and stop worrying about her. Instead, he would return to his lavvu and design and collect the materials he needed to build the sleigh that would carry her away. He would not build it with doubt or worry. He would build it for love and for escape. Mokci leapt down from the boulder and ran away from the village and the missionaries and the wrong direction he had been taking. He would not stalk Rikka. He would invite her.

Back in his lavvu he stoked the waning fire, urging new flames with strips of birch bark, blowing on the blue coals and asking them for warmth. It was a cold night. He had heard villagers complain about how unusually cold the winter was. Apparently, many years went by with little or no snow, and no ice in the fjord. Now the fishermen complained about the frigid winds that blew ice crystals into their eyes.

But to Mokci this winter had been strangely warm. Snow would fall but often it turned to slush. Clearly these Norsemen didn't know what cold was. A winter in Sapmi might well kill them all off. But he was glad that there was enough snow here this winter to allow him to pull out his skis and skirt around the rocks that stood as guardians.

The thought of his skis offered him the design plan he needed. He saw an image of the wild girl last winter. She had joined two skis together and was lying on her stomach head first down a steep incline. She shouted with excitement and exhilaration as her makeshift sled raced down the long, long slope. When it fell apart at the bottom, her laughter broke through the haze of churned snow and filled him with her excitement.

Mokci would take his inspiration from the wild girl but would aim for comfort instead of wildness. He would need crosspieces. Maybe he could get them from Dankert who had a whole workshop filled with planed wood. But then there would be questions, curiosity about his project. He thought about those tall pillars of stone that Rikka had called Sentinels. They trapped some likely pieces of wreckage that the tide brought in. And he would need something to fasten the various pieces together.

Mokci stared at the walls of his lavvu. At the base, the reindeer hides offered him some folds of excess material that he had left to discourage drafts. He set to work on cutting narrow strips of hide. The space was a little less cozy when he finished, but he knew he could fill in with packed snow and wear more layers if he needed. And so, his project progressed as inspiration and experience led his way.

Dagur's head jerked back, yanking her out of sleep. What was it? Something had changed. She had missed something important. She looked at Rikka and saw that the utter stillness had been broken. There was a change in the girl, the first change in days. Her tapered fingers crossed over one another and seemed to vibrate against her neck, a force of life. The stillness of near-death had passed.

Dagur reached over and lay her hand on top of Rikka's as lightly as a feather. Yes, there was movement; life was returning.

"Urd," she called in a whisper that wanted to be a shout. "Urd, she's coming back, Urd. Wake up. Feel this."

Urd rolled over on the pallet next to the kakelovn. "What's the noise?" She pulled the blanket over her head trying to find her way back into sleep.

"Urd. Wake up. It's Rikka. Urd. Now. Wake up."

And she did, shot up and stumbled towards the baking table that had become Rikka's bed. She had lain there for three, maybe four days now, absolutely still except for the ragged movements of her chest, never seeming to take in enough air to support life.

"What is it? Better or worse?"

"Look at her hands. Look where they are."

"Did you put them there?"

"Of course not. Why would I do that? You think I'm playing games? She moved them!"

"When?"

"I don't know, I was asleep just like you."

"There's life in this girl. Let's bring it forward."

Urd, still in the work dress that she had worn day and night ever since they found Rikka, unfolded her body and hobbled over to the stove. "This is perfect now." She sniffed at the black brew that had been steeping for three days. "Here, taste this. I think it's perfect."

"Ja, that's how it should be, like a syrup. Chaga and rhodiola, a perfect balance. It will be stronger now, should settle that maelstrom in her. Not an easy thing to do when a whirlpool wants to spin in only one direction. She can fight against it for so long but it's impossible to break out of."

"I think you're right. But what caused it."

"Any number of things. Look at her life. But I'll bet what pushed her over the edge was a man."

They looked at one another.

"Of course. If you're standing at the edge of your life, a hard hard life, and you need someone to save you, it's going to be a man. But like as not, he'll push you over the edge instead. And then he'll stand there, watching you fall, and cry out "Wait, hold my hand!""

"Enough of that now. How can we best get this blessed brew into her?"

"As we did before… with a poultice."

"Or with a drip cloth."

They placed the cloth between her lips, and drop by drop, the thick liquid forced her to swallow. Then the two women looked at each other and nodded, satisfied that this would be enough for the time being. Now they would just watch.

"What's that nasty smell?"

"Maybe the illness," Dagur said.

"No, not that smell, the really nasty one."

They both sniffed everything around them, noses pointed at one possible villain after another. When they faced one another still searching, they broke into a hearty laughter. "It's us!"

"Come on then, let's do something about it. I haven't washed in a month."

"And all this tension … well, I guess we should clean up a bit," Urd said sniffing at her armpit in disgust. "I'll get the wash basin and warm water from the next room."

She blew out a lungful of air and got to work filling a copper basin and the bread rising bowl with water as hot as she could manage. She got two bathsheets, one for each of them and dragged them back into the kitchen.

Dagur looked at the set-up and laughed. "Really? Do you imagine that we are going to stand in here and dab our dirty bodies under these filthy dresses? That will do little good when our clothes smell like something dragged out of the marsh in July."

"Not a bit of it," was all Urd said before stripping herself of dress and underclothing and dropping them to the floor.

Dagur guffawed and did the same herself. But instead of bathing, she first picked up all their clothes and stepped out into the snow naked as a babe, she laid the clothes stretched out on top of a snow bank.

"There, that will fix you. A bit of fresh air for you; a basin of hot water and soap for us two fine ladies." Back in the kitchen she looked at the long naked body of her friend and laughed. "What a stretch of skin you are!"

Urd looked back at her and simply said, "Well, you aren't, you saggy old bit of nothing much!"

"And what happens if Pernille walks in?" Dagur wondered.

"The old Pernille would have us out in the snow rushing to gather our clothes before we ran off to Russia with them in our arms."

"And the new Pernille, the one whose husband is looking at her as if she actually exists and he's glad of it?"

"That Pernille might laugh along with us and maybe even join in, though that would be a stretch even for her."

"Oh no, I forgot about Dankert," said Dagur running towards the door to grab her clothes from the snow.

"Calm down. He'll need to spend some time with his awful parents. They won't let him go until they have passed on every bit of slander in their bags of misery. And it may not be easy to convince them that he should bring Agnes here for a time."

"Hah," Dagur guffawed. "I'm sure the grand lady of the estate will be delighted to rid herself of the child. Agnes is probably the smartest person on this island, and she isn't one to hold her tongue." Dagur wrung out her washcloth and reached over to Urd. "Here, let me scrub your scabby old back. You seem to be molting."

"That's called reincarnation. I'll be like new when you finish abusing my poor skin."

Dagur didn't notice when Rikka, as silent as they were boisterous, blinked her eyes, giving herself a broken picture of the two old women rollicking naked around the room. She returned to her dark cave of silence.

Mokci shook his head, awakening to where he was now, in this misplaced lavvu waiting for Rikka. He held a long strip of the hide that he had cut and spliced for the sleigh he would build. He stroked the piece, ran it through his fingers, remembered the killing of a buck, the old one, no longer able to keep up with the herd that he once led. He had fallen behind as he felt the flow of the young surrounding and passing him.

Again he pulled the length of hide through his hands, letting his fingers feel the variations in the density and thickness. Where were the weak spots likely to break under stress? Where did the strip gain girth and strength? Why was he thinking about these subtleties? He was not the noadi weakened by age, seeking an aspirant to take his place. He was not his grandfather, but his grandfather was claiming space within him.

"Do not do that, Grandfather. Do not try to control me from within my own thoughts, my own heart. You must look to others. I cannot follow you. Not now."

A whisper slid around the circumference of the lavvu and then rose through the smoke hole into the sky. His grandfather left no words behind. Mokci realized the old man's power was waning, his energy spent on this long struggle to bind his grandson to him. There would be no passing down, no inheritance. Perhaps it was time for the old ways to rest, but how could one who knew so much of the inner qualities of every tree, rock, constellation, and creature let go of the knowledge, let it fall from his mind down through his heart and onto the barren rocks and be gone? Mokci felt an old wind turn cold and dry. It rustled through the birch twigs on the floor and died. He wanted to cry.

Mokci tied a simple knot in the end of the hide strip. It didn't need to be a complex knot. Sometimes the simple ones were the strongest. He liked the feel of that knot, its roundness and honesty. Then he tied another one, a brother, right next to it and pulled it tight. And another and another. Yes, this is what he would do today. The blue hour, the sun skimming the horizon, the second blue hour, once all had passed into darkness again, and he would tie knots until the whole long strip was shortened and strengthened. He looked up through the smoke hole and saw nothing but darkness, not a star nor moon nor sweep of aurora borealis. Instead, a plush blanket of cloud muffled the brilliance above it.

And he was below. They all were, the whole island, perhaps the whole world. Maybe his grandfather was above it, beating his huge round drum held close to his chest. Maybe he was sending out his last joik in that voice that sounded as if it were wrapped in reindeer velvet. Maybe he was gone. And maybe Mokci's last chance to follow him, to take on the robe of the noadi had just slipped into the darkness of this night never to be gained again.

Mokci called out to his grandfather as he tied more knots, each one tucked tightly into the last. And what for? His voice followed a memory of his grandfather's voice in a chant that must be the last unless it was the first. It traced the circumference of the lavvu and then spun out in ever broadening circles, until it must have grown too thin, too attenuated by its reach, and faltered, sounding like no more than a leaf landing on moss, a fingerling sinking into the sand, lips closing over a whisper. And so, he tied more knots.

An inner voice asked him, "And what will you do when all the knots are tied?"

And his outer voice answered, "I will untie them."

"Will that answer your questions?"

"What questions?"

"The ones you are hiding from?"

"Maybe. If not, I will tie them again."

And so the long night passed into the darkness of another day as Mokci sat by his fire tying and untying his chain of knots, waiting for a reason to stop.

"Is Rikka still asleep, Onkle?"

Dankert was hard pressed to answer his little passenger. The distance between his parents' house and his own seemed to have stretched out ten-fold with the awkward weight of Agnes on his back. This was harder than skiing with a pack of provisions during his stint in the army. Those provisions tended to stay in one place and didn't constantly tickle his neck with tiny kisses. Moreover, he was no longer in the good shape of his army days when he patrolled around Trondheim on skis.

"We will see, little one. We will see," he panted.

"If she's awake, can she go skiing with us, Danky?"

"Please don't call me that," he snapped. Then he caught himself. "We will see. First, I just need to get this gear off and get inside. We will see."

"I think she will be awake and if she isn't, I'm going to call out to her and wake her up like Mama used to, 'Henrikka, you get yourself up right now and give me a hand!'" She shouted as they reached the door and her onkle crouched down to unburden himself of the wiggling load he carried.

As Dankert unburdened himself, he glanced at the heap of old clothes lying in the snow bank next to the door. Was this a new method of doing the laundry, just letting it lie in the snow? Using snowflakes instead of lye soap? Or maybe these were rags meant to be thrown out. He shrugged and opened the door. "Come along, Agnes. Let's see how Rikka's doing. Quiet now, we don't want to awaken her."

"Yes I do, Onkle Danky. Yes, let's wake her up."

"No, darling. See, she's lying there just as she was when we left. That means she still needs to sleep, so let's whisper. I wonder where the others are. Someone should be watching her."

"Maybe they had to pee. They're old, you know, and old people have to pee a lot."

Dankert thought he heard a snort, but when he looked at Agnes, she was stone-faced and looking around as if to find something.

"What was that noise, Onkle?"

"You heard it too, did you?" He scanned the room. "Maybe it was the water pipes letting off steam." He heard the noise again, this time louder. It worried him. He thought he had the problem worked out. There had been no one else on the island to consult about his plans to devise such a system. Now, if the whole system blew apart, the naysayers would raise a glass to his arrogance and stupidity. Skøl!

Dankert scanned the room then traced the circumference where the pipes ran. Where he could, he had run the pipes behind the plaster walls. Had that been a good idea? It would have been easier to trace a problem if he could actually see steam or bubbling hot water inside the room proper. "Agnes, go upstairs and see if you can find Pernille."

"Why, Onkle?"

"I want to see where the problem is and I want you to be safe."

"I want to stay next to Rikka."

"You can do that later. Hurry now."

"I'll be quiet and safe. I'll climb on the table and lie quietly."

"No, you'll go upstairs now!"

Dankert wanted to yank her by the collar and shout at her, but he caught himself. Calm down. Calm down. It never works to push the girl.

"All right then, Agnes. I'll lift you up and you can lie still."

He wasn't hearing the noise anymore. Perhaps it had worked itself out, although he knew few problems did that. He would keep up his examination and hope for the best. He hoisted Agnes onto the table and adjusted the blankets so she could lie curled like a seahorse against her big sister and Dankert continued his examination of the room's circumference.

Agnes squirmed around trying to move ever closer to Rikka, hoping to steal some of her big sister's warmth. She tugged at the bedsheet that she was lying on. What was it doing there? The sheet wasn't helping Rikka or her and it dragged to the floor below her. She peeked over the edge of the bed and tried to pull the sheet up. It wouldn't come, and there was that funny noise again. It sounded a lot like her grandfather's pig when she pulled its tail. The harder she tugged the louder the noise. Maybe it was two pigs. But did pigs hiss as well as snort? She hadn't heard that ever. Sitting up now with her legs hanging over the edge, she was better able to get a good hold on the sheet and yank with all her might.

"Pssst, psst, Agnes, let go." That was no pig. Pulling herself around onto her belly, Agnes lifted the sheet and saw two old creatures, naked as wrinkled babies. They were huddled together on the floor, their knees pulled up to their chests. Agnes giggled, "What are you doing down there?"

"Hush Agnes. Please, Dankert can't see us this way."

"I can."

"Well, it may be alright if you do, but not Dankert."

Agnes broke into giggles again, loud ones. Dagur and Urd were the strangest sight she had ever seen, all knobby and wrinkled, all curled up trying to hide themselves. She jumped down from Rikka's bed and slipped into their cave, crawled between Dagur and Urd all the better to examine their skin, so loose and bumpy and soft like when she stroked a frog. It was a very pleasant feeling. Looking dead serious she promised not to make any noise, a promise she would gladly have kept if her two old friends didn't look so funny, so oddly folded and scrunched up. Their dark little world under the baking table, under Rikka's bed, was a place under the sea, a dark cave of sea anemones and nåden.

"Agnes, can you do us a favor? It's difficult, but I think you might manage it."

Agnes nodded. She knew she could do anything they wanted.

"Can you get past your onkle and fetch our clothes from outside?"

Agnes nodded. That would be easy.

"Can you do that without him seeing it?"

"He already saw it, but he didn't know it was your clothes. I did. Mama says that men don't notice. Is that what she meant?"

"I'm sure it is."

"Well, I can get the clothes and he might see me pick them up, but he won't notice what they are." She asked why they wanted the clothes, which Urd thought an odd question but she had already noticed that Agnes was an odd child. She warned her, "Don't let your onkle see you bring them in here. He mustn't know."

"Of course not. Mama calls it woman's business, not for the eyes of men." Urd found it hard not to laugh aloud. The child didn't miss a thing. She slid out from between her two old friends and across the floor without making a sound, keeping low. Urd, peeking out from behind the curtain, saw that Dankert was on hands and knees partially hidden by the kakelovn. Good, that would help.

Agnes sorted through the pile, took out the oldest pair of underpants, and stuffed them back into the snow for safe keeping. Then she gathered and shook out all the other items and squished them together into an ungainly ball. Using her elbow, she pressed down the latch on the kitchen door, peered into the room, and seeing her onkle's rear end sticking out from behind the kakelovn, she breezed into the kitchen.

Dankert looked back over his shoulder. "What have you got there, Agnes?"

"The laundry."

"What are you going to do with it."

"It's clean now. I'll put it all away."

"Do you know where everything goes?"

"Of course, Onkle, don't worry. I'll take care of everything."

"I'll bet you will," he answered and turned back to his work.

Agnes scuttled across the room humming her favourite tune, "Sula meg lit." Without a moment's hesitation she tossed the pile of clothing under Rikka's table.

Then Agnes climbed up onto Rikka's bed and stroked her sister's beautiful face with its long narrow nose and dimpled chin. Placing a finger at each corner of Rikka's mouth, she pulled her lips upward into a smile. It didn't look right, didn't look happy, more like a troll's grin meant to fool you into trusting. Agnes let go of her sister's lips, letting them fall back into sleep. She was so still, so deeply asleep, Agnes realized that she might never awaken. The thought made her cry, but she cried in complete silence, and then she pinched her sister and pinched her again harder, making pink marks on her face. That pleased Agnes. Her sister didn't look so dead then, so she pinched her face more, all over, leaving those marks on her cheeks, her forehead, her chin. She pinched her ear and then hissed into it, "Wake up. I hate you." But Rikka slept.

Dankert watched what was going on. "Agnes, stop. You're hurting her."

"She can't feel it. She's dead.

He ran over to the table and put his ear to Rikka's heart. "No, Agnes, she is the same."

"I don't want her to be the same. I want her to wake up. I want night to end. When will the night end?"

Dankert looked around trying to find something, anything that would give Agnes hope, but there was nothing. Defeated, he whispered, "It's always night."

Rikka floated just under the roll of the waves. The water was warm, friendly. It whispered in her ears. A mouth to share the catch with. Wind in the water, in her ears. A small laughter. The sound of rope sliding through hands. Oar slapping the waves. A child humming. Something under her, rats gnawing on bones, baby bones, the hardanger fiddle squealing, blown away by the wind.

Her mother calling her. Her mother calling her through the green light. The sea, the sky, the green light humming, muffled by the clouds. The swish of skis. A whisper circling her bed. Wake up. Wake up. No. Sleep. Sliding. Slicing. A chunk of grey rock rips free from the face of the Thorn. It crushes moss, tips and tumbles down, down, until it breaks the crest of a wave and sinks, sending up sighs of bubbles bursting on the surface.

There was nothing. There was nothing, then there was pain, some creature crawling on her face, pinching it, then the pain. But that was all right. She hadn't felt pain, hadn't felt anything for she didn't know how long. She felt herself rising, very slowly rising, from some deep place. Underwater maybe. Had she been lying on the floor of the sea? Could she do that and still be alive? Not alive? But she couldn't breathe in water.

It didn't taste like water. No salt. But it sounded like water filling her ears, tapping on her eardrums, a soft rhythm, like inhaling, holding, exhaling. Her face, small pains. Did she still have a body or had it floated away? She pulled her memory down over her neck and lower. Shoulders, breasts, arms like long strips of seaweed, fringes on the ends dancing in the tide. Sea anemone. Her filaments waving in the water, reaching out for something to sting. She would like that. She would relish the taste of stinging anything that touched her. She felt nothing but the water weaving around her waving filaments. No body, just a stalk clinging to a stone on the sea's floor. Her whole life, a dark place in a black sea.

Just the sound of water passing through. And a voice with a sting more painful than her own.

The voices came from the front room, angry and aggrieved. Herr and Fru Lorkman had arrived and they were not at all pleased by being put out like this on a Sunday morning, or any time for that matter. The fru was shrill in expressing her anger; the herr kept stomping his feet to rid himself of the snow on his boots.

"Couldn't you at least clean off the front steps so a person could enter without this load on his boots!" Poor Pernille, the one unlucky enough to be in the vicinity, tried to welcome and apologize for their discomfort while also trying to calm little Ragna down. The baby screamed the moment the Lorkmans entered. She was digging her tiny fingers into Pernille's collar bone as if trying to scale a mountain.

"Where is everyone?" Lorkman demanded. "Where's my son?"

"He's here. I'll find him. May I take your coats?"

"Well, somebody had better."

"Please, make yourselves comfortable. He might be in his workshop, or perhaps … never mind. I'll find him."

"A cup of coffee," her mother-in-law demanded.

"Yes, I'll get Urd to see to that." She wondered if she should put their minds to rest about Agnes. They must be horribly worried about the child's whereabouts. No wonder they were so crabby.

As she rushed out of the front room, she noticed that her in-laws were seated at the dining table, looking far more peeved than worried. "Just look at this table," Fru Lorkman hissed. "At least they have someone doing the cleaning. Where's my help? Am I supposed to do everything myself?"

"Oh, close your mouth and stop whining, woman!"

Pernille rushed to the kitchen. "Where's my husband?" she asked the room in general.

"Behind the kakelovn." Agnes answered. "He's looking for the noise. Or maybe he's hiding."

"Maybe we all should," Pernille whispered and Agnes nodded with an exaggerated cringe on her face.

"Come on out, Dankert. You have some explaining to do, and they are in no mood for games. And where's Urd? We need coffee. And more. Come on, everyone. We have to face the monster."

Urd slid out from under the table and, offering no explanation, slipped over to the counter to make coffee and dig up something to offer by way of honeyed bread. Dankert also came out of hiding looking abashed but determined to face his monsters. Of course, they would be furious about the missing child. It was foolish of him to imagine that they didn't care at all. He sighed and straightened up, heading towards the door to the dining room. Behind him, Dagur who had considered staying under the bread table scooted out hoping no one noticed. "Bring that coffee as soon as possible," Dankert said to Urd. "Pernille, perhaps you should stay in here with Agnes and Ragna. I'd rather they didn't have to listen to their outrage. I'll apologize profusely and come up with some explanation…"

"No, indeed you won't!" hissed Pernille. "It's time you stood up to them. You did nothing wrong. You saved a freezing cold, frightened and lonely child from a barn in the middle of the night. Please, Dankert, do not apologize. They are at fault, and that fault runs deep."

Once again, Dankert looked at his wife as if she were a revelation standing before him. He found the grace to smile and thank her, before heading out of the room to face his parents.

"Yes," he whispered and held out his hand as if he would take her with him for support. She touched his face instead. "Do it, husband. It's time."

Dankert entered the dining room with a newfound sense of determination. He could feel the change in his posture. His shoulders felt broad, held back instead of caving forward. His chin led the way. He nodded at his parents but gave no welcome.

"Dankert, where is she?"

"Where is who?"

"That young woman, Henrikka is her name? She hasn't shown up for work in four days. A lazy slut just like her mother," his father claimed.

"You never should have hired her. I told you so, and now look at the house! How can I be expected to keep things up? You know how frail I am."

Dankert hadn't imagined they were looking for Rikka, but then he remembered that she had started working for them when Johanna was no longer welcome or capable. The thought of Rikka in their house made him shudder. Why had he ever allowed that? Why had he not realized that it was up to him to quash that idea? And why had he never taken the responsibility to get Johanna out of there? And then he realized, it was not because he didn't know what harm was being done to her. It was because he couldn't admit that harm was being done. Dankert felt something inside himself wither. He had not had the fortitude to stand up to his parents, not even to the snivelling of his mother. He had tried to compensate for their cruelty by offering kind efforts, efforts that never added up to any significant help. His efforts had been feeble. Shame washed over him. Was that to be his epitaph? A feeble man making feeble efforts?

"You're here because you want Rikka to clean your house? You want Rikka to do your bidding? You're furious because she hasn't polished the silver this week? She hasn't washed your bed sheets or peeled your potatoes? What is wrong with you? Never mind. I know. You are both soulless. You came all this way to complain about the poor service you're getting from Rikka who is lying in the other room on the edge of death? And what about Agnes? Agnes who you sent out to the barn to sleep in the hay. It's winter and you sent her out there to freeze to death. A small child. And you have said nothing about that. Where do you think she is now? Lying in the straw, curled up next to Bestemor? Sipping hot chocolate or maybe dancing with the elves? Did you even check on her? What is wrong with you? Are you so full of hatred and selfishness that you have no care? You have no heart, not even half of one between the two of you?"

The door to the kitchen opened and Urd, with a look of stubborn righteousness, entered with coffee and sweet bread that she slammed down on the table.

"Thank you Urd. Please take that back into the kitchen and share it with the others. These two will be leaving now." Urd smiled and curtsied in a way he had never seen her do before.

"Thank you, sir, we will all enjoy it, especially Agnes."

"You're welcome, Urd. Please see to it that she is not disturbed by hearing the discussion in this room."

"I will gladly see to that. We will sing a song together."

Lorkman stood with his hands behind his back and his chest puffed up. "You will not talk to me that way. You will not tell me what I can do or what I am. No son of mine will ever talk down to me."

"You're right. I don't think I'll have a need to talk to you at all in the future."

"That will be a future with no inheritance from my estate."

"That is as it should be, Father. I have already inherited far too much from you. It's time that I learn to be a man in my own right. I need nothing from you."

"And nothing is what you'll get."

Fru Lorkman looked from father to son, stunned by the quiet but impervious wall of hatred that had just arisen between them.

"But," she said.

"But nothing. He is not my son. He is not your son. He does not exist." And pulling on the coat he had just shed, he walked out the door, forgetting to take his wife with him.

"How could you?" she asked. "How could you deny us?"

"It is done. Go home."

"Then you can keep Agnes and see what that's like."

"I will. I certainly will," Dankert said. He would keep her and so would Pernille until such time as Johanna could take her back. Or forever.

Silence reigned in the kitchen, silence and stillness. Everyone who had two functioning ears on her head stood in tableau surrounding the bread table. The concentration was intense. There was a common sense that everything in their lives had just changed, and for the most part, the change was profound, and it was good. They joined hands. Smiles lifted faces.

Agnes bit her lip, unable to hold in her happiness. She was the first one to move, the energy in her bursting out so that she had to laugh and skip around the room touching everyone in it. Urd looked at Dagur and they joined the laughter. Pernille, her head spinning with what all this meant, a house filled with life, the corners, the rooms, all holding people and their stories and their love and their arguments. A family.

Urd shook her head thinking of all the work that faced her, and all the helping hands and all the chaos. She laughed.

Dagur took Ragna from Pernille who looked exhausted. She laughed in the babe's face all wrinkled and smeared with drool. And Ragna laughed with Dagur, sensing the change in the house.

At the kitchen door, Dankert stood stock still, his mouth open, his eyes darting around the room.

"Come on, Dankert," Dagur whispered. "They are all waiting to see you. You have a family now. It just opened up before our eyes and ears. Come on, you wonderful man. Lead your family." He listened to the laughter and commotion in the kitchen and was almost afraid to join it. What had he done? Would Pernille kill him, run away from all the noise, the laughter, the fights that were certain to ensue? Well, he had done this thing, and now they would see. Now they would see what life might look like.

When he stepped right into the room everything stopped. He noticed that Pernille was biting her bottom lip. What did that mean? Agnes was staring holes through him and had her fists clenched at her sides. Only Rikka's body, inert as ever, seemed relaxed.

And then Urd looked around at this paralyzed crew and called out, "So who's going to help me make a meal, a big, big meal?" And all that tension exploded in the air as everyone found a way to pull together a feast.

Dankert called out, "We'll use the big oak table in the dining room. Finally, there will be enough people, enough family, to fill all the seats."

Urd began giving orders. The space was filled with energy and commotion. Someone had to take charge. "Dankert, build up the fire. Please. Pernille, you can be in charge of the stew. There are plenty of root vegetables and a shoulder of lamb in the larder. Dagur, try to make some working space on that counter. Agnes, do you know how to make sweet cakes? Good then, let's do it. We'll be squeezed together since we don't have the bread table available, or does someone want to carry Rikka to the guest bedroom?" A unanimous NO answered her question. Rikka belonged in the centre of whatever they were doing. "All right, then. If Rikka were to wake up, I'd tell her to go get the whale fat from the bucket and make something delicious with it." Those who knew the story of Rikka and the whale fat laughed along with Urd.

The kitchen was noisy and crowded. Pernille looked around shaking her head. Yes, she thought, I could live with this.

Johanna drew open the curtain over the window by the day bed. She was trading warmth for light. Then she stood in the doorway, waving to Otten. When he saw her, she opened her arm out to her side and then curved it back in to her heart. Otten's heavy steps lightened.

"Velkommen," she called out.

"Takk," he answered. "No rorbu," he said, but Johanna looked puzzled. "Ingenting." He pointed to her stove.

Some words were similar in both languages.

"Um, book, shirt, penger," he said tugging at his own shirt, but he stopped when he saw the look of terror on her face. He pantomimed picking up the aforementioned items, taking them over to the stove, opening the door and throwing the lot of them inside. He slammed the door and threw his hands up in the air. But then he remembered, they ate fisk for dinner every night, every single night, so he tried "fisk man!"

"Fiskere?"

"Ja, ja, fiskere," and then he repeated his pantomime. "They threw us out. They threw our belongings into the fire. We have nothing!"

Johanna didn't have to understand every word. Her schoolgirl English, never very strong, had faded into the fog of her mind, but she knew what had happened. Those fiskere, mostly from different islands in Lofoten, some from as far away as Portugal, had used that rotten old rorbu season after season. They relied on it as their retreat from storms, from delays in the fishery, from icy hard work on the open waters of winter. The shopkeeper should never have rented it out to these missionaries, but a krone is a krone and shopkeepers live on such.

Johanna was caught between pity and outrage for her new friends, and a understanding of the needs of the fishermen.

Neither were in the wrong, although the fishermen had probably been brutal and the Mormons were just ignorant. She thought about going to the shopkeeper and confronting him, demanding that he at least refund their money so that they could find another place. She thought about it, and she knew it would do no good. He didn't need her meager business. She had no standing in the community, just a reputation for madness and whoring. He wasn't responsible for the actions of the fishermen. Let those meddlers from the "new world" deal with their own problems. In fact, let them get off this island and leave the God-fearing Lutherans to their own ways. And she, Johanna, was in no position to tell him -- the supplier of all the goods on the island-- what he ought to do. No, it as was useless as shouting at the sun to make it light up the sky.

Was there someone on the island they could board with for free? Not likely. Should they return to America? Had they the means to do so? Johanna marvelled at the clarity that came to her after weeks, maybe months of dull confusion, but that clarity led her to no solution.

If I offered to let them stay here, we would all be driven off the nearest cliff! That was not something that could be done: a single woman with three foreign men in her little house. Even though her daughters were not around ... and here Johanna shook her head violently because she had not given thought to her daughters, her three precious daughters. She had no idea where they were, alive or dead or being mistreated or having forgotten their mothers' existence.

Where were they? My dear God, she thought, what am I thinking? Why am I concerning myself with these foreigners? Where are my daughters. Johanna wanted to run over to Dagur's house. She would have the answers to her questions. Maybe the girls were all visiting Dagur. Maybe they were fine and happy and growing taller. She couldn't even remember when she last saw any of them. Was it yesterday, last Christmas, did they ever exist or were they dream creatures? Were they huldras enticing her, enticing men, enticing dreams with which to sink her into the sea?

Maybe Ragna was running in circles now on her bandy little legs. Maybe Agnes was in school. Maybe Rikka was a mother herself.

She inhaled deeply to ward off the thoughts. She knew her mind wasn't steady, that it was clouded by a thick mist that swept away her good sense. She sat down on the daybed inhaled deeply again and again until a thread of clarity unwound in her mind. Follow the thread. Don't question it. Just follow it through the mist. Her feet slid across the floor, never lifting but keeping contact with the surface of something solid. She found herself at the door once again, opened it and followed the thread step by careful step from one illuminated patch of snow to the next until she reached Dagur's workshop. She called into the darkness, "Dagur, are you there?" No response. Then to the house where she knocked at the door. No one. She opened the door. Again, no one. Just cold air, dead cold, not so much as the scurry of a mouse inside. No one had been there all day, all week, even more.

"Dagur, please, where are you?" Somewhere in the darkness, did Dagur lay dead, her old body crumpled in a corner like so much packing tissue, weightless, dry? She felt her way through the dark in the little rorbu, so much like her own except with bits and pieces of nests and shells and sea-smoothed glass that cluttered all the flat surfaces. She couldn't really see them, but she knew they were there, even though Dagur was not.

In the centre of the room, Johanna's head hit something, and the delicate pieces tinkled lightly, brushed her face and twirled in the wake of her steps. She remembered; it was a mobile of bird skeletons, tiny, fragile and sweet. They were Dagur's pets, each one sweeping the air in its flight around the centre of the room.

Johanna laughed. This was so like Dagur. She loved the

creatures, collected their fragile bones, strung them together in sometimes beautiful, sometimes bizarre replicas of living birds or birds of her eccentric imagination. If she couldn't save a suffering creature, she could at least create for it a new life in a form that could only sprout from her old woman's brain.

But where was Dagur? Johanna inhaled deeply. No latent cooking smells hung in the air. She had not been home for some time. Had it been spring or summer, Johanna would have assumed she was out gathering one life form or another: shellfish, mulder, mushrooms or bark. But not in the dark, not in the icy winds. There was no help for Johanna, no suggestions, no solutions. She felt her way to the little table and sat down. Rubbing her hands lightly over the surface, she found Dagur's teacup. She lifted it, cold. She swirled it and smelled it, camomile. Relaxing. Dagur always made it for her: "Drink this, dear, it will help you relax," and then she would stroke the back of Johanna's hand so she couldn't pick up the cup, and they would both laugh. Johanna touched the surface of the tea with her tongue. A film had gathered there. How long did it take a film like that to develop? Certainly more than a day. A week? Maybe longer? She had no way of knowing.

What day of the week was it and for that matter what month? A horrible sense of aloneness lay over her. This condition of hers, this state of being, it separated her not only from those she loved and those she despised but also from herself. She was two people, the one sitting here trying to sort things out and the one who left this plane of existence to do God only knows what. And where was God in all of this? She remembered feeling God. When was that? His hands had hovered just above her head and she could feel little tingles of excitement, of things being right, of her self wanting to fly. That was so good, she was so happy.

Dagur looked at her gnarled hands. The veins stood high above the bones as if trying to break out of their cage of mottled skin. She pulled on the red mittens with an eight-pointed white star knit into each. There now, that was a more comforting sight even though the wool scratched her abused hands. She had not taken sufficient care of the mitts, dropped them in the boot corner every time she came inside, and every time she promised she would pick them up and dry them between two pieces of muslin. That always did the trick, but she always failed to take that extra step, even here at Pernille and Dankert's house where she should show respect for the shipshape orderliness of her hosts' space.

"Where are you going?" Agnes asked. She was using her teeth to scrape the sticky bread dough off her hands.

Dagur was reluctant to answer her. The child had not mentioned her mother in days. Had she given up on her? Dagur didn't really think that possible. Agnes was surrounded by love and busyness in this house. Maybe she had been starved for happiness and baking and laughing. Maybe standing around Rikka's makeshift bed in the center of all that activity was a hundred times better than the loneliness of her grandparents' house where coldness and criticism must have been served up as a main dish every day. Dagur didn't allow her mind to linger there. No one would want to live day and night in that house. Think of Johanna. No, don't. The guilt welled up in Dagur. She had done nothing about the treatment Johanna endured there, and she figured that she didn't know the half of it.

"I'm going back to my house to pick up things I need for Rikka."

"Why, is she sicker?"

"No, Agnes, she's getting better." She looked at the wide-eyed expression on the child's face and added, "Maybe not completely better, but… hopeful. Here, let me show you something. She pulled a chair over beside the baking table and waved Agnes over to stand on it. Agnes climbed up and stroked her sister's face, kissed her on the cheek. Dagur took the roll of paper from a shelf and held it to Rikka's chest. "Here, put your ear to the other end and listen. Agnes picked up the roll and put it to her ear. "Now, put the other end back on Rikka's chest. There, right where her heart lies under her ribs."

Agnes complied with wonderment in her eyes. "Like this?"

"Yes, like that. Now listen, be very still and listen. Then tell me what you hear."

Agnes's attention was total. When Dagur took a step forward, Agnes put her finger to her lips and shushed her friend.

"What do you hear?"

"Du dupe … du dupe … du dupe … du…"

"Yes," Dagur interrupted. What do you think you're hearing?"

"Her insides. I'm hearing inside her."

"What part of her are you hearing?"

"I know. It's her heart. Yes, I can feel my heart make that sound sometimes, but I can't hear it. I can hear her heart!" She listened some more and then asked, "Is that what's wrong with Rikka? Is her heart wrong?"

"No, I think it's stronger. I listen to it every day. I think she'll wake up soon. Maybe you would like to be her listener while I'm gone. Listen and remember what you hear. Is it louder or softer, faster or slower? Can you do that?"

"You know I can! I will listen to her the whole time, Dagur. I promise. And I'll remember so I can tell you when you get back."

"You won't need to listen the whole time, just every now and then. I know you'll do a good job. Maybe someday you'll be a nurse."

"No, I'll be a doctor. Nurses are good, but I want to fix her."

Dagur smiled, nodded. Indeed, she thought, a doctor. Well, I'll be sure she becomes a doctor who knows about all that's secreted away in our flowers and bark and in our hearts. She looked into Agnes's clear blue eyes and the child said, "I'll write down what I hear. I'll put the time of day or night, too. Then you'll know."

"You're a wonderful help, Agnes." Dagur held back a chuckle; surely the child didn't already know her letters. She looked forward to seeing those notes.

After she left the house, Dagur carried that smile along on her walk home. It was good to get out into the quiet, to put one foot in front of another however slowly. It was wonderful having all the people she cared for together in the house, all except Johanna. And what of her? Could room be made for her too? There were enough rooms, enough beds, even enough food. But was there room for all that emotion? How would it be for Pernille who she knew had always been jealous of Johanna, aware of her feelings for Dankert, and worse yet, his for her. It was a fine skein of twisted emotions they wove between them all. Dagur's foot broke through a sheet of ice that she hadn't noticed, too deep in her thoughts of the miseries love brings. The wet cold seeped in through the seams of her old boots. They were beyond repair and she'd have to gather the materials to make a new pair before next winter. Oh hell, maybe she'd be gone before then.

Dagur looked to the horizon where the violet sky was pulling up rays of orange light from the low sun. Clearly it was growing stronger, skimming the horizon for a bit longer. Soon it would master the darkness altogether. Then spirits would rise with the sun each day. There would be new buds on winter's naked branches. Surely all the miseries that plagued them would thaw and dissolve in the sea. Rikka would awaken. Dagur was as sure of this as of the lightening of the sky. But they were not there yet, and she was not yet finished with slogging along her path, one foot reasonably warm and the other as cold as a corpse. She stomped the cold foot against the ground and some of the water gushed out from the broken seam. She stomped again and she thought of the chant Pernille told her had propelled her forward in her journey to get the mushrooms for Rikka. Chaga, chaga, chaga. Dagur tried the chant on to see if it would work for her. The result was a chaga, slush, chaga, slush. As she rounded a deep curve in her path, Dagur spotted a favourite resting place, the large flat rock that served as a bench for lovers, dreamers, and the weary alike. She saw a figure sitting there; which of those was he? The dark form in the purple sky sat motionless, head down. A rosy light was growing out of the gloom. It seemed to emit trails of orange and gold that took hold around whoever sat on the bench.

She approached slowly. The slight tremor between his shoulders proved he was not made of wood or stone. Dagur sat down leaving a careful distance between them. When he didn't respond she greeted him. "God morgen, Mokci."

He did not respond but lifted his head and nodded.

"Are you here to witness the lightening?" He shook his head.

"Do you mind if I sit with you for awhile? I can be silent if you like." They both sat in silence as the orange and golden streaks tugged at the purple blanket of sky along the horizon until the light appeared to shred the dark, bundle it up and carry it away. She watched his profile out of the corner of her eye as it lightened in the skimming sun. He was a beautiful man, almost ethereal in stillness. She turned her head directly towards him. "Mokci, I haven't seen you for awhile. I've been away, staying at Dankert's house." He looked over at her, turning his head for the first time.

"Why were you there?"

"Rikka is sick. We took her there to look after her."

Mokci sat up straight and looked into Dagur's eyes. "What's wrong with her? Is she all right now?"

"I think she's getting better. She has not been conscious for five days now, but I see improvement. I'm sorry, we didn't think to find you and tell you. We've been so focused on her, but that was thoughtless of me. Of course you needed to know. I didn't even tell Johanna, but that was because I was afraid of how it would affect her. That too was a mistake, I think."

"Who has been caring for her? Is there a doctor on this island?"

"Urd and I have used our knowledge, and little Agnes has been by her side all the time. Pernille and Dankert do everything they can. I have given her healing balms and listened to her heart regularly. She is not worse, but she is still deeply asleep."

"I must see her. Help her. Will Dankert allow me?"

"I think so, Mokci, he respects you. I respect you. Maybe you are exactly who she needs right now."

"We must go," he said standing up.

"First I need to gather supplies from my workshop and find something for my foot."

"What's wrong with it?"

"My boot burst open and my foot is freezing in the slush."

Mokci's attention shifted directly onto Dagur. "Here," he said. "This is for you then." He held out a beautiful pair of boots. She took them and admired the skins they were made from, the upturned toes and the colourful ribbons that reflected the sunrise.

"What?"

"They are Rikka's, the ones she made."

"She doesn't make boots. These are Sami boots. They're beautiful."

"Thank you. I helped her."

"You taught her?"

"Yes."

"Why hasn't she worn them?"

"I'll explain later. Now we put them on you." He leaned down and pulled off the sodden boot her foot was trapped in."

Dagur protested. "No, no, I can't put my ugly old foot in those. They're for Rikka. Just give me back my miserable boot. I'd rather go barefoot than ruin these."

"I'm sorry, Dagur, but you must wear them. When Rikka wakes up she will want you to have them. She will want to do something for you."

"But why?"

"I think you know why. Come on now," he said holding out his hand to receive her old foot, gnarled as the root of a wind torn aspen. He pulled a piece of soft reindeer hide from his pouch and rubbed her foot dry. Tears clouded Dagur's icy blue eyes. She couldn't remember a time when she had been treated with such care and tenderness.

"Thank you, Mokci."

He nodded as he laced up the boot and held his hand out for the other foot. "You must wear both," he said. "Otherwise, one foot will be tripping over the other all the way back to Dankert's house."

Dagur stood up straight, feeling the fit of the boots. They were too long by a big toe's length, but as she worked her foot around, the extra width of her splayed foot took up the slack. "Why did you two to decide to make them?"

"They are for Rikka's climb."

"The Thorn?"

"Yes, you knew about it?"

"I thought it was only a dream. But she has been preparing, designing, sewing, thinking and you have been helping her. Right?"

"Yes. It is a dream but not only a dream … a quest."

"How do you mean?"

"Rikka needs to separate herself. She has to go where those around her have not gone. She needs to see far away."

"Does she need to kill herself while doing so?"

Mokci took a moment to answer. He understood the worry on the old woman's face.

"No. I will help her, step by step," he promised.

"You will go with her?"

"No, she will not have me."

"But how can she learn on her own? It's too dangerous!" Dagur stopped in her tracks, caught at Mokci's sleeve and turned him around. "Look at it!" she demanded. They both stood facing the dim outline of the dark form that thrust up out of the sea rising to an impossibly sharp peak.

Fear and anger shook her voice. "Step by step, you say. How are you going to teach her step by step if you aren't with her? I know, you probably spent your whole childhood chasing up cliffs to save reindeer from plummeting to their death. You've made her these boots thinking they will carry her safely to the heights she is determined to reach. Now listen to me, Mokci, she can't do it. Look at that peak, Mokci. No one could stand up there. Imagine her there, balancing on a pinpoint in the wind with no foothold. Please stop encouraging her."

"You will have to trust me, Dagur. I will help her climb. I will not let her fall. Trust me."

"Then we will have to go now."

"Ja, vi gå."

"You are a good man, Mokci. You are just what Rikka needs right now."

They began the trip back to Dankert's house. Crisscrossed with rivulets of run-off, the path was breaking way for springtime. Mokci walked a steady patient pace while Dagur tried to hide the fact that she veered and stumbled while never quite falling. Her eyes were focused on the beautiful boots that didn't belong on her feet but would take her back to the girl lying on the bread table surrounded by love.

The conversation between Mokci and Dagur dwindled as the path twisted and bent back on itself to maneuver around outcroppings of granite and to avoid time worn runnels that carried away the melted snow. Sure-footed Mokci took his time but never let Dagur think it was to accommodate her awkwardness in the new boots.

Dagur was quite aware that she had become a stumbling old crone. Where the path diverged to meet Dankert's stone path, the walking became easier as it was carefully laid with large flat rocks exposed once again to the air. It had taken Dankert well over a year to find, transport and lay those slabs that created a passable entrance to his home. Dagur sighed as her tortured feet made contact with that solid and stable surface.

"Ah, home again," she said. Mokci looked at her in bewilderment.

As they neared, the door flew open and Urd ran down the pathway to throw her arms around Dagur. "Oh, you're back, you old fool."

"So what did you expect?"

"I expected you to be quicker about it. And look at you. Where did you get those boots? And who's this leading you through the muck?"

"Urd, this is Mokci, our friend ... Rikka's friend. He has come to see her."

Urd looked him up and down, squinted her eyes and scowled at him. "Well then, he had better go in and see her."

The kitchen was warm. Steam rose from a kettle. Agnes sat on the edge of the kakelovn's base drawing on a length of brown parchment, her back to the door. Pernille was lying out shards of tile in shades of blue, grey and black, placing them one way and then another. Mokci scanned the room and settled on a form lying on the long table in the centre.

Urd stood still watching the silence, the focused intent of everyone present. It was a room permeated by attention to details, a room silent except for the hiss of the kettle.

Then Mokci stepped forward. He stood over Rikka watching her inhale, watching her exhale, watching her. He matched his breath to hers. The old women backed away from the table but never took their eyes off the two. The only sound in the room was the sibilance of tile fragments sliding across a concrete surface as if to find their spots in the sea of fragments.

Mokci walked to the other end of the table, folded back the soft blanket that covered her feet, and slid his hands under her heels. He held them both as if comparing their weight then pulled off the woolen stockings that covered them and began to stroke first the tops of her feet and then the bottoms. He inhaled in long pulls, held his breath, then slowly exhaled as he caressed her feet. The old women watched, slightly embarrassed to be witnessing these actions, so intimate, so alluring.

Dagur let loose a sneeze that shook the room. "I'm sorry. Forgive me. I'm so sorry," she begged, shattering the contemplative mood that had blanketed the room. Agnes jumped up and ran over to Mokci who smiled and kissed the top of her head. Pernille, who had never met Mokci, dropped a handful of glass shards onto the floor. Her head swung back and forth, trying to catch up on what was going on and where all the people had come from.

Mokci, that must be who the young man was, yes, Rikka's friend Mokci. His clothes were made of skins. His hair was dark, his skin the colour of aspen leaves when they cover the ground just before the snow falls. All three women were silenced by the intimacy of the young man holding the feet of their friend.

Agnes broke the silence. "She's sick, Mokci. She just sleeps and she never moves and never eats. I took care of her when Dagur was away." Mokci picked the child up and hugged her until she cried. She hadn't cried at all before but Mokci's hug released a tempest in her, so he rocked her and kissed her cheek and whispered things to her until she suppressed her fears.

She said, "Look at this, Mokci." She squirmed out of his embrace, ran over to the kakelovn, and picked up the parchment.

"This is for Dagur, really. You can read it too."

Dagur joined the two and stared at the child's depiction of Rikka's heartbeats.

"I see," Mokci said.

"What are they?" Dagur asked.

"They are frogs, see, Dagur?"

"Umm, and when they are jumping high that means...."

"That her heart beat loud."

"All right ... and when they stay on the ground, they are too tired to jump high?"

"Yes, yes, yes! You can read them. I told you I could write."

Mokci frowned and asked, "What about when there are no frogs, Agnes?"

"That means I had to eat dinner."

"How did you listen to her heart?"

"With Dagur's tube."

"May I see it?"

Agnes jumped down from her chair and ran to the herb cupboard, took out the listening tube and handed it to Mokci. He held it in his hand, pondering it and then he put one end to Agnes's heart and the other to his own ear, surprised by how the sound of beating when it was isolated ran straight to his ear. He shook his head and smiled at Dagur. "Where did you get the idea for this?"

She just smiled and nodded as if the source didn't matter one way or another.

Mokci bent over and lay the side of his head on Rikka's breast. Pernille jumped up from her seat on the floor and ran over as if to push him away. A firm hand from Dagur stopped her. No need for the girl to embarrass herself or make so much noise that Mokci couldn't hear the sound travelling through the listening tube. The expression on his face exuded wonderment and also a bit of worry. The frogs at times leapt sporadically.

Mokci looked around the room filled with girls and women. If he walked into a lavvu on most days, he would find the women of the family seated around the fire, drying sedge, making coffee, drawing thin strips of hide between their teeth to make bindings. This was not so different. He smiled at Urd and then at Pernille.

"I have entered your home uninvited and have not greeted you."

Pernille looked down at her legs that stretched out from her seat on the kakelovn's base. She straightened her skirt and nodded, unable to find words. Dagur introduced them and Pernille noticed her boots.

"Where did you find those boots? "

"They're Rikka's, I hope I haven't ruined them forever. Mokci taught Rikka to make them. I never should have worn them."

"Yes, Dagur. Rikka wants you to wear them."

Pernille poked at the sharp-edged fragments of glass next to her. Her hand, none too steady, caught on the keen edge of a clear shard. Blood beaded on her fingertip until it grew too large and dropped onto the crystalline piece she meant to pick up.

Mokci turned again to Rikka. The room had grown silent, everyone aware of the need for absolute quiet as he lowered the listening tube to Rikka's breast. Mokci's eyes were closed, his head held sideways in concentration. He listened. Everyone listened. Agnes held the palms of her hands against the bottom of Rikka's feet. Dagur pressed her finger sidewise against her nostrils suppressing any vagrant sneezes. Pernille stared at the bloodied shard that was turning a reddish brown.

Blades of light sliced the dark water. She heard them slap-slapping against her skin. Herring glittered past, slid over her belly, nibbled her lips. They wrapped her like a silken shawl. A giant cod whispered in her ear. 'You don't belong here. Rise up'. He opened his grinning mouth and sucked in the silver herring. 'Rise up. Your shoal is waiting for you.' He nudged her.

'No, follow me,' called the ninth daughter of Agir, her seaweed hair trailing after. "We'll dive to my father's hall where the music winds through channels and we'll dance with my sisters in our cave beneath the sea. You will have onyx and emeralds from lovers, a crown of glittering phosphorescence. Better that than rise to the surface with the big-mouthed cod and hang from the rack to dry."

And the daughter of Agir dove down and the cod arose with Rikka between his teeth. Catch. Release. The water beaded on her face, released salty tears. She could see through the skim of water that could no longer press her down. She could see him, her love, through the shimmering above and heard her name, 'Rikka, Rikka, I'm here.''

Mokci watched her face, a film of seawater slid over it, obscuring her features. The sound of her breathing was moist. He covered her face with his palms and wiped away the salty water. His fingertips slid down to the pulses in her neck where he held absolutely still, feeling the gentle beat. They did not quite match, the right one slightly stronger. In one long stroke from neck to feet he felt the pulse, the life in her trying to claim her place in the living world. He turned to Agnes standing on a stool next to him. She put her arms around his neck and he lifted her onto Rikka's body, the child's face on her sister's breast, belly on belly, feet on knees.

Dankert came downstairs with the sleeping Ragna in his arms. When he saw his friend Mokci standing over Agnes, over Rikka, he stopped. Silence held the room. He looked down at the sleeping baby, carried her to the table and gently laid her alongside her sisters. He kept one hand on Ragna's chest, felt the peaceful rise and fall of her breath. His attention turned to Rikka's pale face, to Agnes stretched atop her, and then to Mokci who looked as if all this strange tableau were a normal piece of life.

"How is she?" Dankert asked.

Mokci didn't answer, but Dagur moved in closer to Dankert and said, "There's a change. I'm not sure just what it is, but there is a change."

"Worse?"

"No, I don't think so. Just different, maybe like a lightening."

"How do you mean?"

"A rising," Mokci said. "Surfacing."

Dankert didn't ask from where.

Agnes shifted, rubbed her nose back and forth on her sister's chest and murmured something.

"What's that, Agnes?" Dankert asked.

"The bubbles are gone."

"What bubbles?"

"The little ones that are always popping inside her."

Dankert looked at Mokci for some explanation. His friend smiled and nodded.

"All right then," Dankert said, "I guess that means she's getting better. She'll come back, right?"

"Yes," Agnes said. "I can get off her now. Just put Ragna on top of her. That should be enough."

Though he couldn't quite laugh, Mokci smiled and tousled Agnes's tangled hair. Dankert swung her down to the floor. "Go fill out your diary."

"They're charts!" Agnes demanded, but her scowl slid into a smile.

Pernille watched from her seat on the hearth, not knowing what to believe in: her husband's optimism, the old women's mushrooms and roots, Mokci's hands running over Rikka. She snorted. Maybe Agnes's leaping frogs. It all seemed ridiculous. It all excluded her. She had nothing to offer. Sometimes she didn't even feel sympathy for her friend. The perpetual centre of interest lay there in the middle of the room on that same table they had both passed out on after downing the bottle of aquavit. She had thought they were friends then.

Pernille stood up, stretched, put on Dankert's warm boots and went outside. A rising sun shot golden rays along the horizon and illuminated a small fleet of fishing boats headed for home. The fleet was followed by a squawking flock of kittiwakes. She wondered how many of the boats carried a goodly portion of cod, how many only the fraction of their catch allowed by the League. Either way, there would be cod and there would be roe and there would be the herring that escaped the cod. She would bring back fresh fish. Everyone would need to eat, maybe even Rikka. It would taste so good that they'd have to notice her.

Pernille picked up her pace, determined to be first in line at the dock. From the opposite direction she saw the young boys pumping their legs as fast as they could to be first on the dock to claim space at the table.

"Slow down, Halvard, you're going to break your leg. Then you'll be last," said the runner-up.

"You think they'll take you on the boat next year if you've got a gimpy leg?"

"They'll take me, alright. I'll be fourteen before the boats go out, and I'd be faster than you even with a broken leg." Halvard tagged in first at the table. "And even if you could run faster for once in your life, your knife will never be as quick and as sharp as mine." He held his blade up to catch the sun's beam and flashed it in his friend's eyes.

"Ja, maybe, but you sure make a mess with that knife, no matter how sharp it is. They'll be tossing those tongues and cheeks back at you again. You're no champ when it comes to carving. You make everything into mince."

"Well, this is the last year for me. Then you can be Chief of Tongues and Cheeks."

"And you can be puking your green lungs out over the gunnels day after day."

"Not me! My father taught me how to ...."

"Hei," Pernille interrupted.

"Oh!" said Halvard, "Excuse us, Frøken Pernille, I was just trying to teach this youngster here the best way to fillet the cod that are coming in."

"Yes, I overheard your lesson," she laughed. "And I'm not Frøken Pernille anymore. Please call me Fru Lorkman. I'm married." She noticed that young Halvard was tripping over his long tongue as he tried to cover his mistakes. "Don't worry, I'm just here to get the first and finest of the cheeks.

"You're just in time, here come the cod." A line of fishermen slapped down the first of the lot onto the table.

Pernille turned to the younger boy. "Pick out twelve of the biggest ones and take great care to cut those cheeks cleanly, no ragged edges. Can you do that?"

"You had better trust me for the job, Fru. Lars is not as experienced as me."

"And you, Halvard, are not as careful as him. No thank you." She patted his head to underscore the insult. Pernille took a square of brown paper and handed it to Lars to wrap the cheeks in. The boy did a tidy job and kept his head down so his victory would not show on his face. He would tell his younger brother about how he won out over Halvard. Then his pride could light up the room.

Pernille held her packet of fish cheeks close to her chest. First ones of the season. There had been earlier fleets of the island's men, but they had not been allowed to sell their catch to the islanders. The squire would take his full share before a single cod went to the families.

Each step I take will carry me home again. I belong. I'll cook for everyone. Alone, the way I know best. Potatoes in the pantry, still firm. Butter, hopefully Urd hasn't fallen behind on churning. Oh no, old Bestemor has gone dry. Not to worry … salted butter holds. Wish I had dill, fresh dill. Dried will do. Soak it in camomile. My secret. No one's ever found out. Tastes like July. Roots: carrots, beets, parsnips. No parsnips, too sweet. Wish I had a lemon. Wish I had a bucket of lemons. No just one would do. Cut through the sweetness, give it zest … like the red tile … the red tile… red? why not? Blood of the sea. Blood trickling from the throat of the cod where Lars has sliced with his careful knife. Sea urchins with red spines. Careful. Starfish. Yes, red. I'll use it even if I have to soak the tiles in my own blood. But could I use those red spines in my mural? Could I scoop up a bright red urchin? Take it home? Save the spines. Scrape out those five orange nuggets that cleave to the shell and crown the potatoes with them. I ate those once. Delicious, salt of the sea, my friend said. "Try them" and I did. Raw. I almost fell in love then. Almost, but too scared. I'll feed them to my husband, and I'll feed them to Mokci. Then I'll know what no one else knows.

She picked up her pace even while her feet sloshed in the empty space of Dankert's boots. She recalled the chaga chant that had carried her far and fast. It wasn't what she wanted now. Red spines, salty brines, heart climbs… home. Low tide exposed pools filled with rocks, tiny caves where creatures crept and waved a tentacle. With the tip of her boot, she altered their landscape. Salt water spun. So much light now, a generous sun crept up to the sky's knees. It was a blooming sun, one that would light the island for longer today than yesterday, longer yesterday than the day before. A fisher's boat, its bow upturned to push the tide, its sail propelled by a nimbus of light, promised spring, promised new plans, new work, new love. Pernille's hand skimmed the water, stroked the spines of a crimson pin cushion. It let loose its rock, agreed to come with her, no prying needed. She tucked it into her parcel, amazed at how the world applauded her today.

There was her house, her house, in the distance, she hardly recognized it in its glorious cape of gold. She remembered the first time she saw it, another large block of white signifying the owner's wealth. She had despised it for that, where others saw it as a sign of success, of superiority.

She had also grown up in a white house and learned as a girl that one white house always married another white house. Hence, she was now Pernille Lorkman of the matching white houses. She would like to paint it red like the rorbu. Ah, but maybe that was the answer: a large white house dripping red light from its roof down to the sea. That was one benefit of a white house, it could catch the light of the early sun like it had today. And it could become a pallet for the winter lights. She could add the emerald green, the violet and the rose, watch the colours flow from the house, across the snowy fields and into the sea. In her mind the colours of the sea, the Thorn, the moon implied a restricted palette of black, blue, bits of white. Where had that idea come from but from the tiles she had chosen, the ones that felt right in her hand and, therefore, in her mind. Let the sea be the sea in all its blue glory, a hundred shades of blue if she had them, but the sky would be alive with all its colours and she would add her house, hers and Dankert's, would reflect all the colours of the island. She would ask him tonight, in bed, if he could find more of those broken tiles.

A shock of energy ran her spine. there was so much to do, so many tiles to trim, to choose, to compose her picture with. The

thought of how much work lay ahead was daunting but
exhilarating too.

She had already made a good start. The roiling sea with its
white caps and dips, its inky blues and almost turquoise, she now
realized were beautiful and true. But there was so much more
waiting to be painted. It was like a painting, but more than a
painting because it had depth, sharp edges countering sustained
flows of colour.

Pernille looked at the sky and laughed out loud. Maybe she was
the only person in Norway, maybe in the whole world, who used a
tall cylinder of concrete as their canvas, bits of broken tiles as their
paint. But no, no she realized that as often happened, she was
forgetting the rest of the world. She had seen in one of Dankert's
architectural books, a picture of a mosque,

Where was it? In Egypt? No, another one of those countries
filled with fruits she had never tasted... was it Israel? No, maybe
Afghanistan. He said it was the blue mosque. She had stared at it
trying to imagine the different shades of blue based on the
lightness or depths of the grey and black tones of the photograph.

Now she would design her own mosque, her place of
contemplation and revery but using her own colours. they would
be the colours of her island and those of her imagination.

SECTION THREE:

Johanna stepped out the front door, a shawl around her shoulders and mitts to hold the tea in its tin cup. "God morgen. Good morning," she said holding the cup out to Otten. "Te?"

"Takk." Otten thanked her.

"Vaer så god," Johanna curtsied.

"Du look well ... i dag, Johanna. Jeg hope du ar ready for our ... liten ... service," he said with great sweeps of his arms to propel him through her language.

"Yes, I am klar. Who comes?"

"Vi ska see. Maybe the whole island will come. Maybe the priest will come. Du må make big tea." He laughed and then laughed harder when Johanna joined in.

"I make very big tea, chamomile."

"Look there," called Cecil from the other side of the rorbu. "I've just been down that path there," he said pointing. "Someone is coming ... here! Look I knew someone would come. Really, we aren't alone."

Pride and anticipation brought colour to Otten's winter-white face, but as the figure reeled its way closer, he realised that it was the drunk who followed them singing one night, the drunk who came around almost every day now to ask for coffee that they didn't have and wouldn't drink if they did have it. Otten sighed and then shook his head as if to loosen sea water from his ears.

"Let's go inside now." Otten ushered his friends in, hoping a closed door would waylay the weaving steps of the drunk. Johanna took the hint and hurried inside, her elbow brushing against Otten. "Forgive me," she said.

"You need no forgiveness, Johanna."

"Oh yes, I need forgiveness. I now learn what I ... trenge."

"Ja, I also learn," he answered looking as far away from her as he could manage. Trenge, he would have to learn what that meant.

Otten had been spending more time studying his Norwegian ordbok than the Bible or the Book of Mormon. If he were to sway the hearts and souls of these islanders, convince them to leave their poor life on this island and come to Idaho, he needed to express himself in their language.

The little room was warm and clean. A lovely rose afghan laid over the day bed and Brother Rose had cut sturdy chunks of driftwood to make stools for their guests. He had even dried seaweed and plaited a seat cover for each of them, seven in all.

"The stools are wonderful, Rose," Cecil said. "You amaze me with your talents. Where did you learn to make those seat covers?"

"My grandmother. She took care of me when my parents were busy with other work, you know, sewing, harvesting, yard work. She would sit for hours piecing together long narrow strips of fabric that used to be dresses, tablecloths, work pants, whatever. Then she would braid them and spiral them into rugs. She taught me how to braid. I'm sure it was frustrating for her. I was no genius. She said I had ten thumbs but they, too, should be put to good use. Never idle. I'd stare at my hands and imagine what they'd look like if they really had ten thumbs. It terrified me, so I made sure to prove her wrong. If I can do nothing else on God's good earth, I can at least braid. Oh, and I can thread a needle, any needle with any thread," he laughed.

"I sew," Hanna said. "Henrikka sews. She sews pants and boots."

Rose smiled and nodded, wondering what Johanna really meant, surely not pants and boots. He reached out and clasped her hand and smiled.

Otten slapped his hand away from her. "That is inappropriate, Brother!"

Johanna pretended not to take notice of what just happened. Instead, she walked over to the stove and checked the kettle. Was it too early to make the tea? Should she sweep the floor once again?

What she really wanted to do was go into the sleeping room and hide from what was becoming all too clear. She enjoyed having these three men around. They brought laughter into her empty shell of a home. They called each other brother and they now called her sister. They helped her forget who really belonged there. But she hadn't forgotten. Johanna lay down on the bed and pulled the comforter over her head.

Here was warmth and here was silence, and where was family? What of her girls? Where had they all gone? One by one they had been taken from her. Except Henrikka. No one took her, she just left, maybe with Mokci. Good for her. She could make her own decisions and he was a wonderful man, even if he was Saami. There was no evil in him, just love. Lorkman had taken the little ones. She couldn't let her mind dwell there. They were lost to her, may as well have died as go to him. Better dead than … she couldn't even think about what would happen to them in his hands. A huge knot was growing in her gut. It stretched and pushed outward on her belly like a Nokkan breaking through the wall of her womb. Intense pain overwhelmed the misery of her loss. She would burst soon, and all that evil would drain onto the floor. It would flood the room and ooze into the kitchen where the poor missionaries in all their innocence would drown in the mire.

There it was again. Johanna shivered convulsively. She had allowed herself to fall into the maelstrom once again. She knew how to avoid the fall. It was simply an act of will and when she could grasp her will, shake it, demand it to hold her above the spiraling cone, then she could face her life.

A thin voice as gentle as a baby's kiss filtered through the wall from the kitchen. Singing. One voice. A man's voice singing the words of a hymn her father used to sing. A lullaby for baby Jesus. Johanna hadn't heard it since it passed her father's lips, but his voice was gruff as a walrus's. This voice was so sweet that it made her cry. She stood up, put her ear against the door and was drawn back into the kitchen where a small knot of people had collected. The singer had his back to her, but she recognized him by the wild hair and his poor coat. It was the drunk, his body swaying ever so slightly as he sang yet another verse of the hymn. Silent tears ran down the faces of the listeners. Her tears were less silent, but they felt like love let loose.

Although he understood only bits of the lullaby's lyrics, Otten, too, was held in the beauty of the song. This man in rags, smelling of vomit, had just brought love into the room. "Thank you, Brother. Thank you for reminding us all that God would have us gather together as a family, and the baby Jesus is at the centre of that family. I would welcome all of you," he said sweeping his arms around to enclose the few who attended, "to join us in a prayer for this, our family in Norway."

The few looked at him wondering just what he was saying. But they bowed their heads for the incomprehensible prayer.

"Brothers and Sisters, we are a family and God is our father." He looked around the room. His congregation looked back at him, all four of them not counting Cecil and Rose. "We are Latter Day Saints. We believe that God the father, his son Jesus Christ and the Holy Ghost will guide us and guide our families into Heaven." Otten saw incomprehension on the faces of his congregation. Off to the side, Johanna leaned forward with parted lips as if to better understand his words.

His flock sat silent, one leaning forward in anticipation, another staring out the little window behind Otten, a third blinking her eyes to keep herself awake. Otten stretched out his arms once again to encompass them all, but the gesture failed and his arms fell, his hands clasped together and he lowered his head in silent prayer. Johanna bowed her head along with the others. A seagull screeched. A dove landed on the windowsill and, looking in at the strange tableau, tapped on the window. The door opened letting in the scent of spring and Dagur. She scanned the congregation.

"Am I welcome to enter?" she asked in English.

"Yes, yes. Please do." Otten rushed across the room and took her by the arm. "I didn't know you spoke English! Can you help me?"

"Yes, I can, but do I want to? What are you trying to say to these poor souls?"

"I want to tell them that I can lead them to eternal life."

"Oh, the priest has already promised them that."

"Yes, but he's wrong. He's taken the wrong path."

"Of course, I know that much. But I don't know that you have a better path."

"You are a fine woman, Dagur...."

"That I know too, but don't try to flatter me."

"I want to tell them about the Mormon way of life. I want them to know that they can choose a better life, that we will help them attain it."

"I can translate for you, and I will tell them these are your promises, not my own. But first you should offer them all coffee. They are about to fall asleep."

"Not coffee. Latter Day Saints do not drink coffee."

"That's silly!"

"No caffeine. It's not wholesome. The acid eats away at the body."

"It's your sermon that's deadly. Look at them."

"I'll give them chamomile tea after I tell them what awaits them in Idaho."

"You're a silly man, but your intentions are good, I know. I will translate for you, but I will first tell them that these are your ideas, not mine."

"That's fine. I don't hide my beliefs."

"All right. But they will be very disappointed about the coffee. It's probably what they came for in the first place."

"They came because God sent them!"

Dagur chuckled. "Let us start before the sun drops into the sea again. And I need something to sit on. I am not meant to stand before a whole congregation. Maybe you should sit down too so you don't look so much like the captain of a ship."

Otten did as he was told. He began, "I want you to close your eyes and imagine the golden fields of Idaho and Utah, the waving vistas of grass, as gold as your sea is blue."

Dagur interrupted. "Vistas? What are vistas? Keep your speech plain, man. I haven't studied at university!"

He nodded and took a deep breath. "The wheat is our sea, with its own tides and sumptuous waves."

Dagur shook her head. "Sumptuous? What does that mean? Can you just say beautiful or crashing maybe?"

This was harder than Otten had imagined. "The wheat is our sea, and it feeds us just as we take care of it, plowing and threshing..."

"Threshing," Dagur asked. "Is that English?"

Otten pulled himself up from his stump, and grabbing the imaginary handles of his imaginary plow, he pushed the soil around the tight space of the room, wiped his brow and setting the plow down he took up the handle of his hoe and began planting. Then he stood back, hand shielding his eyes and watched the wheat grow tall. His audience leaned forward in their seats.

Now he needed his scythe which he swung mightily around the edges of the room much to his congregation's delight. Encouraged, Otten held out one hand to Dagur and the other hand to the woman from down the path as if inviting them to dance. But the pantomime took them in another direction. Unfolding his invisible blanket, he handed two corners to Dagur and the opposite corners to the neighbour and showed them how to toss the grains of wheat in the air over and over. Those still seated cast their eyes up to heaven and down to their boots as if they could follow each grain on its ascent and descent. The drunk sneezed and rubbed his nose: the chaff clearly irritated his sinuses.

The small congregation stood up and clapped. They smiled at each other and even laughed aloud. This was, perhaps, a church they could believe in.

Only Dagur remained serious. She had witnessed something in the threshing dance that spoke to her. She pictured that golden field, grass reaching up to a cloudless blue sky. Grass so tall you could drown in it. She was a girl with a piece of wheaten bread thick with slabs of warm butter. Surely there would be butter. She would sit in that field, big as the ocean but warm and gold as butter. The wheat grew so tall and thick she couldn't breathe, couldn't find her way back. She turned, forced the stalks of wheat aside only to find more wheat and more and more and no fish and no sea. She heard the scythes coming, swinging blindly through the fields. They didn't see her hidden there, until after.

Dagur shook the vision from her mind. Everyone in the room was laughing. She wasn't. There was something disturbing here. Norwegians were drinking chamomile tea. They were shaking hands with the Brothers. What sort of church was this? Approaching Otten, she tugged at his sleeve. "I won't translate for you anymore," she told him.

"I cannot blame you," he responded shaking his head. "I don't think my actions here would be approved by the diocese. I may have made a terrible mistake. Should I tell them so, Dagur?"

"I don't know. I do not understand your religion. Maybe you should tell me what it really is, not this dance party, I'm sure. They will expect more of the same, you understand."

"Yes, I do. I will have to pray for guidance tonight."

"Who will listen?

"God. I hope. Or maybe the angel Moroni?

"I don't know that angel."

"Oh, he's American, I think."

"Ah, not an angel for Norwegians, just for Americans. I guess he doesn't help out Chinamen or Africans."

"Don't try to confuse me, Dagur. And that's not true. He sent Brother Cecil, Brother Rose and me to Norway, didn't he?"

"If you say so. I wasn't around when he talked to you."

"He did not talk to me. Please Dagur, I'm befuddled"

"Befuddled? Is that your angel name?"

"Stop it, please. I'm just trying to figure out how to complete my mission."

"Well, there should be one of the big ships coming close to shore soon. They'll be loaded with cod, but there should be room for you if you're serious about escaping. And that's a pretty fine solution, don't you think?"

"I never know if you're teasing or helping or just being obstreperous."

"There you go again. Just when I think you really are trying to talk to me you spit out a word like that to prove how superior you are."

"But…"

"But think on this: We are talking to each other only because I know three languages and you only know American."

"Three, really? Three? O God, I am unworthy."

"Yes, you are. We all are. But let's try to understand each other."

"Takk, Dagur. Tusen takk."

"Vaersågod, Brother. "

"Now, Dagur, may I get your advice?"

"On?"

"On how I can better reach the souls of my congregation?"

Dagur smiled at his use of the word congregation but decided she had tormented him enough for one day. Maybe it was time to help. "Actually, Brother, I think you had the right idea today. These folk were looking for something to lighten their lives, and you gave it to them."

"Surely not! You said yourself they only came for the coffee."

"Surely yes. Did you notice how happy they were, even without coffee, even with that wretched yellow stuff you offered up? They were happy and they were listening."

"Listening to me make a fool of myself!"

"No, listening to your story of Idaho and a new way of life. They aren't stupid. They know they were being invited into something better."

"Really? "

"Yes. Do more of the same. Add a few words of Norwegian any time you can so they'll know you respect them. You can tell your stories by acting them out, and then you can draw them into the action and into the stories. Think about what you most want them to know and then follow your instincts."

"Hmm. It would be easier if I could just give them translations of The Book of Mormon."

"Lord in Heaven, no. Then you would lose them all. They would keel over from boredom. Why do you think none of them go to the Rose Church? You had a good idea when you used your body to tell them a story, and as you learn more Norwegian, you'll be ready to add some fine points. Have fun with them."

"I like your idea, Dagur, but what would the church think of my methods? It just isn't the way we do things."

"You mean it just hasn't been done that way. Be courageous."

Brother Otten straightened his spine. "I will go ask the Lord. Thank you Dagur."

Dagur pulled her fisherman's cap down over her brow and opened the door.

Johanna followed her old friend outside but stopped to take in the new smell of the world. All those cod that had swarmed through the waters surrounding every island in the archipelago had laid their many many eggs, been caught in nets and dragged to their death. The smell of them wafted through the air creating arabesques of odor. She loved the tang of them, salty and sharp and clean. Soon they would be slit and gutted and tied by their tails to the tall racks, hundreds upon hundreds of them. Each day the tang of them would intensify and morph into an odor that only a fisherman could love. Every stinking, dehydrating carcass meant a family would eat, would be able to buy what foods they couldn't grow themselves, like sugar, like coffee. Johanna smelled the air and then returned to her rorbu to make herself a cup of precious coffee. The missionaries would just have to suffer the aroma of temptation.

Brother Cecil had kept the fire burning in the stove. He rolled one of the stumps close to the heat and placed an extra mat on it for Johanna. When he saw her take the small can of coffee from the cupboard, he took it from her hands and used her rolling pin to grind the beans to a fine powder.

Meanwhile Johanna set water to boil. "Would you like to try a small cup of coffee?" she asked Cecil with a sly grin.

"No takk, Johanna, I will enjoy the smell only."

She tsked, tsked her tongue and wagged her finger at him. Their communication of gestures and bits of two languages was developing into an art. They all called it Norglish and didn't worry too much about precision or confusion. Good will promoted understanding.

With her coffee in hand, she thought about those fields of wheat Brother Otten spoke of. What must they smell like? Was it like the sea grass when the tide was out? But no, there was no tide, just field upon field of gold. Was corn sweet or bitter, and what did it smell like if you left it too long? He said it was a yellow spear of a fruit with a thousand kernels for a sheath. He said they smear it with butter and the butter drips down your chin. They must be very wealthy to treat butter like that.

She tried to visualize those fields. He said they were like the sea, but if the sea ran yellow it would surely mean the end of all times. And if their fields ran blue, would they mould in the hot sun? She would like to paint a picture of those fields. What if she painted a field of wheat and a field of corn, which he said grew as tall as a man, and then let the tides of the blue Norwegian Sea rush in to slap the verge of those fields? I would like to paint this picture in my head, she thought. I would like to see these two worlds meet to make a new place where I could be at home. I would like a warm home with a big kitchen for Henrikka and Agnes and Ragna. He could play his fiddle and make us all laugh. Just think of it: golden wheat, the fiddle to dance to, my children, all of them around me. Then I could be a real mother again.

These men, they call themselves missionaries. I don't think we have a word for that, for men who travel far in the world to bring a new religion to people. That caused mountains of agony when the followers of Jesus tried to do the same thing. Why do men want to change the beliefs of other men? Why not just love what you believe to be true and leave the others alone? But, maybe they do have some final truth and maybe that truth can make me happy again. Would my children be happy in a new land, a yellow land? Ragna wouldn't know the difference. Agnes would be so interested in things that were unknown to her that she'd be happy exploring the fields, especially the corn fields. But Rikka … what of her? She would have to leave Mokci. Or would he come too?

The wind pushed the wings of her shawl in one direction, then the other. She shadowed her eyes with her hand and looked into the deep blue sky where a kittiwake hovered in one spot, its wings spread wide and canted at just the right angle to freeze it in time. How could it do that with all the forces of wind and change, just hang there as all passed by in a tumultuous flurry to move on? It would be so much easier to give in to the forces and soar. She would like to paint that bird too, but how to paint its impossible stillness when any viewer would think it was in flight? And why would it work so hard? Why refuse to move ahead?

Johanna looked back at her home. She could see Cecil and Rose through the little window facing the sea. They were laughing, full of joy and the desire to lead others to a new life. She wondered, Could I? Could I leave this land, its profound blackness speckled by a million stars in winter? The endless gold and blue of summer when the sun refuses to set? Could anywhere else be as beautiful as this? Perhaps not, but perhaps it could be more welcoming, and it would be new and just maybe she would be new again.

"Cecil, Rose," she called. "It's time to find my daughters."

The brothers pulled on their coats and hurried down the path. "I know where they are. My daughters. Will you come with me?"

"Of course!"

"Which way?"

She pointed.

Rose elbowed Cecil and said, "Let's sing "The Morning Breaks" as we hurry along.

"Yes, ja, yes, yes, it's perfect."

They followed singing one of their incomprehensible hymns.

Angels from heav'n and truth have met
and both have record borne;
Thus Zion's light is bursting forth;
Thus Zion's light is bursting forth
To bring her ransomed children home.

The brothers grinned at their friend. "Did you like it? It's called 'The Morning Breaks'."

The title made no more sense to Johanna than most of the lyrics. "I understand light and children and home." Tears filled her eyes

"Yes, Johanna. It's about bringing the children home. That's why we chose it. Now let's go do that!"

Cecil, the one facing east, was the only one not to celebrate. "Look. Who is that? He's driving that horse at a hard gallop."

Johanna knew. All her joy drained. "It's Lorkman. He goes to my rorbu.

The three looked at the madman and Rose said, "He'll find Brother Otten there..."

"Sitting at the table"

"Drinking chamomile tea."

"In my rorbu!"

"Hurry," Cecil pulled his friends down the verge to the sea. They ran to the Sentinels, their feet sloshing through the rising tide. Inside the brothers opened their coats and pulled Johanna into the cover of a woolen tent, a tent within the frame of the Sentinels. They kept their heads down, their black hats tilted and covering Johanna's geldpale brown hair. "Shouldn't we go and..."

"No," Johanna commanded.

"Will he hurt Otten?"

"No, he will shout, he will threaten, and then he will tell the priest that there is a man, a heathen, living in my house."

"In sin," Rose answered with horror and held Johanna more firmly.

"Yes," she whispered. "That will happen."

"And we will be expelled."

"Spat upon."

"Our mission destroyed."

Under the flickering light of her candles, Dagur stroked the birch box her husband made for their last anniversary together. She ran her hand over the high surfaces and let her fingers dwell in the valleys below. Somehow it still smelled of birch and she wondered if it was just the memory of a smell that brought his presence back in such a rush. He was a rough man, one who had no use for what he saw as her flights into realms where his mind couldn't follow. He couldn't see what was clear before her eyes. He scoffed at her collection of bones and her meticulous care of them. Yet it was he who spent hidden hours carving this box for her, carving a network of intricately woven bones into the dense wood. He had examined those bones as closely as she had.

She poked at the bones, picking up one and imagining what function it could fill for the creature pushing to be born from her mind. Initially her creatures had tried to replicate nature. Of late, she had begun to tamper with nature's plan. A bird's skull with its eye socket holes could become a basket carried by a knock-kneed urchin. Why not have one of those swinging from the ceiling with all its avian friends.

"Now, where's that jar of beeswax? Ah, right where I put it." She dipped a finger into the jar and pulled out a pebble of stiff wax which she rolled between her thumb and middle finger until it softened and released its rich scent. Each of the selected bones was treated with the wax which made it glow and appear to be alive and vital. She lay them on the table and arranged them with utmost care. It was essential to hold her breath as she looked for the perfect alignment of bones. Once she had that figured out the difficult part would begin. Her precious silk thread was hiding from her. "How do things get so out of hand," she wondered. "Oh yes, there it is by the windowsill. You haven't totally lost your wits as yet, Dagur."

But something drew her eyes and ears away from the search for thread. A wild noise filled the darkening air: horse's hooves, a whip slicing the silence, the manic outrage of a man. Lorkman. It could only be Lorkman. Not at her rorbu but at Johanna's. 'Oh God, who's inside,' she whispered. It hardly mattered. Whoever was inside was about to become the victim of his fury.

Lorkman had leaped from the carriage before the horse had fully stopped. The tail of his long coat caught on the frame and ripped the silk lining. He yanked on the coat tail, cursing the horse for its stupidity. Then his attention turned back to the door which he banged on with his crop. "Open up! Open up! Now." He heard a scraping, perhaps a chair. "Hurry up. I'm coming in." This time he beat at the door until his crop snapped and just as he was ready to thrust his full weight against the door, it opened.

"Please," said a very large man, holding out his hand. When he saw that it was not going to be shaken, he used it to gesture the angry man in. "Would you like to take a seat?"

"Where is Johanna and what are you doing in her house? And you can speak English to me instead of mashing my language."

"Please, sir," answered Otten. "Come sit by the fire and I will tell you anything you need to know."

"What I need to know? Oh no, you will tell me everything I demand to know. And I don't sit on stumps."

"Then here is a chair. Excuse me for not understanding. This will be more comfortable on your aching bones. A man of your age deserves comfort," Otten's voice was as gentle and understanding as Lorkman's was brash. "May I get you a cup of chamomile tea?"

"You may shut your mouth and answer my questions."

Otten cocked his head to one side and raised an eyebrow. Perhaps it was best to let the man vent his rage. Instead Lorkman sat down on the chair and Otten sat on a stump. The man seemed to approve of the arrangement. "Where is Johanna?"

"She has gone to collect her daughters."

"Where are they?"

"At Dankert and Pernille's home."

"Why are you here in her house?"

"Because she has been sick and disturbed and had no one to care for her. And we had lost our lodgings."

"We?"

"Yes, my brothers and I."

"And you are the Mormon missionaries, I suppose."

"Yes."

"And you thought it fitting," Lorkman sneered, "to move into a house with a single woman, one of loose morals and mental incompetence?"

Otten was horrified. "No, no, that is not the Johanna that we know. She is gentle and kind. She shares the little she has with us and with others who have even less."

"Yes, I'm sure she shares … many things," Lorkman sneered. "The whole island knows of her sharing."

"I can't listen to you slandering her. She does not deserve it."

"And you do not deserve to be on our island, seducing our women and trying to seduce our souls. I will see to it that you and your brothers, as you call them, are removed from our island, our archipelago, our nation, very very soon." He stood up, brushed off the back of his coat as if he had been sitting on a dirty floor, and opened the door. There stood the old hag. "Out of my way!" Otten demanded. Dagur stood in her place, arms folded over her chest.

"I'll be sending you away with the rest of the trash," Lorkman hissed at her.

"No, you're the one the island will spit out into the sea. I know your secrets, Lorkman. Others know them too, but I'm the one who is not afraid to call them out in church. And when I do, the whole community will pile on what they know, and the priest will have to stand behind his congregation, not behind you and your money."

"You know nothing about me."

"You look less than certain about that," Dagur said offering him a sweet if somewhat sardonic smile. "Good day, sir. Best to go home and get your coat mended. The lining has been dragging through the mud."

Lorkman tried to rip the ruined lining off but only managed to tangle his foot in it. Fortunately, he had a riding crop in hand and a horse he could beat all the ride home. Dagur waved him a friendly good-bye, clapped Otten on the back and said, "Tea? It's already brewed."

"Ah yes, it seems that many things are brewing," Dagur chortled.

"Please, take the chair," Otten offered.

Dagur sniffed at it and shook her head. "No thank you. There's a lingering smell of nasty about it."

"Then take this cushion and choose your favourite stump," Otten laughed. "I wish I had a grandmother like you."

"And now you do." She patted him on the back and fluffed the pillow before she sat down. "We have some planning to do. The storms of spring are on their way and I think they'll be raging this year."

"Skøl."

"Skøl."

"Skøl"
"Skøl"
The word chased itself around the big dining table in Dankert and Pernille's house. The celebrants were seated on curved benches that followed the oval lines of Dankert's oak table. Master, mistress, friends and servants all raised a toast to the new day. Little Agnes helped Urd and Dagur bring out the whole mølje. Agnes carried her favourite treat, breaded cod tongues that the old women allowed her to fry in a deep bath of butter. She loved the sound they made as the crispy pieces sizzled in the pan. There were even cod cheeks supplied by the village boys who worked on the docks.

Mokci poked at the kamsemager. He recognized it as the stomach of a cod but had never eaten it with liver stuffed inside. He eyed the steaming bowl of potatoes and hoped they'd reach him soon to neutralize the liver flavour.

Rikka, sitting shoulder to shoulder next to him laughed at his discomfort. "It's all right," she said patting his arm. "The flavour is only half as bad as the texture. Here, try some of this." She scooped some curls of butter-fried cod skin onto his plate. Now, that was something he could appreciate. "This butter is from a cow?" She nodded.

"It's not like our butter," he said," but it tastes similar, very good," he smiled.

"I remember the butter you put in my coffee. That was from reindeer. Delicious, just enough different to be surprising. We don't put butter in coffee. But I loved it." Rikka bit her lip. Was that too much? Loved it? She focused on her plate. She could feel Mokci looking at her bowed head. What was he thinking? What was she thinking?

"Rikka, when you were sleeping so long, I just wanted to hear your voice again. I am glad to hear it today. I want to hear it every day."

Rikka's eyes remained rivetted on the boiled potatoes. She poked at them with her fork; the right words tumbled through her mind, all of them sounding wrong, insufficient, or terrifying. She lifted a piece of potato to her mouth but couldn't open her lips. So tired. Maybe she could go back to sleep. It was too soon to be here, awake and expected to say something. "I want my mother," she mumbled.

"What? I can not hear you."

"My mother. Where is she? She's been gone a long time."

"She is at home, Rikka."

"Why isn't she here?"

"She has been sick."

"Who takes care of her?"

"The Mormon men have been staying with her."

"Staying in her rorbu?"

"Yes, I think so. I have not seen her for awhile."

"Are they good to her?"

"Yes, I am sure they are. They are kind and helpful."

"But they're in trouble. The missionaries and my mother. They are in trouble, aren't they?"

"Why?"

"Because they are Mormons. Because they are men and she is a woman. Because they can't live together like that."

"I understand, Rikka. That is not the way of things here. But it is working for them. And nothing else was. Maybe it is right."

"Not for the church! Not for the island."

"Would you like me to go and talk to them?"

Rikka finally looked up at him. She stared at his beautiful eyes, so full of compassion, and she laughed. The sound of her laughter was jarring. It had the sharp edges of a clam's shell. The room went silent.

Then the laughter stopped. "No Mokci. You cannot go there. Please. You don't understand. You are wonderful and kind, but you just don't understand." She looked at his sad eyes and added, "No more than the missionaries do." Rikka stood up, a little wobbly on her legs, and walked out of the silent room.

Mokci stood to follow her, but Dagur stopped him. "Leave her, Mokci. She has been away for so long. She needs time to herself."

"I would only comfort her."

"You would think you were comforting her, but her comfort is in silence now."

Mokci looked at Dagur, almost resenting her but knowing she was right. He sat down again and stared at his plate of mølje. He wanted to feed Rikka. He wanted to hold her. But Dagur was right. He would only suffocate her and she needed to breathe deeply and alone.

The glasses went on clinking, the noise level had risen four-fold, and the sopranos were outdoing the altos, as usual at such a feast. Ragna, bouncing in Dankert's lap, was blowing spit bubbles of joy and clapping her hands. Urd knew the melody the others sang but she belted out her lyrics in Finnish. Agnes ran in and began orchestrating the song of the moment which inspired Mokci to drum out a powerful rhythm on the tabletop. And empty bottles of aquavit jiggled as if they were nonce again being shipped across the equator and back. Dankert handed off Ragna and pulled Mokci away from the table partly to confabulate and partly to protect his masterpiece from the drumsticks.

"Come on, Mokci. Let's go out to my workshop. I have something to show you."

Mokci scanned the happy gathering. Being a part of this feast was the closest he'd come to feeling at home. These happy people could just as easily have been seated around the central fire in a family lavvu, legs thrust straight out in front of them, soles warming at the fire and the stew pot being passed around. But he pulled on his boots and followed Dankert willingly enough. Halfway to the workshop he saw Rikka and Pernille walking in a straighter line than that of Dankert and himself.

The workshop loomed in the late afternoon light. This was a long structure, big enough to house timber and tools, and space to build skis, perhaps benches and certainly a family dining table. He noticed that at the far end sawdust gave way to an office area. Immaculately clean, it housed bookshelves, a desk with a green shaded oil lamp, elaborate sketches of projects past and present rolled into tubes or hanging from the walls like fine art. Some were even framed and hung with precision. He stood. He stared. He wondered what he was doing there in that wondrous space.

"Come over here, Mokci. I've got something I want you to see." Dankert grabbed hold of two corners of a large tarpaulin and whisked it aside like a magician. The boat. There was the rowboat that Mokci had been filching for the last few months. After he first took it to

look for trails or at least handholds on the Thorn, he worried about getting caught and being accused of theft. They would probably throw him off the island. But when that hadn't happened, he decided that no one cared about the old thing with its loose gunnels and splayed bow. In time it had become his own, at least until the local fishermen returned to the island and the cod found their way home. And all along, it had been Dankert's boat and he never left the island during the winter.

"He must know," Mokci had said to his boot laces. "He knows and now he will torture me with what he knows me to be. A thief."

"I'm sorry, Dankert. I thought it was abandoned, hoped it belonged to no one."

"That was pretty much the case, Mokci. I was tired of the old relic. Didn't seem worthwhile to drag it all the way home, so I just ignored it. I should be thrashed for leaving it on the shore where some drunk might take it out on an icy night and end up with the bottom feeders of the sea. But it was you who took it out, you who made a few critical repairs. I saw you working on it. It took awhile to realize it was you, but the lights were flowing in the night sky and I recognized you, emerald green though you were."

"You forgive me?"

"You should forgive me for not telling you that you could have it. Fix it up. I imagined you and Rikka rowing out to the Thorn together."

"I would only do that once it was safe!"

"I know. I brought it up here for some final touches. Thought you might like to paint it. It's yours."

"You would allow me to take Rikka out in it?"

"When she's strong enough."

Mokci shook his head.

"What's wrong, Mokci?"

"I can not believe you would let me take your daughter out in any boat, even a seaworthy one."

"Daughter?"

"Yes, Rikka, your daughter. She has told me your secret."

Dankert bit his lip. There it was, all the lies and half truths and deflections. Now Mokci was involved in the mess. "I am not her father."

"She told me you were. She said you would not admit it, maybe you did not want to be held responsible for her. I do not understand these things. I do not think Rikka understands either."

"No, how could she? I don't understand how that whispered lie became some sort of truth in the eyes of the islanders. But somehow I let her believe it while never admitting to it."

"Why?" Mokci's eyes showed his confusion and disbelief. Nothing like this would ever happen in his siida. It would be an abomination. Hide a child's parentage from her? No.

"Because the truth," Dankert murmured, "would be worse."

"I do not understand."

"Of course not, Mokci. Neither do I really, but I remember sitting in the Rose Church. I was maybe about twelve years old. The priest was giving a fiery sermon, one that stuck with me though I hardly understood it. That thundering voice of his drove it into my thick skull. I guess I remember it because he seemed to look straight at my father, or perhaps it was me he looked at and said, "The sins of the fathers will be visited upon their sons to the third and fourth generation."

Mokci looked at Dankert in confusion. This language was outside his reach. Or maybe the meaning was unfathomable. He couldn't even ask a question.

Dankert saw his utter confusion and tried to put in simple language something he had never expressed before. "My father is evil. His actions will send him to Hell if there really is such a place. But I must also carry the burden of his sins. That's what our Bible says, and I know it to be true. My only choice is to try to do right, and sometimes I don't know how. There doesn't seem to be a right way, only many, many wrong ways."

All the words, all the meaning seemed to be sucked out of the space they stood in. Mokci slowly reached out his hand and touched Dankert's arm. "What is this thing, Dankert?

It must be a very dark sin to live on in all those sons."

He thought about what his people passed on through the generations. Their skills, their tools, their reputations. Did they also pass on the evil in their hearts? His grandfather had tried to pass his strength as a noadi to Mokci. Had he managed to do so, or would all his powers and knowledge die with him? Would his generation be the one to reject the old ways? He didn't know, but he did know one thing: "Dankert, you are a good man. Your father has not changed that. If he is bad, you have made up for it with your goodness."

"A good man doesn't allow an evil man to persist in his sins," Dankert whispered.

"A good man can always be better," Mokci suggested.

"I'll try making that my motto." Dankert chuckled. "In the meantime, consider this workshop your own space. Look over here. I have this old sofa back here. There's a pillow and blanket. Do you think you could sleep on that? And there's a little coal stove to heat up your coffee or whatever. That way you can work on the boat and not have to make your way back to your lavvu all the time. And you're always welcome in the house."

"Why are you doing this for me?" Mokci asked.

"Two reasons," Dankert said looking down at his boots. "There are a lot of females around here. Had you noticed?"

Mokci chuckled.

"I could use some male companionship," Dankert admitted. "But beside that, I think Rikka should stay with us while she is so fragile, and you are the closest thing to a cure that I can imagine."

"All right. Thank you, Dankert. We will try it out for awhile. I would like to work on the boat. And I think you know that I want to be with Rikka more than anything."

"Good. That's settled. And maybe I can show you my plans for a really fine boat. You might have ideas for it."

"Saami boats are very different from your cod boats. I would like to share ideas. I would like to work with you."

Dankert went over to his desk and took a flask from the bottom drawer. "Here's to our new venture. Aquavit?"

"Skøl," Mokci laughed.

"God help us!" Dankert added as he poured.

When Dankert managed to weave his way over to the house, he found Pernille and Rikka sitting on the concrete base of the kakelugn. They were both moving pieces of tile and glass around the base. He leaned against the wall and watched their total absorption as their hands danced over the fragments. "What are you two up to?" he asked, concentrating on not slurring his words.

Pernille didn't even look up. "You're drunk, husband."

"That is the truth. And why are you not drunk, wife? You had tossed down a bucket of

aquavit when I last saw you."

"That was a very small bucket you saw. Now let us concentrate while you go sleep it off. It's hard enough to find the pieces I need without your generous help."

"What are you looking for?"

"The right shade of blue to define the edge of night over the sea."

Dankert frowned. "Shade of blue ... at the edge of night?" he stammered. "Why, I think there are more blue tiles in that old tobacco tin out in the workshop. I'd offer to get it for you, but I just might fall asleep on the way over there."

"I think, husband, that you are making things up."

"Well, I think, wife, that you should trust me."

"Usually I do, but I know where drunkenness leads, and it isn't the path to good sense."

Agnes followed Rikka outside She made just enough noise to let Rikka know she was approaching, but not enough to pull her away from her thoughts. Draping Pernille's coat over Rikka's shoulders she sat down on the edge of the boulder and tried to see what her sister saw out there.

"I was deep down when I first saw my father." Rikka's voice seemed to rise out of a dense mist. "His scales glittered in the dark and he was huge. His long lips curved downwards and when he spoke, his teeth gleamed with phosphorescence. He said he was glad I had come. He had been waiting to take me to the cave. I would love it there, he said. It was emerald green and full of pleasant dreams. I didn't know if I should believe him. The daughter of Aegir had tried to lead me down and I had known not to follow, but now I didn't know because this was my father, or so he said. But I knew that Dankert was my real father even though he wouldn't own me. I never knew why. Now it didn't matter. He wouldn't have me, so maybe I should follow this cod."

Agnes tipped her head to the side, baffled.

"Rikka, we don't know our father, do we? We know we are sisters and so is little Ragna. and Johanna is our mother. She tries to love us. Can we go back inside now?" She reached for Rikka's hand and held on tight, just as tight as she could.

Rikka stood up and squeezed Agnes's hand. She looked at her little sister as if she hadn't seen her for years. "How blue your eyes are, Agnes. Dark blue."

"So are yours, Rikka. Don't you know we're the same?"

Rikka and Agnes sat together, tipping in towards one another. Pernille came out and saw them. She felt a wave of jealousy. Sisterhood, something she had never had though she had come close to it with Rikka. Was that feeling still there or had Rikka left it behind in the depths she inhabited through all those days of unconsciousness? Pernille could hear the faint buzzing of their conversation but not the words. She was on the outside. Maybe all she needed was to reach out.

"Hei, may I join you?"

"Hei Pernille," little Agnes called out. "Come sit with us." She scrunched her skinny body even closer to Rikka to make room.

"Hello Pernille," called Rikka. "Please join us. We're talking about what we want."

"Surely you're not hungry again already!"

"Definitely not. I mean what we want from life. Agnes says you have to know that if you ever want to amount to anything."

Agnes nodded, "That's what Dagur taught me. And I think Dagur is right, always. Even when she's cranky."

Pernille laughed and asked, "Is this a masquerade party? Do we all have to wear someone else's coat to be part of it? No, never mind, I see what we're doing. We're all seeing what it's like to live in someone else's skin. Right?"

"Maybe so. Maybe that's a good idea," Rikka said. I'm wearing your coat to see how it feels to be married to a wonderful man and live in a big comfortable house."

"I'm wearing Urd's coat to see what it's like to live on fermented whale fat. Yuck!"

"And I'm wearing Dankert's to try to imagine carrying so much responsibility. You know, I don't want all that responsibility. I just want to create. I want to be an artist. I want to be a mother, but I don't think I can, and that saddens me. I can't make a baby, but I can build something of beauty. Tell me more about what you want, Rikka. I don't believe it's just about wealth or a husband."

"No, You're right, Pernille. I want to make my own decisions."

"About what?"

"About everything. I want to make pants for women. I want to pray to whatever idea of God pleases me or none at all. I want to climb the Thorn. I want to go north with Mokci. I want to love

277

Mokci and be loved. I want to never see Lorkman again. I want to travel to strange lands that terrify me. I want enough coal to keep warm. I want my mother to be well and Ragna to grow strong."

"Hmmm. Doesn't sound like much," Pernille chuckled.

"Sounds like a lot to me!" Agnes said, eyes wide and incredulous. "I just want to be a scientist, probably a doctor."

Pernille and Rikka looked at one another and came to an instant decision. "Then we are agreed. Pernille and I will see to it that you become a doctor or a scientist, but I hope a doctor, one whose charts are full of leaping frogs."

Agnes's face lit up. "And Dagur and Mokci will be my teachers. And you'll be my patients. Thank you so much. I'm going to run back to the house now and see if anyone needs my help. Maybe Ragna."

Pernille and Rikka sat in silence. Rikka scratched at some calcified algae on the boulder. "What has happened to our friendship, Pernille? We get close, we support one another, we get nasty drunk together, and then we part. Why is that? Don't we need each other?"

"Yes. We need each other, and we forget we need each other."

"Let's make a pact … to be there even when we would rather go our own ways."

"Even when I'm jealous of what you have…

"…and I'm jealous of who you have."

"All right. Let's see if they've brought out the aquavit yet."

"Lord help us."

Rikka stood up. "I'll go look for those tiles, Pernille. It's worth a good search. We haven't had any luck here. By now I know what you're looking for. And my legs could use a stretch."

"True. Sometimes my husband has a good idea or two," she smiled. "And I can tell by the way you've been scrooching around that your skinny bum must be killing you here."

The night was dark and a shower of glistening stars catapulted through the sky. She could barely discern the outline of the workshop across the field. Her body had become accustomed to lying flat for almost a fortnight, and now it took a bit of concentration to move one foot in front of another, for the second time in one day but it felt wonderful. There was a sense of floating, almost like being under the sea again but with the flickering lights of the sky above her and the fresh coldness of the soil beneath.

The workshop door was a heavy one that opened by sliding along iron runners. She put her shoulder to it and it slid open with a sigh of ease. The area inside smelled of milled wood and something tangy. She stood still and inhaled the warm air. A flicker of flame blinked behind the office area. Dankert must be drunker than she had thought. She couldn't imagine him being so careless.

Rikka made her way behind shelves laden with books. Wouldn't they just catch fire in a flash! Then she could decipher the source of the flame, a small kerosene lamp hanging from a rafter. She would have to give him a good lecture when she returned to the house. She'd let the lamp burn only as long as it took her to find the can of tile fragments.

"You could have given me a hint, Dankert," she mumbled, as she got down on her knees to feel around under the sofa he had mentioned. It was blacker than black under there, so she straightened up and carefully lifted the lantern off its hook. She had often wished for a lamp like this in her rorbu, but now realized that the smell of it negated any benefit. Bending down by the sofa once again, she maneuvered the lamp along the floor to give its best light, but its best light did little to illuminate the underside of the sofa.

"All right then," she mumbled, lay flat on her belly, and reached her arm in wide swoops. "If there are any small biting animals under here, please announce your presence."

"Only me," came the answer, and Rikka knocked her head

against a leg of the sofa.

"It is me, Rikka, only me. I was asleep."

"Mokci!"

"Yes, Mokci, not an animal that bites."

Rikka sat stunned, no longer remembering why she was on this dark floor in this darker workshop. "Mokci? Why?"

"Dankert told me I should sleep here."

"Why not in the house?"

"Maybe he is not willing to have me in there, not in a bed, not with so many women and girls there."

Rikka stared into the dark. She wiped her hands on her skirt and brushed the dust away. "And maybe he had a plan."

Mokci had no answer for that possibility, but he pulled the blanket off his legs and wrapped it around Rikka's shoulders. "Are you cold?"

"No colder than in my long sleep."

"Please, Rikka, come up here, alongside me. I will make you warm. Come on, there is room for two here."

"Did you and Dankert come up with this plan together."

"There was no plan. Just two men who had too much to drink."

"Are you still drunk."

"Not enough that I can feel it. Not enough that I would do anything careless with you."

Rikka knew she could trust Mokci. Then she thought again. Trust Mokci? Why? She remembered the night he went to her room and never came out again. But did she know the full story there or had she just been so jealous she couldn't see another truth.

"Did you spend the night with my mother?"

"No. Why do you ask that?"

"The night she danced naked. You were with her."

"Yes, I took her to her room, and I laid blankets on her. She was crying. I climbed up to the high bed and kept watch on her. When she slept soundly, I put more wood on the kitchen fire and then I left. Everyone was asleep or gone. I am sorry. I wanted to stay all night and be sure she slept, but I thought that might cause trouble. I looked in on her the next day."

" It would be better if I just lay down here on the floor. Is there an extra blanket?"

"No, just this one. But I will lie on the floor and you can have the sofa. Or I can carry you back to the house if you prefer."

She was so tired, her head so heavy, that she just said, "Move over."

And he did. She watched his shadowy form reposition itself against the back of the sofa to make room for her. Then he lifted the edge of the blanket to welcome her in.

What am I doing? Rikka thought, but Mokci held out his hand to help her up and utter weariness held her other hand and gently pulled her in.

"Good night," Mokci whispered.

"Good night."

The last thing she felt was his hand sliding under the blanket and over her neck where it rested until she fell asleep.

Dagur pulled her husband's fishing jacket tightly around her neck. The smell of tar, sweat and fish guts still clung to the fabric, just as it once clung to him and hence to her. She missed him, the old bugger, missed his sardonic jabs at her and the comfort of his arm hooked around her neck: a sign of his love as well as camaraderie. If he were here now what would he think of the choices she was making? Stepping out the door, she could see only a faint echo of the path ahead. This time of day, at this time of year, still held that Arctic darkness that could swing into light in no time at all. By this hour, the aurora had melted into a luscious sunrise. To the east, the Rose Church looked like no more than a dark hole in the brightening sky. Although ominous, the church pulled her in its direction.

The path was slippery from water that gathered during the day and froze at night. Each step required a negotiation with fate, but each step drew her closer to her purpose. She walked around to the back where the rose garden had lost its glory. An iron bench rested against the back wall of the Rose Church and there Dagur would sit and wait until he arrived... if he arrived at all. She felt her head nod and jerk. Footsteps. Just as she stood up to greet him, the minister sat down on the bench next to her.

"Don't bother, Dagur." He tugged at the cassock twisted around him. "This is an informal meeting, and I hope you will respect the need for privacy and discretion here."

Dagur squinted at the rose garden, a small forest of thorny black stalks. Not a single petal of last year's blooms remained, just these canes shrouded in a thick layer of straw, in need of the sun's warmth and light.

"I am aware." She turned her head to face him. "I am not aware, though, of what you have to say." Instead of looking at him, she focused on those forlorn stalks and imagined them festooned in roses the colour of new blood.

"It's about the note you wrote me," he said in a whispery voice. "You told me something that I have long wondered about."

"That's right. Did you credit my words?"

"Yes. I didn't want to, but you made me aware that I have suppressed what I really did know about that man. I didn't want to credit it, and I am ashamed of that. Now the sin belongs not only to him but to me also because I lacked the courage to acknowledge it."

"Then you must do so now or carry it to hell when you die."

The minister flinched. "You are blunt, Dagur. Blunt but right. But there is something I will need."

What do you want from me? "

"To forgive me. And then I can do what my conscience demands."

Dagur was amazed that the minister showed her this respect. She wondered if she could ask for one more thing - or would that tip the balance that was so finely weighted in her favour at the moment?

"I forgive you and I thank you. Courage that comes late is courage much considered. May I ask one more thing of you, something that would certainly heal someone in great distress?"

The minister wondered what new weight would be put on him now. He squared his shoulders. Inhaled. Nodded his head once.

"Bring Johanna Nielsen back into the church."

"Would she choose to come?"

"Yes, if she knew that you were going to cleanse her name in front of the congregation."

The minister looked down at his hands twisting in his lap. "That would be very hard."

"Being shunned as a whore ever since her daughter's birth was harder by far. She has not been welcomed into any decent home, and you slammed the door of God's house in her face."

The minister stood up, trod the pathway through the rose garden, back and forth, a thorn snagging his cassock as he passed. Then he got down on his knees, his hands folded together on the bench and whispered to his God, "Forgive me for I have sinned."

Dagur stood, straightened her skirt, and almost, but only almost, put her hand on the poor man's head.

Johanna heard a timid knock at the door. She pulled the knekkebrød from the oven and set it aside to cool before greeting the woman with the eyes of a frightened stoat. "Fru Henriksen, velkommen. How good to see you. Have you come for the service?"

"I think so. May I? I don't know, really, why I came, but I often hear the singing as I walk by, and every time I think it sounds so happy. I want to be happy with those people."

"Please, make yourself comfortable. Or, since it's a bit early, maybe you'd like to help me set things up for the others."

"May I really?"

"Ja, of course," Johanna said.

"How can I help?"

"I've made this flatbread. You could cut it into squares, maybe twelve pieces. That should be enough for everyone to have a bit with their tea. Here's an apron. You're small enough to wear my daughter's."

"Thank you," Fru Henriksen said tying a firm knot behind her back. "I like your little rorbu. It feels friendly."

"Well, you must especially appreciate the fine furniture then. Did you notice all the tree stumps in place of carved pews?" Johanna laughed. "Look out the window, here comes Brother Cecil with more firewood and a song."

"Aah, so he is the one with the beautiful voice! I always open my window when I hear him singing. Imagine having a man with a rich tenor voice like that. His name is Cecil? How clever."

Johanna looked down at her feet so the amusement on her face wouldn't show. "Yes, it is a fine voice, and he is a good man, very young, but kind and of high moral standards."

"Really? And is he married?"

"No, no," Johanna assured the young widow. "He is here at

the bidding of his church."

"What is that bidding?"

"To convert us heathens and bring us to the Promised Land, which in this case is called Idaho."

"I-duh-ho"?

"Yes, it's in America."

"What's it like there?"

"Huge fields of wheat and corn, and many sisters and brothers and treadle machines for sewing clothing and many cows and chickens and a big church for all of them to go to and pray. I think."

"Is our ocean there?"

"No. No ocean. Maybe a stream, I don't know."

"When are they going? Are you going with them? Can anyone go?"

"I might, but I don't want to leave my girls. I can't answer all your questions. I don't think they know when they're going. You can ask them anything you like. They are friendly, but their Norwegian is appallingly bad."

Just then the door was kicked open and Cecil entered with his load of firewood and the last chorus of his song.

He and Fru Henricksen looked at each other and a red blush rose in each of their faces as if they had a shared indiscretion to hide. They stared at each other until Johanna saved them with an introduction. The fru turned back to her work over the knekkebrød, placing the pieces in a tidy pattern on a plate. Cecil dropped the firewood off next to the stove and excused himself.

Looking downward as if speaking to her shoes, Fru Henricksen said, "I like the beautiful way you sing."

"Thank you. You are beautiful too," he answered, aware that something was wrong in the way he said that. "I am Brother Cecil. What is your name?"

"Fru Henricksen."

"I'm glad to meet you, Fru." She giggled and covered her mouth. He didn't know why, but he knew he liked her laughter.

"Are you staying for the service? We all sing together then."

"I want to go to I-duh-ho with you."

Absolutely delighted, Cecil took her by the hands and did a little dance of sheer happiness. "Wonderful," he said, and danced her around again.

Johanna shook her head and laughed. This is moving along faster than I imagined, she thought. "Cecil, go outside and welcome the others in." She followed him out the door and took hold of his arm. "I see you like Fru Henricksen."

"Yes indeed. Fru, isn't that a beautiful name!"

"Umm, Cecil Fru is not a name, it's means Mrs."

Cecil's face sank along with his heart. "She is married?"

"Not exactly. She is a widow. Her husband died the night of their wedding. She has been alone ever since. I wanted you to know that. Her Christian name is Liv."

"Liv," Cecil let the name linger on his tongue. "That sounds like an omen. I think she will leave this island with me."

"It's just the right colour to stand out against the sea and sky, a good idea in waters as rough as ours." Dankert had handed Mokci a large can of white paint. But Mokci had put the can aside and chose the deep blue instead. He wasn't interested in being spotted or saved.

He had made daily trips to the base of the mountain, each time scouting out an ascent. Eventually he spotted a ledge that might be made accessible. He chipped away at small crannies that became toeholds. Because the nascent pathway wound both upwards and counter clockwise, it offered a much broader view of the Norwegian Sea to the southwest. As he chipped away at the gneiss, he wondered just how much Rikka's body could handle. She was light on her feet and when they walked together now, she managed to keep up with him but her breathing was shallower and she often reached for his arm.

The sun on its ascent was casting its glow on the mountain and brightening the unshuttered windows of houses, small and large, so they seemed to be the source of light. Mokci ran his hand over the next small step he had just carved out of the great wall. It was neither flat nor smooth, but its roughness promised more security. Sometimes he was lucky, and the mountain offered its own natural steps where he need only wipe away the waste of a white tailed eagle. He looked behind himself at the spiral he was creating. If he could reach the ledge before the light gave way to purple evening, then tomorrow he would carry up the supplies he needed to turn the ledge into a sanctuary.

"Mother, let me help you with that. It's too heavy for you," Rikka said taking the basket of wet laundry from her mother's arms.

"I'm much stronger than you imagine, Rikka. While you were sleeping under the sea, I was learning how to be a strong woman again."

"Who helped you? You do look healthy, even happy."

"Brother Otten," she said and then laughed. "Well really brothers Cecil and Rose, too."

"How did they help?" asked her daughter.

"We sang together, cooked and cleaned and prayed together. They are wonderful, really kind. Did you see what Brother Rose did to that windowsill?"

Rikka turned and saw that an intricate little fence woven out of willow sprouts guarded the sill where the doves liked to lay their eggs in the spring. No more disappointment and tears need be shed now that the eggs were so gently cradled from rolling to the ground.

"What an interesting thing for a man to spend his time doing," Rikka said.

"I know. That's the way they are. People gossiped about the three brothers living in my house with me. I'm sure the stories flew all around the island about the heinous sins in this little rorbu. But the gossip faded as more people came on Sundays to sing and pray and learn of a new life."

"But what does the good pastor have to say? I'll bet he's breathing brimstone in the Rose Church."

"No. Believe it or not, he visited just a few days ago, and he was gracious. He spoke with respect, asked many questions. He and Brother Rose spend hours together now. They are trying to understand one another's beliefs. Sometimes the discussions get a bit heated, but then they find some point they agree on. They seem surprised rather than outraged."

The two women lifted an old and often mended comforter out of the basket, each taking two corners and giving the weighty thing a good shake before hoisting it over the clothesline.

Johanna said "We have both spent time in the dark, Rikka, and maybe we will again, but if so, next time we will know that the dark is susceptible to change if we let the light in. That's what I've learned from those crazy Mormon missionaries.

"Do you think they tell the truth?"

"They tell their truth, and they have every right to it, just as the Lutheran's do. Just as the Saami do. Speaking of Saami?" Johanna raised an eyebrow and looked into her daughter's eyes.

"I love him."

"And he?"

"Loves me."

"But you are frowning…."

"Yes."

"Because?"

"I can't see it, can't see how we would live together, where? Both of us would lose everything we know. If I went north with him, would I be despised by his people just as he is despised by most of our people?"

"Maybe so. And would that ruin your love?"

"Maybe."

Johanna shook out one more item from the basket. They both looked at it and laughed.

"That's my first dress," Rikka said.

"It was my first dress too. See? Here's the black vest that goes with it."

"Was it really yours first?"

"Yes, then yours, then Agnes', now Ragna's. A real family tradition. Look here at all the little repairs I've had to make over the years."

Rikka had to examine it closely to find the subtle telltale stitches that held the dress together. "This is our family, isn't it!" she laughed. "Others would have thrown it away years ago, but this shows how we are all stitched together."

"Yes, we are. Isn't that why it is so difficult to uproot yourself? There you'd be, whipping around in the wind, no clothesline to hold you in place next to your sisters, and me."

"A whole new world!" Rikka whispered.

"A choice of two new worlds: living with the reindeer in Lapland or living with the wheat fields and sewing machines in Idaho."

"Or I could just stay here."

"Yes, but I don't think you will, my darling. I don't believe you will."

"What about you, Mother?"

Johanna smiled shyly. "Brother Otten counsels me to come with him when the ship leaves. He says that the girls will be welcome there too."

"He loves you."

"Yes, I think he does."

"And?"

"He doesn't know what I know. He doesn't know that the demons will come back again and again and again."

"How can you be sure of that?"

"They never go far; they just burrow in deeper and wait for the right time."

Rikka looked at her mother's face, the beauty of it only slightly marred by the lines of anxiety. "I hope, Mother, that they will tire of you and shrink into nothingness."

"Perhaps they will. And now, aren't you supposed to meet Mokci."

Rikka looked at the sun rising a little higher every day. "Yes, you're right. He told me to wear the pants I made and the Saami boots. 'Dress warmly,' he said. "I hope he wasn't expecting me to head north to his homeland today," she laughed.

Mokci ushered Rikka into the rowboat. She sat gingerly on the soft cushioning of reindeer hides and balanced herself between the gunnels. She noticed that there were carefully wrapped provisions between their two seats and some tin cans rattling around on the floor. Just before he seated himself, he pulled in a rolled up tarp. Rikka was glad to see that because the skies were looking restless. "Where are we going, Mokci?'

"You will see. You will see, my love." He picked up the oars and began rowing with a fierce intensity. His back was to the Thorn and she, facing it, watched it slowly inch closer to them. "Maybe I'll take you to where the giants live."

"Oh, that would be nice, I'm sure," she smiled.

"Or maybe we'll head south to Afrika."

"Oh, I don't think I brought the proper clothes for that."

"Well, in that case I will take you to the Thorn and we'll see what's been happening there."

"That seems a bit more reasonable," she laughed.

And yet, it wasn't. They had just reached a point at which there was no line of sight between their boat and the island when dark clouds rushed along the horizon in a great and sudden hurry to reach land and cause havoc. Mokci jettisoned his plan for the climb up the Thorn to the ledge. Instead, he altered his course and aimed for the protection of the cave he had spun around in on that emerald green night months ago. He manipulated the little rowboat away from the oncoming storm and into the mouth of the cave.

The water worked its way in slow circles turning the rowboat around and around in a dance, a dream. Mokci controlled the boat with one oar so the motion was more trancelike than terrifying, though there was a sense of danger that Rikka could not suppress.

The walls of the cave seemed to slide past and one tall fissure in the rock wall caught her attention with each rotation. She wanted to explore it not just with her eyes but also with her hands. How deep into the mountain did it go? Could she fit into it, maybe just her arm, slide her hand over the satiny walls within? It seemed to belong to one of her underwater dreams. Had she seen it in that subconscious state of her sickness? She could imagine it in the palms of her hands, the slickness, the invitation to go deeper. On the next revolution she reached out her arm as far as possible and managed to touch, just for a moment, the sleek surface.

And then Mokci called out. It was the sound of pain, and the boat whipped out of his control. Rikka reached forward. He dropped the oar and was gripping his wrist, pulling at something imbedded in his hand. She knelt on the floor of the boat, pulled his hand towards her. The boat spun with the will of the swirling water, out of his control, dizzying. In the green light of the pool, she could just discern a splinter of wood jammed into the pad of flesh below his thumb. He winced. His eyes darted from the splinter to the walls of the cave. Rikka bent forward, pulling his hand closer. She sank her teeth into the blunt end of the splinter and tugged, tugged. He winced She pulled again, her teeth firmly imbedded in the wood. And finally it released, drawing bits of flesh with it. Mokci tried to draw his hand back but she wouldn't release it yet. She sucked the wound, licked the flesh surrounding it until Mokci's shoulders began to let go. His eyes closed, and the boat continued to spin.

"Mokci, are you alright? Mokci?"

His eyelids were closed, his breathing heavy and ragged. She stroked his face, loving his skin, the supple leathery texture of it. She cupped her hands under his chin, her fingers tracing his cheekbones; how prominent they were, how perfect in that green light. A shudder ran up his body landing in the open cups of her palms.

She wondered if he was asleep. She hoped he was; her fingers wanted to explore his body without awakening him. She ran her open palms around his neck, slid her fingers under his collar and let them explore his shoulders, his chest. Mokci had no hair, just this tawny perfect skin which rippled under her touch. Was he awake? Was he feeling her hands? Did she dare …? But her hands could reach no further. And what if he awoke? Was he hiding from the invasion of her hands? Would he spurn her? Pull her hands away? Reject her? She listened to his breathing, shallow and ragged. His eyes were closed. Her hands rested on his chest, feeling his heartbeat, his warmth, his desire. And she wanted more.

Why was he so still? Was it some sort of trance or was he pretending not to feel her hands? Her mother had always warned her, but her mother wasn't in this spinning cave of green. No one else was. No one else could see them in this strange light, and so she let her hands travel down his chest until they reached inside his leather pants that smelled of feral animal. Her hands wanted to clutch what she found there, but she didn't want him to awaken, not yet. Just let her be, let her explore. She imagined that she was under water again. The giant cod rubbed against her, suckled at her breasts. She wanted to push the ugly creature away, leave her alone, dive back into the inky depths of the sea. But her mind didn't want what her body yearned for. She waited, watched his erratic breathing and her hands held what she wanted. She felt him grow inside her grasp, didn't fully realize what she was doing, but she had no intention of letting go. He shuddered. She pulled away, suddenly scared.

His lips moved and then he whispered to her, "Lie back. There is a blanket there. Lie back."

She did. His eyes were still closed. Was he awake? Dreaming? Angry with her? She didn't know, but she did as he asked, and then he was on top of her, his hands suddenly alive and moving over her body, his tongue circling the nipples of her breasts. She was panting, all resistance flowing out of her body which wanted more, more. And more came. She reached for him, guided his penis toward its berth where he entered her slowly, gritting his teeth to slow down the desire, to hold back, to feel everything that lay beneath him, inside him. Rikka gasped again, afraid of what she felt, braced against the pain and inviting more, deeper, forever. She didn't understand what was happening to him. His whole body shuddered. Her body stung, arched, reached for more.

As the boat continued its circling of the cave, Mokci lay back.

Rikka turned her eyes up to the ceiling of the cave and his followed.

"Can we live here," she asked. "In this light? Can we just love each other? Spin forever?"

Mokci smiled, drawn to the dream.

"Give me your hand."

He looked at her doubtfully, but as she sat up in her seat, took his hand, and licked it like a cat, any dream seemed possible. "You won't be able to row back. No, don't shake your head. I will do it."

"No."

"Yes, I will. Do you think I could live here all my life and not know how to row a boat?" Rikka took the oars, canted the angle with care, and putting her strength behind the oars she showed that she could maneuver the boat. It took exactly four circuits of the cave before she gained the feel of the current. The tide was going out, so she knew that night was falling. And so were the stars. She let the current pull her towards the cave's entrance. Her timing was almost right but her feeling for the current caused her to miss the opening to the sea. "Let me do it," Mokci said reaching for the oars.

"No, this is mine to do, and I can do it."

On the next try she maneuvered the boat through the cave's entrance, Rikka worked with the tide instead of against it and soon they were in the open water. Dancing streaks of green and violet light beckoned her, wrapped the boat in a blanket of colour. The violet wound through the rose pink, the colour of the flowers that proliferated around the church in the summertime. As she rowed towards shore, she took furtive glances at Mokci. He had given in to her ability to take care of herself, take care of him if need be. His eyes closed, the tension in his neck released. Let her do what she could do. They would drown together or they would reach the shore together. He closed his eyes.

Rikka's arms ached. Her time lying on the table in Dankert and Pernille's kitchen had left her weak. She had not needed any strength, not used any of her muscles for the days and days she had floated under water, and now they ached. Well, let them ache, let them scream at her; now she had to wake them up, remind them of what they could do when called upon. She would not fail this challenge. She watched the lights change the colour of her lover's face. Lover. No, she would not fail him or herself. The little boat seemed to have a will of its own, and that will along with her own brought them to the shore where the bottom of the boat scraped the gritty slope.

Rikka balanced the boat as it bucked and swayed. She looked back at Mokci who lounged like a sheikh. Her oar scraped bottom and with two more pulls, she leapt out of the little boat and landed, face down in the icy water. Mokci vaulted from the boat. Landing on solid ground, he lifted a sodden Rikka from the water. Drenched as she was, she weighed far more than he anticipated, and a trail of salt water and gravel marked his effort to carry her.

"Let me down!"

"No."

"Mokci, let me down. I can walk."

"Maybe, but you will not last carrying all the water with you."

She fought in his arms, slapped at him, hit his throbbing thumb. Mokci gritted his teeth and dropped her on the shore.

"I can't go home like this." Rikka cast her sodden jacket aside and tried to wring out her shirt which held tenaciously to her body. Her teeth were chattering to one another. Too cold. Too cold. She stared down the beach, past the marina where the fishing boats lay at anchor. "It's too far."

Mokci held out his hand for her and pointed in the opposite direction. "But my lavvu is close," he said.

Rikka scanned the shoreline to see if anyone was watching them. Hard to tell in the blue hour when everything seemed to hold a mystery inside itself. Was that boulder hiding an angry fisherman? Were there eyes in that naked birch tree? But Rikka's chattering teeth told the truth: she could not stand this icy cold weight dragging her down. Mokci hugged her, squeezing some of that sea water out of her clothes. She watched the trail of water return to the sea. "You're right," she said through chattering teeth. The lavvu was just up the beach and in the opposite direction of the village.

Wanting to carry her home -- to his home-- Mokci lifted her and struggled his way up the beach. She flailed like a reindeer fighting for its freedom. Mokci only held on tighter and soon the lavvu was in sight, a vague triangle encircled by shuddering aspens. "I will build a fire. You can take off your clothes and I will wrap you in hides."

Rikka relented. Her legs wouldn't agree to take her in any other direction. Each step accomplished, each breath expended, brought her closer to a dry place, a place that would soon offer a fire, a place to lie down, a place offering something hot to drink. And then she could sleep. She had never been so tired.

Close now she could hear the hides flapping in the wind like raven's wings fighting against a storm. Mokci was staggering under her sodden weight. She wriggled loose and beat him to the lavvu. A few embers in the fire ring emitted a feeble glow. They could be revived. She knelt and blew on the orange glimmers, reached around for any bits of bark or grass to urge a flame out of hiding. She didn't hear Mokci enter.

"Let me take over there," he whispered, leaning over her bent back.

"I can do it," she said huffing

"I know, Rikka. You think you can do anything. That is fine, but you can also let me help while you get those wet clothes off. Here, take this skin. Put the fur side next to your skin and I will keep your fire alive."

Rikka's hands shook with the cold. She turned her back to Mokci, peeked back over her shoulder to see if he was watching her, judging her body. But Mokci was focused on the feeble flame, blowing gently at its base, so she reached for the reindeer hide and wrapped it around herself, lay down on his pallet and turned her back to the tiny fire. Her whole body shook. She pulled the hide tighter and closed her eyes. She could hear Mokci talking to the infant flame, could hear that flame whispering back to him as he blew at its base. And she knew that he would take care of her, and love her. She wondered if that would be enough for him, for herself. Her teeth chattered together against the cold. Again, she tightened the wrap of the hide around her shoulders, around her feet, and fell asleep.

Mokci

Once the fire whispered to him that it had caught, that it would grow and drape the whole lavvu in warmth, Mokci sat staring at his love curled up like a sea mollusk in its shell. He hoped she would stay with him for the whole night, maybe longer. I will make her so comfortable that she will want to stay. He reached for the bag that held the flour and then for the dwindling supply of reindeer butter. He worked up a dough and patted it into shape. He would let the dough rest while he put on his other pants and went outside. There he was met with a sky filled with dancing streaks of violet piercing through the blanket of green that rippled and swayed in the night sky.

Mokci pulled the salty air deep into his chest and held it there. He felt the end of winter cling to his lungs. He felt the birth of spring blow out between his lips. His grandfather was stirring up the love he had for the polar north, and Mokci couldn't tell whether the song – the joik that filled the skies –was coming from his own throat or from his grandfather's. Somewhere in the sky the notes that came from him intertwined with his grandfather's notes, and deep stirrings of love reached out to his own lavvu wherein his lover slept. He sang out to her. He sang out to him. For a moment he thought he could bring them together, but the soaring conviction of his joik seemed to twist around on itself and tie a knot that his song could not loosen.

He knew what his grandfather wanted and why. He wanted his grandson, not just for himself but for their people. He was dying and it was time for Mokci to return and take up his place in the siddha. His grandfather told him as a child that his task in life was to assume his grandfather's role in the community, and all his childhood training, all his skills with the reindeer, with the siddha, with hunting, with communicating with the spirits of their people: they all led towards his real purpose, to lead the siddha as their spiritual guide. To refuse this position was to refuse his heritage, his own people. And all his life, up until the time he left them, funneled towards becoming their spiritual guide, the wise man who reminded them of who they were even while the Christian missionaries lured them into a whole new way of being.

And then the sounds of the night, of two different voices travelling in opposite directions, spun together in the wind and settled in silence. Mokci stood. He breathed deeply and tried to see something, anything, in the dark distance. He couldn't see the future, nor his direction in it. He only knew that he must see his grandfather and he must be with Rikka. And how was that to be achieved?

He heard Rikka rustling around in the lavvu and realized that his singing had awakened her. Right now, he would go to her. Later he would make a decision, but he knew that no decision was right. Betrayal, one way or another, betrayal. There was love. There was duty. There was where the two intertwined and spun dizzyingly in his heart.

"Mokci," she called.

He entered the lavvu and stood staring at Rikka wrapped in the skin, her long legs extending out from the cover. She smiled at him. "That was beautiful, almost like two voices, different in tone, but somehow still one. How did you do that?"

"I had help from my grandfather," Mokci responded.

"And?"

"And what?"

"And what did the two of you say to one another?"

"He said he is dying."

"I'm sorry. And does that mean you need to go back?" She tried to ask this in a neutral tone, not showing the panic she felt. "Are you going to leave?"

"I have to."

Rikka gasped. She had tried not to, but this news was her

greatest fear. They had made love, and now this? Images of her mother, Johanna, flashed through her mind. Was she, Rikka, going to fall into the same sad patterns that had trapped her mother? Now she could see how easily it happened. Urges turned into huge mistakes. She already felt pregnant. Could it be?

Mokci walked over to her. She was rigid, no longer the soft, yielding girl he held so recently. He felt her panic, knew the cause. She turned her back to him and tried to keep herself from crying, from letting go of whatever dignity she might still have.

"Your song...."

"Yes, my joik. It is how I communicate with my grandfather."

"That doesn't make any sense. How can that work? How can he hear you and you him?"

"That is hard to explain."

"Try," she demanded.

"I can hear him. He can hear me. The distance doesn't matter."

"Yes it does. It has to," she countered.

"But it does not," he insisted. "Rikka, try to trust me. I am not leaving you. I want you to travel with me to see my grandfather and to introduce you to my siddha."

"Why?"

"Because I want to be with you always."

"Where? Do you mean here or in Sapmi?"

"That is what we need to decide together. Do you want to live here always?"

"No, I guess not. This place has always been cruel to us, to my mother especially. I've often wondered if somewhere else people are kinder. Are they kinder where you come from?"

Mokci had to think about the differences. Were his people kinder or just more likely to accept one another's weaknesses? He had no answer to that. All he knew was that his Sami community understood working together. Be they herders or mothers or small children, they all had their jobs to do, and they did them together.

His job was to succeed his grandfather, and it was an onerous job and a profound honour which, if fulfilled properly, would comfort his people in hard times and nourish their bellies and souls in good times. Their welfare depended upon the reindeer that needed to be cared for: milked, bred, led across the vast and mountainous landscape of the polar north, groomed and butchered. And this difficult life needed a leader whose strengths, both physical and spiritual could be relied upon. There were no other contenders for the job. The siidha had known since Mokci's birth that he would be the next noadi.

Rikka stared at Mokci. Who was he? If she went with him, who would she be?

She had known contempt all her life, contempt for her mother who refused to divulge the father or fathers of her children. She had heard Johanna referred to as whore and witch. Why did men pull her into their bed one night and throw her out of their house the next morning before washing their hands and faces, before going to church and singing about God's love and mercy?

"Rikka. Rikka, tell me what you are thinking."

Silence.

"Rikka?"

"I'm afraid."

"What frightens you?"

"You."

"Why?

"I'm afraid that if I go on this journey with you, your people will hate me for my place in your life. That girl who loves you will hate me more than anyone here could hate me. I wouldn't blame her."

"I never made her any promises."

"But you took what she offered, and what did she get in return?"

Mokci stared at his open hands as if an answer might lie there.

None spoke to him. "Not enough," he admitted. "But I always told her she was not the one I am destined to marry."

"That must have been horrible for her."

"I do not think so. She just rolled over and said, 'Let's do it again then, while you're not married.'"

"Did you do it again?"

"Yes, and again. But no more."

Rikka knew that bedding down with a man did not mean there was a promise made between the sheets. And if there happened to be a promise made, that did not ensure that the promise would be kept. Was there a man anywhere who could be trusted?

"What is her name?"

"Vivvå."

"That's a strong name. I'm afraid of her ... of you and her together."

"We are not together, Rikka. You and I are together, and we must find our way of being together."

"I'm too tired of this, this way of planning a future. I'm tired of so many things. And I'm hungry, so hungry and cold." She could not hide her tears, those tears that made a lie of her strength and her abilities.

"I can fix that." Mokci knelt by the fire and picked up the round breads from the warming stone. The outside edges had charred a bit. He rotated them and let the other side char just around the edges, then went to his sack and fished around for the coffee jar. The water was already heating by the fire, emitting a fine cloud of steam. He made the coffee with a meager dab of reindeer butter melting on top of each cup.

Rikka noticed the charring on the bread. "Why did you let the outer edges turn black?".

"It makes the bread more interesting, more like the way our mothers made it. In my lavvu we all char the edges."

"But it tastes burnt."

"Or it tastes like home."

"Are your lavvus all charred around the edges?"

He laughed. "Yes, they do look that way after a time."

"Do you ever get worried that the lavvu will burn down?"

"It happens sometimes. Then we rebuild. There are always more poles, more reindeer hides."

"When a house or rorbu around here burns down, it's considered a tragedy. Everyone comes together to rebuild."

"With everyone living in their own lavvu it is not that difficult to rebuild, and neighbours and family help out. By dinner time everything is back to normal." Mokci gestured towards a cushion near the fire. "You sit here. You will be warm."

Rikka adjusted the reindeer skins to best cover her body. Mokci folded another skin into a large rectangle. "Here is a cushion for you."

He organized the reindeer pelts around her shoulders and down her legs. Then he took her feet into his lap and massaged the warmth back into them. "You will have to stay by the fire until you have thawed out," he laughed. He brought cups for the coffee which he poured from a dented pan, and Rikka cringed as he dropped another dollop of reindeer butter into each cup.

She lifted the cup to her lips and then held her breath at the smell of the reindeer cream. She took a sip from the hot cup and waited for her stomach to revolt against the fat, the feral smell of it. But it didn't react; rather, the warmth of it followed by the animal scent was reassuring, comforting.

Mokci no longer looked like a boy. His stature had changed, matured. He was a man. It was that simple. He was a man and he held himself like one: taller, quieter, his step more sure of itself.

"Mokci, I will go with you, as far as I can go and for as long as it feels like the right path. I will stand by your side." She felt Mokci's hand on her cheek. His smile settled her heart.

"Then you trust me?" he asked.

"Yes, but I wish I knew how to behave in your siidha. And how to understand your people when we don't share a language."

"My mother will help you with all of that. Here," Mokci said, "I will teach you something that you can practise ahead of time. Scoot over."

Rikka made room for him next to her around the fire. She watched Mokci grimace as he folded his legs back at the knees and sank his bottom between them until it almost rested on the floor. His face certainly didn't look rested. Rikka tried to copy his pose, hopefully with more grace. "Ouch, ouch, my knees don't like this."

"But look, you are doing it already, with no practise at all."

"Um, yes, but I may never be able to stand up again," she laughed.

"Let me help you. See, you are already like a Sami woman," he said.

Rikka would have laughed too, but her attention was pulled to the walls of the lavvu which were billowing and snapping. 'This is no wind,' she said. 'It is her, isn't it. Your Vivvå is out there. So what happens next?"

When he didn't answer she filled in the possibilities: "You ban her from this island? You ban her from the siddha? You find her another man? You make room in our bed for her to squeeze between us? What? What is your solution? Hers seems to be to tear this lavvu apart and maybe tear me apart. What do you have in mind, Mokci?"

Mokci turned and walked out of the lavvu. He knew that this wind that tore at the skins of the lavvu was more than Vivvå. This was the power of his grandfather, of his people, demanding that he return. He would go. He would take up his role and he would prepare them to welcome Rikka into the siddha as his wife.

Rikka pulled the hides more tightly around her. She stared at the fire, at the embers that baked their bread, at the pot that heated the water for their coffee. What now, she wondered. I can't leave until my clothes are dry. I can't leave without knowing if she is gone, if he is gone, if I'm really alone here. She went over to where her shirt, pants, stockings and boots were letting off steam. Too much steam. They were far from dry. She could not go out into the cold night and make it all the way back to Johanna's rorbu, and certainly not all the way to Dankert and Pernille's warm home. She put more aspen on the fire. There was more than enough to get her through the night, and that night which was so raucous just a few minutes ago was now so silent that Rikka felt abandoned. She was abandoned. Well then, she would make this her own home for the night. There was still some coffee teetering on a flat stone next to the fire. She sat down beside it and took stock: clothes - wet; boots - soaking; coffee - still warm; walls - holding back the wind and hopefully holding back the spirits or whatever that was screaming around the lavvu earlier.

"I don't believe in spirits that have bodies. The one cancels out the possibility of the other. That means that there is no such woman as the one that circled the lavvu and tried to scare me away. No such woman and no such spirit. It didn't happen." Rikka muttered to herself.

It was a night of small sounds and restless sleep. The hides kept slipping off her naked body where she lay near the fire. She would tug the vagrant hide over herself only to feel it sliding towards the fire. Her restless body could not give in to defeat and she woke repeatedly with the sense that she had been wrestling with cloven-hooved beasts. The lavvu was alive with the sounds of something small, and no doubt furry, chewing on a coffee bean.

She opened one eye, two ears. What was in the lavvu with her?

Rikka shifted her position so her back was to the fire and her eyes could scan the area for the intruder.

"A lemming! I haven't seen one of you for ages. Look at you! For such a little monster you sure make a lot of noise."

The lemming leapt at the sound of her voice.

"Don't worry little one. I don't eat lemmings, though I might be tempted right now."

The tiny creature stood on its back legs and wiggled its nose at her. His face was the colour of charcoal underscored by an orange neck and mantle. After his long winter sleep, he was now hungry and more curious than threatening. She searched for something for the creature to eat. She gathered the fine crumbs and dust of the bread they had baked on the rocks near the fire. Then she searched the food sack for a bit of reindeer butter, mixed the two together and created a tiny bun for the lemming. She held her hand out to the creature and he moved in closer, close enough to grab the treat she had made. Sitting on his haunches, he watched her intently as he nibbled away at his meal. Rikka smiled and reached out to stroke him, but he would have nothing to do with that. Instead, he swallowed the last bits of bread and then rushed to the walls of the lavvu where he began running around the circular wall. His scratching noises were familiar and, in a moment, Rikka realized that the sound he made was the same sound she heard during the night. It was not the sound of a mad woman threatening her safety.

"All right then," she whispered to the lemming. "It was you making the racket

last night. And here I lay blaming that mad woman. Enjoy your meal. Thank you for guarding my sleep. You can run around all you want in here, little Fuzz Ball. I'll be leaving as soon as I can get dry boots on. You can come with me if you like. I'd love a faithful companion."

Her voice caught on the word faithful. She held out her open hand to him. "Fuzzy, that will be your human name. I'm sure you already have a lemming name, but I doubt you can tell me what it is. My name is Rikka."

Fuzzy made a sound, almost a chortle, and curled up inside her damp boot. "All right then, make yourself comfy. you little beast." Rikka lay back down, taking her cue from the lemming. Morning would come, and if there was no Mokci standing by the fire or curled up next to her, she would leave with her new friend, the lemming. In the night, in her dream state, she heard voices around her, teasing the edges of her reality. One of the voices sounded like her mother, screaming for her. Another sounded like Mokci speaking in hushed tones of a journey he must take. But in the hour or so that she got real sleep, the fatigue in her body convinced her that these voices was no more than a dream.

Morning did come, and there was no Mokci. She poked at the fire, a mere lump of fading coals incapable of giving any true warmth. She reached out to the boot and gave it a gentle shake. Her friend tumbled into her lap and looked at her in full expectation of something more to eat.

"We are out of food, my little friend, but my clothes and boots are dry enough and it's time to go. Nothing here for us." She poked at the spent embers. She looked around. What had been a nest for her and Mokci was now a sad refuge for an unwanted girl and a cheeky lemming.

The wind had faded from tumultuous to timid and the ebbing tide sucked the storm's detritus down the beach and urged it back up again to form fleeting patterns on the gravel. The sky was as pink as rose petals. Her island was awakening. Was that singing she could hear or was the wind playing tricks on her?

The lemming skittered around over rocks and between the branches of a naked shrub. Sometimes she thought he had run off, perhaps turned around to find the lavvu again. Then his perky little head would pop up from behind a pile of driftwood.

"Come here little one. Do you want to be carried? " He came closer as if in answer. Rikka picked him up and tucked him into her jacket pocket. He blinked twice and curled up. I must show him to Agnes and Rana, she thought. Would they be with Johanna or with Pernille and Dankert? Johanna's home was closer; she'd start there. The little creature in her pocket gave her reason to move forward.

Rikka picked up her pace, almost running around boulders and skipping over tide pools. She kept her eyes focused on the next step and the next, suddenly impatient to be with those she loved and who had for their whole lives loved her.

And here she was now, just short of the breakwater, the piers, the cod-laden fishing boats with their prows curved upward towards the sun infiltrating the blue hour. On the horizon she could just make out her home.

"We're almost there, Fuzz. My sisters will be so excited to see you. Better brace yourself for cuddles and kisses." Fuzz disappeared deep into her pocket as if he knew that something terrifying was coming.

Rikka squinted. Someone was on the path up to her home. No, two people walking close together. Not Johanna, smaller. A small woman or girl. And a man close by her side, almost skipping up the path. It had to be Brother Cecil, and the girl's slight limp identified her as Fru Hendrickson ... Liv.

Rikka squinted into the new sun no longer hidden by the pall of winter. It had not yet risen high enough to light up Johanna's little house. Instead, an unusually bright light emanated from the one window that faced the Norwegian Sea. She could just make out movement inside the kitchen.

Was it Sunday? A church service with the Mormons? There was also more movement on the pathway to the rorbu. More people arriving. Who?

By his stagger, Rikka identified the old drunk. Behind him came the priest; now there was something to think about. Some people she couldn't recognize but there were more arriving than would ever seem possible for a Mormon service.

"Get cozy, Fuzz. I want to catch up with the others, find out what's going on." Fuzz tucked his head deep down in his woolen burrow. Rikka could pick up threads of the conversations but none of it was making much sense to her.

"No, he'll never get past the gangplank."

"…wouldn't mind moving to a warmer climate. Where exactly is Idaho? Is it near California?"

"Maybe, but probably closer to Minnesota. That's where most of us Norwegians land."

"….just trying to keep track of my congregation. Why are so many leaving?"

"I hear that those corn fields bring in enough to make a millionaire of a hard working…."

"Ach, don't believe everything you hear."

Rikka climbed the path in a hurry, taking in as many stories, details, and absurdities as she could manage. This was no church service. It was beginning to look like an emigration meeting. Was her mother going to America on a boat? What kind of life could she expect? And was marrying Brother Otten? He was a good man but good enough to follow halfway around the world? And what would become of Ragna and Agnes?

Did they have a say in the matter? Agnes wanted to be a doctor or a nurse and take care of the people on the island. It might be a far-fetched dream, but the girl had the intelligence and the spirit to do wonderful things with her life. Surely this island was in need of a doctor, a nurse, or a healer like Dagur, and Dagur would not be around much longer. Then who would take care of the sick? Who would aid a mother during a difficult birth?

Rikka turned around to face the rising sun and the sea,

breathing in the azure blue of the sky as it melted into the indigo of the sea. Blue upon blue and a hundred more shades of blue where the soft belly of the waves painted a view of her world. And how could that be replaced by endless fields of corn? Yellow and brown and more yellow and more brown blowing in a hot wind over flat ground. Dust. Dry bones. Idaho. No Mokci.

Her head ached. Would everyone she cared about leave? Would it just be her and Dagur left behind, two women without a man to care for them or be cared for by them? Well, so be it. She thought of Pernille and her tile project, how the kakelugn was being transformed into a tower of art, of the many shades of blue needed to depict the beauty of their island in the sea. I have to see it again, she thought, see how high the tiles ascend the cylinder in all those shades of blue. Pernille understood the depth of beauty that was their sea. And the sea was the source of their life's work. It gave to the islanders the cod that grew as thick as corn stalks in Idaho. It gave them life and it brought them death. And that was how things were supposed to be. That was their life.

The chatter in front of her and behind her was all about finding a new life. She understood the appeal of adventure and change. Young men on the island often complained about never having a home of their own, of how they had to pay landowners for the privilege of working their land. Never a hope of owning their own. Merely cotters, borrowers of a piece of land on which they could build a small house that they would never be able to call their own.

Rikka had always thought the system unjust. The landowner's property was enriched through the labours of the cotters, and the cotters were endlessly indebted to the landowner for seed and implements and loans that could not be paid off.

Rikka spotted Dankert in the procession headed for Johanna's rorbu. She called out to him and he waved to her, ended his conversation with a young man.

Rikka ran to Dankert with an idea that was just blossoming in her mind. All that land between his house and his father's, all of it lay idle.

"Dankert, why are you here? Are you actually thinking of moving to Idaho with the Mormons?"

"No, my darling girl. I am not. I am Norwegian and always will be. I heard that a Mormon representative was here to lure our people to their Promised Land." The irony in his voice made it clear that he was not here to jump onto the ship.

"I'm glad to hear it. But why? Do you hope to scuttle their plan?"

"Well yes, that's my mission. I want to make those young men a better offer."

"Oh, I'm so glad to hear that. I was afraid for a moment..."

"But you needn't be. Too many Norwegian men have left this island in despair. They have been used and abused by those with large land holdings. I will not be one of them."

"What do you have in mind?"

"I will offer the cotters full ownership of the land they cultivate and the homes they build. In exchange they will work hard to improve the land for their own benefit. They will not be taking anything from me, and I will not be taking anything from them."

"Does Pernille approve of your plans?"

"Pernille is the author of my plans. She will settle for nothing short of them. She said, 'Let the fishermen be fishermen and let the land workers reap the benefits of their toil. We benefit from their toils, but we take nothing from them.'

"I pointed out to her that there are other landholders nearby, very nearby, who will resent this generosity. 'So, let them stew in their own resentment and greed. We do not need that land except as a buffer between us and your parents.' I laughed my heart out. The woman is so astute, has such a vision of what is right and what is wrong, and my parents are hopelessly lost in their greed."

"They will hate it, fight it," Rikka countered.

"Exactly," Dankert agreed. "And now let's get to that meeting. The boat will come in soon come in. We will see who fills it and who decides to stay."

"Well then," Rikka responded, "it must be time to make up my mind. Go to a new world or stay with the old? I only wish I knew. Why is it all so difficult to decide? Let's go in, Dankert. I feel the ground shifting under my feet, almost as if I were trying to balance myself between two different worlds."

"Then you need to decide, my little fugl. You need to decide where to make your nest. With Mokci, with us islanders or with a new and foreign world." She warmly remembered the old nickname Dankert had given to her as a child – fugl: "little bird".

"There is no Mokci. He has made his choice and left."

"That may be true, though I hardly think you've given him a fair chance. How do you know he has left?"

"Because he's not here. He has answered his grandfather's call and his lover's demands."

"Just don't let your aching heart make your decisions for you," Dankert counselled. "All is not what it seems … at least not always."

"That's true, Uncle. But since I might be leaving, don't you think it's time for you to be honest with me?"

"About what, Rikka? I thought I've always been honest with you."

"You know what!"

"Oh, that old business. You mean … am I your uncle, your father, your cousin, or your grandfather?"

"That is what I mean. Now that I'm grown up, I think I deserve to know the truth."

Dankert looked into her sad eyes. She had lost so much and yes, it was time for her to know the truth, to have some sense of where she belonged in the family. He knew that she would be disappointed that he was not her father nor her cousin. She would be disappointed and probably very angry, but it was time. He took a deep breath and finally let the truth escape from his lips.

"I am your brother."

Rikka stared at him for a moment that stretched out against the sky, against the sea, against everything she had believed.

"No, how can that be? It cannot be. Listen to what you're saying to me. This is no joke, and it's no time to be teasing."

For years and years, she had tried to convince herself that Dankert was her father. Even though Johanna had tried to convince her that her real father had died at sea. Even though she had met her father in the form of a giant cod during her illness. Dankert had been in love with Johanna, that much she knew for certain, so it was logical in her lonely mind that he must really be her very own father. Rikka shoved her fists into her pockets, too late realising that she had just punched Fuzz who let out an enraged squawk and leapt from his warm shelter. Rikka pushed aside the turmoil in her brain and chased little Fuzz under a boulder tipped against a larger boulder. Rikka fell to her knees and began scraping away soil and pebbles. She dug like a dog mad to free a bone. "Fuzz, Fuzz,'" she cried. Everything else fell away: Utah, family, the recruiter inside her mother's house, and all these islanders looking for a new and golden life. She felt Dankert's hand on her shoulder: warm, stroking, full of understanding, her brother's hand.

What swarmed through her head like a nest of honeybees, was the implication, no, the truth of her parentage. Her mother would always be her mother; her sisters her sisters, but her father was not the drowned fisherman her mother married, was not Dankert, her brother. And then she knew who it was. She knew whose blood she carried, and the knowledge was like cold poison scraping through her veins. Lorkman.

Hanna

Johanna's rorbu was full of the scent of cardamon and toasted poppy seeds but overwhelmed by the odour of sweat and salt; it held more visitors than seemed possible: young men with big rucksacks and little enough to put in them; even more women who were being promised sunshine, security and treadle sewing machines.

"Every woman will have a husband," a man said with a grin. "No more husbands lost at sea as they so often are here."

The air reverberated with questions. How many hours will it take to get there? What will we eat if our stores run out? What do you mean 'no alcohol'? This could all be a huge mistake. I can't swim. How much money? Can I pay that later as I earn it? What if? And where will we sleep? Are there beds or will we sleep on the decks? What about rats; surely there will be no rats aboard. What about wind? What about storms? What about the wrath of God? What if? and What about? And where's the spokesman? I have to ask him about and about, and about.

"No, you cannot come. You're drunk and if you came to this meeting drunk, that means you'll be drunk whenever we need you to be sober. No sir. You're staying right here."

"Excuse me. I have a question. Or two."

Agnes held Dagur by the elbow and seemed to steer her to the front of the crowd. In a voice that must have been walking the earth for a century, Agnes politely commanded others to make way for Dagur as if she were the queen of the expedition.

"Please, Peder, find her a comfortable stump to sit on," and Peder did as commanded. "And now Peder, I smell my mama's crispbread. If you stand and keep Dagur comfortable, I'll bring back sweet things that just came out of the oven. And there will be one for you," she offered in such a sweet voice that Peder was glad to do her bidding. In the meantime, Dagur began challenging the agent in her blunt manner with questions about multiple marriages, about stealing land from both the white population and the natives. When he finally managed to brush her off, he could only hope that others wouldn't confront him in the same way although it had happened on many an island and in many a port.

Dagur took one last stab at the man who held the information they all needed. "What would the Mormons, or should I say Latter Day Saints, do for a girl like little Agnes here?"

"She would live in the women's house and learn from their skills until she reached the age of marriage."

"And when might that be?"

The agent shrugged and decided this would be the last question for the old woman. He tipped his hat back and looked straight in her pale watery eyes. There'd certainly be no question of whether or not he'd let the old witch on board. "Does the girl sew?"

"Of course, all girls sew. And some do far more," she said nodding her head in Agnes' direction. "This girl will be a healer ... a doctor."

"No, that is not a suitable calling for a woman, much less a child. Eventually, she might be able to work with the midwives. They, too, are healers."

Agnes, with cracker crumbs stuck to her lips answered. "Of course, I have already learned about birthing. I will also learn about cures and poultices, and healing herbs. I will be a doctor."

"Then you will stay on this island."

"Yes," nodded Agnes. "I will stay here and become a doctor. I already have the best teacher. Can we go now, Dagur?"

Dagur nodded and took her hand. She knew that no matter how strong this girl was, she was about to lose her family, but she could also tell by the set of Agnes's jaw that her decision was made.

A slow stream of downhearted islanders left the meeting,

either rejected, or realizing it might not be their destiny. As the crowd cleared inside, those who had been accepted by the agent broke into small groups and began sharing ideas for what they could squeeze into the one allotted trunk per adult.

In the kitchen area, Johanna was still pulling flatbreads from the oven as Otten carefully stoked the fire.

"Johanna, I have something I must talk to you about."

"And what is that?" she asked, not caring what he had to say, just that she had this good man standing by her side, one who would not go to sea, one who would stay and love her and her girls.

"I have talked to my brothers."

"And what did they have to say?"

"That if I take you to my community in Idaho," he said staring at the salt stains on his boots, "the elders will dictate who will marry whom. You would have no say, no ja or nej, and no more say would I have."

Johanna had expected something like this.

"So, you will go without me?"

Otten stared at her and slowly shook his head. "I will go nowhere, nowhere on earth, without you. Let's look at another way. Will you marry me … here and now, within your own church, within your own country? Because … nowhere without you." He had been gently bouncing Ragna on his chest, but now he stood as still as one of the pillars in the Sentinels.

"Can you do that? Can you make such a decision … to live here, to become Norwegian, speak our language without wringing its neck?" she laughed. "Can you live without your religion?"

"I don't know. But what I do know is that I won't live without you and the girls. I cannot. I will not."

"Perhaps we should go and have a meeting with the priest, see what wisdom he has to offer."

"Shall we clean up this mess first?"

Johanna bit her lower lip. "No, let's go visit him now. I think Agnes is with Dagur peering into a tide pool. I have no idea where Rikka is. In fact, I haven't seen her for a long time. Maybe she's with Mokci. I hope so. Let's go now and find our way, a way of being together." Johanna tore off her apron, dropped it onto a stump, and said, "It's time to be happy."

As Otten pulled on his huge black coat and held the door open, she wrapped a shawl around her shoulders, took his hand and stepped outside. So often in the past she stepped out this same door, took a deep breath to brace herself, and headed for Lorkman's house to serve those dreadful people. This time, however, she stepped out to take the arm of her betrothed. Together they would visit the priest, that same priest who had thrown her out of the church. Was she nervous? How could she not be?

Looking down the slope of land to the main path below, Johanna saw her eldest daughter and Dankert walking together like brother and sister in the direction of the Lorkman estate. "What could they be up to?" Johanna asked. "They seem to be on a mission and in a hurry to complete it."

"Look," Rikka pointed to the west where a dark horse was barrelling towards them.

"Good for you, Midnatt. You finally broke loose. I don't know why it took so many years. Old Bestemor spends half her life breaking out."

"Will he carry us?" Rikka asked.

"I'm sure he'll carry you. It'll save time. You can tether him by the workshop, and then go to the kitchen and see what Pernille has achieved. I'll be right along."

Rikka felt a surge of energy pass through her as her brother made a stirrup of his hands and vaulted her onto Midnatt's slumping back. The horse was old, but he knew just what she wanted. He trotted down the road, kicking up clots of snow-infused mud. Rikka tugged Midnatt's mane and looked ahead to the big white house where her brother and her friend lived.

Dismounted and with the horse secured, Rikka rushed down to the house and ran inside without knocking. There was Pernille down on her knees buffing the residue from the glistening tiles. The kakelugn was completely transformed. It soared to the high ceiling in its coat of stars and sea and swirling lights all emerald and amethyst.

"Rikka, there you are. Come on."

They stood on opposite sides of the tall oven.

"It's finished. Look, I think we can wrap our arms around it if we really stretch." They reached their arms towards one another and hugged the magnificent creation.

"It's amazing, Pernille," Rikka said. "Anyone who doesn't love it would have to be blind."

"Look at what it does when the sun's light hits it through the window."

"Amazing."

"But look over here, Rikka." She pointed to a wooden chest sitting on the counter where Rikka had lain unconscious for so long.

She moved forward, touched its smooth, oiled surface. "English oak, just like the dining table. It's beautiful and made by Dankert for his sister." How she knew that the conversation had been recently had between Rikka and Dankert, Rikka didn't know, but she was grateful for the ease in this new way of addressing the relationship.

Rikka bent over, smelled its satiny gold surface. "Beautiful! But why for me?"

"You will need it."

Rikka opened it slowly, checking the range of the hinges. The inside of the box smelled of camphor. Its lid was carved with designs of the gods who lived under the sea. It held numerous compartments which Rikka started poking into. There was a box of kennekkebrød, crisp and salty; Norwegian raisin buns; and plenty of flatbreads. Next to a cloth bag filled with last autumn's apples, there was a large round of cheese and two smaller rounds of sweet gjetost. A good space was devoted to jars of clean creek water, an item often forgotten on the sea, Pernille told her, but crucial to good health.

"You'll find many things in this trunk. Dankert has built it, of course, and Urd and Dagur have augmented it with what they thought best: no fermented whale fat, I promise. But there's plenty of smoked cod and every other sea delicacy we could find. And eggs, stored in waterglass. Oh, and a tin of coffee."

"But why? Why all this trouble for me."

"Because we love you. Because we can't hold you back. Because we know, one way or another, you're leaving us."

For several reflective days, Rikka spent treasured time with her brother and his wife, her sisters and her mother, absorbing for a lifetime all of their love and fear, planning her voyage and imagining what she would find in the land of golden fields and the cautious unknown. She spent hour upon hour with her sisters, wrapped up in their sweet, small embraces and bathing in the newly found, tentative love surrounding her mother. She knew that there was always going to be that lingering darkness in Hanna's head, but somehow felt that the darkness had lifted some and might stay lifted through sheer, blind force of will and the constancy of Otten's kind companionship. Rikka battled her rage and her hurt towards Mokci and there were days when it shattered her wholly, but she knew what she must do, and she knew that that decision was entirely hers – hers alone.

Deep into the last night on her home island, Rikka sat with Pernille and Dankert, sharing memories and even revealing old secrets that no longer held any power over them. Pernille knelt nightly before the kakelugn and pleaded with whatever power it held, to watch over Rikka on her journey. The kakelugn was tall and filled with light, as a beacon that could guide Rikka through foreign lands, foreign ways of life. The thought, however fanciful, was just enough of a sedative to put her worries for her friend aside.

And on that last early morning, the two women slept, curled up like cats on a hearth.

Mokci found the lavvu empty, nothing but cold grey ash in the fire pit, a trail of coffee grounds across the floor and a small pile of rodent scat. No heat to the fire. No sign of his love anywhere. Rikka wasn't there; she hadn't waited. Mokci started a fire with a handful of shoe straw borrowed from the ring of sedge. He would change the sedge in his boots before heading out to find her. There was no way to know whether she was nearby, at Johanna's house or even gone visiting Pernille and Dankert.

He was jolted out of his thoughts by the blast of a horn. He didn't need to hear a second blast to realize what the first one meant. He ran out of the lavvu but not onto the trail towards the village. Instead, he headed over the escarpment behind his lavvu. From there he could just see where the deep bay lay, the one place on the island where a large ship could moor.

He was running now, running and scrambling but mostly scrambling until he realized he could just see the chimney on the steamer, and in the harbour, a long line of passengers rising out of the fog and onto the deck. He did not see Rikka among them. He scanned the line of passengers again and again, and finally she fit into the disembodied line-up. She turned her head from side to side, her hand shielding the glare from her eyes. And then he saw her eyes find his form on the escarpment, and they held him fastened to his spot for what felt like ten lifetimes, until he shook his body free and began to run.

The steamship's blast deafened all extraneous noise until finally, with a great grinding of gears, the ship pulled away from the dock accompanied by the cheers and tears of those left behind.

That morning, Dankert had brought Midnatt to the kitchen door and carried Rikka's trunk out to the sled that the good horse then pulled to the largest dock on the island. Dankert had arranged with a deck hand to deliver the trunk to Rikka's berth and to direct Rikka personally to that berth.

The steamer's railings were now lined with passengers waving goodbye - perhaps forever - to the family members and friends below. Calls back-and-forth were lost in the viscosity of the fog. There appeared to be no pier, no pathway, and no gangplank most of the way up to the boat. All was lost in a disturbance of air, a downward pressure on the heads of those left behind. And above that fog, Rikka's head, her long blondish-brown hair floating on the surface of the fog below was pushing towards the gangplank. She thought to herself that she would not stop at the railings as everyone else seemed to be doing. She could see no one there, no one that she dared call out to, wave to, shed tears for. Not now. But she stopped and looked just the same; she could not help herself. Her hand shaded her eyes as she investigated the fog over her island, looked at the black mist-streaked face of the Thorn, the mountain she hadn't climbed, and was now leaving forever.

And then she saw him on the escarpment that loomed over the harbour. Mokci had come back for her. She turned and ran, along the railing, past those still waving and calling to their friends and family, past the piles of luggage, to the place where the gangplank had been and where now, there was only a growing gap of swirling black water. The ship's horn sounded again. She looked at him - all she could do now.

He began to scramble down the cliff, over thorns and moss. She could just barely see him through the fog. But he made it to the wharf and for a moment, she was terrified that he was going to swim after her. But he stopped. He lifted his face to her and watched while the sea foamed and roiled along the ship's hull. The ship heeled hard into a turn and she lost sight of him. She ran to the stern and watched as he dwindled into a small black figure, and then disappeared altogether, into the mist and fog that now covered the island, the Thorn, the wheeling kittiwakes, and all that she had once known and would see no more.

APPENDIX

Writing with Doreen

by Alanda Greene

Doreen keenly hoped for and anticipated with both joy and trepidation that *The Thorn* would come to fruition with publication. Her trepidation was fueled by unwarranted concern that her research had not been thorough enough, that she had missed important details, that someone in Norway would find the flaw. She'd express her concern from time to time and we'd always end up in laughter as we fabricated what that imaginary reader might possibly find. Her research had been thorough, her words respectful of the people and their history. Deep down she knew, as did I, that no one would find fault. From her dedicated research and writing skill, she crafted this wonderful story. Knowing what it means, meant, would have meant to her to see it in book form brings an ocean of joy to my own heart. We worked together with our respective writing projects for a long time. In addition to my own pleasure, I also feel huge gratitude to Ingrid for all she has done to make sure the novel came to be a book.

Doreen's and my history together as friends and colleagues predated by many years the connection we shared with writing, which began nearly thirty years ago. Born from a conversation as a gathering of friends expressed their desire to write, we formed a group to nurture and support this shared aim. Over the years, the group showed a mostly constant membership. For several years we drove weekly to Nelson for writing course sessions with Kootenay School of the Arts (offered in the glory days of government support for the arts in our region) and had the good fortune to be mentored well. Doreen commented several times how much she appreciated the influence of these classes through Tom Wayman, Verna Relkoff and Almeda Glenn-Miller. Tom was our consistent guide who coaxed possibilities from us and encouraged us to use our words well. He accommodated the challenges of the ferry and teaching schedules by altering his own class timetable to make it easier for us. Doreen mentioned often her gratitude from what she learned through his teaching and his advice about our group: "Guard it with your lives. You've got something really special happening there." We knew and we did.

Yet, years went by and lives changed as work, additional creative pursuits, and community involvements adjusted priorities. Finally, it was just Doreen and I who continued our regular meetings. Both of us were writing novels and appreciated the focus of bringing work to the other for feedback. From meeting monthly, we went to every two weeks, and in the last year of her life, to every week. She knew time was running out and she wanted to finish that story. But she never wavered from also requiring that I submit work for each session, never wavered from reading it and offering intelligent, honest and supportive feedback.

In all our years of writing together in a group of various numbers, Doreen set the bar high for quality of feedback. Hers was always kind but never at the expense of thoughtful and honest analysis. She wanted to know where her own writing needed to be honed, strengthened, enlivened and she was committed to offering that to all of us and eventually just to me. On our very last meeting, five days before she died, she wanted to know why I hadn't sent a piece for her to review in this session. She expected to offer feedback and insisted I read something to her for comment.

She demonstrated that it was authentic feedback that was required, that unkind or harsh feedback had no place and

neither did words of praise that had no substance. I think
this quality was part of what Tom recognized and was why we
did guard our group. One dimension of Doreen's
commitment to kindness was in the characters of her novel.
"I don't want to feed any negative stereotype, or any
stereotype at all. I have to find ways to show their humanity.
It has to be loving but can't be sentimental. Loving isn't the
same as being nice. Spare me from nice." These are examples
of phrases she expressed when exploring both the characters'
behaviours and how her words could possibly wrongly
portray them.

Yes, high standards for herself and consistently coaxing
the same from all of us. The other dimension that suffuses
the memories of our time working together is her humour.
Doreen was so funny. She saw the humour in her own work,
in that of others, and in our often clumsy attempts to convey
meaning that was ambiguous or awkward. When the signs of
dementia began to appear, she was distressed but that didn't
stop her from finding the humour in it. She struggled with
remembering details and dates, but when she gave feedback
on my writing and talked of her own, she grasped the big
picture, the over-arching themes and direction, the way
metaphor wound its way through her story, how repeated
vivid images of colour and landscape bound *The Thorn* with
visual meaning. I'd remind her often that the lower order
thinking skills were slipping, but the higher order ones were
taking all the juice and functioning in a high octane zone.
She appreciated that. Her comment: My memory is a
sleeping creature curled up in some dark corner.

In the last couple of years, I'd often head home after one
of our writing sessions and my stomach would be sore from
laughing. We commented regularly how we both recognized
that although things could be dire and the prognosis grim,

that was no reason to abandon seeing the humour in the situation. So, when for a time she could no longer swallow and required a feeding tube and a stand that held a bag for intake, she personified the tippy, metal support as a new character in the house, Ichabod. She wrote:

Ichabod regrets the day he first laid eyebolts on her, knew there would be trouble trifold: she seemed the fussy sort. Their relationship grew and had its challenges. Ichabod's backbone aches, rigor mortis of the spine. He watches the human bend, arch, twist from the waist. Some consolation - he's good at spinning. Her tube wraps around his spine, trips her up. He'd like to have a brow to furrow like hers but he'll settle for pissing her off.

I miss her. I miss her loving friendship, her creative inspiration, her intelligence and love of ideas, our conversations and her writing support. That *The Thorn* is completed feels wonderful but it doesn't resolve that she isn't still here. Her voice appears now and then when I'm writing and can channel her perspective, encouragement and insight. Best of all, her laughter.

EDITING *The Thorn*

BY LUANNE ARMSTRONG

I have never before edited a book when I didn't have access
to the writer to do the actual work. I did edit a wonderful
book by Sigurd Askevold, (the former French teacher at
PCSS) but I had his son to consult and a finished
manuscript that only needed to be cut down a bit.

But editing *The Thorn* was a different process. When I work
on a book, any book, I read it once, fast, then again slowly
and then again. I take it for walks. I think my way into it. And
then I usually talk to the writer and say, what did you mean
here, and how did you want this to go?

So, it was a huge leap of faith for Ingrid to bring me this
book and for me to take it on and believe I could edit it into
a finished publishable manuscript.

When I first read *The Thorn*, I could see immediately there
were some knotted things, structural issues, pieces that could
be moved around, put here or there. But there was so much
more than that. Here was a deep and powerful story; here
were people in the grip of huge forces they could barely
contend with. I had to go deep, think about the imagination
and the power of the writer who had dreamed this story into
being. What was the vision? What was the big dream this
writer had seen?

It took a while. There was no way I could go fast with it,
even though there were other projects that needed work, and
other writers that needed support. I had to dream my way
into the book. I would edit until I got stuck and then I would
walk, and the book would hover just outside my
consciousness while I sat and talked with the lake and the

mountains and then I would see where the story could go next. I would rush home, holding the thought, and go back into it.

It was a complicated project; it holds a lot of characters for one book to contain and a lot of stories, and I knew nothing at all about the people and the land and the culture and the history. But I understood it. A love story, a freedom story, a story of yearning and need and courage is the same in any culture and any time.

When I was done the first edit, I went back and did a second and then a third and each time, I saw something new. I never changed the language or the words. My pact with this book, and with Doreen, was that it was her book to be told in her words. But I moved them to where they wanted to go.

The only section I took part in rewriting was the ending, because there wasn't one, and there had to be. No book truly has an ending, of course. The characters live on in some alternate universe and their lives unfold there. I've always had trouble with endings. But a book must end and the readers sigh and come out of the story that has held them in its spell.

I loved this book. I loved working on it. I miss the conversations the writer and I could have had about how things could go and what needed to be. But I am very glad to have been part of the process of bringing it to life and to readers and friends everywhere. I am so grateful that Ingrid asked me to come into this process and trusted me to move the book forward. It will always live in my mind and heart and that is a good place for it to be.

Doreen's Legacy

by Ingrid Alina Zaiss Baetzel

My mom was a lot of things – a writer, a poet, a potter, a gardener, a teacher and a million other wonderful manifestations of a life well-lived, with choice and purpose. She had a great big brain full of beauty and love and pain and curvy and straight lines. She got everything done and did it all well. She spent a lot of time on her own, in the soil and the clay, often talking to herself, spinning tales and coaxing green shoots and starts into full bounty. As a writer and teacher, she wove brightly and deeply with her words and drew unimaginable things out of young minds with her fierce creative spark and direct manner of high expectations in herself and others. She was not to be messed with, but her tough, no-bullshit personality was threaded with a silliness and a zest for creation that has, in my life, been unmatched.

She became visibly sick only a little more than a year before she died in March of 2020. Cancer took her body and saved her from the desperate slide into what quickly was showing itself as dementia. It was early years for her with her mind slipping, and only in the smallest of steps, but it was obvious to her family and closest friends, and it terrified her. She was never scared of cancer, but she could not tolerate what was happening to her mind. But, before it came to be more than she could tolerate, she chose her own way out with medical assistance and left this realm to the rest of us along with her legacy – and this book.

The Thorn was so close to completion, we called it a finished work. It really just came down to polishing and sewing together some small components we could only guess at as a team who knew her and loved her. She had, indeed, laid the clear groundwork and done the gorgeous brunt of the work. She did her job, and a few of us brought it home as a team.

Her friend of decades and writing colleague, Alanda Greene, sat many a day over many a year with her listening to her process and helping to soundboard her ideas. She was instrumental in mom completing this book. She knew it well and has signed off with deep love on what we have pulled from mom's clear message and brought to the page. Thank you, Alanda, for knowing her and for loving her so well. *The Thorn* is here because of you being there for Doreen.

Luanne Armstrong was fundamental in marrying her perspective with mom's and getting inside the manuscript with her deft eye for structure and content editing. The work that terrified me, she handled with grace and efficiency and I am indebted. I spent many months working on the copy edit, diving deep into mom's well and trying to bring the book up to air, clean and cohesive, but without the profound efforts of these two women, I would have likely stayed underground with it.

Geoffroy Tremblay of EncreLibre Publishing has been a magic maker with design assistance, support, and bringing *The Thorn* to physical form. His friendship with Doreen transcended the process and he brought all that he knew and loved about her to the game.

Jacqueline Wedge worked tirelessly, patiently and with a chasm-deep love on the cover image, listening to me, drawing my unmanifested thoughts out through conversation and sketch. I am so grateful for her artistry and friendship.

I am, again, indebted and gobsmacked at the depth of relationships mom fostered with beautiful minds in our region. We are richer than we understand, and we can do it all. Thank you to all who contributed - for your friendship, keen eyes, creative prowess, and absolutely steady hands and hearts.

This book is a gift to us all from someone who loved us and profoundly encouraged us to keep gloriously creating. She brought it out in the people she encountered and affected with her power and vision. I am so proud of her, of this work, and of the time she spent earth-bound. She was a human; she was a warrior, a back-to-the-lander with high aesthetic and immaculate taste; she is still here – in these pages.

-Ingrid Alina Zaiss Baetzel

CPSIA information can be obtained
at www.ICGtesting.com
Printed in the USA
BVHW071222180921
616989BV00003B/13

9 780993 791185